the Lonely Crosses

Richard Lory

Arctic Road Publishing
Puposky, Minnesota

Arctic Road Publishing
195 Arctic Road NW
Puposky, Minnesota 56667

Publisher's Cataloging-in-Publication Data

Lory, Richard
The Lonely Crosses / by Richard Lory
p. cm.
ISBN-13: 978-0-9790890-0-8
1. Sexual abuse victims—Fiction.   I. Title.
2. Self-defense—Fiction.
3. Chippewa National Forest (Minnesota.)—Fiction.
4. Minnesota—Fiction.
5. Family—Fiction.
PS3612   2008   2006910237
813'.54

Printed in the United States of America

1 3 5 7 9 10 8 6 4 2

This book is printed on acid-free paper.

BOOK DESIGN BY RICHARD LORY

To purchase this novel visit your nearest bookstore or order online at:

www.ArcticRoadPublishing.com

†

It is not the size of the army that victory in battle depends,
but strength comes from Heaven. —1 Maccabees 3:19

Today I will stand up to that bully. —friend from 2nd grade

†

the Lonely
Crosses

CHAPTER 1

The strong current of the Clearwater River had him in its deadly grip. From out of the corner of his eye he could see that the girl was following his progress in the cold water of the river.

"Don't you dare drown before you pay me!" yelled Elsie as she ran along the bank, coiling the hard rope into her left hand. The rope was a log-lasso made from, well—an old lasso.

Before today, Richard had not yet fallen through the rotten ice of Clearwater River, as had previously succumbed—one by one and day by day—the other members of his crew. By furiously treading water, he had managed to keep his head, shoulders, and chain saw above the surface of the river.

"I can just touch bottom with my tip toes," said Richard as he bounced along like a kid in a pool. "But I took water in my waders and it's getting cold in here," he complained, while not mentioning about the next sheet of ice that he was rapidly approaching. If he hit it, the current would pull him under.

"Catch the rope if I miss."

Richard hoped that Elsie's aim would be true, and the rope would become a lariat, not a noose. "I take back all the mean things I ever said about you," he yelled over the rush of the river.

"What mean things?"

Elsie let fly and threw the rope over the chain saw, down Richard's Statue of Liberty arm and over one shoulder, catching him as if he was a lost calf that had wandered away from a cattle drive. She then braced her feet and held against the current as her prize swung in an arc toward the shore.

Freshly captured, Richard reached up with his soaked, but free, right hand and cut off the engine switch of the still snarling chain saw. After insuring that water could not be drawn into its carburetor, he could then fully concentrate on protecting his own lungs.

Since he was near shore and anchored somewhat by Elsie's light weight, the current was not robust enough to pull him any farther downstream. Richard would not have to spend the rest of the day drowned under a sheet of river ice, staring up at a blue sky of oxygen two frozen inches from his face.

It was early spring and the river was frigid liquid, but Richard was slightly shielded from the cold by his insulated chest waders and the warming effects of adrenaline. Time would soon eliminate both of his protectors.

A mossy-backed, primordial snapping turtle, larger than a wicker basket, had been dislodged from the hidden undercut of the river and was busy swimming slowly away from the commotion. Richard took time from his soggy predicament to watch in awe the old armored reptile, its neck thicker than a man's wrist and its head as large as a football.

"I'm not carrion yet, big guy, so just keep swimming."

Big Thomas Thorson, solid but slow, was second to reach Richard. Thomas was half Ojibwa Native, half Irish, and half Norwegian—poor math perhaps—but he really was a man and a half. He was the oldest member of the crew, the strongest, and the hardest to coexist with. He liked working with Richard—by default—because no one else could tolerate Thomas Thorson for any length of time.

Thomas had made it to the edge of the river. He salvaged the chain saw from Richard's grip and passed the machine to Elsie. Then he turned back to Richard, placed one of his big hands over Richard's forearm, pulled him clear out of the water, and derricked his catch to the safety of the river bank.

Though an ignoble retreat, Richard was glad to be on dry land.

"Thanks, Thomas."

A rumbling sound came from somewhere down in the big man's chest. "Urrrr-ahh, grrr-ahhh, yurrr-wet." It was the same phrase, but without the "wet," that Thomas would utter when talking about beer, food, the ladies … anything.

This had been the final hour of the final day before the start of an ice-out break from work. They were to have two to three weeks off, waiting for the last of the rotten ice to abandon the river and for the water level from the spring melt to subside. Richard was the last of his crew to be baptized. He had believed he was going to remain a heathen. Now he was slogging up the bank, his chest waders full of ice water.

"God, I thought I'd made it, then crack and splash, so fast I can't hardly remember what had happened." At least a warm spring sun was shining, the wind was calm, and he had dry clothes: a faded blue cotton T-shirt and green nylon jogging shorts left in his truck from yesterday's post-work run.

Big Thomas Thorson, Elsie, and the rest of the crew were trailing Richard through the woods to the field where their trucks and cars were waiting. Richard had been a regular crew member at the start of the project, had evolved into a de-facto crew boss, and finally had molted into an actual paid crew boss—at the insistence of the other workers. The two original crew bosses had lost their jobs through various derelictions of duty.

"Let me help you take off those waders," said motherly Elsie, a pretty little red-haired, green-eyed farm girl who was working on the crew to support her four small tow-headed girls—left penniless and homeless by a runaway father. "Don't forget to call me when it's good to come back to work. Baby needs a new pair of shoes," an old saying that just might be literal in Elsie's case, though Elsie's youngest was no longer a baby.

Elsie and her Nordic brood lived with her grandparents on her mother's side, crowded into a small farmhouse on fertile land in the heart of Clearwater County in northern Minnesota. The only items of value that she had managed to salvage from her lost farm were an old red Case tractor, several head of black Angus cattle, a dozen or so brown-egg laying chickens, her four children, and her dignity—still intact, though somewhat battered by her ex-husband.

Elsie's dark, wavy red hair was normally swept behind ears that stuck out a bit too much from her head. Somehow, Elsie's ears made her look even more pretty and feminine. During her riverbank chase after Richard, that dark red hair had escaped from behind her ears and was now catching and reflecting every passing sunbeam. Or so it seemed to Richard as he studied Elsie's tresses swaying to and fro while she struggled to remove his waders.

"I have everyone's number," answered Richard. "So I'll call the crew back as soon as the project is ready to resume. I'll also try to convince the project supervisor to get us over in the woods before the water recedes, even if we only clear deadfalls on the riverside for a while."

One by one, the crew left the field in their various cars and trucks, each driving away too rapidly for the bumps of the pasture, as if they were escaping from a long church sermon, instead of a day with chain saws and wood and cold river water.

Thomas was the last man to say good-bye, "Urrr-ahhh, God be with ye... ummm," and then he too bounced away in his old truck with the familiar spiderweb-cracked windshield.

Elsie was left with damp Richard. "Don't scare us like that again," she said as she raised her fist like a girl and punched out like a girl and hit Richard's shoulder like a little hammer, which he didn't expect and wasn't ready for.

"Ouch," was out before he could stop it, but he acted as if it was just a joke. "All right, slugger, I'll be more careful, and you'll get paid for your work. Fair?"

Elsie took a towel from her truck and had Richard bow down as she dried his head. The towel smelled of dog hair and chickens, but Richard didn't say anything in deference to his sore shoulder.

"We should have gotten off the ice a week ago," stated Elsie, like this was a fact that could be blamed on someone. "You guys just don't know when to quit." Guys, as in males. Blame assigned.

"In hindsight, I suppose you are correct," defended Richard as well as he could, bent forward like he was, studying a large beetle that was crawling on the ground between his feet, while Elsie was getting rougher with the musty towel.

Elsie removed the towel from Richard's head and pushed him straight with her hands, much the same as she would with a little boy whose mamma had caught him playing in mud puddles wearing his good Sunday shoes. Certainly not like with an older, grey-haired gentleman. When Richard looked up from his bug, he was smiling, staring into the beautiful, somewhat angry, green eyes of his female co-worker. He did not look away from those eyes soon enough or say anything clever quick enough.

"What are you looking at?" she asked accusingly.

"Listen," he said, finally turning his gaze from the girl's green eyes, to look back over his shoulder and up the gentle hill that ran away from the river. Saved by a flock of sandhill cranes. At least a dozen of the large birds were gliding downward from high thermals, their deep, resonant, rattling calls announcing their springtime approach from Dixie. "The flock must be headed to Red Lake up on the Indian Nation." Richard concentrated on not looking back at the angry girl with the rough towel and the dark green eyes.

Finally, "They do look nice," agreed Elsie. "I took my girls up to the Agassiz Wildlife Refuge one spring. We watched the cranes as they came in to land in the marshes."

"I love how you know so much about wildlife," said Richard. Elsie would often tell him things about the natural world as they worked on the river.

"Part of that is from the fact that I grew up on a farm. The rest is just curiosity." Elsie leaned against Richard's truck and pushed her hair back behind her ears. "I miss my farm. Maybe someday I can get another place, but I just don't see how that might be possible."

"Your girls must feel the loss of their old home. I hope the change has not been too hard."

"The children dearly love my grandparents, but it is a strain on them sometimes. Too little space and too much youthful energy for such a small place."

When Elsie finally left, Richard peeled off the remainder of his wet clothes, finished drying off with Elsie's dog-chicken smelly towel, and put on his running clothes and dusty jogging shoes. His nerves were jangled by his cold immersion in the river and by Elsie's zealous concern. He needed a run to calm himself.

Richard drove up and out of the river-cut lowlands and onto a nearby highway-topped ridge. The new, smooth blacktop road had been built so the local farmers could get their milk to market. It was the least-traveled country road that Richard could ever remember seeing, a nearly perfect place to run, where even the resident dogs were friendly. He took off on his amble. "Oof-ah, oof-ah, ouch, ouch, ouch." Richard believed that beginning a run with these soreness sounds would help him get into the rhythm of running, a mental massage of sorts. "Ouch, ouch, ouch, ouch!" Soon he was smoothed out and limbered up.

A half-hour run would be enough today, thought Richard, around fifteen minutes east and then turn back. Most of Richard's running was measured by time—not by distance. This was because he was always traversing new and unmeasured places: sandy farm paths, sparsely-used country blacktops, and even the bike and snowmobile trails around Lake Bemidji State Park. Often, he did not know exactly where his runs would lead or how long they might last; it depended solely on how he felt as the run developed and on what nature and the weather had to offer.

A clan of farm children, all ages of boys and girls, were sliding on saucers down a long, steep hill that ended at a small pond. Their rocket descents would finish with the saucers shooting out onto the slushy ice of the pond. The tall hill itself was covered in some snow, lots of mud, and a beginning of new grass. The kids waved to him as he ran by. Richard hoped that the children's mothers had buckets of laundry soap at home. The scene of the children playing reminded Richard of his own childhood, back when youngsters were expected to be bruised, scratched, and muddy.

He ran past the hill with its children, and on for another mile or so. Far ahead, he could see a gang of dark birds at the left edge of the roadway. Evidently, a squashed critter was providing daily sustenance for the county's scavengers. There were a dozen crows, two vultures, and one white-headed eagle. The black crows were keeping the eagle from his share of the dinner.

Another eagle arrived from the sky, tipping the balance of power away from the crows. Apparently, two eagles outnumbered a dozen crows. The vultures, a neutral country to the eagles and crows, were content to continue their feast unmolested.

The crows were too busy with their harassment of the eagles to pay much notice to the approaching human. Richard was getting very close to the melee. He wished that he had his camera with him, this would make a great picture. Just then, the scent of the carnage reached his nostrils. Skunk.

"This is where we part company, my dear," said Richard, as he turned and ran back from whence he had come. A little less than three miles would be just fine today.

The odors in this direction were much more pleasing, at least to Richard, if not to the dark birds. The heavy, sweet scent of yarrow covered the road in places like an invisible blanket. He remembered that it was the leaves of this plant that released its perfume, not its clusters of small white flower heads. Spring dandelions massed in huge numbers on many of the steep hillside pastures, turning their ground completely yellow. Small bees were already out looking for early nectar.

Clans of purple loosestrife were just beginning to shoot their green spikes heavenward; later in the summer they would grow as tall as Elsie's children. Listed as a noxious weed in Minnesota, state law required its destruction. But along this quiet country road, their rosy purple flowers were tolerated by the locals, so it was safe. Richard commiserated with its plight and its convict status.

CHAPTER 2

The ride back home took less than an hour—from about the center of Clearwater County to about the center of Beltrami County. Most of Clearwater was green ash trees mixed with sugar and red maples, tall bur oak trees, and cottonwoods—a finger of hardwood forest that jabbed north out from its palm in central Minnesota.

Just over the Clearwater County line into Beltrami County the great northern forest began, stretching north of the border deep into Canada and east into the Boundary Waters and its wilderness. Cedars and other conifers, birches, willows, and the favorite trees of the pulp companies: balsam fir, poplar, and aspen, both bigtooth and quaking. Most of the old-growth white and red pine had been cut in northern Minnesota by the beginning of the twentieth century, but Beltrami County still had a few stands of the old giants, a wall of which greeted Richard as he passed over from Clearwater County.

Richard's own land was covered with quaking aspen. These were one of his favorite trees because he loved how its leaves would shake with the slightest breeze, shimmering their light green undersides. An old, ten acre field, carved in a gentle S-shape, lay at the front of his forty acres. Normally dark green and light tan and flowered, now it was turning from burnt black to fresh green grass. His sons and a few of their friends had helped burn the field while remnants of snow still held guard in the woods, protecting the surrounding forest. The fire would kill most of the ticks—a springtime threat, and would also stimulate the growth of wildflowers—a springtime treat.

Around the perimeter of the field Richard had mowed a half-mile course. Two laps pushing the power mower, fifteen minutes each, was all it took to cut out a nice path. It was one of the few places where he could gauge how far he was running. The ground of the field was soft and forgiving to his knees, but after the springtime burn, a few laps around the course would leave traces of soot on his white socks. Another hard, cleansing rain was needed to remove the last of the ashes.

A log home stood at the back of the field, set up against the edge of the woods. The house, built with the help of Richard's children while they were still very young, was now too large for just one lone person. Richard drove up to his home, sending a group of brown and buff flicker woodpeckers into bobbing flight, white patches on their rumps flashing like the tails of startled whitetail deer. As soon as he entered his home and had closed the door behind him, the flickers returned to continue their search for ants.

A shower taken and clean clothes having been donned, he loaded his camping gear and tent into the back of his truck. Richard planned on spending several days camping and hiking in the wilderness of the Chippewa National Forest, twenty miles to the east of his homestead. He loved exploring the new sights that could be found in the clean freshness of springtime in the northern forest. He placed his camera bag on the passenger seat, first checking that he had plenty of film.

Before he left, he filled the bird feeders with plenty of sunflower seeds and topped off the hummingbird feeders with freshly made sugar water. The seed would last the few days that he planned to be gone, but the sweet liquid may or may not be enough. It seemed that the more nectar he put out, the more hummingbirds he attracted. He guessed that there were at least twenty hummers feeding at his three stations, though it was hard to tell because of their speed as they swirled around the front of the house. Besides, to Richard one hummingbird looked about the same as another, the only distinction being between the guys and girls.

"Come and get it," said Richard as he hung the last sugar feeder.

He could hear a lone hummingbird as it hovered close to his ear, seemingly impatient for this large mammal to leave its territory. At least it wasn't hovering in front of his face, a tactic that was even more distracting when it occurred.

Richard drove to the east side of Beltrami County, deep into the Chippewa National Forest. There was a primitive backcountry site near North Twin Lake. There he quickly set up camp, though his skills at tent assembly were rusty. He stretched a rope between two trees and leaned or hung the majority of his gear against or from the rope. Anything that needed to stay dry he put in his tent. Then he carried an armful of firewood down from the back of his truck. Good, dry slab wood with thick bark would give off just enough smoke to keep any mosquitoes at bay.

A few long casts were made with his closed-faced spinning reel, more to limber up his elbow than to try to catch anything. Not many fishermen used closed-faced reels, but he did because they were easier to use from canoes, his favorite mode of water travel.

Richard placed the fishing pole against his rope and walked the shoreline, peering into the water. In one direction from the camp the shore consisted of sand and weeds, a shallow beach where children could safely wade and explore. Small sunfish darted to and fro, but nothing larger or more aggressive. In the other direction the water was slightly deeper. Here cedars had dropped into the water every ten or fifteen yards. This made for great cover for crappies. Richard could not see the silver and black fish, but knew they were waiting in ambush at the tip ends of each submerged tree.

A loon called from out on the lake. Richard thought it was too early in the day for loons to be calling to each other. Maybe it was predicting rain for later tonight.

He thought about starting a fire to cook something for supper, but decided first to visit two nearby friends, an old couple, Teddy and Clara Zemm, who lived near the turnoff to the trail that led to this part of the forest and to the camp that Richard was now occupying.

Teddy was an old World War II veteran. Italian campaign. He had met his wife in a field hospital while convalescing from shrapnel wounds taken to his legs. From the sound of their stories, it was love not on the first, but maybe on about the fiftieth sighting.

They were still up and glad to see him; they did not get much company this far into the forest. "Well, hello, Richard; come on in," said Clara. "We were just about to have some stew."

"Made from our own vegetables from our own garden, and young venison that your son Foster had given us last winter," said Teddy.

"You can join us," ordered Clara as she set another plate.

"That sounds really good. I'm starved," said Richard.

"We like best the venison that you and your son Foster always give us because it is from younger deer," said Teddy. "We're glad you are not horn hunters. I'd rather eat swamp grass than some of those old bucks."

"I cut the potatoes big and greasy, just the way you like them," said Clara to the two men.

It was apparent to Richard that Clara had gained more than just a few pounds over the past winter, though she still looked healthy. But her husband Teddy appeared to be much worse than Richard had remembered from last summer. An arduous life spent working in the out-of-doors, a long fight to push the Nazi army out of the Italian mountains, and just too many years on this earth were taking their toll. Richard kept his concerns to himself.

"I set up camp on North Twin Lake. My plans are to spend a few days there if the nights don't get too cold," said Richard as he studied a picture frame full of medals that Teddy Zemm had brought back from Europe.

"It must still be in the forties at night," said Clara. "Won't you about to freeze to death sleeping on the ground like that?"

"I'll be double sacking a pair of warm sleeping bags, so that should help, but my metabolism likes to fall to zero when I sleep."

"You should be thankful, young man," said Clara. "My Teddy doesn't have a metabolism, day or night, summer or winter."

Teddy Zemm defended himself, "My hands are still strong— strong enough that I could crush the neck of the bastard that attacked our niece's friend up on the Paul Bunyan Trail. A fourteen-year-old girl. Raped her and kicked her half to death."

As Teddy's thoughts were progressing from his strong hands to killing the little girl's rapist, Teddy's natural-born anger had rocketed to red face and spitting spittle.

Teddy's outburst and the information that it had revealed had taken his guest by surprise, but Richard kept his mouth closed and his face rigid until his own feelings, rushing through his brain like an adrenaline shock, could subside enough that he could control them. Richard was glad that at least one other male in the county was yet man enough to be able to become furious at the evil of predators.

"Poor little thing," said Clara.

Teddy put his hands down on the table, the better to concentrate on what he was feeling and saying. "Samantha said that her friend was in the hospital for some days, then at home for a long while before she let herself come back to school."

"I think she wanted her bruises and cuts to heal before she went out in public again. That took a long time. I remember how long it took for you to heal in Italy." Clara was remembering the war. "Some of those wounds, they..." She got up from the table to stir the venison still warming on the stove.

"They have not caught her attacker yet, but I don't seem to see any deputies in the area, so I wonder if they are even trying," said Teddy.

"We are keeping our niece close by when she visits. The road and the trail are off limits unless we are with her," said Clara.

Clenching and unclenching his fists, Teddy Zemm asked his wife, "What was the girl's name? Samantha told us before, but now I can't remember. My mind is leaking like a sieve nowadays."

"It was her friend Sally. Norwegian stock, I think; people been up in this area for decades, since the first loggers came here." Clara stopped her pot stirring, the better to think, her mixing spoon held up in her left hand like the queen mom's wand. "You remember her, Honey, she was the dark-haired girl, real thin—no development as yet—if you know what I mean; skin as white and clear as fresh farm milk. She came over with Samantha and they both helped us pick and preserve our tomatoes."

"Sure, I remember her now. She really liked helping out. I think she did more than Samantha did. It seemed odd to me that Samantha would have a friend that was so much younger than she was herself, then when I asked Sally—she said she was the same age as our niece. Before, I had thought she was ten, maybe. Certainly not fourteen."

Teddy Zemm's eyes were filming over; the old soldier was getting upset again as he spoke of his niece's friend and the day she came to help the old couple with their garden. He turned his gaze from his audience and looked at his medals, "I must have killed many good

13

men in that war, fathers and husbands, parents' sons. But nowadays, when a man defends his child from perverts, some politically correct district attorney wants to put him in prison."

The tough and tender veteran stood and took the frame off the wall and brought his medals closer to his tired eyes. "Richard, I have already told Clara to give these to you when I die, you deserve to have them for what you did."

Clara took the frame from her husband's strong hands and set it back in its place on the wall. "All right, enough of this. I don't need two vigilantes getting themselves all worked up into a posse. Let's get back to our supper and, God willing, change the subject to something more pleasant."

Clara talked as emotions subsided, the visible anger of Teddy Zemm and the hidden fury of Richard, bending the two men's steel hatreds to softer issues of gardens, fishing, and the rebirth of spring-time in the north.

The rest of the evening was warm and pleasant, though the news of the attack on the trail lingered in Richard's mind. He did not want to stay too long since he knew the Zemms were used to getting to bed early, so as darkness approached he took his leave and said his last good-byes.

"I better be going," said Richard to the pair. "I'd like to check my camp one last time while there is yet some light left."

"If you catch any crappies this trip and don't want to clean them, just drop them off and I'll take care of them," said Teddy. "Then we'll have them someday when you can visit again."

"Sounds like a fair deal," said Richard.

Richard was tired himself. The chain saw work clearing water-logged trees from the Clearwater River, his cold baptism in that river, the ridge run, and the pitching of his camp, coupled with the sharing of warm stew with his old friends, all were rapidly catching up with his old body. Back at camp he went directly to his tent and his double-stuffed sleeping bags. No campfire tonight.

The prophecy of the loon had been accurate. A thunderstorm came in the night, lightning announcing the first of the rain, then gently settled into a steady patter against the fabric of the tarp that Richard had the foresight to stretch over his tent. Normally, he would have loved the fury of the beginning of the storm, and its quiet, rainy aftermath. But tonight he had his own storm to contend with.

As he slept, thoughts of the dark-haired girl, Samantha's friend, swirled around inside his head. He had met Sam on several occasions, but never Sally; still, his dreams created the girl until she was a real memory. Richard awoke in the night, from the new image of Sally and from the old reflection of his own daughter, Jeanette. Both girls had been 14 when their lives had been forced to change. Richard breathed into his crumpled sweatshirt and concentrated on thoughts of his new life with his youngest boys—his new free life, until he was asleep again.

CHAPTER 3

Running was his way of staying sane. For that reason, early the next morning, Richard was running up the packed clay road that led from his primitive camp on North Twin Lake to the gravel surface of the Forest Service road that passed in front of the home of Clara and Teddy. The residue of sadness and anger of last night's dream was fading from his mind as he ran.

Forest Service Road Number 2213, as shown in red and white on the Chippewa National Forest map, led from Turtle River to the Carter Lake Trail System: a maze of trails for snowshoes and skis in the winter, for hikers in the summer, and for hunters in the autumn. Springtime—the animals pretty much had it to themselves. Richard loved the forest in the spring, with so few people around and so much new to see and feel and hear.

His primitive camp was one of several that Richard's youngest boys, Joshua and Foster, had discovered during their explorations of the national forest lands. Between Richard and his sons, someone would be staying at this camp almost every day during the spring and summer. Besides just enjoying the activity of camping, Josh and his older brother Foster used the primitive camp as a base from which to fish the depths of North and South Twin Lakes and the other waters in the surrounding area. Richard often used the camp as a home away from home, spending his time running, hiking, and just generally out exploring the natural world that the Chippewa Forest offered.

It had rained hard the previous two nights. But the unimproved road he was running on had already dried sufficiently to make the mud firm enough for solid footing. This was low country, inhabited mostly by maples and basswood, guarded by random sentinels of tall, white birch trees. Richard loved the trees. Loved them more than he loved the deer and the other animals that made the Chippewa Forest their home. Animal lovers had it wrong, it was the trees of the forest that were truly eternal, that made this place magic.

The ascent of the mud path was gradual, so much so that it seemed almost like a level surface. Only while going back downhill would the incline be noticed, and only then because Richard would feel much stronger, a result of gravity's slow release of kinetic energy.

A comfortable pace had brought Richard up the two miles on the packed mud road to the gravel-surfaced Forest Service road. Because of the rain, the local traffic had packed the gravel stones of this road into its underlying base of sand. Later, in the drier summer, the gravel would resurface to impair a runner's footing. Then a person would have to find firm, clear lanes in the middle or on the edges, where the cars and trucks of the tourists had not turned up the small, sharp stones. But for now the entire surface was smooth sand, perfect for running.

On the right, toward the southwest, was the entrance of the short drive to the home of Teddy Zemm and his wife Clara. The couple were already out working in their large vegetable and flower garden, getting ready for the upcoming season. Richard had first met the old veterans one morning long ago while he was out running and they were walking their daily summer constitutional. Later, a deal was struck by which Richard would do small favors, such as helping to split the couple's winter supply of firewood, and in return Teddy and Clara would leave him yesterday's newspaper. Richard could see from where he was that the newspaper was already in the plastic holder under the Zemm's post box. He would retrieve it on his return trip.

Richard waved to the couple when they saw him, then he took a left turn onto the forest road, away from the Zemm homestead. This direction led to Drury Lake, Rice Pond, and Nelson Lake, all smallish bodies of water, with Rice Pond being the largest, and most isolated, of the three. Forest Service Road 2213 ran right by Drury Lake and Nelson Lake, but Rice Pond was hidden from sight by almost a half mile of forest.

A long hiking trail, created from an abandoned logging road, led to and around the west and south sides of Rice Pond. In the winter the trail was a favorite of snowmobilers, but not many people hiked it in the summer because it was too far to walk the south perimeter of the pond. Rice Pond was almost a mile across, larger than many lakes, but with a great deal of shallow water along its reedy banks and bays.

If asked, Richard would say that he ran to keep from getting fat, which was partially true. But the real reason was for his soul. His runs smothered the memories of the night his young daughter, Jeanette, had been gang raped, and of the next day when the predators had tried to murder her. With a rifle, Richard had managed to save her life, but defense is not an option in Minnesota. One of the rapists had been shot in crossfire by one of his fellow rapists. At the time it seemed logical to the police that Richard must have done it, so after two years and three trials, and with the assistance of a crooked district attorney (a family friend of the rapist gang), the state was finally able to force a conviction.

Ten years in prison had trashed Richard's life, perhaps worse than the rape had trashed his daughter's life. Memories that should have been of Richard being a good dad raising his children through their teen years were instead replaced by a long, violent ordeal of survival in prison. Richard had somehow made it, but not without many deep, unseen scars. He had come to hate all predators, like the ones that had hurt his daughter. Not just an aversion to, or even anger, but deep, cold-blooded hate.

Richard never did understand why a jury could convict a father for protecting the life of his only daughter. It also pissed him off to no end that nobody, or at least so very few people, would bother to listen to his side of the story. Especially since the forensic evidence proved him right. But it had taken two years for the local boys to bother to get the FBI to do the test that could clear him. An FBI Lead Analysis test. When the test finally did come back, the DA was able to pull his lawyer tricks in the trial and have his state experts dance around the true meaning of the results of that test. The true meaning being that the stupid rapists had managed to shoot themselves.

Now Richard was trying to begin a new life, but convicts seldom get closure. "Just one step in front of the other, that's all. Relax, and enjoy the wilderness," Richard told himself. "Think of your sons, Josh and Foster, living near the wilderness that they have come to love."

If Richard ran far enough in this direction, a dozen miles or so, to where the national forest started to blend with remnants of settlers' old farmsteads, he would come to where the boys were staying with their girlfriends: sweet Eileen for Josh, and the often bad-tempered Sally Jean for Foster. Probably not bad matches.

Despite their dad having been missing from their lives for so many years, the boys had turned out well. Richard remembered when they had come to visit him while he was in the prison camp at Lino Lakes. By then, many years had already passed. The boys were not much taller than their dad's five foot seven, but they were lean and tough from having to survive on their own in a town that had sided with a gang of rapists against their sister and father.

As Richard ran, he passed Drury Lake on the left, a small lake whose shallow shoreline was littered with dead tamarack trees and thousands of cattails from last summer's growth, a perfect place for ducks and beavers. Another mile or so farther, Richard passed the entrance of the hiking trail to Rice Pond, then to Nelson Lake, with its rafts of puddle ducks recently arrived from the bayous of Louisiana. Four miles so far, now to turn around and run back to his camp.

Soon he had returned to the entrance of the trail to Rice Pond. Too much stored winter fat was causing Richard to have to strain too hard. "Always keep it aerobic, even if you have to walk at times," thought Richard. So he decided to stop running and to hike down the trail to Rice Pond. He would probably be the first to see the pond this year.

The sweet scent of clover permeated the trail. The clover had been planted years ago by a local hunting club for the benefit of ruffed grouse. Long after the hunters had forgotten about their project on the trail, the clover was still coming up and the grouse were still having an annual feast. Ahead, revealed through tiny openings in the small, new leaves of the trees, Richard could see glints of light reflecting off the water of the pond. In another month he would have to get much closer before the pond would reveal itself.

The water looked clear and cool. Richard had finished the last of his own water a mile back, but as thirsty as he was, he would not drink any of the cold liquid that lay in front of him. Giardia. Passed from beavers to the water they swam and worked in, and thereby on to unsuspecting humans. Or maybe it was the other way around, with humans infecting the beavers. Scientists weren't exactly sure.

Because of the possibility of giardia, Richard knew he couldn't drink, but he could splash the cool water on his face. He stepped onto a flat rock at the pond's edge and knelt down to spread the curtain of dead, dried rushes that remained from the previous year. As he did so, in Richard's mind, in that first microsecond, he thought how odd it was to be looking at a dark blue gingham dress floating on the water at the pond's edge. Before the remainder of the second could pass, Richard had jumped back onto solid ground, his heart pounding hard in his chest.

He had learned in prison to react in that first, unthinking second. Thinking could always come later, but only if one was still alive.

Richard's mind began to catch up with his reflexes. He realized that he had seen, near the top of the gingham dress, a girl's long black hair floating limp on the surface of the water. The girl's hair had been as shiny as the water itself, like a crow's wing. He also realized that he had seen a pair of legs, below the knees, and the bare feet of the girl.

Frozen, holding as quiet as a newborn fawn, Richard studied the woods around him, watching and listening for anything that might reveal another person or persons. Several chickadees flitted into the branches of a nearby birch tree to clean its surface of insect pests, some of the birds swinging upside down on the branches to perform their service. A brisk staccato drumroll filtered down from another birch tree deeper into the forest—a woodpecker. Two red squirrels played a lustful game of tag, running dizzy circles around the trunk of a great spruce. But as for noises human or evil: nothing.

Stepping back onto the rock, he knelt down to the body and pulled her closer to the shore until he could turn her face up and lift her out of the water. "This girl is so light, even wet like this," thought Richard. She was young and pretty and she was Native; that much was plain to see. Her raven-black hair fell past her shoulders. Richard carried her up to the clover of the trail and laid her down to check her, just in case. But she had been dead for some time now, though Richard could not guess for how long.

"Did someone kill this young girl?" wondered Richard. "What a waste."

The cold water ran off her cold body and out of her dress, into the bed of clover that she was resting on. Her damp hair was already drying from the strong breeze that was channeled between the trees of the clover path. Her eyes were a deep brown. They must have been very pretty in life, but were vacant in death. He closed her eyes with his palm. Richard straightened her raven black hair to make her more presentable. A person should have dignity even in death.

Though a casual observer might not have been able to discern it, a firestorm of emotions was rising again in Richard's chest and in Richard's mind, bringing back feelings of hurt and dread from years ago. Fear could be, and very often was, more deadly to an attacker than anger. Unfortunate for some few unlucky predators, fear did not always freeze their would-be victims.

The girl looked like she must have been in her late teens or early twenties. A delicate chain hung loosely from her neck, but the end of the chain trailed into the edge of the girl's mouth. Richard gently opened her mouth. At the end of the chain was a small Celtic cross pressed between two of the girl's teeth, like a World War II dog tag would have been jammed between the teeth of a dead soldier for later identification. With some considerable force, Richard removed the cross from the girl's teeth.

The cross was similar to those crucifixes Richard had seen the Spanish guys wearing in prison, with a little Jesus welded onto the front. But this cross had a circle of silver halo as well. There were light scratches, or a worn design, on the back of the cross. Richard took off his bifocals to look closer, but could not make out what the faint marks might be. He couldn't be sure, but it seemed that the front of the cross was really the back, updated with the welded Jesus. The back of the cross was perhaps the front of an older, original cross.

The only obvious injury was to the side of the girl's neck, slightly toward the front of her throat. A dark purple, almost black bruise had formed there. Looking closer, Richard noticed another bruise, very small, on the right edge of her lower lip.

Richard gently folded her arms across her chest. As he did so, he could feel scratches—small cuts on the palm of her left hand. Again he took off his glasses, this time so he could inspect the girl's palm.

Bringing her hand close to his eyes revealed shallow scratches and many little holes, like pin pricks, only larger and deeper, like a dozen sewing needles had been used to tattoo her hand.

Setting her arm back over her chest, Richard rocked back onto his knees and took a deep, calming breath. Unconsciously, he touched the top of her head with his hand. He had done the same thing many years ago when he had first laid eyes on his broken daughter, Jeanette. That time, when he had brought his hand back, there was his young daughter's blood on it. He had closed his fist around her blood. Today when he brought his hand back his palm was once again damp, but it was only water. Nevertheless, Richard shut his eyes, his mind, and his heart, took another deep breath to bring himself back to flesh and blood, and closed his fist down tight.

CHAPTER 4

The girl's damp and drying hair clung to the sides of her face, partially obscuring her appearance. Richard brushed her hair away as well as he could. He believed that she must have been terrified before her death, but her face showed only calm. "And maybe fierce determination," he said to the young Native girl lying on the fresh clover of the trail. If determination is something that could be frozen on a dead girl's countenance.

It was unlikely that anyone would be coming down here this early in the spring, and besides, Richard wasn't sure he could carry the girl all the way back to his camp. He left her resting on the trail as he went to get help, looking back one single time before he lost sight of the pond. The girl really did look like she was sleeping, with her eyes closed and her arms on her chest, her hands crossed over each other as if in prayer. Richard could imagine that he saw her chest rise and fall as she breathed. If he had been here just a few hours earlier he could have saved her life as he had once saved his daughter's. His daughter could have been this girl. This girl could have been his daughter.

Walking back up the trail, Richard paid close attention to the ground. In many places he could see where a car or truck had driven down to the pond. The tracks were sharp and clear. Last night it had nearly frozen, and the ground, shaded as it was here, was still firm. Richard would come back as soon as he could and use his camera to take pictures of the tracks.

Once back onto the forest road, Richard began to run again, a slow and steady jog, enough to cover ground, but not so fast as to exhaust himself. He had things to do yet and wanted some energy left with which to do them. At the Zemm's mailbox he stopped to retrieve yesterday's newspaper. Nothing on the front page about a missing girl. Just a long article about how good it is that there are no gangs in the Bemidji area, and how wonderful it is for the tourists. Flipping pages as he walked up the Zemm's drive, he quickly scanned each article. Nothing about the girl on the inside either.

Richard walked to the cottage of Teddy and Clara and asked to use their phone, first giving them a shortened version of his discovery. The old couple looked as if the news was about a death in their own family. It was personal for Teddy and Clara.

"I left her where the trail passes by the west side of Rice Pond. Nobody will be going down there this time of year."

Clara was really upset, almost in tears. "Poor little thing. What a waste."

"We should go down to the pond and bring her back home," said Teddy, meaning his home, not the girl's, though perhaps any home would be better for her than where she was. The awful news had made Teddy look years older, weighing his shoulders into a tired stoop.

"Never mind, my friend. The county deputies will have to check the scene when the paramedics arrive. Maybe they will find something that can help find the girl's killer," said Richard.

Teddy's shoulders straightened as he clenched his fists. "You can find the killer, I know you could." Teddy's eyes grew brighter, almost feverish.

"Richard needs to stay out of trouble," reminded Clara as she moved to her husband's side.

Teddy put his arm around his wife, but his eyes kept their feverish shine. "I know you could."

Before calling dispatch at the sheriff's office, Richard called his youngest son Josh and told him what he had found, who he had found. "I was tired after jogging from the middle camp at North Twin down to Nelson Lake, so on my return trip I stopped to check out the trail to Rice Pond. I found the girl floating in the reeds at the edge of the water. She looked to be really young, early twenties or maybe even still in her teens."

"What a waste. I can imagine what you were feeling," said Josh.

"I lifted her out of the water and placed her on the trail. It was clean there because clover had already started to grow. I think she had been dead for some hours, but she almost appeared to be alive—just sleeping on the grass."

"Don't let this get to you, Dad. You need to stay out of trouble," warned Josh. He was worried that his dad would again let his heart get him into trouble.

Richard called the police and told them to drive to the Zemm homestead. Teddy, in turn, could give his instructions to direct the officers to the hiking trail leading into Rice Pond.

Eager to get to his camp and get his camera before the deputies showed up, Richard explained what he wanted Teddy to do, talking over his shoulder as he walked to the door. "I told the cops to meet you here at your place, so you can tell them how to get to the trail into Rice Pond. And also, do you have today's paper yet? I want to see if this girl is missing—is being missed by anyone."

"It came early this morning, as usual; but there wasn't anything in it about a lost girl," added Teddy. "However, now that I think of it, as I was jumping channels on the radio late last night, there was something on one of the country stations about a convenience store clerk, a Native girl they had said, that had closed up her place of work at the end of the night shift, but had forgotten to lock the place or turn off the lights."

"So was there any explanation as to why the girl would forget to close up the store?" asked Richard.

"The radio guy said that the police figured she must have gone out partying with friends because she had left her own car in the lot."

"I told my husband that sounded like a stupid thing to say," said Clara, "what with all our Minnesota girls going missing and gone the past several years. When will the cops and media people ever learn?"

Not having to add anything to Clara's sentiments, since Richard knew the old World War II couple understood just how he felt about predators. He just said "yeah" and "bye" and took off running out the door.

Going downhill on the dried mud road leading to his camp at North Twin, with his mind racing around the events of the morning, Richard covered the distance in no time. He threw his camera bag onto the passenger side of his old Chevy's bench seat, then turned up the mud road to the Forest Service road, and drove to the entrance of the trail to Rice Pond.

Thank God the tracks were still firm. Richard thought that he should be able to get some good pictures. There were only a few shots left in the camera, which he quickly used, but he had the foresight to bring an extra roll. Reloading the camera, he noticed that the tread marks that he had followed appeared to have been made by a tire with a chunk of rubber missing. Maybe over an inch in diameter. The marks it left in the mud reminded him of the holes in the ends of the little screws he used to hang his pictures with. "What are those things called?" he asked of himself, knowing that it would come to him if he would just take time to think. Absent minded, or slightly dyslexic like his two youngest; 5 seconds, ...10 seconds, 15 seconds, 20 seconds… "Oh yeah, torque," he remembered. Torque screws—their small holes starlike. "Yeah, like little stars," he concluded.

He remembered that he used torque screws because their heads were smaller than those of sheet rock screws, so that their heads fit into the holes in the plastic picture frames that he used for the wild-life and nature pictures that he liked to take with his 35 millimeter… "Slow your mind down! You are wandering off," he commanded of himself.

He worked his way down to where the girl was lying. It wasn't part of his original purpose, but once at the pond's edge, with a camera in hand, he decided to take a few pictures of the girl and of the "crime scene," as it was. Richard imagined that the police would take their own pictures, but insurance never hurt.

Task completed, he walked back to where he had left his truck. If only by shear luck he had timed it well, because the flashing lights of an EMT truck, followed by two patrol cruisers, floated miragelike over a slight rise in the road, about a mile away. At least their sirens were off.

"You must be Richard Bede," stated the passenger-side paramedic as the driver dusted the EMT van into a landing next to Richard.

"Yes, I am."

"Like a bead of sweat, I suppose."

"Not that kind of bead," corrected Richard. "B-E-D-E, as in 'The Venerable Bede,' Saint Bede, a seventh century English historian and theologian. My family originally came to America from Cornwall. That's in England." It always bothered Richard that Americans knew so little of their history and heritage.

"Well, so where is the body?"

"Right down this trail here. There are some tire tracks pressed into the soft ground of this old path. Maybe your deputies will want to take a look"

"If a civilian vehicle could make it in, then so can our EMT truck," boasted Mr. Passenger-side as he waved his driver onward. The police cruisers followed obediently in his wake.

Walking after the procession, Richard got to the pond just as the two paramedics were loading a black body bag into their vehicle. The pair of deputies, one for each cruiser, were standing where Richard's dead Native girl had lain. They were scuffing the clover as if the soles of their boots could make this problem go away.

The largest deputy, name tag "G. Mandible," seemed to be in charge, or at least doing most of the talking. "Are you the guy who found the body?"

"Yes, I am. I was out running this morning and decided to look at the pond on my way back to my camp. When I knelt down to splash some water on my face, I saw the girl floating face down at the water's edge. I pulled her out and carried her to where you found her, but she was already gone."

"Isn't it too cold to be camping?" asked Mandible's partner.

"I like the springtime," said Richard. He figured the deputy didn't need a better or longer explanation to be sidetracked by. The facts alone would probably be confusing enough.

"Did you try anything to save her?" asked Deputy Mandible.

"I checked her to determine if I could help her, but it was obvious that she had died some hours before."

Mandible turned to his partner as he spoke. "Right. So, then you called us, and here we are. Well, she appears to be the girl that went missing from the convenience store up on the highway. Too bad, a nice looking girl."

"I should bring to your attention that there were tread marks, many of them, on this old logging trail. I told the paramedics about them before they drove down here. When I first walked to the pond I did not notice the tire tracks, though they should have been obvious to me. Anyway, after I had found the girl, I looked around, and there they were."

"Maybe the tracks are from the vehicle that the girl was riding around in," theorized Officer Mandible. "The district attorney figures that she must have gone out partying after her shift, left her own car at the convenience store, where we found it. She must have grabbed a ride from someone she knew. These Indians are a little wild like that sometimes."

Mandible's partner added, "We will call the state BCA and tell them about the tracks. They can check them out if they want to."

"Couldn't hurt, I guess," agreed G. Mandible as he shrugged his considerable shoulders. "They might want to take a couple of pictures or a cast or something."

The EMT truck was already leaving, so the officers did not see a need to hang around. The space where the girl had lain was just wide enough in which to turn around their cruisers, then they, too, sped off.

After their engine noise faded away, Richard walked over the area, looking one last time at the scene. Nature and the pond had already returned to normal, it seemed. The clan of chickadees had returned to perform their acrobatics, while the woodpecker had resumed his drumming in the high pines. The last to come back to life were the pair of randy red squirrels, who chatted their scolding of Richard. Perhaps they thought he had tried to bring the law down on them for mating without a license.

At the water's edge where Richard had first parted the rushes to discover the Native girl, he re-enacted his earlier actions and tried to remember—something—anything. There was nothing significant from his memory, but as he looked into the water, he saw yellow. A glowing golden-yellow.

A flower. Maybe a yellow pond-lily, slowly growing its way to the surface. Richard knew from past experience that this pond and the slow stream that fed into it would eventually be covered in floating spatterdock, as his grandmother used to call it, as soon as summer was fully underway. But this far north it was too early in the season for even half-developed water plants. The ice had melted not long ago. Nothing on the bottom had even started to grow.

Fishing the flower out of the pond, Richard saw that it was a rose. Not a wild plant at all, though it was aggressive enough to stick him with its thorns.

"This must be what had marked the girl's hand," said Richard softly to himself. He carefully turned the yellow rose in his hands. The flower was bright and new, a beautiful specimen of its race, recently picked and recently drowned with the young Native girl.

"She must have held tight to it even as her life was fading away."

CHAPTER 5

Josh had already arrived by the time Richard returned, his new 4x4 parked at the top of the hill overlooking North Twin Lake. The small parking area was like a pumpkin patch with foot trails for its vines, twisting in different directions from the main plant. A short trail led to a large, open camp with a white sandy beach, Josh and Foster's favorite camping spot. In the past, campers and swimmers would drive all the way to the beach, but half the distance down the side of the hill, erosion had cut a steep gash across its face.

Boulders the size of old Volkswagen bugs had been set across the path at the top of the hill, thereby gating the trail from vehicle traffic. And a forest ranger, using sentence-to-serve workers from Beltrami County jail as slave labor, had engineered a restraining wall at the cut, to repair the damage and slow any further erosion. The men and women of the crew had set treated railroad timbers as narrow steps, leaving a barely negotiable, steep descent from the higher section of the trail to the lower section. The forest ranger then created a short section of trail around the stepped wall of the timbers, leaving a safer and easier path to navigate to the beach.

The other two trails, each much longer than the rocky beach trail, began together as a single entity, then split apart from each other fifty yards or so deeper into the forest. One trail wandered off to the east, snaking along a wide ridge covered in Norway pine. The scaly red bark of the trees lent a tint of color through all the seasons, while the great height and openness of the Norways gave that part of the forest a tall, cathedral-like feeling. This trail would eventually dip down to lowlands and to a camp set on an isthmus dividing North Twin from its smaller cousin—Bass Lake. The isthmus was favored by tourists since it was bounded by two beautiful lakes. As lovely as it was, the boys seldom stayed there because it was a poor place to catch fish. The lake was too shallow and warm for the smallmouth bass and crappies, too open and sandy for the toothy northern pike, and who knows what something it was too much or too little of to keep the bright little bluegills and pumpkinseeds away. A fishing mystery.

The middle trail, vaguely positioned between the other two trails, veered sharply to the south, zigzagging downhill as if a reckless skier had set its course, dodging mature basswood trees understoried with vast multitudes of younger maples. At the end of this descent rested a secluded camp set on a small, hatchet-faced projection of land, about one acre in size. Across from the mainland camp was an island, tiny enough as to allow a clear view of the rest of the lake, yet large enough to shelter the nest of a pair of mergansers and their fuzzy family of ducklings—seemingly there to compete with the boys for the good fishing that the spot offered.

Josh had guessed correctly that his dad had bivouacked at the mergansers' camp. "On the way over, the radio was reporting that the girl had been found," said Josh. "Luckily, they haven't mentioned you by name, just that a local guy was out jogging and came across the body."

"That's good. I don't need to have anyone bringing attention to me, especially since I plan on doing some of my own investigating. Hopefully, they will continue to relegate me to obscurity."

Richard also wanted to fly into a tirade about the EMT truck and the cops driving over the tire tracks. Couldn't the officers perceive that those imprints, fossilized into the mud of Beltrami County, just might be evidence? But he knew that once the floodgates of criticism were opened, there might not be enough time in eternity to quench his ire. Instead, he calmly asked Josh if he could use his cell phone. Richard had yet to buy one of those infernal contraptions, preferring instead a measure of peace when he was in the forest, but today Josh's portable phone and its connection with the world would be a godsend.

From the back of the spiral notebook that he always kept in his truck, Richard retrieved the number of a trusted investigator at the state BCA—acronym for Bureau of Criminal Activity. When he was going through his own various trials it had occurred to him that the criminal activity in the acronym might be referring to how the state handled the evidence. But it turned out that the BCA was decently competent. It was the local boys, the district attorney and a few of his quislings, that were the weak link in the system. Proof came one day when a state technician from the BCA lab, Agent Michael Kieran, called Richard's wife and told her that the district attorney had been holding back the findings of the DNA evidence concerning who had attacked Jeanette. The same district attorney that had called Jeanette a liar after she had named her attackers.

"Michael, this is Richard Bede. I'm calling from my camp on North Twin Lake in the national forest up here by Bemidji. That's the Chippewa National Forest. The camp is located on the west side of the forest, about twenty miles south of the town of Blackduck."

"What can I do for you?" asked Michael Kieran. The tone of Agent Kieran's voice was not quite one of irritation, but he knew that a call from Richard was probably not good news.

"I found a girl this morning. A Native girl...murdered."

The sound of paper rustling and a pen clicking. "OK."

"I need your help—she needs your help—to work up the forensics so the circumstances of her death can be determined."

"What about the local coroner?" asked Michael.

"I need the forensics determined—accurately."

"Are you afraid that something important might get missed by the authorities up there?"

"Yes. The story line is already being formed by our local district attorney that this Native girl went out partying after her shift at her workplace, a convenience store up on the highway. The local radio stations were playing this version even before I had discovered the girl's body."

"How did your district attorney come to the conclusion that the girl was out partying if her whereabouts were still unknown by the authorities?" asked Agent Kieran.

"The place was found the next morning with the doors unlocked and the lights on. Her car was still in the lot. So from those facts came the official conclusion that she had gone off with some as yet unknown friends to have a good time."

Richard's poor choice of words, "to have a good time," dredged up bad memories of his daughter's ordeal. After Jeanette's rape, the district attorney had used the local newspaper to announce to the citizens of Bemidji that Jeanette had a night of fun sex.

Michael Kieran, sensing in the quick silence that followed, that an inadvertent similarity to past events had stayed Richard's speech, took up where the thread of logic was going and offered his assistance. "I was scheduled to go up to Thief River Falls in two days, to go over their evidence concerning a college girl gone missing. I'll leave now… um… tonight—I first need to tie up some lab work down here. But I'll call our Bemidji office—Jeff Haltman. He's new but he's good, real good. I'll have him hold the body and keep an eye on the autopsy."

"Make sure that your agent has the coroner use a sexual assault kit to collect evidence," added Richard.

"Of course."

"Sorry. The messed up tire tracks have me a bit rattled."

"What tracks?"

Richard informed Michael Kieran of the smashed tracks and the rest of the events, the rose and the scratches to the girl's palm, the blue gingham dress, everything he could remember. Kieran was really pissed about the tracks. Then Richard remembered the photos he had taken of those tracks, the revelation of which improved Michael's sour mood by some minuscule yet discernible degree.

"Put the rose in a baggie and place it in your freezer. The action of the lake water would have almost certainly washed off any blood, but we never like to take anything for granted."

Clicking off Josh's cell phone, Richard sat next to the now empty fire ring and organized his thoughts. The effect of the morning's long run was catching up to him; normally he'd have taken a short nap by now, but there were as yet other elements of the slowly burgeoning murder investigation that needed to be set in motion.

Brain organized, Richard requested a line of action for his son Josh. "On the way out, stop by the Zemm's cottage and ask them to keep an eye open for any unusual traffic. When they are out working in their garden like they are today, they can see most of what goes by on the road. Maybe we might get lucky."

Richard took a roll of film from the pocket of his running shorts and handed it to his son. "Take my pictures into Wal-Mart and have them developed. Be sure to use the one-hour service. There will be several pictures of the tire treads and of the girl."

Thinking for another moment, he added, "There is a photo lab girl on the day shift, has a longish crew cut of green, pink, or blue hair depending, I imagine, on what day of the week it is, and she is always wearing a multitude of earrings; she does the best job of developing. Tell her the pictures are for me, she'll know. When you get the pictures back, look them over and make eight-by-ten enlargements of any that look promising. That will take another hour or so."

"Consider it done. Then meet you here this afternoon?"

"No, not here. Meet me at home later this evening. I want to first see if I can talk to somebody from the girl's workplace. The radio said that she went missing from the Put-N-Go Gas and Convenience store."

"I'll come by around two or three this afternoon. That should give me plenty of time to get the film developed and the pictures printed and enlarged."

Richard remembered that the second roll of film was still in his camera, not yet shot to its end. "Stand over by that tree, Josh, where my fishing poles and stuff are leaning against the clothesline, and I'll use the last of this film to take your picture." Four, three, two, one—the screen of the camera back-counting to its finish—the arrival of which was announced by the soft whirring of the rewind motor.

Josh left for his assigned duties at Teddy and Clara Zemm's home and the photo lab at Wal-Mart. After his son had departed, Richard took some clothes from his tent, but otherwise left his camp as it was and drove over to his home, twenty miles west of the most western edge of the Chippewa National Forest. He needed a post-run shower before his visit to the deceased girl's workplace.

CHAPTER 6

Revived by a cascade of rusty hot water, Richard backtracked the same twenty miles, to the edge of the national forest, to a convenience store sandwiched between old and new Highways 71, near the tiny village of Tenstrike.

A short, round man in his mid-to-late fifties, with just a few lost stragglers of dyed-black hair carefully plastered in an arc across his forehead, was mumbling complaints as he feverishly stocked the shelves of the all-inclusive gas-grocery-bait shop. The three tiers of his name tag announced, Bob—Put-N-Go—Day Shift Manager. Richard introduced himself, trying to link his civilian persona with the more official persona of BCA Agent Kieran, without formally grafting himself onto Michael's profession or organization.

Bob was sceptical until Richard gave him one of Agent Kieran's business cards and suggested that he call.

"No, that's all right," said Bob. "I don't need cops butting into my business over a young girl that can't take her responsibility serious and gets herself into this mess. Now I have to cover for Miss Frontera every evening until I can find a suitable replacement."

Richard guessed that the mess was her being dead. Harsh thoughts angered silently inside his head, "How so very ill timed for the man."

Richard held his tongue and instead said to Bob-The-Day-Shift Manager, "Can I see the tapes from your security cameras? They might give us a clue regarding her departure from the store last night."

"We don't have any cameras anymore. Had one, but it broke, so we never replaced it. That's not really our legal requirement," added the manager. Then, poking an errant strand of hair back to its proper assigned place, "I can't tell you anything that the sheriff's deputies don't already know. Now if you don't mind, I really need to get back to my napkins."

"One last thing. Can I see your time sheets for the night that Miss Frontera went missing from your store?"

Manager Bob led Richard to an office next to the men's bathroom and brought up a time sheet on the dusty screen of an old computer.

"It shows here that I had Lennie and Cindy scheduled to closing for that evening, but Cindy was marked for an hour less," said Bob. "If business is slow, then sometimes one girl will leave early, which is all right with me because it saves the store some money."

Richard thanked the man, bought a plain Hershey bar with which to feed his chocolate-craving monster—with its "Feed Me Some Chocolate and Nobody Will Get Hurt" mentality, and departed from the store. But not without first noticing that one of the counter girls, a tall brunette covered in pizza flour, seemed to have taken an interest in his conversation with the manager. The girl had the lithe look often associated with women athletes. Richard wondered if her close attention meant anything more serious than just idle curiosity.

Pushing through the store's ubiquitous glass exit door, Richard felt that he should stall for time. He looked to see if the place had an air pump, which it did. Stuck on a front corner of the building was a hose for free air—free air not yet being extinct from the rural petrol stations of northern Minnesota. He pulled his old truck to where he was sure it could be seen from inside the store and began to check his truck's quartet of tires, all the while observing the pizza girl as much as he could so as to make himself all the more obvious.

The girl took the bait. Carrying a miniscule box of trash to the dumpster, she stopped on her way back, kneeling behind the truck's passenger door to hide her considerable height.

"My name is Cindy Heath." Probably the Cindy with the missing hour. "Are you a state cop? If you are, I'd like to talk to you about my friend, Lenora. But not here; I can't talk here."

"I'm not a cop, but I'm working with one—BCA Agent Michael Kieran. I'm meeting with him this evening." Richard handed the counter girl one of Agent Kieran's BCA cards.

"We'll be getting together at my home, over by Puposky. Turn off Highway 15, six miles north of the Buena Vista Ski Hill. Then turn onto County 202, a gravel road, and you will see a log home on the north side, fourth mailbox down. The house is set at the back of a ten-acre field, near the edge of the woods. My name, Richard Bede, is painted bright green on both sides of my mailbox. Can't miss it. Can you be there around six?"

"I'll be there". Cindy Heath unfolded her long legs and stood, her top half far above the box of the truck, and, checking that she had not been seen, strode back to the store. "Gotta go now, before the boss sees me and has a fit. He's so anxious that there will be bad publicity for the store, it's made him awful to have to work for."

~

Back at home Richard lay down on the old couch that he kept in his farm-style kitchen, naps with sunlight, fresh air, and a view onto his field being his preferred mode of rest during the day, and the kitchen having been built with two generous windows, one on the west wall facing the nearby woods and one looking south onto the open field.

Because of his long morning run, Richard slept soundly, waking two hours later to Josh's light knocking on the glass of the sidelight of the east door, the main entrance to his home. He yelled for Josh to come in, the door not being latched or locked, just held closed by the pressure of last winter's insulating felt.

Josh came through the living room and into the kitchen where he cleared a space on the table for the pictures he had gotten developed. "All the photos you took came out fine, though the treads could have had better contrast. You had a similar problem this winter with taking pictures of deer tracks, remember?"

Richard scooped up several of the photos and began to study them as he spoke. "That's right, I remember that. The deer tracks I wanted to shoot looked good to my eyes, but the camera flattened the view and lost the contrast that I needed."

"You were really disappointed because the white snow would not allow pictures of what was so clear to our eyes."

"I am still not sure what I should do to fix the problem. Perhaps a light could be used to illuminate the tracks from the side. That might create more contrast."

"Or maybe use a hand sprayer with colored water, to darken the snow just a bit. Or is that too crazy?"

"Not too crazy if it works. You would be surprised the lengths that photographers go to in order to get a good picture," stated Richard as he continued to file through his collection of murder-site images. Richard was one of the multitude of amateur photographers who had to continuously struggle to figure how to get good pictures. Most of his successes were the result half of effort and half of luck.

By six everyone was assembled in the kitchen, seated around the long trestle table that had been the final project that Josh and his dad had been able to complete before the third trial had taken Richard from his family. Handing everyone his or her choice of steaming hot black tea or ice cold root beers, Richard introduced Cindy Heath to his son Josh and to the BCA agent, Michael Kieran.

"Michael helped me, unofficially, on my own case. He made sure that tests that should have gotten done, were done," said Richard, "even if months and years late." Not said: If only Michael could have made the police interpret the evidence correctly in court when they had testified.

"I was very young when you and your children were going through 'The Trials,' as they are called by my family, but my mom remembers it quite well," said Cindy. "I would often hear her talk about your case as I was growing up, so it is as if I had learned about your troubles firsthand."

"Right, 'The Trials' is a good name for my family's ordeal," said Richard. "I have often been asked if I believe that I was put through a gauntlet of double jeopardy. I can easily say now that I know I was, because I could feel it, not just know it, but really feel the effects of being tried over and over again."

"Triple jeopardy," said Miss Heath.

"I know exactly what it was that our country's founders wanted to prohibit when they wrote the Constitution," said Richard, "before lawyers had not melted its meaning away."

"By the way, my mom thinks you got a bad deal."

"My dad did get a bad deal," said Josh. "But this time the bad guys will lose. With the assistance of Mr. Kieran here, we will find what happened to your friend," vowed Josh, in a tone that was somehow both friendly and aggressive. Josh pushed his long black hair back from his forehead as he spoke. He was slightly taller and thinner than his older brother Foster, but his fine features would become just as intense when he became angry, and that anger always lasted longer.

"I did most of the forensic testing surrounding Richard's case," said Michael. "My lab proved that Richard's daughter, Jeanette, had been telling the truth concerning who had attacked her."

"The local paper never corrected their initial false assertions, the version that the DA had given them," said Josh.

"Also, the Lead Analysis test was done by the FBI, not my lab. The results of that test strongly suggested another shooter, that the dead rapist had been killed by one of his rapist gang, but the FBI did not type a conclusion into their report as one might expect."

"That means that the bullet fragments from the dead rapist did not match my dad's other bullets," said Josh. "This fact was somehow ignored in the trial, the last trial, the only trial where the test was ever used."

"Our job today," said Michael, "is to keep the authorities focused on the facts, away from their perceived politics of this present case."

"According to the hourly news coverage coming over the radio waves, the local authorities were already trying to downplay the events surrounding the Native girl's disappearance. Would her death change their direction, or just make it more difficult to create their version of what may have happened?" said Josh.

Looking at the pictures of the girl lying on the clover of the trail, Cindy's eyes almost teared, but she held it back. "Lennie was my best friend, from when we first met at the high school in Blackduck where we played on the basketball team together. She was better, faster than I was, but I was just plain tall, as you can see, so we played the game well together—complimenting each other." Cindy Heath was a very focused and determined young lady. "Believe me when I say that I am going to make sure you guys find who did this to Lenora." A promise. "And pay the bastards back," she added.

Agent Kieran took over the questioning of Ms. Heath, recording her responses on a small tape recorder. Richard and Josh sat silent, not wanting to interfere, but also not wanting to be caught on tape, which would make their own involvement too apparent to anyone who might ever listen to the recording.

"Lennie would have never left the store unlocked," said Cindy. "She never partied like the radio is hinting at, like she was wild or loose. We had fun, dates and such, but neither one of us drink much at all. That is just not what we are about. And, too, Lennie was really into the Catholic Church in town, the brick one by Bemidji State."

Cindy's gaze rose to the heavy beams crossing the ceiling, as if Lenora's face could be seen there, as if she were talking directly to her lost friend. "We took our faith seriously and both tried to follow the Commandments as best we could. Lennie was more successful, I would believe, than I was," she added.

Cindy had rested her elbows on the table and had clasped her hands together, fingers entwined as in a prayer. "Lennie had better morals than most people."

The tall brunette's knuckles were turning white in their prayer, revealing anger her voice seemed not to belie. After a few moments of silence, she spoke again, "One of the radio stations from town keeps repeating what the cops and DA have said, which is bad enough, but then the station adds things to make it sound like 'dead Native girl' and 'drunk' are synonymous." At that, Cindy dropped her hands into her lap and looked down as if to study them. Richard could see that her anger was mixed with a heavy sadness, and, he thought, perhaps something else, something that eluded even Richard's prison-trained skills of observation.

"Can you think of anyone who might have had a conflict with Miss Frontera?" asked Agent Kieran.

"No. Not at all. She, we, stayed away from anybody who might be troublemakers. And I'm not aware of any animosity between Lennie and anyone else that we might have known. My gut feeling is that she was taken by strangers, perverts or such."

It was apparent that Agent Michael Kieran did not like, but had to accept and acknowledge, the possibility. "I agree. It seems Minnesota is in the midst of an epidemic of assaults against young women." At that, Michael turned off the recorder, ending the official statement.

"Our epidemic started fifteen years ago, about the time Richard was arrested for defending his daughter from her rapists. Back then the state was not ready to accept the premise that people should be allowed to defend themselves from these types of criminals. They still are not ready as far as I can tell, even after the abductions and deaths of so many girls and young women."

Sensing that Cindy was beginning to stress again, Josh changed the subject to the pictures hanging on the kitchen walls, scenes from nature and photos of animals that his dad had taken in the local area and in the Boundary Waters wilderness near Ely. Soon they were busy talking about canoeing and camping in the wilds of the Chippewa National Forest in north central Minnesota, and the canoe wilderness nestled inside the Superior National Forest in Minnesota's Arrowhead Region.

As the meeting ended, everyone exchanged numbers and agreed to meet again in a few days. Josh would be the default contact because he had a cell phone and could always be reached. Cindy Heath left first since she had to go into work early the next day. That gave Agent Kieran an opportunity to again look over the pictures Richard had taken of the tire tracks and the girl.

"I don't see anything significant," said Michael, "other than the star-shaped impression on the track here, and the fact that this is most likely from a truck tire. See here, it is wider than most car tires, and the tread is more prominent. Well, I'll take the set of copies you made for me and study them again tomorrow when I'm not so tired. The drive from the Cities seems to be getting longer, every year older I get." At that, Agent Kieran left too.

Richard and Josh walked out onto the side porch to see Michael off. It was getting late. Evening twilight was arriving with a shroud of cool air and a companion of fine mist. Michael Kieran's taillights faded away as he drove down the long drive and turned toward the highway.

"Michael seemed to be tired," said Josh. "Weary, is more like it."

"His lab must be very busy. When I was a boy, Minnesota was a very peaceful land. Now our state is infected with violence and crime, especially against women and girls, but the politicos and the media refuse to acknowledge the problem. Michael and his lab workers are fighting an uphill battle."

After a few minutes of being misted by the night air, like plants in a sunless greenhouse, father and son went back inside to the relative warmth of the kitchen, and sat shortway across from each other at the trestle table that they had built together during Richard's brief spell of bail-set freedom, many years ago.

Yes, many years ago, but Richard knew that a large part of his soul would always be stuck in the past, trying to fill in those missing years of his life.

Josh pushed the "evidence" pictures aside and dumped out a small oatmeal box full of packets of vegetable and flower seeds that his dad had bought in anticipation of northern Minnesota's springtime: a cool hope for a warm summer.

"I dug up that space where Foster had parked his broken-down Oldsmobile," said Richard. "The grass was dead and gone anyway. I'll plant that first, with flowers and some of the tougher and more cold-loving veggies."

"Then you'll have a flower garden in the shape of a classic '56 Oldsmobile. That's cool."

"That will leave three more vehicle spaces I can dig and plant. Let's see: where the old Ford truck had been, the Cadillac with the roof of the back seat cut away..."

"The Caddy was Foster's field-hunting car," said Josh.

"...and some small car that you guys had left."

"We really had a junk yard while you were gone." Josh spread the seed packets over the table. "Well, let's pick what would look good in your '56 Olds garden."

Richard leaned over the table to help in the selection. "Zinnias did really well last year. So did moss roses, but I couldn't find any seeds in the stores this year for some reason. Nasturtiums, cosmos, flax...I'll put Mexican sunflowers in the middle. The edges can be planted with radishes and alyssum and leaf lettuce. Broccoli can be hidden in with the taller flowers."

"These Sweet Williams look nice," suggested Josh.

"I don't know how well they will grow, but I'll try them and see."

Josh put the picked seeds to one side, next to the photos of the tire tracks, the trail to Rice Pond, and the dead girl. The "evidence" picture of Miss Frontera looked less like evidence and more like a picture of a pretty girl sleeping on a bed of clover. Josh couldn't help but notice.

"Well, what do you think?" asked Josh. "Will we be able to catch her killer?"

"I don't know, Josh. I'll have to let my mind work this over while I'm sleeping tonight. But I know that I'm not going to leave my camp set up at the lake. For one thing, it's starting to rain, and besides, I need the phone and computer that I have here at home. I'm going to drive over and disassemble my camp tonight before it gets any later, darker, or wetter."

"I can help you take down your camp," said Josh. "But first I have to stop at my place to check on Barker. I need to feed her and let her out for a few moments. When I'm finished taking care of my dog, I'll meet you at North Twin and help you break camp."

CHAPTER 7

There was an old farmer's joke that went something like: "A traveling salesman was lost way out in the countryside, and so he stopped to ask directions from a farmer. The old geezer thought and thought and thought, then finally, after many, many minutes of deep contemplation, announced to the salesman that 'you can't get there from here.' "

Beltrami County, north of Bemidji, made that old joke a reality. There was no good connection between the east half of the county and the west half. One either had to use Island View Road, set just a few miles north of Bemidji, or you had to drive much farther north up Highway 15 until you came to the Nebish Road. This left a great block of land, most of which was Buena Vista State Forest, without a hard surface east-west passage. In the middle of this block of forest, starting behind the county's only ski hill, was a mud and gravel road that could sometimes be used by 4x4's in dry weather. That was it.

In reality, there was a logical place for a good east-west route to exist: halfway between Island View Road and Nebish Road was Highway 22. But 22 only ran west of 15, not east. A driver coming across the county would get to Highway 15, then it would end, "you can't get there from here." This probably made sense in 1902 when the roads were laid out following the ancient trails of the Ojibway and the newer tracks made by the settlers' oxen.

This evening Richard just wanted to drive directly, or at least as directly as he could, to his camp, so he drove south on 15 to Island View Road. This route would be the quickest and shortest possible, considering that the rain had once again made the dirt shortcut into impassable mud.

Island View Road, and the Forest Service roads that branched off the main roads, were all wonderfully scenic in the daylight, but twisty and treacherous at night if speed was desirable. Richard preferred to slow his old Chevy truck and take his time. Safer that way—what with this evening's intermittent spells of rain and mist and rain again, and besides, driving this unhurried pace gave him a better opportunity to review in his mind what had happened so far.

Few as they were, what did the clues mean … the dead Native girl—murdered is what Richard believed to be obvious. The blue dress she had worn to her death. Blue gingham. The rose, the cuts on the girl's hand, the lack of official interest. What else? A Celtic cross bitten into the thin space between two of the girl's teeth. That must have taken a great deal of force and determination on the part of Miss Frontera. What else? Thoughts muddled aimlessly inside Richard's mind as he drove through the dark.

When Richard arrived back at North Twin Lake he saw that a badly beat-up, very dusty white van was already parked in the area above the Twin Lake campsites. Leech trappers often preferred vans because they were as tough as trucks while being much more secure than trucks—a few pails of leeches were worth hundreds of dollars.

"Must be someone setting out his leech traps tonight," thought Richard, as he parked his truck a short distance from the van.

The season for capturing the slimy, squirmy invertebrates had just gotten underway. When they were teenagers, Richard's sons had caught leeches every year, spring and early summer. Made some good money, but the days started early and the hours were long when the hunt was in full swing.

The sky had calmed itself to a fine mist again, while the low clouds thinned to reveal a slice of moon that had been waxing from new to quarter the past few days, so that its moonlight, filtered by the misty clouds, gently washed the forest in an opaque luminescence.

Guided by the dusky moonshine, Richard slowly walked the winding trail to his camp. It was darker in the forest, with just enough light to allow Richard to find his way, aided by the fact that he knew the twists and turns of the path by heart. As he neared the lake, he could discern the opening in the trees that was his camp. Something or someone was standing near the fire pit in the middle of the camp's clearing.

Richard stopped and stared at the apparition. His vision lost hold of the form. Not enough light. Richard moved his eyes to the right and left—an old night-fighting trick learned at Army basic training. The rods of the eyes, located toward the edges of the insides of each eye, would be activated if a soldier did not stare directly at the enemy. The form reappeared.

Richard saw a long, faint glint of steel, reflected from where the man's hand would be if his arms were being held loose at his sides. "It can't be Josh already, can it?" wondered Richard. His son could not have gotten here already, though he certainly would have driven much faster than his conservative-driving dad. It is possible—maybe—but not likely. No, this wasn't Josh, or Foster either; the man standing in his camp was huge—tall and wide, like a great block of humanoid flesh. Perhaps a ghostly reincarnated Neanderthal or the legendary beast Sasquatch.

Richard knew that fear and trepidation might impede his thought processes, so he would have to devise a strategy soon or be at the mercy of circumstances. He decided to use threats and antagonism to test what he now knew to be a stranger in his camp. If it was Josh or one of Josh's friends, there would be no harm done, except the teasing that Josh would for sure throw his way; but if the intruder had hostile or criminal intent, then his plan should set off the trespasser. Better to act while Richard was still hidden in the shadows of the path.

Richard shouted, "Why are you in my camp? What did you steal?" No response from the dark form. "I'll get the cops on you!"

Between "cops" and "you" the intruder had pivoted and rapidly accelerated into a full sprint toward Richard's voice. But Richard had, aided by quick reflexes and adrenaline, also spun in his tracks and started to dash back up the trail. Richard was not a fighter. Richard was a runner. But not a fast runner; time would be needed in order to outdistance his pursuer, probably younger and stronger than he was, which would most likely be the case or the man would not be giving chase in the first place. The initial turns in the trail had given Richard a chance. Each time his attacker's footfalls had come close to him, another invisible turn would give Richard an edge. He could hear the man—and it was definitely a man's voice, he could be certain of that now—as the man cursed tree branches struck during the pursuit of his quarry.

Each time the man would begin to close the gap, a new twist in the trail would buy Richard a reprieve. Richard could hear the man's breathing becoming more labored. With time and conditioning being Richard's allies, the contest might yet be won.

"Thank God I know these trails as well as I do," thought Richard.

Just as his confidence began to grow—he could win this race, a leathery root reached out and tripped him up, like a disembodied hand in one of those 1950s monster movies that Richard loved so well in his childhood. But that was far in the past; fear was always fun in imagination, not so much when it was steeped in reality. Richard crashed.

"Dammit," grunted Richard. Fortunately, he was tough from his daily regimen of running, and lucky to hit the hard path evenly, so nothing was broken. He immediately pushed his body back up, more like bouncing off the ground than landing on it, to continue his fast escape from the man with the glint of steel in his hand.

The attacker, having certainly heard Richard's fall, must have been encouraged, because he increased his speed considerably, as a swift cheetah in the final seconds before it takes down its prey. The trail broke out into the open area where the vehicles were parked. Richard fell again, slipping on something slimy. "Maybe an oil slick from one of the parked vehicles," he reasoned. As his legs swept sideways from under him, he rolled as he hit the ground and then came back up running again, his hands and most of his body covered in the mud that the mist and rain had reconstituted from a solid into this viscous substance. At least it wasn't oil.

Richard ran back into the darkness of the forest, picking the short trail this time, the one that led to the camp with the good swimming beach. He knew that the old scar on the trail's face lie just ahead, now repaired with jail sweat and oak railroad timbers. A wide arc in the trail, providentially placed before the timber-built retaining wall, would hide Richard from his pursuer for a moment.

Slowing imperceptibly, Richard timed the placement of his right foot onto the top timber and vaulted into the air. Flexing his knees like a parachutist about to end his airborne descent, he came down with a slight jolt, much better than he would have thought possible—given the antiquity of his bones and the dimness of the trail.

Reining himself to a slow jog, Richard looked over his shoulder and saw his assailant appear around the curve. He hoped that the man was as tired as he sounded and would, in the dim light of the forest, focus on his fleeing prey and ignore the trail. Like the slow motion fall of Saddam's statue, the man went over the retaining wall, his last step not finding anything more solid than fog and mist. The thuds of meat and bone against old oak timbers were painful even to Richard's ears.

Timing his escape to coincide with the crash, Richard cut off the trail and bolted into the woods, finding a fern-filled hideaway behind the broken top of an old aspen tree. His heavy breathing immediately began to slow, another benefit of being in good shape. Even if his fallen attacker could hear anything above his own rasping gasps, he would not likely hear Richard's quiet heart.

"Damn Jesus, Damn Jesus to hell!" yelled the sprawled attacker. The man rose to his feet, albeit with apparent pain, and walked the rest of the way to the lake. His progress was relayed clearly by the shuffling of his bruised and battered legs. Finding the beach empty, Richard's attacker returned to the timbered wall and stood before it, for what seemed like an eternity, searching for something at its base. When he found what he had sought, his dropped weapon, the man laboriously climbed the timbered wall, not seeing the faint path that circumvented the repaired cut. The giant stopped at the topmost beam and stood in relative silence.

A frog hopped by Richard's face, apparently unaware of the new life form hiding under the broken tree top. The mist once again turned into a light rain, its soft patter on the half-rotten leaves of the forest floor muting the sound of the frog as it jumped about its business. Scattered clumps of violets added their sweet, delicate fragrance to the musky effusions of the decaying leaves. If not for the cold and the rain and the man with his weapon, Richard could take a nap right there. He felt safe in his hidden lair. A long time passed.

The rain stopped, allowing a dense fog to take its place, rolling up from the lake and into the forest where Richard was hiding. Anything lower than twenty inches was invisible. Richard was lower than the required twenty inches and invisible. The fog reminded him of a war movie he had seen when he was a boy. While crossing an open field, a company of GIs had been ambushed by German machine gunners, but when the guns opened up the soldiers fell into the cover of the fog. As long as they did not move and stayed quiet, they were safe. Richard remembered to stay still and be quiet.

A large, dark, great horned owl glided by silently and landed high in a nearby basswood tree. It called into the night, "hoo-hoo-hoooo, hoo-hoo," which sounded like, "eat...my...fooood, ...I'll...eat...yoooo." Perhaps this fearsome feathered predator thought Richard was after his little frog.

As if spooked by the calls of the owl, the block-headed man left his own perch on top of the retaining wall and slowly proceeded to walk back to the parking area.

Listening in the silence of the rain-soaked forest, Richard could easily judge the man's progress. Without hound dogs or a battalion of National Guardsmen to ferret out Richard, and acres of forest tangle to hide in, he could hold to ground for hours if need be. But another sound reached his ears, the sharp whine of a small motorcycle, that Richard knew would be a bright red Honda, to be more specific. His other young son, Foster, was ripping down the service road to the open area where the vehicles were parked, Richard's truck and the big man's dirty white van.

Josh must have sent Foster to help his dad disassemble the camp. Not good! Not good timing at all! Richard crawled from under his lair and jogged up the hill, quietly pursuing his pursuer, trying to time his entrance at the forest parking area to coincide with Foster's arrival. Demons from hell could not have made more noise as Foster did as he broke into the open and drove his snarling motorcycle up to the side of his dad's truck.

"Foster! Watch out! That guy has a weapon—don't let him get near you!"

Warning given and received, Foster dropped his snarling motorcycle against the side of the truck—undoubtedly adding another dent to the multitude of previous injuries, and stepped into the clearing to face the dark and approaching hulk. The last time Foster stood his ground against an armed attacker, Foster had ended up with a hefty bill for the attacker's teeth, courtesy of Beltrami County's dishonest and pervert-sympathetic district attorney, DA Foat—Foat the goat, as the ladies in the county offices had named him.

Apparently realizing that he was larger than the newly arrived motorcyclist, the man closed the distance between himself and Foster. But like the half-life of a deadly radioactive substance, the distance continually halving itself without ever completely closing the gap, the big man would never be close enough. Before the hulk was as near as he needed to be to strike, Foster smashed a hard fist into the front of the man's blocky head, knocking the attacker backwards into the mud. As yet an unbeliever, the big man brought himself to his feet and, weapon still in hand, again lunged at Foster.

There was another appalling thud.

It reminded Richard of an earlier sound that Richard had heard years before. He remembered, long ago, when the kids were small and they lived in their rural home in Adam's county in central Wisconsin. Richard would sometimes take them on bike trips to the little town of Adam's Friendship. Inevitably, as they passed a certain decrepit farm-yard in the middle of their journey, a very mean pit bull would chase them and try to bite the kids. Only luck had kept them safe.

One evening as they rode back from the town of Adam's Friend-ship, as daylight was fading into darkness, they approached the pit bull's favored ambush site. Richard had previously armed his children with flashlights, with instructions to ride as fast as possible past the farmyard and to direct the disorienting beams of their flashlights into the dog's face if it got too close. But the dog had timed his ambush more accurately this time, cutting a low intercepting angle toward Jeanette. As the dog pulled next to Jeanette, she blinded him with her flashlight. The dog kept running alongside of her, snarling and snap-ping at her, but he could not see well enough to make the kill. Though Jeanette was frightened, she held her light in the dog's face.

This drama continued at a high rate of speed; dad could not help and did not know what to do. But then, up ahead, everyone could see a looming metal post—square, heavy steel, about four feet tall, the kind used to house telephone connections. And everyone could also see that an impact was inevitable. The pit bull, barking and growling madly, crashed his chest dead center into that steel post. The sound of that long ago collision was unforgettable.

It was the same sound tonight.

Foster's fist collided with the side of the big man's head, sending him back into the mud. The attacker had enough. He struggled to his feet and ran off to his van.

"Leave him go, Foster. He might still have his weapon, so better to be cautious."

The attacker started his van and spun in the park lot and flew away up the muddy road, muttering incoherent obscenities as he drove away, "Daa Jeeze, daa Jeez to heh."

Foster, searching the scene of the short fight, found what he was looking for. "Here's his weapon, Dad, a knife. He had dropped it on the second shot."

"And probably couldn't think clear enough to remember to pick it back up. Don't touch it, though. Maybe the knife has that guy's fingerprints on it. Let me get a plastic bag from my truck."

"Agent Kieran can have it checked," said Foster.

"Right."

"Did you know that guy?" asked Foster.

"No, never saw him before. Actually, I still haven't seen him. Just a big blob in the darkness. I'm not sure if I'd recognize him even if I saw him tomorrow in the daylight." Richard spoke as he collected the knife with a pair of pliers and placed it safely in a clean trash bag from his truck. The steel glint that so scared the piss out of Richard turned out to be a long thin fillet knife, speckled with pits of rust and dried fish scales, but otherwise as sharp as a straight razor. "Christ Almighty, you would have been sliced to ribbons and infected with a case of tetanus all in one swipe," complained Richard.

"Et tu, Brute."

"Yeah, me too," agreed Richard.

"Well, let's close your camp. You'll be safer at home, and you can call Mr. Kieran and inform him about what happened here. Do you want me to stay over with you tonight at your place?"

"No, I'll be safe enough at home. Besides, I think that my attacker has had enough for now. He'll be crawling back to the hole where he came from to lick his wounds, I'm sure. Not only did you clobber him, twice, but he also ran off the oak embankment on the trail to the beach. You should have heard the crash he made."

"Ouch. I imagine."

"I wonder if Josh is still planning on coming over to help us take down the camp?" asked Richard.

"No, he was tired, and his dog had eaten part of that new couch his girlfriend had talked him into buying. Josh said he just wanted to throw Barker in the back yard and relax in front of the television."

"I once lost a ski boot to the teeth of a growing puppy. But a couch?" wondered Richard.

It didn't take long to disassemble Richard's camp. He didn't have much equipment with him, and they didn't bother to fold the tent since it was wet anyway. Tomorrow Richard would have to spread it out to dry, outside if sunny, inside if not.

Foster followed Richard's truck until clear of the national forest, then split off toward Turtle River and his girlfriend, Sally Jean. She would gently comfort him tonight, but not until after first scolding him for getting himself into such a perilous situation.

"Thank God for Foster," thought Richard as he retraced the curves of Island View Road, winding his way back home. "I'd hate to have to escape from that guy right after I had finished one of my distance runs; that would be a disaster."

Once home, Richard threw his dirty clothes and his wet camping gear in a corner of the kitchen. The mess could wait until tomorrow. Then he made a call to Agent Kieran.

"Hello, Michael, I have a bizarre ending to report about today's developments. I surprised a very large person snooping at my camp."

"Was he trying to steal something?" asked Agent Kieran.

"I don't think so; I think he might have been specifically looking for me because he was holding a knife before I even had a chance to speak to him. Luckily, I was able to run away from him."

"Good thing you keep in shape."

"I may be in good shape, but I was also tired from my run earlier this morning, and I fell twice."

"So you were just lucky," said Michael.

"Well, he didn't know the trail like I did, and I could hear him having to bust through branches as he ran after me. Then, after he took a nasty fall, I was able to slip him."

"He couldn't find you?"

"No. I hid in the forest." With a little frog for company. "The man's breathing was so laboured that he couldn't hear me even if I had made a sound, which I didn't."

"That's good; so there was no actual contact then?"

"Not with me. But Foster clobbered him, twice."

"Good that you did not have to commit the crime of self-defense again."

"I was hiding off the trail that leads to the beach; I can show you where tomorrow and you'll see where the guy ran off an embankment made of oak railroad ties."

"That must have hurt. Do you think he was injured enough to need a doctor or go to the hospital?" asked Michael.

"I would have thought that he would have broken all his bones, but he got up after the fall and walked down to the beach and back."

"I'll have a police check put in tonight with all the area hospitals, just in case."

"So, then I heard Foster's motorcycle. I could recognize its sound; besides, I figured, Josh must have sent his brother to help disassemble my camp. So I left my hiding place and ran to the vehicle park to warn Foster. The big man—he looked to be huge—went after Foster, which was a mistake since Foster knocked him over hard."

"Sounds like a repeat of that trouble Foster got into a few years back, when you were still in prison."

"Right. That's just what I was thinking. If you don't mind, when and if you type an official report, it might be just as well that you keep the information about Foster's combat tonight to yourself until we can figure out who killed Lennie Frontera."

"I planned on doing exactly that; no need for too many people knowing what we are up to and interfering with my investigation. I've had too many things compromised in the past. In your county," he added. "This time we're going to get our man."

"Not to change the subject, but what did you think of our Miss Cindy Heath?" asked Richard.

"I think that she really wants to catch her friend's killer. She could be an important asset to our investigation. I also believe she might know Lenora's attacker, though she might not realize it at the present time. I think that the attacker was a patron of the convenience store and marked his next target while posing as a customer."

"I suppose you're right." But Richard had an uneasy feeling about Cindy Heath. Just why, he wasn't sure. He couldn't characterize his misgivings, let alone be specific. "Call me early tomorrow, before noon, Michael; give both of us time to digest what has happened so far. Oh, yeah, before I forget, when Foster hit the man the second time, the guy dropped his knife. I picked it up, cleanly, and put it in a plastic bag."

"Good, I'll collect it tomorrow when we meet."

Clicking off the phone, Richard went outside onto his porch. The low, misty clouds had at last blown away, revealing a shimmering light show dancing in the northeast sky. The moon had fallen below the western horizon, so there was complete darkness with which to see the aurora borealis. Springtime was not often the best season for viewing the northern lights, but tonight would be an exception. Soft curtains of blue, green, and white were waving across the sky. At times the translucent lights would almost disappear, and then they would slowly rebuild themselves to another peak of intensity, and then again suddenly die into near disappearance, only to recreate themselves into a fresh apparition.

Orion appears to have tripped, as Richard had done earlier that evening, and was halfway through the process of falling into the far western horizon. "Perhaps this portends poor hunting for the both of us, now that winter is over," thought Richard. He hoped not; there was greater game to be caught than snowshoe rabbits, whitetail deer, and ruffed grouse. The clear sky was quickly letting what little heat there was to escape into the heavens. Soon the cold night air of this northern Minnesota evening succeeded in sending Richard back into the warm comforts of his home.

His last thoughts were of the owl, and the little frog hiding under cover of the fog.

CHAPTER 8

Despite all odds, and the haunting memory of a dead Native girl, Richard had managed to turn in early and, thanks to the long run of that morning, to sleep the deep sleep that results from physical exercise, thereby allowing him to wake just as the sun was rising. After a hot shower taken, not so much to get clean as to limber up his old joints and sore muscles, he spent the first two hours in his yard, splitting poplar firewood that Josh had salvaged from a resort that had been cutting clearings for more cottages. Poplar wasn't the best firewood, but if covered and dried correctly, it would work to heat the house, a superior fate for the wood to that of being thrown onto huge slash piles and incinerated with showers of kerosene.

A faint ringing from the phone in the house, barely discernible to anyone that might be outside, sent Richard on a full run. Agent Kieran had said that he was going to call before noon, so Richard figured that this must be Michael calling like he promised. The voice from the receiver was female.

"Cindy Heath here." Formal, but to the point, and not Kieran.

"Let me catch my breath, Cindy. I just ran in."

"I was wondering what you were planning on doing later today. In an hour I get off work, so I wanted to offer my humble services, presuming there is anything I could do to help." Miss Heath definitely intended to impose herself into the workings of this investigation, that much had become abundantly clear even to Richard's leisurely thought processes.

Not wanting Cindy Heath to be present when he and Michael went over the case together, Richard silently edited his schedule for the day, leaving out mentioning this morning's upcoming meeting with Michael. He liked Cindy, but he didn't really know her; besides, there was a disquieting feeling he had about her, one he couldn't quite put a name to.

"I was doing some outside work this morning. I like to get something tangible accomplished every day to satisfy the work ethic, but maybe I can call you later this afternoon and let you know what I have decided to do, that is, if I can think of anything to do." Miss Heath agreed to that plan, though Richard could sense an anxiousness, or so it seemed. Maybe not, maybe just his imagination.

Hearing an engine approaching his house, not his imagination this time, Richard tried to identify the vehicle. It was not Josh's truck or Foster's red Honda motorcycle. Two possibilities eliminated.

It was Agent Kieran. Michael had chosen to arrive without first calling. Unless Richard had, at some point this morning, not heard his phone ringing, lost in his thoughts and the whacks of the splitting maul.

Michael and Richard went into the kitchen and sat at the trestle table, which by now had been commandeered as a command center of sorts for the investigation, photos and notes spread hither and yon across the expanse of the old, scarred, pine table.

"The preliminary results from the county autopsy indicate that our victim was raped and beaten before being drowned," said Agent Kieran.

Richard did not answer.

"I had one of my men at the BCA lab check the rose," said Agent Kieran. "Nothing. Any blood or skin that may have been scraped onto it must have washed off in the lake water."

"Pond," said Richard, more curtly than intended. He was troubled by the girl's senseless death, the dearth of clues and witnesses, the lack of interest by the local authorities, and the total insensitivity of the local newspaper and radio stations.

Agent Kieran sensed that the events of yesterday must have brought back hard memories for Richard, so he quickly shifted focus from that of the girl. "The pictures you took of the tire tracks will be effective for matching to a vehicle when we find the killer. Which we will," added Michael.

"The girl, Miss Frontera, was a Christian—the cross," concluded Richard. "And she was dressed nice. A blue gingham dress. How many young ladies would bother to dress well nowadays?"

"Do young ladies ever wear gingham anymore?" asked Michael. "There might be something there, Richard. That is what is making you suspect something, but you can't quite put your finger on it, and that is bothering you."

The possibilities exhausted and the coffee growing cold, Michael took his leave. Richard gave him the glint-possessed fillet knife that his attacker had dropped the previous night. As they were stepping out onto the porch, Foster rode up on his snarling motorcycle. The three men talked for a few moments before Agent Kieran drove off to town. Foster followed his dad into the living room, through the center hallway, and back to the kitchen.

"I see that you threw all your camp gear into the corner over there. Well, I had better spread your tent out on the porch before it has a chance to get moldy."

"Thanks, Foster."

Most of the water would have dried last night under the influence of the arid wood heat, but there might yet be some slight amount of moisture hidden in the folds of the crumpled tent. Richard had started a fire in the stove before turning in last evening, spring nights in northern Minnesota falling toward freezing even when the days were warm.

"Do you want to drive to Rice Pond and see where I found the girl? I can call Miss Heath and have her come over, then we can all go together to examine the site."

Foster agreed, Richard called Miss Heath, then father and son stacked more of the poplar wood while they waited for Cindy Heath to arrive at their place. When the posse had assembled, they piled into Richard's truck for the drive to the pond. Each day more and varied types of tree were leafing out, while the trees that earlier had awoken from dormancy were slowly becoming a darker green. As is his usual practice, Richard took his camera. Perhaps, he thought, to capture the perfect light green of this newborn forest growth.

Though their planned expedition was to a woodland pond set at the end of a damp forest trail, Cindy was wearing a dress, albeit a country-style garment, looking like a throwback to the war years of the forties—brown, faded cloth that came to the exact middle of her knees. In style and general ambiance the dress harmonized with her auburn hair and the strong, thin build of her tall frame, as if she was planning to work in a World War II Victory garden, not visit the site where her dear friend had so recently been found dead. At least her feet were combat ready, dressed in white, ankle length work socks and an old pair of red, white, and blue hiking shoes, now faded to pink, cream, and baby blue.

The ride over to Rice Pond was mostly in silence, save the good radio advice delivered in a rude manner by Dr. Laura.

Disembarking at their destination, Cindy spoke, "The funeral for Lenora will be in two days. That is the earliest that the body can be recovered from the coroner. I'll be there, of course, along with a few family members and close friends."

"I am very sorry about what happened to your friend," said Foster, with sincerity if not with great eloquence, appearing relaxed standing in the center of the trail, his short, black hair making him look very young, in contrast to his large, rough hands which belied the years spent, while he was yet in high school, working on a dairy farm north of Puposky to help support a fatherless family and to pay restitution for friend's-of-rapists teeth.

The day was bright, but cooler than yesterday, and as a result the trail had become firm again. The three vehicles of the authorities and the night's rain and mist had erased the last vestiges of the truck tracks, so the walk to the pond was mainly a nature hike.

"Teal," whispered Foster. "They're cupping their wings to land in the pond."

"I see them," said Cindy, as she crouched down to conceal at least some of her height.

Two small ducks, with green chevrons on grey wings, set their wings and glided below the level of the treetops. The hikers moved quietly to the pond where they could observe the pair of green-winged teal that had landed in front of a facade of reeds and saw grass along a fold of the pond, about forty yards from the hikers.

Keeping her sight on the teal, Cindy kneeled at the shoreline, dipped her hands in the pond, and splashed a little of its water onto her face, then patted off the excess with the bottom hem of her dress. As she did so, a small cross on a fine chain fell from the front of her dress and hung over the water, catching the reflected light of the pond as the cross swung back and forth from Cindy's neck. Richard did not know how she came to posses it, but he recognized the cross.

Cindy stood and put the cross back in her dress, against the bare skin of her chest.

"I wonder, if those birds could talk, if they could tell us anything about Lenora and what happened here?" Cindy was conversing with herself as much as with her present companions. "I wish I could talk to the animals."

They continued to follow the trail as it curved past the south side of the pond. Snow had left the trail before ice had left the pond, so the path was already green from the clover while the pond was still washed in the browns and greys of last autumn. Cindy spotted a fat porcupine high in a poplar tree. The branch it was on seemed much too small for the animal's weight.

"I don't think it is smart enough to know it is too high up," said Cindy. "That branch must surely break."

"Green poplar is tough and springy," said Foster. "But you might be right; there has to be a limit."

They watched the porcupine as it ate the greenish bark from the branch it was holding onto.

For a while longer they enjoyed the wild beauty of the pond and its inhabitants, then they departed the national forest lands and drove back to Richard's home. Their talk during the ride back was lighter, if unenlightening. The ride itself was uneventful save for a large herd of Holstein cows that somehow had managed to escape the bonds of their barbed-wire captivity and flee their peaceful fields for the rather questionable freedom of Forest Service Road 2213.

As Richard slowed his old truck to a mere crawl, the black and white cows converged on the vehicle and crowded around, shoulder to shoulder, the better to lick last winter's salt from its blue surface. Cow spittle soon turned the truck's windows into opaque surfaces.

"If Michael could fingerprint cow tongues, we could identify these bovine culprits in court and make them pay for slobbering my truck."

Upon arriving at Richard's home, Cindy said that she would call and check later, then she departed. Richard and Foster watched her drive the quarter mile field road as she left the property, then they went inside to cold glasses of grape juice, Richard's third favorite drink, next to cereal-soaked milk, and frigid, post-run water. Richard heated his oven to 425, a temperature memorized out of necessity to bachelorhood, and cooked a thick pizza for the two of them.

"It's not delivery, Dad, it's French," said Foster, referencing an old private joke salvaged from a TV commercial for that brand of pizza.

Foster was hungry from the fresh air and the short hike, and the general principle of being young. After dinner, Foster, in deference to the heartfelt pleads of Richard, who hated any kind of dish washing, cleaned the two forks and the two plates, then dried his hands on a dish towel and sat down across from his dad at the kitchen table.

Their talk consisted predominantly of deer hunting and making plans for deer hunting. There would have to be more archery practice this summer if they were to be ready at the beginning of this autumn's season. And equipment would have to be updated or repaired. As they talked, Foster's big hands absentmindedly found the pictures from his dad's last two rolls of 35-millimeter film. The girl lying in the grass at Rice Pond, the tire tracks with the star-shaped cutouts, the water's edge and the thick reeds that had hid the girl's body, floating unseen, face down in the water.

There were also pictures of North Twin Lake, and the middle camp where Richard had been bivouacked prior to his finding Lenora Frontera. Pictures of trees, flowers, ducks that were too far away to make a good picture, an eagle, two good sunsets or sunrises. There were the end-of-roll pictures that Richard had taken of Josh at the North Twin camp.

Foster, shuffling back through the pictures as he listened to his dad, came to a daylight picture taken of Josh at his dad's camp. In the photo, a short rope had been stretched taut between two nearby trees, like a clothesline strung at chest level. Most of the camp gear had been leaned against or hung from the rope, a simple plan of organization performed by Richard in deference to his chronic absentmindedness. Josh was posing for his dad's camera, leaning against a maple that anchored one end of the rope.

Richard had recognized early on that his two youngest boys, though certainly not geniuses, had been blessed with the uncanny ability to automatically recognize their surroundings and to find their way back from wherever it was that their youthful excursions might have taken them. As young as two years old, when their mom and dad had been busy building the family's first house, Foster and Josh would escape their prison of a crib and slink off into the small woods surrounding the building site. There, hidden in the dense growth of oak trees, baby pines, and tall ferns, they would play and explore for hours, then later manage to find their way back when hunger or mom called them home.

Now, as Foster studied the photograph of Josh at his dad's camp, his unconscious mind automatically sorted all the elements in the picture and compared it to the pile of camping gear thrown into the corner of the kitchen. Inner processing completed, Foster returned to conscious mode and announced his findings.

"Your grapple hook is missing."

CHAPTER 9

Like an old, slow computer freshly supplied with additional facts, Richard's mind gradually began to generate newborn connections, "You're right. It was not loaded last night."

"Correct."

"And because we know, per that picture and my old memory, it had previously been with the rest of my gear—that means when camp was broke, the grapple hook was not on the rope where it should have been."

"Correct."

"Therefore, someone took it from my camp before I had returned and surprised the hulk."

"That must be what happened," agreed Foster. "So, who took your grapple hook, and why?"

"It is improbable that my camp was visited on the same night by both a thief and an armed attacker, so they must have been one in the same person."

"But why take an inexpensive grapple hook, and leave the much more costly fishing poles?" asked Foster.

"That man had a knife in his hand before I spoke to him, and he continued to pursue me to the beach at the west camp when he could have escaped in his van. He was not a startled thief. He had been waiting for me, and because it was I who had found the girl at the pond—that must be the connection."

"But how would Lenora's killer, and it must be her killer, how would he know that it was you that found the girl? And how would he know that you were camping on North Twin?"

Richard had to think about Foster's questions. The whole thing didn't make any sense. Something or someone was missing from the equation.

"I don't know," said Richard. "I just don't see how."

"OK, let's get back to the missing grapple hook," said Foster.

"Well, we know the grapple hook was not taken for its monetary value," said Richard, "because it isn't worth very much. Its value to the hulk must have been in its intended use."

"What were you going to use the hook for?" asked Foster.

"I was going to clear enough branches from the shoreline to make an open area to swim in, for later in the summer. A small opening would also give me a place to pull up my canoe."

"The hulk must have needed to fish something out of the water, too," figured Foster.

"He must have lost something in the water," said Richard.

"Then are you saying that: the grapple hook was taken to retrieve something?"

"Not something," stated Richard. "That is not a question we can answer. Somewhere."

"Maybe somewhere...lost at your camp...or maybe from Rice Pond?" Foster answered his own question, "Right!"

Foster helped his dad load an old aluminum canoe into the back of his dad's truck, then kicked his motorcycle to life and took off.

"I'll stop by my place and get my chest waders and spotlight. Even in daylight, the powerful spotlight will allow us to see deeper into the water."

"Good idea," agreed Richard. "You get your light and whatever else you think we will need. Then we'll meet at Rice Pond and see if we can find what it was that the hulk had lost in the water. If it's the correct somewhere, it might lead to the mystery something."

After Foster left, Richard put his swim trunks on under his work pants in case he had to dive in the pond to retrieve whatever might be there, then he rechecked the rope holding the canoe in the bed of his truck, and drove off.

When Richard arrived at the entrance to Rice Pond he saw that the trail was still firm from the cold day, so he took a chance that he would not get stuck and drove most of the way to the water's edge. Dragging his canoe the remainder of the distance, not difficult to do over the lubrication of clover and grass, he pushed its nose into the frigid water and, paddle in hand, pushed away from the shore.

Later in the summer the water would be murky from the season's algae bloom, as dark as coffee, but now it was weak meltwater tea, only slightly stained by tannin released from decaying oak leaves. Last autumn, leaves had fallen into the pond from the few oak trees hiding among the stately white pines on the far shore of the pond. Now they were doing double duty as mulch for the forest floor and a natural dye for the pond water.

Richard searched the bottom with his eyes, looking for anything that might not be from nature. The sun was still in the sky, but the pond, created in lowlands and surrounded by the forest of high pine trees, was already dimming into twilight. Foster's searchlight would soon be needed. So where was Foster? Richard surmised that his son must have had to recharge the searchlight before leaving his house. Like most of the other things that Foster owned, it had not likely been in a ready condition.

Ultimately losing sight of the bottom, Richard paddled back to his truck and jumped out onto the shore to wait for his son. At length, he could hear an engine up on the forest road, not Foster's motorcycle, maybe Michael Kieran or Cindy Heath. The noise slowed and, it seemed, turned onto the trail.

"Damn, I hope it isn't a busybody, come to snoop around where the girl was found," thought Richard. The information about where the girl had died would be leaking from the local cops just about now.

A dirty white van, "the" dirty white van, sped down the trail to the pond, blocking in and almost crashing into the tailgate of Richard's truck. As the van's gears were mercilessly ground into park, Richard's former assailant from North Twin ejected himself from the driver's door. The great, dark hulk from the night before was still a great, dark hulk in twilight. Black, actually; with a black keg for a head, set with black, spiritless shark eyes. Black fists the size of coffee cans.

Though panicking as the great hulk of the man charged toward him, Richard wondered how a giant black rapist could have remained undetected in northern Minnesota.

Why did Richard's first thoughts always have to be about something other than survival? At least his second thoughts were directed toward self-preservation. Richard turned and dove into the pond, swimming underwater for the sanctum afforded by far distances. As he surfaced, his attacker crashed into the water and began to swim after him.

"Damn Jesus. Damn Jesus to hell." The hulk's vocabulary had not improved from the previous night.

The man was a good swimmer and probably faster than Richard, but of all the physical contests that Richard might get into and lose, there was one that he knew he could win—swimming underwater. His first love of running and the last few pounds of fat that stubbornly resisted melting away allowed Richard to hold his breath underwater for a very long period of time and to breaststroke under that water for a considerable distance, all while keeping warm—or if not warm, at least not dead from hypothermia.

Toward the end of his time in prison, Richard had been assigned to a forestry crew clearing brush and trees from the parks around the Twin Cities. At the end of a few of their work days the crew had been allowed to swim at a lightly used beach at one of the smaller lakes. Not being able to compete with the younger and stronger convicts at anything else, he had challenged the other members of the crew to a contest of swimming underwater. One by one, he swam against his fellow crewmen to see who could go the furthest before having to surface for air. It was no contest. He could easily beat the toughest con at this one single challenge. So today he knew he would, again, have the upper hand. At least he hoped so.

Mimicking games of tag played with his children when they were young, Richard waited until the man got close, then he dove straight under, picked a random direction, and swam away. When he came up again, his attacker wasn't even looking in his direction, let alone any nearer to him.

The game continued for some time, to no avail for the man. The only problem for Richard was the pain the frigid water caused his head every time he dove underwater. He realized that he would have to get out soon or risk hypothermia, even with his layer of insulation. He would have to end the game—now.

Richard had worked into the middle of the water, which he knew from fishing the place with Josh, was deep for a pond, thirty feet or more. As the man neared again, Richard dove straight down, but deeper this time, and without setting off in any new direction. The surface of the pond being lighter than the depths, Richard could see the man's legs as he passed over. He reached up and caught the cuff of one of the man's pant legs and pulled him down.

It was unlikely his attacker had gotten a chance to get a full breath of air before being pulled under. At first, the man tried to turn and dive toward Richard, but by holding onto the pant cuff and sinking ever farther into the depths, Richard managed to keep the man's hands away from him. Again the man tried to turn, with the same result, but now at an even greater depth. They had sunk so far down that the light from the surface was lost. Two of the most terrifying things that can happen to any person are to have one's lungs run out of oxygen and to be caught underwater in total blackness. In panic and abject fear, the man began to kick so violently that Richard had to let go to save his arm from injury.

At separation, Richard took off in an oblique angle toward the surface and came up a short distance from where the latest action had started, inhaling a great breath of air as he surfaced—his own lungs having run out of oxygen. He need not be concerned with proximity to his attacker. The man was trying, with great difficulty and severe coughing, to make it back to shore.

Richard swam after him, and being a part-time ass sometimes, yelled after him, "Hey, wait, I want to talk to you some more." Very cold-blooded and crazy, his children would say, but a cold-blooded crazy act that might ensure that his attacker would quit the game and leave the area, thus allowing Richard the chance to get the hell out of this hypothermic water. "You can't quit already. I haven't shown you the bottom of the lake yet. Don't you want to see the weeds?"

The black hulk did not see the humor. "Damn Jeez...cough, hack... God damn...uhh." He spit up or thew up water.

Richard continued to swim after the man; the predator had again become the prey, but on firm ground the man might regain his lost courage. Still, Richard knew that time was on his side since Foster would be arriving soon, though Richard would much prefer to avert another confrontation between his son and the big man.

Once on shore, the man did turn again, but Richard just treaded water. "Come on in," invited Richard, "the water's fine."

Richard was cold, but the big man must have been colder, even out of the water and standing on dry land. The hulk was shivering violently, virtually like a seizure. A strong wind and a setting sun were not helping him. His large, hyena teeth were chattering like a dry crankcase.

A standoff. At length, between gnashes of his teeth, the man cursed at him, "Da...it Jesus! 'snap, snap, snap' God...am 'snap' Je...'snap' to hell!" His voice was more foghorn than human. But with the chatters and snaps of teeth, rather comical.

Richard could not help himself. He laughed and laughed at his would-be killer. He laughed until his body became warm from the mirth.

The black man was furious. If he caught Richard now, he would have killed him twice. Luckily, the cold would not go away. The giant hulk gave in and left the pond, backing his dirty van all the way up the trail.

As Richard sloshed out of the water, Foster came roaring down the path on his motorcycle. He must have seen the dirty white van turning back onto the Forest Service road. "Dad! Are you all right?"

Yet suffering the residual effects of his ass-ness, he answered, while still laughing, "No, Foster, he killed me." That brought a smile to Foster's wide face.

Thanks to his hasty retreat into Rice Pond, both his pants and the underlying swim trunks were soaked, as well as his shoes and the rest of his clothes. Luckily, there was a pair of new shoes and a freshly laundered change of running clothes in Richard's truck, the set that he always kept in case he found himself a good place for running, and which, thanks to the cold waters of Clearwater River and Rice Pond, was lately doing double duty as post-submersion survival gear. As he changed into the dry clothes and running shoes, he explained to his son what had happened, and then started his truck, turned the heater on high, and tried to thaw his frozen body.

Foster, having gotten into his chest waders, walked into the pond and began to search the bottom with his searchlight. Richard watched from the warmth of his truck, soaking into his body the heat that he could not yet feel but knew must be there. Just as Richard thought that they would have to come back the next day, Foster yelled that he saw something shiny, like a fishing spoon. Foster was standing in the same reeds, or very close to, where the girl had been found. Pulling his left shirtsleeve up to his shoulder, he reached down into the water and came up with a short, but heavy, gold colored chain.

Not wanting to leave his heater, Richard wisely and patiently waited for Foster to complete his search of the area around the reeds. Nothing more was to be found.

As Foster removed his waders and threw them into the box of his dad's truck, Richard inspected the newly discovered treasure. It was a brass bracelet consisting of a chain and a curved bar. A type of ID tag that Richard remembered to be popular back in high school. The kind of heavy bracelet a man might wear. The identification tag was engraved with an alphanumeric series: PMB 185-417.

"License plate?" questioned father and son in unison.

CHAPTER 10

The next morning Richard was still puzzling the meaning of the letters and numbers on the bracelet, PMB 185-417. Last night, after having been escorted by Foster as far as Cindy Heath's convenience store on Highway 71, Richard had sat in his truck and observed the vehicles that came for gas and groceries. Both the cars and the trucks had license numbers with three capital letters followed by three numerical digits. At least for the Minnesota licenses.

Other states might be different, Richard did not know; all he knew about license plates was that Colorado plates had a little mountain on theirs and New Mexico had a yellow sun. And also, remembering way back, he thought of the civilian plates that he had seen during his Army service in Germany. All the German plates had three-letter designates for the town of origin of each vehicle. Therefore, a game could be played whereby the number of distinct German towns could be "collected" during drives around his home base of Pirmasens.

PMB 185-417. Maybe the technicians at the BCA could make a match. Richard had tried calling his own BCA agent, Michael Kieran, the night before to inform him of the bracelet, but had only gotten Michael's answering machine. Now that it was the next morning, he tried again, this time with greater success.

"Hello, Michael, this is Richard. I called last night, late, and missed you. Got an answering machine instead. Did you receive my message about the bracelet with the possible license number?"

"Yes I did. I was waiting to return your call until my field agent in Bemidji got back with me on the forensics that he was processing. Anyway, as far as the letters and numbers you gave me, they do not match any current Minnesota license plates."

"What about other states?" asked Richard.

"My lab people in the Cities are checking that now."

"And nothing on the forensics?"

"Agent Haltman just informed me that the knife had no prints, but it did have a quantity of fresh fish scales stuck under its hilt. Smelt."

"There are no smelt around here that I know of, but Lake Superior has runs in the early spring. One year, while the boys were still young, I took them east of Duluth, along the north shore of the lake, where we tried to net smelt. We didn't have much luck."

"Little fish, right? Like sardines."

"Yes. When we lived in Michigan we would catch pails of smelt. Then we would clean them with a scissors, dip them in a special crumb batter, and fry them by the dozens. I love them, though they can stink up a kitchen fairly awful."

"Smelt really are smelt," concluded Michael.

"I should add that smelt are not de-scaled when they are cleaned. Like sardines, their fine scales are eaten along with the fish's body; so someone would have to process buckets of smelt to get very many scales under their knife's hilt."

"OK, so we might be looking for an extremely successful smelt fisherman. God, what clues!"

"Anything else, Michael?"

"Just that the BCA lab in the Cities does not know what caused the star-shaped cutouts on the tire tracks. And also, your helpful girl, Cindy Heath, might be a jealous lover."

"She has a wandering boyfriend?"

"More likely a girlfriend. Agent Haltman interviewed some of Lennie Frontera's friends. It seems that Miss Heath had a crush on Lenora, but the feelings were not reciprocated. Frontera was straight; she only dated guys—God-fearing Christians, and few of them at that. I believe that Miss Heath forgot to mention this item when you talked to her during your trip to Rice Pond."

"You believe right." Richard's intuition about Cindy Heath had been accurate, presuming that his intuition had to do with Cindy Heath's love of Miss Frontera, not something else, extra, and as yet undiscovered.

"Miss Heath is of now an official suspect as far as I'm concerned," said Michael, his voice revealing that he was clearly irritated.

Irritation at Cindy for leaving out the information about her love for Lenora, her licentious love, not her friendship love, or irritation because Cindy had unnecessarily made herself a suspect, Richard wasn't sure which his friend was feeling.

"Half-truths and omissions are usually as damaging as outright lies," finished Richard. His eager helper had become a possible, though unlikely suspect.

After the talk with Michael, Richard next tried calling Foster, but could not make the connection. So he tried calling Josh's cell phone instead. Better luck there. He explained about the love situation with Cindy and her friend. The past love with her passed friend.

"That is a complication that we did not expect," said Josh. "Why do you think she was hiding this from us?"

"Maybe for sinister reasons, but more likely just an old habit of privacy."

"Sure, that would make sense," agreed Josh.

"I don't want Cindy finding out that we know this about her, so be careful what you say around her. And get ahold of Foster and tell him about the new development."

Richard spent the rest of the morning watering black cherry and basswood saplings that he had planted in his yard the previous spring. The entire State of Minnesota was still in a rain deficit of almost ten inches—as measured back the past 12 months, so the land, after the first flush of melted snow, was already dry and getting drier. The boys had burnt his field at the exact opportune time; a few days later would have been too late.

As Richard took care of his trees, he reviewed in his mind the facts to date: tire tracks cookie-cut with a star-shaped design, small cuts and pin-pricks on dead girl's hand, a worn Celtic cross bitten into the teeth of said dead girl, one aggressive yellow rose, a blue gingham dress, a brass ID tag lost and found at Rice Pond, PMB 185-417, a knife with smelt scales, and one large, half-drowned black attacker somehow hiding among the Ojibwa natives and the Scandinavian descendants of far northern Minnesota. It occurred to Richard that Teddy's niece's friend, Sally, attacked last week, might have something in common with Lenora. But what? Dark hair?

Richard turned off the water hose and went inside to fix his midday dinner. Two quart bags of perch and crappies, the last that Joshua had given him from the past winter's ice fishing. They would be enough for this meal and for three or four re-heat meals. If freed bachelor Richard had to cook, he always tried to prepare several meals at once, a common practice among his species. As the oil was heating in the fry baby, he called his daughter living over in Packerland.

"Hi, Jeanette. What'cha doin?"

"Hi, Dad. Not much. The girls both have a cold, so we are lazing around the house today. When Nick comes home I'll get out to the stores for a bit. My way of relaxing."

Nick, a Navy reservist and a cop-in-training in Green Bay, was Jeanette's boyfriend and the father of Jeanette's two girls, Christy and Christen. Jeanette was a good mother to her two blond-haired, blue-eyed hellions, and a loving wife to her husband, though she could not bring herself to make the marriage paper legal. The rape of her little body when she was fourteen and the brutal assault on her mind during the subsequent police interrogation, coupled with the district attorney calling her a liar in the city newspaper and the community's reaction to that "fact" had made her fearful of fully trusting anyone outside of her immediate family. Jeanette had "issues" as they like to say on the talk shows.

"Foster called me this morning and told me what was going on over there. Dad, stay, stay, stay...out—of—trouble."

"I will, of course I will," assured Richard, more in self-defense than out of parental concern for his offspring's worries. He related the events of the past days and described the evidence and the people involved as he saw it, including the new evidence-gossip, per Agent Michael Kieran, about Cindy's love for her former teammate.

Jeanette, retaining her concern for her dad, was nevertheless very interested in hearing about what had happened. She was, after all, a cop.

After Jeanette had graduated from the high school in Bemidji, she had taken law enforcement classes at Bemidji State University, a five thousand member college crowded into a section of the south shore of Lake Bemidji, directly across the lake from Lake Bemidji State Park. The college and the park were connected by the Paul Bunyan Trail, a favorite trail where high school and college kids liked to run and bike and roller blade. Where dark-haired Sally had been raped and beaten.

After two years spent at BSU, Jeanette had moved to Green Bay where she had finished her law enforcement classes at a technical school. She had stayed with her brother Foster, who was at the time living in Green Bay and making good wages working for a concrete construction company. There she had met Nick in one of her classes and moved in with him, a love circumstance that soon bore many practical consequences—they had tutored each other into earning their respective graduations.

Jeanette wanted to be a probation officer, but in Wisconsin there was a requirement that all law enforcement types had to first work as police officers for a minimum of two years. So now little Jeanette was a street cop patrolling for one of the suburbs outside of Green Bay. The practical experience had made her mind much sharper, quicker, and attentive to detail.

As Richard finished his exposition of the facts with the bracelet, Jeanette said, "The number is like yours was, only bigger. I should know because I wrote you countless letters over the eight and a half years that you were gone. Remember?"

Like when Foster had commented on the incomplete topography caused by the missing grapple hook, Richard's lethargic mind once again slowly clunked the pieces together. Several moments of phone silence, and then, "You are absolutely right, Jeanette. Bigger means later, 926 convicts later, to be exact. That would be a year after I got to Stillwater. Maybe more."

"What about the letters, Dad?"

"So simple, how could I have missed it? Except that I always said my number in pieces of two, 18-42-91. Anyway, the letters: PMB is Prison Motorcycle Boys. White boys!"

"So, a white boy ex-con attacked the Native girl."

"Maybe, but it does not feel right. The PMB guys hate all the sex offenders. And what about my black attacker? PMB boys hate blacks too, so how does that fit together?"

"You can have the BCA agent check the number for you. See who it is."

"I don't want the police knowing about this PMB guy. Not yet". Except Jeanette, of course, his daughter-cop already knew. "If this particular ex-con, whoever he is, is not directly involved in the death of the girl, the police will just scare him off and then we will lose the connection and whatever information it might bring."

"So what now?" asked Jeanette.

"Simple. You have a computer hooked to the Internet. Look up the number in the Minnesota corrections department web site; it will be there. While you are at it, look up sex offenders recently released to the Beltrami County area. Black ones."

Richard could hear his daughter's key taps over the phone as she worked her computer and wiggled out the information. "Chad Rochambeau—prison number: 185417, address: 1725 Revolution Lane, St. Paul, Minnesota. Released in 2002. Assault, some smaller drug charges. Age 27. I don't see anything for a telephone number."

"I know Chad, not real well, but well enough. He was my barber in the prison at Moose Lake. Nice kid. Talked like he really wanted to stay out of trouble. He had an older brother, Trent Rochambeau, who had gotten in much greater trouble while doing time at Stillwater Prison, so Chad wanted to stay clean for his mom's sake. At least one son come back home."

"You don't think this Chad guy would get in trouble again?"

"If trouble came his way, he might handle it in his own way; Chad Rochambeau was an amateur boxer on the street. He was not a big guy, so if you didn't notice his shoulders you would mistake him for an average person. Two black rapists did just that in the chow hall at Moose Lake. They tried to strong-arm him out of money, or yeast for making hooch, I can't remember which. Chad's white-boys said that when the two rapists tried to attack him, he hit them so hard they about came out of Africa. Those were their words, not mine, but the sentiment was believable. Still, I can't imagine him hurting a girl."

"Well, Dad, either the Native girl lost Chad's bracelet at the pond, and it must have been this Chad's because it was a man's bracelet, with Chad's prison ID number. Or your black attacker had it for some unknown reason. Or this PMB guy was at the pond the night the girl died. Any one of those three possibilities could have happened, though I doubt your black attacker would have had the bracelet. That leaves Chad and Lenora. Per logic, sans information we are not yet privy to, that leaves Lenora. Or maybe not. Maybe any of the three."

"It would make a vast difference if I knew which." Richard was aware that he would have to talk to Chad in person. He would have to go to St. Paul. "I'm going down to the Cities and talk to Chad if I can find him. I'll stay at Terrie's place in Minnetonka."

Terrie was Richard's oldest son and richest offspring. Richard liked staying there because Terrie's home was a mere hundred feet from a beautiful paved hiking trail, which in turn led to a spacious park. Like so many outdoor opportunities in the Twin Cities area, a great place to walk, hike, and run.

After the call with Jeanette, Richard packed for his trip, as usual taking a great deal more than might be warranted for such a short excursion. Then he called Joshua and Foster and told them where he was going. Foster agreed to check with Agent Kieran daily to see what, if anything, had been found, and to pass on any current information. Richard also asked Foster to see what he could find out about the little dark-haired girl, Samantha's friend, Sally.

"There must be a connection between Sally and Lenora," said Richard. Like dark hair is enough of a reason to be raped, beaten, and killed.

"The only connection you will find is that both girls were attacked by evil," said Foster.

"Perhaps you are right. Just evil."

The drive to the Cities was picturesque, but slow, a result more of Richard's driving than of road conditions. Richard had forgotten to call Terrie and let him know that he was coming down. When he got to his son's home in Minnetonka, nobody was home and the door was locked. Richard metamorphosed into his running clothes in the cab of his truck and took off on the long and pleasant run that he had been anticipating. Even the temperature in the Cities was warmer than it had been back home, which was to his liking since he preferred warmer weather for his outings. Fewer clothes and more sweat.

Upon Richard's return from his run, Terrie was waiting in the front yard for his dad. Jeanette had already called Terrie to let him know what had transpired the last couple of days and of their dad's plans to talk to the convict Chad Rochambeau the next day.

"I have an idea," said Terrie, "about finding your convict person. Traffic will be miserable driving in St. Paul tomorrow. Instead, let me drive you tonight in my BMW. We can get down there quickly in the evening, and I can find my way better than you. Afterwards, I can take you to a nice restaurant for supper."

"OK, I can concentrate on the business at hand since you will be dealing with the navigating. Just let me shower, and we will be off."

The distances in the Cities were not really that great, it just seemed so in the daytime traffic. At night, places grew closer together. Soon Terrie had his BMW in front of 1725 Revolution Lane. Terrie stayed with his expensive vehicle as Dad walked to the house. A newer white Jeep Wrangler, with hot-pink wipers and pink seat cushions, was parked in the drive. The diminutive 4 x 4 needed a wash, covered as it was with mud and smeared road salt. Richard always wanted a white Jeep Wrangler; if he ever got one, he'd keep it clean.

Chad met Richard at the front door. "Richard, how you been? What brings you here?" The young convict reached out a powerful arm with which to shake the old convict's hand. Chad Rochambeau looked younger than his 27 years, with a smiling teenager's face, tan and healthy looking. His secret weapons, his oversized shoulders, moved under his silver-buttoned cowboy shirt as if independent from the rest of his otherwise normal body.

Richard told him about finding the Native girl floating in the pond.

As Richard spoke, tears clouded Chad's eyes and spilled down his cheeks. Chad said he knew the girl. Lennie had been his girlfriend back when he had lived in Bemidji. He had kept in touch with her and had spent time with her during his infrequent excursions back to the North Country.

"I loved Lenora," said Chad. "I always wanted to get back with her, but trouble and distance kept interfering with our plans."

Richard told him of the bracelet that had led him to Revolution Lane. "You must have given it to Lenora as a present?"

Chad's tears stopped and his hazel eyes grew hard and flat. Time passed in silence. Finally, "I lost it in Stillwater. Lennie had smuggled it in to me during a visit. It was a present from her. I kept it hidden from the guards until my rapist roommate ratted on me. When I got back from the barbershop, my stuff had been searched and that was the last I ever saw of the bracelet."

"Was this roommate a large black man?"

"He was black, but not big. You know him. He was your roomy before you changed units, then I got stuck with the bastard for a while. Eugene Euglena. I remember that you hated him, too."

Richard did hate him, even more than he hated the pair of sex offenders that had tried to kill him in Stillwater. Euglena had caused him endless grief with his petty harassments. Richard had never told anybody but Foster and Joshua, but Euglena was the only convict that he had seriously considered killing. If Richard had been kept as his roommate any longer, who knows what may have happened?

"Right, he always wore a greasy do-rag on his head. I remember him."

"Euglena was in for abducting runaway girls from the St. Paul bus station," said Chad. "He would take them back to his place and tie them up and rape and beat them until they were broke. Then he would pimp them out. He specialized in little white girls. The city newspaper said that when he was caught, there were two young girls tied in a back room, beat so bad that they had to be hospitalized."

"Right. He was not a pleasant person, to say the least. But here's the problem: Euglena ratted on you, you lost your bracelet to a prison shakedown, and then it turns up in the pond where I found Lenora. So my question is: how did your bracelet get there?"

"I don't know."

Richard and his friend sat on the steps of the porch and talked. Chad was visibly hurt by the news of his past girlfriend. Richard tried to reminisce about their shared time at the prison at Moose Lake, but Chad kept asking about Lenora.

"Did Lennie hurt before she died?" asked Chad. Pleaded was more like it, rather than asked as if a truthful answer was expected.

"I don't think so, not too much anyway," lied Richard. He knew that in a day or two, or a few at most, that Chad would lose the denial that was protecting his breaking heart. Chad would realize the truth, but he would not hold Richard's soft lies against him. Chad would know that sometimes convicts had to have ways to blunt the pain. That is something learned in the loneliness of prison.

"That is good," said Chad.

Soon Chad would come to understand that, after being brutally raped and humiliated, knowing that she was about to die, she fought to keep the evidence of who had attacked her. She had gripped a rose tightly in her hand, until its thorns drove themselves into her palm. She had bitten a cross into the space between two of her teeth, in a fierce determination to keep it in her possession. As she was dying, she had won the battle.

With this understanding, Chad's heart would harden, and then he would be very dangerous. Chad would try to revenge Lennie's death.

"Chad, did you get a 'Confiscated Property Sheet' after the guard's shakedown?" asked Richard.

"I was given a paper, but the chain was not listed on it. I figured that a guard must have kept the bracelet for himself, but I didn't press the issue and maybe get segregation time."

"Or Euglena stole the bracelet and then ratted on you to cover its missing."

"Christ," cursed Chad softly. "I should have smashed that damn molester to dust when I had my chance in the chow hall."

Richard had gotten something from Chad. Lenora had been his girl. And the bracelet was definitely a connection to the rape and murder. But how? Perhaps the answer was obvious. Eugene Euglena, that's how. Euglena, the beater of lost girls, was somehow connected to Lenora's rape and death.

"I really should have killed the scum when I had the chance," murmured Richard to himself.

"What? What did you say? I was thinking about Lennie and didn't hear you clearly."

"Nothing, Chad. I was just mumbling something to myself about what I need to do."

Richard talked a little more with Chad, mostly about Stillwater and Moose Lake, then of what they had both been up to since their respective releases. Richard told him that he loved Chad's white Jeep Wrangler and was so jealous that it wasn't his. Finally, Richard had to leave.

"I'm sorry about your girl, Chad. We will, my sons and I, try to find who did this to her." The two men embraced each other, as befitted a farewell between prisoners that had spent a time in hell together.

Chad turned and went into his house. Richard walked down the drive to Terrie's auto, stopping one last time to admire Chad's jeep.

"I'd love for you to be mine," thought Richard. "I'd clean those smears off your body."

Then it hit Richard. Another chunk fell into place in his mind. He glanced at the house to make sure he was not being watched, pulled loose a corner of his shirt, and rubbed at a small area of the salt smears; then he proceeded to the BMW.

Four blocks later, Richard took off his now salt-smeared shirt, leaving him clad only in a T-shirt. He folded the shirt-turned-towel into a neat triangle with the gooey smear tucked inside and placed the package onto the floor of the back seat. His son watched with an inquisitive look on his face.

"Cow licks," explained Richard.

CHAPTER 11

Terrie had left early for work the next morning long before his father had arisen. They had stayed late at Terrie's treat for his dad, the Carrbini, a neat restaurant specializing in the diametrically opposed nutritional camps of health food and thick, bloody steaks. Richard had eulogized at length about the revelations emanating from his recent meeting with Chad Rochambeau, explaining the meaning of the smeary cow licks. Chad Rochambeau's white jeep must have been traveling on Forest Service Road 2213 the day after Richard had discovered the Native girl floating in the cold waters of Rice Pond. Richard had reasoned that it would be highly unlikely that his old truck and Chad's jeep would have been licked by separate herds of cows at separate locations.

Richard had told his oldest son that he would be gone and back north by the time Terrie would have completed his workday. Before leaving Terrie's Minnetonka residence, he called Foster to let him know about the white jeep and its impressionistic pattern of probable cow slobber. "Call Agent Kieran for me and tell him about Chad and his jeep. Let him know that I have a dirty shirt that he can have tested for bovine saliva—just to make sure that my hypothesis is correct."

"Kieran phoned your house yesterday," said Foster. "I was over there getting the large sockets so I could work on my van and I took the call when the phone rang. He said that DNA tests revealed recent sexual contact with Miss Frontera by two separate individuals."

"Does Michael know who these individuals are?" asked Richard.

"Yes. Two sex offenders were positively identified by DNA left on Miss Frontera's dress. One, a rapist from Duluth, had been recently released back to Duluth from the prison at Moose Lake. Odis Elvie Blister. It seems that Odis had gotten into the habit of dropping from trees onto women walking at Duluth's Park Point. He was identified and caught by the police because he always wore a football helmet during his attacks."

"Safety is important when you drop from trees, I suppose," said Richard sarcastically. "Another piece of the puzzle can be connected. Odis Blister is from Duluth, where smelt fishing is carried on every spring along the North Shore rivers. Blister must have cleaned his catch over there, and then brought his knife with him. Or took the knife from another Duluthean that had success at smelt fishing."

Foster nodded his head in agreement, as if nodding motions could be discerned over phone lines. "The other man identified had also been in Moose Lake, for false imprisonment and for trafficking in underage females. Eugene Euglena. He is a level three sex offender, so he must be the worst of the worst."

"He is. He is also my ex-roommate. Remember? When I was in Moose Lake."

"Oh, yeah, of course. You know, Dad, in hindsight you should have finished Euglena when you had the chance."

"You think that maybe if I had eliminated Euglena, then Miss Frontera would still be alive. OK, fair enough. But I've spent enough time in prison for protecting females from their attackers; I'll let some other Minnesota-nice person defend the next of our state's victims."

"I guess you're right, Dad. It would be perfect justice if one of the jurors who convicted you would be put in a situation like yours. See if they would stop a rapist to protect their daughter."

A moment of phone silence signalled Richard's agreement. Then he moved on to the topic at hand. "So we know that Lenora was raped by two men before being killed."

"Actually, three. At least three men had attacked Miss Frontera. As I said, Euglena and Blister were identified by matching DNA from semen that had gotten on her dress. But a third suspect was indicated by samples taken directly from Frontera's body. The blood type of the missing DNA is different from that of the other two rapists. The third attacker is O-negative."

"But what about the DNA results from the O-negative samples?" asked Richard.

"The Sheriff's people had somehow ruined that particular sample. It was collected with a hospital sexual assault kit, not from her clothes. By allowing it to get too hot, the sample became too deteriorated for DNA testing. Only the blood type could be determined at Michael's BCA lab," added Foster.

Richard was too furious to answer. A decade ago the exact same thing had happened in his daughter's case. Someone had tampered with Jeanette's sexual assault kit to protect one of the rapists. Likewise, in Jeanette's case, DNA had been left on her clothes and in a condom, so even with the destroyed sexual assault kit, the identity of her three attackers could be positively determined. Once again, the destroyer of DNA had missed the evidence from the clothes.

Richard knew that the same thing was happening again. "DNA does not destroy itself."

"Since we can be reasonably sure that the ruined DNA evidence was purposely tampered with, that leads us to another possibility," said Foster, using up his entire yearly supply of big words in just one single solitary sentence.

"To protect the rapists," was Richard's obvious conclusion.

"Actually, I was thinking about the hulk that found your camp on North Twin Lake and was waiting there to stick you with his germy knife," said Foster.

"That's right. The hulk must have gotten his information from a cop or from someone a cop had talked to—maybe a friend of a cop. Or maybe in the process of filing reports and such a courthouse worker had overheard details of the case." Richard realized that Foster had it right. Someone in law enforcement or the local government had talked to the hulk prior to the attack at Richard's camp.

"Because the cops and our friends had been the only ones who knew about your finding the girl," said Foster.

Then Richard realized that there was a third possibility, or more accurately, a third probability: the district attorney's office.

"What about DA Foat?" asked Richard.

Foster, guessing what his dad must be feeling, let many moments pass, then he changed the subject and broke the long angry silence. "A woman named 'Elsie' called, from your river crew. She asked if you knew when your forestry work on the Clearwater River would begin again."

"I'll call her before I leave the Cities," said Richard, needing to end the conversation and get out once more into the clean air of the running trails.

"One last thing," said Foster. "Joshua talked briefly with Sally, the girl that was attacked on the Paul Bunyan Trail. She works part-time weekends as a volunteer at the same place where he works, out at the language village. She heard about you finding the Native girl, and she said that she has a message for you."

"Good. Have Joshua tell her that I can meet her in two days. I need to rest and unwind from this mess, to have some time to mull over the facts of the case."

"We all need to get reorganized," said Foster.

"Ask her if we can meet at Teddy and Clara Zemm's home. She is familiar with their place and we can have some privacy there."

Having said good-bye to Foster, Richard took a shower before his planned run, preferring to be clean prior to getting sweaty. As the day was in the mid-60s, Richard was indeed sweating as he ran, but only lightly. Miles rolled by as he covered unexplored terrain and slowly disentangled the many mazes of asphalt hiking trails. Other runners were out, too. Most said "hi" as they approached him. A few of the faster runners passed him going in the same direction. Richard had managed to pass one very old lady jogger who was brightly dressed in a red and green Reebok outfit, and later passed a pair of teenage girls jogging to the sounds of 1970s-era rock music.

Just as Richard wondered if he was hopelessly and irretrievably lost, his latest chosen trail emptied into the beautiful park he had found the day before. He walked for a short distance to cool down, then chose a sun-dappled bench set a short distance off the trail. There he could unobtrusively watch the other runners go by as he thought of the case he had become such an integral part of.

The star-shaped cutouts on the tire tracks pressed into the ground of the trail to Rice Pond. Nothing yet with that. One yellow rose. Two possible yellow-rose cuts on Miss Frontera's hand. The cross bitten into Miss Frontera's teeth. That same cross now around the neck of Cindy Heath.

Chad Rochambeau's ID bracelet. How did it find its way into the waters of Rice Pond? Richard's past, hated roommate, level three sex offender Eugene Euglena, must have stolen it from Chad, then years later lost it during the assault and murder of Miss Frontera. Lennie would have recognized the bracelet sometime after her abduction. Perhaps she tore it off Euglena's wrist in order to leave another of her clues.

Therefore, Miss Frontera crushed a thorny rose into the palm of her hand, bit her cross into her teeth, and tore the bracelet from the wrist of one of her attackers and threw it into the water. Lennie must have known she was about to die and wanted only to make sure her killers would be caught. "What a tough lady," said Richard to a pair of Canada jays that had stopped to see if there were any handouts at his bench.

The mystery of the missing grapple hook was solved. It was used by Richard's giant attacker in an unsuccessful attempt to try to find the missing ID tag, which in turn had led Richard to the white-boy PMB boxer with the hard-rock shoulders—Chad Rochambeau.

Chad knew Lenora Frontera. Said he loved her. OK, good so far.

Then the white Jeep Wrangler owned by Chad that was covered with the same cow licks that Richard's truck had suffered on the forest road the day after Lennie had been found dead. That meant that Chad was on that same forest road on the same day—the day after Richard had found Chad's old sweetheart floating at the edge of Rice Pond.

Richard's train of thought was broken by a pretty, pony-tailed girl jogging down the trail. She was clad only in a pair of short running shorts and a pink sport bra. No shoes or socks. Richard watched her disappear around a curve in the trail, then he continued arranging the known facts.

Lenora's gingham dress and a light chain around her bruised neck. There was also a slight bruise at the corner of her mouth. On the end of that chain hung a timeworn Christian cross wedged between Lenora's teeth. The rapists must have tried to remove the chain and its cross, but Lennie bit down so hard that the cross stuck between two of her teeth.

"My daughter's rapists took her two crosses as souvenirs of their gang rape," said Richard angrily to his feathered friends. The pale gray birds flew off to the sanctuary afforded by the branches of a nearby maple tree. "Sorry," apologized Richard.

The attack on Samantha's friend, Sally. With luck, Richard might learn more from Sally when they have their talk.

And don't forget about the fish-scale-embedded knife dropped at the vehicle park at North Twin Lake. Dropped by a very large black male with a foul mouth: "Damn Jesus, Damn Jesus to hell." That could be Odis Elvie Blister, who is now one of two positive matches to the dead body of Miss Frontera. The case was being solved. But what about the ruined DNA samples? Who in the Beltrami County justice system was protecting whom in the sexual predator community?

And, according to his son Foster and the rules of logic, the secret destroyer of DNA evidence is also the purveyor of information to his attacker, the hulk. If the district attorney is once again protecting a gang of rapists by tampering with the evidence, then he would also have a reason to sic the hulk on Richard. Really two reasons. To keep Richard from snooping into the present case, but also to enact revenge on Richard for killing the district attorney's former rapist friend.

"Once a rapist, always a rapist," said Richard to his Canada jay visitors, newly returned to continue their hunt in front of Richard's bench. "Once a rapist's sympathizer, always a rapist's sympathizer."

Thoughts of predators ending young girls' lives were eroding Richard's brain. He rose from the bench, cleared his mind, and began to walk back to his son's house. He would have liked to run back, but Richard did not want to make himself too severely sore tomorrow by resuming his running after too long of a cool down today.

Once back at Terrie's, Richard took his second shower of the day, and then called Elsie at her farm. "Hi, Elsie, I understand you called asking when we would go back to work."

"Yes, I did. But I really wanted to see if my girls and I could visit you at your place tomorrow? Make a day of it, if possible. I heard about you finding that poor Native girl. I thought you might want someone to talk to."

"I would, yes. But not tomorrow. How about in two days?"

"Good. Two days, then. I'll come over in the morning with a farm fresh picnic dinner. It'll be ample enough for noon and evening meals, and possibly leftovers too. OK?"

"I should mention something before you come," said Richard. "Another girl was attacked in the county, assaulted before the girl that I found had been assaulted. I am supposed to talk to her the day after tomorrow at a mutual friend's house near North Twin Lake. That's in the national forest. Anyway, that is why I want the two days, to have some time to reflect on this whole mess before I talk to the girl."

"How old is she?"

"Fourteen."

"I might be able to help you. A female that young might rather talk to another female." At that, Elsie ended the conversation while Richard was yet mired in agreeing with the concept of female assistance.

His old truck repacked, Richard sat behind the steering wheel, thinking, debating with himself what he should do next. Finally, he admitted to himself that he would have to stop by Tony's place on the way out of the Cities. Richard needed to check out Eugene Euglena. He needed more information on the Twin Cities' rapist/pimp/child molester, Euglena. All the same type of animal as far as Richard was concerned, contrary to the rap music gangsta propaganda that some of the new generation of punks seemed to adhere to.

At any rate, Tony would be the one to ferret out information for Richard.

Antonio the ex-prison comrade, Antonio the protector of lost and battered girls, Antonio the rapist.

CHAPTER 12

Antonio de Medici—given birth by his dear mother, Maria Evangilista de Medici, 28 years ago. Richard had first met Tony in Stillwater prison while taking writing classes from a young professor on loan from the local community college.

Tony had been convicted of sticking a Muong gang leader that had attacked him for interfering with the gang leader's prostitution business. Allegedly, Tony had the insidious habit of convincing young prostitutes that they possessed the inalienable right to break the bonds of indentured servitude that they had been pressed into, and to come home with him to his mamma's place where they could become his next girlfriend, or not, whichever they pleased.

One night, a Muong gangster took umbrage at Tony's interference and tried to stab him with a knife. Tony took the knife away from the punk and chased him down the street, eventually running him down and sticking the pimp with his own knife. A clear case of excessive self-defense in Minnesota. Tony was convicted and sent to Stillwater. And made to pay for a pig for the pimp, to facilitate a Muong healing ceremony. That got Tony some considerable razzing in Stillwater.

Tony had become one of Richard's closest friends in prison. A man that, if need be, could be trusted to fight by his side if and when the situation called for it.

The drive over to Maria's place was not very far out of Richard's way. A small remnant of a once much larger Italian community in the city of St. Paul, the houses were crowded together but clean and well kept, each home protected by a moat of green lawn and ancient sentries of huge bur oaks.

Tony came to the door, shirtless as usual, a myriad of colorful Catholic tattoos festooning his entire upper body. "Richard, what's up? Man, it's good to see you." Tony embraced his old comrade from hell. "Come on in, my man." Tony turned and led Richard into Maria Evangilista's home, revealing a tattooed drawing of the Virgin Mary. Mother Mary of God was standing forlornly on Tony's back, posed in front of a rose-covered version of Jesus' cross. The multi-colored picture of the Virgin Mary and her son covered most of Tony's back. Though Richard generally hated tattoos, he had to concede to himself that Tony's were not cheap prison tattoos; these were detailed works of art.

Life was omnipresent in the home of Maria de Medici. People seemed to be everywhere. Mostly young children, but also a few old folk, and spiced overall with a smattering of ages in between, Tony's brothers and sisters, aunts, uncles, grandparents, grandchildren, countless close and distant kin, all mixed in with various and sundry friends of the family.

The air was perfumed with lilac and red wine, with laughter and shouted English and murmurs of aged Italian, and all of this lightly overlaid with the fragrance of tomato steam emanating from an iron cauldron of dark red spaghetti sauce simmering on the stove top in Maria's linoleum-carpeted kitchen. Richard had stayed before with the de Medici, dragging his wretched self, after release from prison, into their midst, where, like a salt block at a deer lick, his sadness had been gradually and inexorably consumed.

Maria Evangilista de Medici spotted Richard as he entered her home, rushed over to him and smothered him in her arms, pressing his body into her bosom while fervently and lovingly kissing his face so very many times over. Maria was a large-hipped woman, but not at all overweight. She had a youthful face framed by two long black ponytails, one at each temple, and beautiful, wide, dark eyes. Her very feminine, sweet voice was spiced with Italian accents. Richard had always loved to listen to her voice.

In turn, Richard held her close and kissed the top of her forehead. "I have missed you," they said to each other.

After countless more hugs and innumerable kisses from the hordes of old friends and adopted relations, and even some from new faces freshly introduced to him, Richard steered Tony into the relative privacy of the kitchen and explained the developments of recent days. About the death of Miss Lenora Frontera.

"The state must not be able to find either Eugene Euglena or Odis Elvie Blister, or they would have arrested them by now," said Richard. "I was hoping that you could check into this matter and see if you can find anything."

Richard had never brought it up with Tony, but he had discovered a hidden secret of Tony's. After prison, after staying with Tony and his mother Maria, even after going back home to Bemidji, Richard had discovered one day while on the Internet that, prior to Tony's conviction for knifing the Muong pimp, Tony had collected a prior court conviction for sleeping with a newly freed but under-aged girl. This liberated prostitute that he had brought home had been much younger than the required eighteen years. Statutory rape. Maybe not violent or sadistic, but still wrong.

With all the pimps and prostitutes, present and ex, and the street people that Tony knew and the convicts he kept in touch with, not to mention the sex offenders he had been forced to take treatment with, Tony had an uncanny ability to know what was going on in the city.

"Let me make some calls, Richard. See what I can help." Tony left the room.

A little olive-skinned girl in a white party dress brought Richard a large drink glass of California Burgundy and a plate of hot spaghetti smothered in Maria's tomatoey sauce. The little girl said that her name was Carmen, and that Carmen was Latin for "song," and that she was Latin because she was Italian and that was like being a Roman, but she didn't know if there were any Romans left in Italy. She was confused as to whether or not there were yet Romans in Italy. Maybe they all came to America, she thought, like her grandmother did. And, oh yeah, she didn't like boys because they were always getting dirty. And she was six going on seven, in just eleven more months. "So what do you think, Mister."

"I think that you have a very pretty dress."

"Thank you, Mister," she said as she twirled around and ran out of the kitchen and disappeared into the multitudes.

Richard liked wine, but had been forced by the rules of probation into a regimen of abstinence from any form of brew, even though he had been clean sober when he had supposedly shot one of his daughter's rapists. If logic should follow the facts, then perhaps Richard should have been compelled to abstain from sobriety. He decided that the rules of the state did not have jurisdiction in Maria Evangilista de Medici's kitchen, and tasted the wine the little girl had brought him.

An auburn-haired beauty walked purposefully into the kitchen, smiled seductively at Richard as she approached him, slid her arms around his waist and pulled him close, kissed his cheek, kissed his lips quickly, and laughed a beautiful laugh that matched the rest of her.

"You don't recognize me?" she asked, still smiling seductively.

His arms loose and worthless at his sides, Richard stared at her. Nothing was registering. He looked into her eyes to see if he could glimpse her soul. Then he remembered, but he tried to conceal his recognition.

He put his arms around the girl and held her tight. "Give me a couple more kisses and I think maybe my memory might be jogged."

Of course the girl was not fooled. She pushed him, or tried to, away from her bosom. "You remember me, you old con."

"Cassandra?" asked Richard fakely. "Is that you?"

"You might want to let go of me before my husband walks in and catches us in the act."

"You have a husband?" Of course she would. Why not?

"Yes I do, and four children, and a dog, and a masters degree in molecular biology from the university, not to mention a great job with one of the pharmacological companies." A long way from when he and Tony had pulled her out of a dumpster behind McDonalds, hungry, dirty, and slapped black and blue by her sadistic pimp.

Richard crushed her to him and gave her a real hug. "The last time I saw you, you were an item with Tony. I thought you two were eternal."

"Tony is sweet, but he will always be a boy. I have a man now."

"I can't believe how much you have changed."

"I can't believe how much I've changed, either. When you came into the house and didn't recognize me, it really struck me how far I have come from the old days. I just wanted to tell you how much I love you for your help back then. You saw something good in me that was invisible to others. Thank you."

If Richard said anything now, he would start crying, and he didn't want to look the fool. He stayed quiet.

"I have to go take my children to the dentist now, so I have to leave right away. But I wanted to say hello, and, well...Richard?"

"Yes, what is it?"

"I need to tell you something, warn you is more like it."

"Go ahead, Cassandra. I am listening."

"My dear Richard, four days ago I had one of my dreams. I saw that you will never be free of the predators." Cassandra's dreams were a mirror on reality. "You will have to fight evil for the rest of your life. And so will the people around you, anyone that you love will be drawn into this fight." She squeezed his hands in hers and turned and walked away, her dark hair blowing back strongly in a wind that was not discernible in the calm of Maria's kitchen. "Visit me next time you are in the Cities," she said, not looking back as she spoke.

Unlike any other might, Richard believed Cassandra's prophecy.

The first sips of wine, like a Catholic Communion, were still sweet on Richard's tongue when Tony returned. "Euglena keeps a second apartment that his probation officer does not know about," said Tony. "That is where he has been rebuilding his prostitution business. As for Odis Blister, eight months ago he jumped ship from the city of Duluth, so to speak. Since Odis is a level three sex offender, the State of Minnesota has been looking for him ever since."

"Do you have Euglena's secret address?"

"Yes. And I'm going with you. Euglena is too ruthless for you country folk," smiled Tony.

The drive from Tony's neighborhood to that of Euglena's was short in distance but far apart in seediness. Like the surface of two different planets: one hospitable to life, the other barren. Tony led Richard to the unlisted apartment of Eugene Euglena and banged on the door. A small, coffee-colored black girl came to the door and opened it up as far as its safety chain would allow. She had fresh and ugly bruises on her cheekbones and over one eye. When asked, she said that Eugene was not there. Her words were still trailing out of her mouth as Tony's boot kicked the door in, tearing the safety chain off the thin moulding it was screwed to.

"Eugene will be mad, mister. Please go before he comes back." The black girl seemed more afraid of Euglena's possible return than of Tony's violent entrance.

"Where is your master—Eugene," asked Tony angrily, seemingly disrespecting the black girl's fears.

"I don't know."

"Or you know and won't tell us," said Tony.

"I really don't know. He hasn't been here for days. Now, leave here immediately or..."

"Or what?" asked Tony.

"Or I'll call the cops on you guys."

The two convicts ignored the little black girl and searched the apartment for signs of Euglena. He was not there.

In a back closet Richard found another small girl, a white girl. She had light blond, almost translucent hair which fell over her shoulders in smooth currents of light.

"Another of Minnesota's Scandinavian descendants lost to the filth of the city," thought Richard out loud, perhaps to the pale-blond girl, or perhaps just to his own anger.

The girl was sitting in the closet, facing the rear, her hands and feet duct-taped to a heat pipe. Her mouth shut with duct tape. She was naked. She was shivering violently with cold and fear.

"Looks like Eugene is up to his old tricks," said Tony as he came up behind his friend.

Richard took the girl by her hair and gently pulled her head back so he could see her face. Her eyes were a remarkable green. He slowly peeled the tape from her mouth and used a jackknife to cut her loose from the pipe. Her back was so cramped that she could not stand. Richard picked her up and carried her from the closet and carefully set her down on her feet in the middle of the bedroom. She slowly straightened her back as well as she could.

Nothing in the apartment was clean enough to wrap her in, so Tony volunteered his shirt. It came to just below the girl's knees like a woman's button-up dress. Richard, thinking how the dark green of Tony's shirt so closely matched the green of the girl's eyes, asked her, "Well, green-eyes, do you have a name?"

The girl stood in the center of the room, shaking like the aspen leaves on Richard's trees. "I should go back in the closet before he returns," said the terrified girl.

Tony, his upper torso now clad only in the tattoos of his faith, turned to the other small girl and asked her, "What is green-eyes name?" No answer. Tony walked over to the little black girl in two long strides. Richard was worried that Tony might kick her in like he had broken the door. But instead, Tony put his arms around the girl and held her tight to his now bare chest.

A long time passed. When Tony let go of her, she managed to stammer through her tears, "Amber. Her name is Amber, with some Minnesota last name. My name is Paulownia Royal, but my friends used to call me Sassy."

"How old are you girls?" asked Tony.

"I'm 22 this year. My mom lives over in Minneapolis, or… at least, she used to," said Sassy, looking down at the floor as a renewed flush of tears washed over her face.

"How old are you, green-eyes?" asked Richard.

No answer.

Sassy spoke for her, "Thirteen… fourteen. Something like that. I'm not sure, exactly."

Tony and Richard decided that Sassy could stay at the de Medici home until her mother was found. Richard would take Amber, since Tony did not want such a young stranger staying with him. Besides, Tony had reasoned, she should go back to rural Minnesota where, he presumed from her Icelandic appearance, she must have come from. Richard thought that Amber could maybe stay with Elsie until the girl recovered some of her previous self, whatever that may have been.

Shirtless Tony took Sassy by the hand and led her to the truck. Richard took Amber again by the hair of the back of her head and calmly but firmly guided her outside.

"I should go back in the closet before he returns," she repeated.

CHAPTER 13

Tony was concerned that someone at the building of Sassy and Amber's prison apartment might have become curious about two men, one shirtless but not tattooless, the other old and grey, leading two very young-looking girls, one black and one white, into a rusty, beat-up Chevy truck. License plate numbers could lead to unwanted police scrutiny, so Tony urged Richard to make a hasty retreat from the Cities, which Richard did, taking just enough time to pour some of Mother Maria Evangilista's sweet red spaghetti into a Tupperware container (Richard would mail the container back on Christmas—packed with his hard-as-rock ginger-snap cookies), and to pour a little of Maria's Burgundy into a rinsed-out pop can. He took a fresh can of cold pop for Amber.

While Richard was provisioning himself in the de Medici kitchen, Amber remained sitting on the rear bench seat of Richard's extended truck, packed as she was with his running gear, camera bag, and the extra coats and clothes that Richard always brought with him on any outing of any duration at all. She was still wearing Tony's dark green shirt-dress with the line of buttons running up the front.

While Richard was packing their lunch, the little olive-skinned girl in the white party dress ran out to the truck and gave Amber some cookies and a plastic glass of milk. Amber drank the milk in one shot and then nibbled on the cookies as she talked with her little hostess.

"You're not from around here, are you," said the little girl.

"No, I'm not. I came from up north," said Amber.

"Did you enjoy your visit?" asked the little girl.

"Not really." Amber hoped she did not sound as pitiful as she must have looked.

"The next time you come down, you can come and visit me. I'll have my mama take us to a museum or something."

"Yes, I'd like that." Amber felt a bit better.

When Richard returned, the shirt-dress girl lay down and slept the first hour of their journey, using a coat for a blanket, burrowing into the jumble on the back seat until she was indistinguishable from the rest of the menagerie. She hibernated until well past the stone walls of the boys' prison at St. Cloud, then she awoke and sat up and stretched. Amber studied the landscape as it gradually converted from cities to towns to farmland to dense wild forests. The fear in her eyes seemed to melt away. She did not speak.

St. Cloud to Little Falls to Motley, large cities to small cities to small towns to little villages; then Leader to Badoura to Chamberlain, quiet collections of old, forgotten buildings. Faint reminiscences of past communities. Continuing to the north, where between Akeley and Kabekona, a Forest Service sign announced that one was now entering Paul Bunyan State Forest. Richard turned off onto a familiar dirt road he knew would lead to a secluded section of the forest. He drove a short distance to where the road ended at a cool, shadowy intersection with another old forest road, and there he stopped for lunch. He turned to hand the can of de Medici pop to Amber. Her eyes were fear again.

Richard did not ask why. "We can eat our spaghetti here, Amber. Grab two plastic forks from that side pocket back there."

The girl did not speak, but did as she was told.

Richard lowered the tailgate of his truck and put the container of spaghetti in the center where man and girl could share its contents. This part of the forest was maple lowland speckled with tiny ponds of captive water. Multitudes of frogs peeped and croaked love songs to each other.

The amphibian crescendo seemed to calm Amber enough to where she could speak, but her eyes were still misty with an unspoken dread. "The Paul Bunyan Trail must be in the Paul Bunyan Forest. Right?" she asked.

"No, it is not. The Paul Bunyan Trail lies up north of Bemidji, between Bemidji and Blackduck," said Richard. "This particular state forest is south of Bemidji."

Amber's shoulders relaxed just a bit. "Oh," she said.

In reality, Richard, like most people who used the trails, was slightly misinformed. A section of the Paul Bunyan Trail did run through the Paul Bunyan State Forest, but east of where the truck was now parked. Also, the trail ended just south of Bemidji, not north; the trail seemed to continue north, but that was another trail—the Blue Ox Trail. Richard's confusion resulted because signs on a short black-top section of the Blue Ox Trail, near Lake Bemidji State Park, were marked as the Paul Bunyan Trail. Just a half mile north of the park, where the trail turns to gravel, the signs correctly state the Blue Ox Trail, but everyone uses the Paul Bunyan designation.

"We are not anywhere near the Paul Bunyan Trail," said Richard.

"Oh… OK," said Amber. Then, after some thought, "So, will we go by the trail when we go to your place?"

"No, we won't. We are not going near there because my home is completely on the other side of the Buena Vista State Forest." The girl's shoulders seemed to relax even more. "The Buena Vista is a different forest from the Paul Bunyan." The girl's shoulders relaxed a whole lot more.

Richard did not speak further, letting the peace of the forest calm the girl. After a time, Amber spoke again. She asked, "We would not ever go by that trail, would we?"

"Well, in the past I have run on the Paul Bunyan Trail, usually after shopping in town. The section near Lake Bemidji State Park is paved, which is great for running. But I haven't been over there lately."

Richard did not mention that his run past Rice Pond, on Forest Service Road 2213, was only two miles from the Paul Bunyan Trail, or that tomorrow Elsie and himself would be driving very near that particular trail to meet with Sally at Teddy and Clara Zemm's place. And certainly not that Sally had recently been attacked while jogging on the trail that Amber seemed to fear so much.

"Why?" asked Richard.

She answered tritely, "Oh, no reason. Just wondering."

Richard accepted that explanation. After a time, he sensed that Amber wanted to say something else. "What is it?" he asked.

"What are you going to do with me?"

"I'm going to fatten you up and use you for bear bait."

Amber almost laughed and almost smiled.

"You will be safe at my home. I have a girlfriend that you will like. A farm girl like yourself," said Richard.

Amber did smile and did laugh. "That would be good."

The girl did not eat much spaghetti. She said there was not any room left in her stomach after the milk and cookies. Richard guessed, from the looks of her ribs when in the closet, that she had not eaten well the past several days and her stomach was not used to food.

Having dined on sweet spaghetti, red wine, and cold pop, the pair resumed their journey to Bemidji. Richard stopped in town, filled the truck with gas and bought four gallons of milk. He gave Amber some change and told her to buy some candy or such.

When she returned she politely asked if she could keep a quarter. "See, it is the old man from New Hampshire. They say that a section of his face has broken off now." Amber showed Richard a badly scuffed quarter, holding it out in her hand as proudly as if it had recently come shiny off the mint.

Richard looked at the quarter lying on the girl's palm. The craggy visage of the old man from New Hampshire reminded Richard of his old friend Teddy. Maybe they were related.

"I like the motto, too," stated Amber.

"Sure," agreed Richard. Live free or die.

Richard drove out of town on Highway 15, eighteen miles farther north, past reed-edged Turtle Lake and sun-sparkled Lake Julia, past the ski hill that stood sentinel at the west edge of the Buena Vista State Forest, then past the tiny hamlet of Puposky with its postage stamp-sized post office womanned by a pair of pretty Postmasters, and finally to the dirt and gravel road that led past the lane to Richard's home.

He turned onto his rough, cratered driveway—the quarter mile path which ran through the center of his ten acre field—to where his weather-beaten log home sat at the edge of the surrounding woods, on the northern border of the small field.

Amber immediately loved the secluded home. While Richard unpacked his truck, Amber explored the large yard surrounding the house and poked into the edges of the woods that framed the back and sides of the yard. A mostly white snowshoe rabbit, as conspicuous as a neon sign now that the snow had melted, broke from the cover of its brush-pile home and loped along the edges of the grass. Amber called after it, informing the rabbit that it should hide itself before it became hawk food. Two red squirrels scolded her for disturbing their afternoon siestas.

Richard left Amber to her discoveries at the back of the field and made several phone calls to check with his fellow operatives. First he called Tony. Sassy's mother had already been found, still resident in Minneapolis but in a new apartment in a different section of the city. At least Tony had been able to reunite his lost fledgling with its mother.

Tony had another useful bit of information. "The girl Amber, she was never raped," said Tony. "Just beat mercilessly and abused."

"No need for a hospital visit, then."

"That's right. All you can do is give her a home and pray."

A call to Foster confirmed that Sally could and would meet with him on the day after tomorrow. Then a call to the Zemm home, where Clara answered and verified that the Zemms knew their place was to be used as the meeting site. Richard let her know that Elsie and her brood would be coming with him to her forest home.

Michael was again not at the local BCA office, but Jeff Haltman, the Bemidji area BCA agent, informed Richard that Michael had some new news for him. Something concerning the chow hall fight between Chad Rochambeau and his two adversaries. Jeff would have Michael call him as soon as he got back.

Richard had to use his calling card to reach Elsie's farm over in Clearwater County. She was at her farmhouse, not outside in the fields, cattle being much less demanding than dairy cows, specially after the calving season. A little girl's voice answered the phone, "Hi, I'll get mommy." And a clunk as the phone was dropped onto some wooden surface.

Presently, preinformed with knowledge from her caller ID, Elsie's voice, "Hi, Richard. Are we still planning on getting together for our springtime Thanksgiving?"

"Sure. I have another visitor, however." Richard told the story of how he came to acquire the green-eyed captive of Eugene Euglena; about how he and Tony had found Amber taped to a pipe in a back closet; cold, cramped, naked, and dying of fear.

"I don't think that she will be a problem for your girls though," said Richard, "despite the trauma she must have suffered. Amber seems to be a relatively normal young teenager. If there is such a thing," he added. "I think that Euglena was still in the early stages of breaking her."

"I'd like to meet this bastard," said Elsie, catching Richard off guard by the uncharacteristic vehemence in her voice.

"Yes. Me too," agreed Richard, in a tone much less severe and much more pensive than Elsie's.

"Death is too good for the likes of him," said Elsie.

"Yes, your are correct," agreed Richard, not mentioning to Elsie that he had considered killing Euglena while in prison.

"How tall is this girl?" asked Elsie.

"Amber is just a tiny girl. Both the girls were small. But I think Amber is younger than the fourteen or fifteen that the other girl said she was. Kind of hard to tell."

"I should have some clothes for her," said Elsie. "Some dresses and blue jeans and such. Girl items."

"That would be good, but all your girls are much smaller than Amber. I think this girl is just under five feet, maybe four–seven or eight."

There was a long silence on Elsie's end. Richard had no clue as to what he had said to cause the silence. Then Elsie spoke again, softer but yet firm, "Let me find the girl something. It's the least I can do for her."

"OK, good," agreed Richard, wondering why finding clothes for a stranger should be the least, and not the most, that Elsie should do, but Richard did not question Elsie's spontaneous concern with Amber's plight. Elsie was a good mother and a genuine Christian, so maybe that was all the explanation needed.

Elsie gave an approximate time of arrival for her and her clan, and whetted Richard's appetite with an encore description of the dinner. Then she had to excuse herself from any further conversation so she could attend to imminent children's issues.

Michael Kieran called a minute later. "I have some information from an incident report filed at Moose Lake Prison, about the fight that Chad Rochambeau was involved in. Rochambeau's adversaries were Eugene Euglena and Odis Blister. Our two DNA matches. In the report, your Chad Rochambeau had stated that two black men had jumped him in the kitchen of the chow hall. They, in turn, said that Rochambeau attacked them because he was prejudiced against African Americans."

"What was the official conclusion?" asked Richard.

"Several bystanders said that Euglena and Blister were harassing Rochambeau, but that Rochambeau was ignoring them. Then Blister said something disparaging about Rochambeau's Christian faith. That got Blister clobbered for his disrespect."

Richard thought for a moment and then asked, "Does the report indicate what it was that Blister said to make Chad go off?"

"Yes, I think so." The sound of pages turning. Then, "Here it is; he said something like: 'Damn Jesus. Damn Jesus to hell.'"

"That is what my oversized attacker said at North Twin Lake and later at Rice Pond. He must have been Odis Blister," figured Richard.

"Another small part of the puzzle solved," agreed Agent Kieran.

Without mentioning Tony de Medici as the source of his newly acquired information, or anything about the two liberated prisoners, Richard told Michael of Euglena's secret apartment. "Your BCA men or the St. Paul police could stake it out, if that is something they might want to do," suggested Richard, but he doubted that Euglena would be foolish enough to return there. The macho child-beater would know that an arrest warrant had been issued for him.

Richard also had his cow-slobber shirt cooling in a plastic bag in the vegetable crisper of his refrigerator. He could drop it off sometime tomorrow if Michael thought it was important enough to be tested.

Michael thought so; the evidence on the shirt could establish part of a time line for Chad Rochambeau, if nothing else. But Michael asked Richard to call first, to make sure he was in the office.

"I don't want your cow slobber to go the way of the other DNA evidence."

After the various and sundry calls were completed, Richard took his bow outside to do some target practicing. It would be a good way to relax. He called Amber in from the wilderness of his yard and from her circumnavigation of its surrounding woods. After a few shots at the hay bale, Amber asked if she could try. Richard took an arrow from the round tomato cage that he used to hold his arrows when he practiced, and taught Amber how to shoot the bow.

"You can aim in two different ways," instructed Richard. "Either sight down the length of the arrow and let your mind tell you where to put the arrow, or line up the front bead with the hole of the string peep."

Amber could not pull the string back with her bare fingers, so Richard showed her how to use his string release—a mechanism that combines a wooden handle with a steel trigger. Her very first shot was remarkably close to the center of the target, then her next several succeeding shots were not so accurate, and finally she improved until once again the center became vulnerable to her aim.

Richard sat at a bench behind the house and watched Amber shoot. When he saw that Amber's arms were beginning to tire, he called her over.

"You'll have ticks, young lady, from going in the woods. Let me check your hair and your back."

"I already caught two crawling on my ankles. Yech!" shuddered Amber.

"Springtime is the worst for ticks. Later in the summer they will go away and leave us in peace."

Richard picked two ticks out of Amber's hairline and one more off her shoulder blade. When he had the girl lower her shirt-dress below her shoulders, like an old lady's shawl, he saw that her back was a mass of old purple and black bruises overlaid with newer red and blue marks. He had not seen them in the closet because of the dark, and not when he put her down in the room because she had turned toward him. He had thought that odd, but she must have been less embarrassed to show her front than to reveal the abuse on her back. Elsie's words of death came back to Richard's mind.

Richard pulled the girl's shirt-dress back up around her shoulders and packed her off to the house to take a shower. Then he retrieved the arrows from the embrace of the straw target and placed them with the bow in the wire tomato cage which was pushed into the ground about forty feet from the bale. The wood and steel mechanical release was not hanging on the bow's string. Amber must have taken it inside the house, he figured, so he quit his search of the lawn and went inside to find some clean clothes for his small guest.

"All I could find was an old pair of Jeanette's running shorts and a long-sleeved shirt that I was given at the Walker North Country Marathon last year. The shirt is too tight for me, so it might fit you a bit better than Tony's dress."

"Just leave the clothes outside the door," shouted Amber, loud enough to be heard through the bathroom's wood-paneled walls.

The shorts were a blue satiny nylon and the long-sleeved T-shirt was deep red, printed over with the name of the marathon and a dark green picture of a running gnome holding a forked walking stick.

"Not that Tony's dress looks bad on you," kidded Richard.

Amber wisely ignored him. "Any shoes?" she asked, speaking over the sound of the shower.

"Not really. But I have a pair of flip-flops that might stay on your feet. And some ankle length white socks that look kind of feminine. You could wear one or the other, I suppose."

CHAPTER 14

While Amber took her shower, Richard went running on the course he had mowed around the perimeter of his field. His heart would pump an increased supply of blood to his muscles, and, it seemed, an increased supply to his brain, allowing him to relax and let the facts of the case organize themselves as they might.

The grapple hook mystery had been solved: Odis Blister had used it to try to recover Chad's bracelet from Rice Pond. He had failed. Foster found the chain, with its ID tag. Jeanette put the puzzle of the number to rest; PMB 185417 was Chad Rochambeau, Prison Motorcycle Boy, who, it turned out, loved Lenora "Lennie" Frontera: our raped and murdered Native girl.

Then there was: "Damn Jesus. Damn Jesus to hell." Big black Odis Blister had been Richard's attacker at North Twin Lake—where he had dropped a scale-encrusted fillet knife, and at Rice Pond—where he had been half-drowned by Richard. Odis Blister could be knocked down both by Chad Rochambeau and Foster Bede.

The case was seemingly resolving itself. Eugene Euglena was the second attacker of Lenora, per DNA testing. But what about the third attacker? And why should the local authorities want to ruin the third set of DNA evidence…which Richard knew they had. And why would a cop or the district attorney send a rapist out to try to kill him. Somebody important in the community must need to be protected.

What else? There were the tire tracks with the star-shaped cutout. A yellow rose. The puncture wounds on Lenora's dead hand meant that she had wanted to keep the rose for evidence—for after her death. And the gingham dress, which might not mean anything, but seemed important in Richard's mind.

Then there were the two cattle-licked vehicles, Richard's old Chevy and Chad's new Jeep, which brought us back to Chad Rochambeau. He had been at the Chippewa National Forest, on Forest Road 2213, the exact day after his lover had died. "God, what does that mean?" thought Richard. "How does that fit in?"

There was Miss Frontera's very old and very worn cross, forced between Lennie's teeth like a World War II dog tag. Was the Christian cross a connection between Chad Rochambeau and Lenora Frontera? But we already have two connections: their love and a gold bracelet.

Does the incident report from the prison at Moose Lake mean anything? Chad was a very serious Christian that took poorly to Odis Blister's disrespect. Odis's partner in perversion, Eugene Euglena, must have stolen Chad's bracelet. Then it ends up at Rice Pond.

Sally, Zemm's niece's friend, had been attacked a few days before Lenora's death. Tony and Richard had found two more victims, the little black girl Sassy and green-eyed Amber. Earlier, Richard had thought that the coincidence of Lenora's dark hair and Sally's dark hair had meant something, but then there came light-blond Amber.

Richard could not reconcile Amber's extreme youth and fragility with the horrors of Euglena. "Someone should kill that bastard, as Elsie had intimated," thought Richard as he finished his few miles.

Amber was sitting at the kitchen table, dressed in Jeanette's blue running shorts and Richard's green-gnome-emblazoned red running shirt, a yellow towel wound around her head. She was talking on the portable phone.

"It's your daughter, Jeanette; she called while you were out. I told her who I was and how I came to be here. We have been talking ever since. Do you want the phone back?"

"No, that's all right. Just let me speak to her when you two are done."

Amber turned back to the phone and her new friend, as Richard cracked eggs for a French toast supper and dropped round patties of sausage into an iron frying pan. "Can you cook this French toast while I have my turn at the shower?" asked Richard.

Not answering, Amber rose from her chair, waved Richard off without interrupting her speech on the phone, and walked to the stove. Richard took that as a sign that she had things under control.

Amber's conversation with Jeanette was still ongoing even after Richard had finished his shower. He turned the phone sideways in Amber's hand, told Jeanette that he would call later, and then signed for Amber to wrap up her talk with Jeanette, which she presently did. "Good-bye, Jeanette. Thanks for listening to me."

"Your daughter is really nice. I never had a sister at home that I could talk to." The long conversation with Jeanette had opened the floodgates. Amber talked nonstop through the entire meal. Richard listened. He was good at that.

It had been a long time since he had anyone stay with him, friend or family. Amber was like having a daughter in his home again. She did not tell him about everything, of course, but she did drop bits of her past life. There had been a loving father that had died when she was seven. A mother who liked rum too much. And finally, about a year ago, a stepfather that, though not often overtly cruel, had much resented Amber's presence in the household. She thought that her running away would be the answer. She said it wasn't, but she didn't say she wanted to return to her mother's home, either.

"What do you like to do?" asked Richard.

"I like school. I'm good in math, especially geometry, and I like science. Botany and geology are interesting."

"Bemidji has good schools. Where did you go to school?"

Amber didn't answer that one. Instead, "I had a rock collection back home, until my stepfather used it for driveway filler."

"I used to collect rocks when I was a young boy," said Richard. "Perhaps I can help you start another collection. A few miles north of here there is an abandoned gravel pit."

"I'd like that. And so would my..." Amber didn't finish her thought.

Richard didn't press. "I just remembered, I have a microscope from when I homeschooled my two youngest boys. I think it is packed upstairs somewhere in my bedroom."

Amber's eyes brightened by several degrees of intensity at the mention of a microscope. "Really?"

"Really."

"My school has a microscope, but only the teachers are allowed to use it. You'll have to show me how to use your microscope, if that would be all right with you."

"We could do that. There is a duck lake about a mile or so back of my home. We could hike there and collect samples to put under the microscope."

"Are there fish in the lake?" asked Amber.

"Just minnows. The lake is very shallow."

"Minnows are good."

Richard's visitor continued to talk about her likes and dislikes, and her former life, without getting too specific. She said she had girl-friends that were loyal. She didn't mention any boys. The microscope came up in her conversation every now and then. She allowed herself to believe that she could have a rock collection again, one that would not be driven over daily.

Richard would have loved to listen to Amber through the night, but he had to get some rest, to recover from his twin runs of today, and to be ready for whatever tomorrow might bring. He figured that Amber should catch up on her sleep too, having been newly released from her cramped prison. Foster's old bedroom had a futon in it, so he directed Amber there. Then he found a Teddy bear that Josh had won for one of his past girlfriends. He offered it to Amber, hoping that she would not be embarrassed by a gift of a Teddy bear. She accepted it graciously.

"Like any little girl would," thought Richard. "How young is our Amber?"

Then aloud, "How old are you, Honey?"

"Eleven. I'll be twelve in October," she said.

Richard tucked her in, read her a scary story from one of Foster's old Richard Scary books, kissed her on her forehead, and wished her a good night and a God bless.

Richard went downstairs to put away the remainder of their meal, made a few marks in his notebook, and then went back upstairs to his bedroom. The drive from the Cities, the morning and evening runs, and the events of the long day threw Richard into a deep sleep.

~

"Sir…sir…wake up." Richard heard the diminutive voice as in a dream. A small someone was standing in the middle of his bedroom. Louder, "Wake up! There is something under my window, trying to eat its way into the house."

"Gnawing?" asked Richard.

"Yes."

"My old adversary. A grizzly-spine-covered porcupine that has been chewing on the frame of my front door for the past month. He shows up every few nights."

Richard took a flashlight from the bookcase in his bedroom and led Amber downstairs and to the front door (which is directly under Amber's bedroom window), and which from the sound of it, was still being consumed. Richard opened the door and placed the light on the porcupine, who, being rudely disturbed from his meal of dried pine board, turned in circles and made loud clicking noises with its mouth. Amber laughed until she could hardly stand. Richard shooed the animal off with a strategically placed broom.

"I should have warned you, Amber, don't ever go outside at night without checking for this guy first. A leg full of porcupine quills would ruin your day for sure."

Richard walked to the kitchen, followed by Amber in her running clothes and flip-flops. Richard knew that it would be a while before he was sleepy again. He poured each of them a glass of milk and found some chocolate: two Milky Way bars. They sat on the couch that was under the south window in the kitchen, leaning against each arm of the old piece of furniture, facing each other, ate their chocolate, and talked. And Amber could talk. She continued from where she had left off earlier in the evening, then, having finished her life story, or so it seemed, she asked questions of Richard and about his family. Richard gave her another half hour, and then sued for peace and sleep.

Amber was content with that, for now. "Good night, Sir," she said. "See you in the morning."

CHAPTER 15

Twenty-two days ago Amber was not a slave. She was living in a poor rural area of northern Minnesota with a mother degenerated into alcohol and drugs, a cruel stepfather, and a little brother that she struggled to take care of from day to day. But she was free.

Then the day came, as she had known it would, when the rage of her stepfather was turned from her mother to Amber's small body. He had left a crescent scar high on her right temple. The next day she walked away, many miles to the closest town with a bus pick-up, and with most of the dollars she had saved bought a ticket to the Cities.

Amber had been saving the money to buy a new bike for her brother. His old bike had been run over by her stepfather, the reason supposedly that Thor, her brother, had left it too close to the edge of the drive. So the stepfather had veered onto the grass and run the boy's bike over, then backed over it to make sure all the metal was bent.

Before she left, Amber told Thor that she would get a good job in the Cities and buy him a nice new bike, but first she would have to arrange to somehow get him reunited with her. Somehow. She didn't know how. But she would figure some way.

"Please don't leave me," said Thor. "I may never see you again."

The little boy hated to cry, but he did.

"I'll be all right," said Amber. "God will protect me." Amber was not so sure that would be true. God wasn't doing such a good job to date.

Thor ran into the house and came back with a small cloth bag of coins. "Here, take this with you. It will help."

She looked inside and counted maybe four dollars or so, mostly quarters and dimes. "Thank you, Thor. It will help."

Thor put his arms around his sister and hugged her, which he hated more than crying, but he could not help either.

He was taller than his sister and stronger, so she had to accept her fate until her little brother decided to relinquish her. Amber believed the bear hug to be less of affection and more an effort to delay her departure.

Amber kissed her brother's face, which, like rock salt on a blood sucker, caused him to let her go. "I promise. I'll call you as soon as I have a home where we can stay," said Amber.

Thor was not convinced. "Take me with you. I won't be trouble to you. I promise."

Promises and promises.

"I only have enough money for one bus ticket."

"We can walk."

"St. Paul is too far." At that, the girl turned away and left her brother standing in the dust of the driveway, turning once to wave good-bye to her little brother.

He could not wave back.

The many miles to the town with the bus pick-up was tiring but not exhausting. Amber sat next to an open window and rested, watching the farms and forests go by as the bus slowly began its journey south. At the first town down the road a very young nun got on and sat next to Amber. The nun seemed too shy to start a conversation, so Amber decided to talk first.

"I am going down to St. Paul, which is one of the Twin Cities," said Amber.

The young nun told her that she worked in a church in downtown St. Paul. She was just up north visiting her folks.

Amber wished that she had folks. Maybe this nun could be a mother to her and her brother, and could get a paying job in a church.

Amber could find her a guy. Amber was desperate. She needed to put a family together for her brother.

"Your hair is very pretty," said Amber. Short, blonde-red hair was poking its way from under the edge of the cap of the young nun's habit. Amber studied her face. It was thin and pretty. Maybe the nun was Irish. "Are you Irish?"

It was a good guess. "Well, yes I am. Some of my ancestors first settled in St. Paul. There was a large Irish community back in the old days. St. Pat's day is still a big deal down there."

"My name is Amber. What's yours?"

"Sister Catherine."

The two girls talked most of the rest of their way to the Cities. Amber wanted to ask the young nun to consider being a mother to herself and Thor, but what a silly question, and how would she start without letting on that she was a runaway.

"Have you ever considered getting married and having a son and a daughter?" asked Amber.

The nun girl told Amber about her big church. Amber thought that she said that the church's name was Tenkay, and that every year a run and a block party is held there to raise money for the poor.

Amber was poor.

The nun told her how to get to the church. Amber tried hard to remember the instructions, but it was difficult to do because she had no references upon which to build a mental map. Their talk trailed off as they approached the Cities. Amber put her head against the glass of the window and closed her eyes. She was scared. She brought up an old image of her father, her real father, just before he had died. He had taken off work early and had come home so he could watch his son and daughter get off the school bus together on Amber's first day. Amber remembered her dad's face, she could again see him, and she was less scared.

"We are here, Amber," said Catherine.

They got off the bus together. Amber was a bit confused by the mass of people at the station. She turned in a circle to take in the place, and when her vision had circumnavigated the scene, the nun girl was nowhere to be seen. Amber had planned to follow her, if at all possible, though Amber had figured that Catherine probably had someone waiting for her with a car. Amber made it to an empty bench and sat down. The crowd was already starting to thin, so that she was not so apprehensive about the crush of people and the noise.

A young-looking black man was staring at her from the other side of the room. Amber did not like being stared at and did not meet his look, but instead turned her head away. When she finally turned back he was standing next to the bench she was on.

"You look kind of lost, young lady," said the man. He had some kind of a rag tied onto the top of his head. Amber thought the rag looked dirty. Apparently her thought was apparent.

"What's a matter, girl? You don't like black people?"

"Oh, no. I'm not prejudiced." Amber remembered the diversity training she had gotten in school, but it didn't help her to figure what to say about the dirty rag.

"You waiting on somebody?"

"Um, not really. I'm just resting before I walk to the Tenkay church downtown. That's all."

"Well, you're lucky today because I'm driving right by there on the way to my place. I'll give you a ride." The man had not introduced himself or asked her name.

Amber was confused as to what to do or say. "That is all right. I would just rather walk."

"Too prejudiced to ride with a black, that's it, isn't it?"

"Oh, no. I'm not prejudiced." Maybe a ride would be all right. The man did know how to get to the church, which Amber didn't.

"Come on and follow me," said the man as he turned to walk away.

Amber followed.

The man drove through the center of the city, past several large churches. Amber thought that she had seen Catherine getting out of a car in front of one of the churches. The man drove to a badly-littered section of town and stopped in front of an apartment building. There were several young blacks hanging out in front of the building. They were listening to a rap song with sleazy lyrics. A lot of bitches and ho's. The man walked around to Amber's door and opened it.

"Here is your church, young lady."

The blacks in front of the building laughed at his comment.

From Catherine's description of her church and from what little common sense Amber had left, she knew that this was not a church.

The man reached into his car and pulled Amber out by her arm, and before she could ask for help from the bystanders or scream, he banged her head against the top of the door opening and knocked her unconscious. When Amber awoke she was sprawled on the floor of what was apparently the man's apartment. Her head hurt and she was dizzy. The man and two other men were standing around her. Amber was scared. She would certainly be raped. But she wasn't. Not then, and not in the days to follow. Apparently, not to be raped was worth forty thousand dollars.

One of the other men was a giant black. The other man looked like an oriental Mexican white guy, with a Midwest accent. Amber soon learned that the large black was mostly stupid and the white guy was mostly mean. Rag head was just ruthless.

A small black female came into the room with a wet wash rag and started to rub the blood from Amber's temple. Ruthless slapped her across the face for her small act of kindness.

"You stupid bitch. What you think you doing?"

The small black girl apologized and left the room.

Mean picked Amber up and flipped her over his back and onto the floor, pulling her shirt off in the process. Amber covered her chest with her arms, but Ruthless slapped her bare back with the palm of his hand and calmly told her to put her arms at her side. She refused. Ruthless slapped her again. She refused again. He slapped.

Each slap would knock the wind out of Amber. She knew that she would lose this contest or die winning. She was too young to have any breasts anyway, so what did it really matter? She relented. She dropped her arms to her sides, revealing breasts that were just nipples. Stupid and Mean laughed at her and picked at her nipples.

Ruthless slapped her on the back again. He slapped her again. And again. And again. And again. The beating never stopped. She would be beat to death, it seemed. She was not raped, a fact which she found curious. Mean wanted to, but Ruthless would not let him. She heard the forty thousand mentioned many times.

Late that night she came to hate black men and white oriental Mexicans with Midwest accents.

Amber was drowning in her fear and her blood.

She hoped for help that would not come. She knew that the sounds of the slaps could be heard in the other apartments, but as the hours passed she realized that nobody was going to call the police. Not for one little white bitch, as she had apparently become.

Stupid pulled the snap open on her jeans and tried to pull her pants down. She resisted and held them up with her hands and yelled at Stupid to stop. Instead he kicked her in the crotch, literally picking her off the ground with the force of the kick. The girl was not a boy, but the pain was still unbelievable. She immediately fell to the floor. Her pants were wet from urine or blood, or both.

Stupid took the bottom of her pants and swung her in a circle. He was so large that it was no more strenuous to him than waving around a rag doll. Her pants pulled loose and came off her legs, stripping her socks and shoes in the process. Amber was left with her panties and very little dignity.

The men took time off to get something to eat and to watch some basketball. Blacks were good at basketball, remembered Amber.

After the food, the game started again. Slaps to her bare back again. She lost her panties and the rest of her dignity sometime later.

Ruthless dragged her by her hair into a closet at the back of the apartment. There he shut her mouth with duct tape and taped her hands to an iron water pipe. When she was not being beaten, that would be her home for the next couple of weeks and more. Amber lost track of the days.

The small black girl would feed her and try to clean her body whenever the men left the apartment. If they got too drunk to leave, then a few meals would be skipped. Amber was always thirsty. The closet smelled of old urine. Amber realized that there must have been many others that had been broken in the closet. Sometimes, Amber had to wet herself too, when the presence of the men kept the small black girl from helping her.

Twice Amber was taped up and thrown into a dirty white van and driven up north to a filthy cabin. The men would have her cook for them and make her clean the place. Amber would keep her mouth closed and her ears open, but the vacation from the closet never meant a respite from the beatings. Once, Ruthless got angry at something that Stupid had done, and took it out on her back. From what Amber could discern, Stupid had raped a girl on a bike trail in the area. So Amber got a tougher beating that night.

Amber knew that she was not breaking as fast as the men had

the LONELY CROSSES

hoped. But she was breaking. Taped into the closet, the picture in her mind of her dead father waiting at the bus stop for his daughter to come home from school was sometimes all that kept her alive. This would not last forever. She would have to relent, whatever that meant, or she would have to retreat deep into her mind and let go of reality.

The second time the men brought her back from the northern cabin, Ruthless beat her harder than ever. He even let Mean help him. Except at the cabin, where she wore a too large gingham dress, she was always naked and cold. Amber was dying. The darkness of the nights in the closet were almost a relief. She would hold out one more day, maybe two, then she would allow herself to drift into insanity.

Ruthless, Mean, and Stupid would never have her.

Hours after the beating, the small black girl came to her and fed her and washed her cuts and bruises. The black girl, in all these many days, had almost never said anything to her. Today she had something to say. She pulled the tape from Amber's mouth, then spoke to her.

"You have to give up, Honey. Or these guys will kill you soon. Do you understand?"

She understood and did not care. "What is your name?" asked Amber, her voice grown as little as her starved body.

"My friends call me Sassy, but never call me that or say anything to me when the others are around."

"Fair enough, Sassy," said Amber, thereby appointing herself as one of Sassy's friends.

"It has been like forever since anyone has called me Sassy. I almost forgot what it sounded like to hear my own name."

"Don't you ever see your friends?" asked Amber.

"No, never. I stay here all the time, except when I'm being rented out, of course."

"You need to get away, Sassy. Why don't you just walk off when those guys leave?"

"Oh, no. Never. Eugene would kill me if I ever tried something like that." Sassy had been broken. Abraham had freed his people a long time ago, but he had never foreseen the rise of pimps.

"Cut this tape then, Sassy, and I'll free the both of us."

Fear flooded over Sassy's face, so much so that Amber felt almost like telling Sassy to forget about freeing her and to tape her back up. The conflict between Amber's will and Sassy's terror was cut short by

127

a knock on the front door.

"My God," said Sassy, "I pray that's nobody come to collect you." She put the tape back over Amber's mouth and shut the closet door, leaving Amber once again in the dark.

An overwhelming fear gripped Amber. The fear of being beaten by Ruthless, the fear of giving in to a growing insanity, the fear of the unknown stranger who is waiting for when she is broke. A perfect storm of fears. Not to mention the constant worry for her abandoned brother. Abandoned because of her mistake.

Amber strained to listen. She thought that she could hear Sassy talking to someone. Then a loud crash and Sassy begging for...what?

Another wave of fear washed over Amber. In her imagination she saw Ruthless breaking down the front door and beating both her and Sassy for their friendship.

The closet door opened. She could sense that it was not Sassy. An old man took her by her hair and bent her head back. His eyes were a deep blue like her father's had been. She thought she saw sadness there. She thought there was also a flicker of a killer in his eyes.

The man peeled the tape from her mouth. She did not dare speak. Maybe this was the man that she was being broke for? The man cut her free of the iron pipe and lifted her and carried her from her prison.

A younger man was also there, as well as Sassy. They were talking about something. The old man set her down on her feet in the middle of the bedroom. She slowly straightened her back.

She was still naked, as she had been for most of the last few weeks. The young man took his shirt off and gave it to the old man, who put it on her and buttoned it up. She could hear Sassy talking to the men. As the worst of the fear left Amber, she could make out some of what was being said. The young man, covered with bible scenes, held Sassy in his arms. When he let go of her, she was crying. She told him that the girl's name was Amber.

The old man took Amber again by the hair and led her away.

"I should go back in the closet before he returns," said Amber. She felt a fool for saying that. She had been closer to being broke than she had realized. She prayed that the old man and his pictured friend would be an improvement over her three previous tormentors.

She was led to a long truck with two bench seats, one in front and one behind. The old man put her in the rear seat, into a pile of clothes and assorted items. They drove to a better part of town and took Sassy into a large white house, leaving her alone in the back seat. She thought about running away, but worried about her black friend. A little girl brought her a glass of milk and some cookies. The milk was so good. She was so thirsty. She nibbled slowly on the cookies, giving her stomach some time to get used to food again.

The old man returned and drove away. She fell asleep for a while. When she awoke, they had already left the city. She could tell that they were travelling north, but on a different route than her bus ride south.

They stopped in a forest for lunch. She asked some questions about a trail. She wondered if the old man was just taking her up north to Ruthless. Maybe he was just fooling her.

Later, at a store, the old man gave her some money to buy something with. She did that, and in her change there was a state quarter she had not seen before. New Hampshire. She read the quarter and decided that it might be lucky. The old man let her keep her quarter.

He drove her to his home. It was a log house in the wilderness. A perfect place to keep a captive without anyone being the wiser.

She checked out the yard around the house. The old man shot some arrows from a bow. Maybe he would hunt her and shoot her with his bow? She tested him by asking if she could try shooting. He let her, showing her how to hold the bow and fire the arrows.

He made her take a shower as he found some clean clothes for her. He said something about a red-haired girlfriend with sticky-out ears.

Amber wanted to laugh at what he said about the hair and ears, but she wasn't sure if it was safe to do so. Maybe the old man had a temper.

After the shower Amber could not find the old man in the house. Then out a window she saw him running around the field in front. She felt free, but maybe it was a trick.

The phone rang and without thinking she picked it up. It was the old man's daughter.

"Hello, who is this?" asked Amber.

"Who is this?" asked the daughter.

"Who is this?"

"Who is this?"

Amber realized how foolish she must sound to the lady on the phone. "I'm sorry. My name is Amber. Amber Tollefson." She tried to explain to the lady who she was and why she was where she was.

The lady understood quicker than Amber might have thought possible. "You are a residual from my dad's investigation, then."

Amber agreed she was a residual. "Yes, I am."

"My name is Jeanette, Richard's one and only daughter."

"Glad to meet you. I am an only daughter, too. But my dad is no longer alive. All I have now is a younger brother." Amber told Jeanette about her brother and her plans to get him reunited with her. Amber may have said more than she should have, but she needed a real live person to talk to, not just the memory of her dad's face. She needed a friend.

Jeanette made herself that friend. She helped Amber to conspire. "Do you think that your brother could make it to my dad's place on his own?"

"I'm sure he could," asserted Amber, not mentioning that her old home was over a hundred miles away. She had already figured that from a highway map from the truck.

"Then don't tell my dad. Just call your brother when you get a chance and have him get himself to your new home."

"You sure?"

"I don't think my dad will turn away just one more stray."

The old man came in from his run, started a French toast and sausage supper, and then took his shower, leaving Amber to take over cooking the supper. When he returned to the kitchen, he asked the girls to finish their conversation, which they presently did.

Amber realized that a daughter like Jeanette could only be the result of a good father.

She and Richard talked the rest of the evening. About her school, his family, their interests. Lots of stuff. It had been so long since she had someone to listen to her. The old man seemed good at listening.

Later into the evening he said that she needed to go to bed. She figured that he must be really tired, what with the long drive and the run, and considering his age and all. She agreed to go to sleep, though she would have rather talked some more.

Sometime in the night she heard a monster eating its way into the house, the noise of the consumption coming from somewhere below her bedroom window. She went and woke the old man.

"Sir!" she said loudly.

It was only a porcupine. The old man said that the animal was dangerous, though he did not seem afraid of it. The little girl thought the porcupine was just funny, though she made a note to stay away from its quills.

After the porcupine episode, they made some chocolate milk. She was still thirsty from her time in the closet. As they drank, they talked some more. She told the old man some about her life, being careful not to reveal any needed secrets. After a time, the old man became tired again. She could tell. They decided to go back to their bedrooms and try to get some more sleep.

Early the next morning Amber snuck downstairs and called her brother. She knew that her mother and stepfather would be out like lights this early in the morning. As expected, Thor answered the phone.

"Hello."

"Hi, brother."

"Amber, where have you been? Do you know how worried I've been these last weeks?"

"I'm sorry, I've been tied up. But I have a home for us now. An old man with a big house in the wilderness. You will love it."

"Do you think he will want me?"

"I talked to his daughter, Jeanette, over the phone. She told me to have you come over here without telling her dad first. She said that you will be able to stay once you are at this place."

Amber gave instructions to her brother, then told him that she would be calling him every morning until he left, then said good-bye before the old man caught her on the phone. "I told you that God would protect me," said Amber.

As she hung up the phone, there was a machine-gun staccato on the roof. She about came out of her skin.

Amber ran upstairs, then walked down the hallway and knocked on the old man's door, as the awful noise continued.

"Sir...Mister," she whispered.

CHAPTER 16

In the morning, lying in his comforter-covered bed, with cool, leaf-filtered green sunlight streaming through his curtainless windows, Richard could hear tapping on his house and on his door.

"Sir… Mister," said softly, yet with concern.

"A woodpecker, Amber. That's all."

"Oh, all right. I'll be downstairs, Sir."

"Richard. You can call me Richard."

"Yes, Sir," said Amber, as she flip-flopped away.

Richard enjoyed a few more moments in bed, stretching his old muscles to warm them. They were sore from his long run in Terrie's park yesterday and at his own field in front of his home. Running two times in one day was probably a mistake, but he needed the second one to get the long drive out of his system.

He could hear noises in the kitchen, then a loud announcement, "Breakfast is ready, Sir."

He finally got up, dressed, and went downstairs. Set at the kitchen table were two large bowls of cereal. Richard could see that Amber had mixed several different kinds of dry cereal in each bowl.

"My son Josh used to do the same thing. He talked me into trying the mixture one day and I was really surprised at how good it was."

Richard sat at his place at the table while Amber poured milk over his concoction. "But it still doesn't make sense to me," said Richard.

"I used raisin bran, Cheerios, shredded wheat, and a multi-grain cereal. I could be a chef someday," bragged Amber.

Coffee was just finishing perking in the electric coffee maker. "That really smells good in the morning." Richard filled his cheeks with cereal, got up to pour himself a cup of coffee, and made it back to his seat just in time for another bite of cereal.

"What are we going to do today?" asked Amber.

"I thought that I'd be in the Cities yet, so I have an extra day to catch up on things. Phone calls and such. But mostly I need to relax and rest."

"Can we go to the lake that you talked about yesterday?"

"I guess we could. But you don't have very good shoes, or I should say, flip-flops, to hike in."

"Would the lake have any ducks swimming on it?"

"I can't guarantee that, but there might be. This time of year there are often mallards and wood ducks sitting on the temporary ponds in the woods."

"I noticed that you have a nice camera. We could take that with us and try to get a picture of an animal or such."

"We could do that." Richard usually did take his camera when he hiked in the woods, especially the spring of the year. The deciduous trees of the forest had that fresh, light green color that contrasted so well with the darker pines, and the birds were really moving about, migrating and settling into their summer territories.

Amber finished her cereal, then ran off to get ready for the hike. Richard took his shower and got dressed, lacing on an old pair of work boots with aggressive lugs on the soles. Then he loaded his coat pockets with a folding knife, cheese, and crackers, and filled a water bottle with orange pop. He was ready.

Amber came clumping downstairs in a pair of old boots that seemed to fit her. "Look what I found. There is another pair upstairs just like these, only bigger."

"Yours must be the boots that Josh used to have. The larger ones belonged to Foster, seeing that he is older. I didn't realize that we still had those old things. I really must go through the house and get rid of more of this old stuff. But I just never seem to have the time."

"I found a baseball and two mitts. We could play catch when we get back, if you're not too tired."

The phone rang just in time to save Richard from more of Amber's plans. It was Josh. "How is your new child getting along?" asked Josh. "Is she bored with country life yet?"

"She is finding all the old stuff that you guys have squirreled away in this house. And she is making tons and tons of plans for herself and me. She likes the country life; she is a country girl for sure."

"That's good," said Josh. "Anyway, I called to let you know that Sally called again. She wanted to make sure that you were going to meet with her tomorrow."

"No reason I wouldn't."

"I think she is anxious to talk to you. She probably wants to tell someone something, and she figures that you are a suitable person to listen to her. That's the feeling I get."

"I hope I can help." Can help the girl and help the case, too. But Richard didn't say that. "I'm going to rest my mind today, and God willing, tomorrow I'll be ready for Sally's story."

"You'll be ready."

"But first I have to take Amber on a hike back to Anderson Lake. It was her idea, but it is a good one. I didn't get back there even once last year."

Josh talked a bit more about the case, and asked more questions about Richard's newly freed guest, then he had to go.

Since Richard was already sitting on the living room couch next to the phone, he decided to call Elsie. "Hi. I was just checking to see how your clothes drive was coming along."

"I found lots of stuff," said Elsie. "The girl is not heavy, is she?"

"No, she's real thin." As thin as skin and bones can be.

"That's good. These clothes should fit her well." Elsie was very concerned about the rescued stranger. "I can't wait to meet her."

"She seems to be nice, and perhaps smart, too," said Richard, as he wondered about Elsie's intense concern with the girl she had not even yet met. Perhaps that is just women sticking together like they always do, he figured.

"What is she doing now?" asked Elsie.

"She is getting ready for a hike back to Anderson Lake. She talked me into that, then found an old pair of boots that Josh used to have, so now I have no excuse not to take her on her excursion."

"You'll have fun," said Elsie. "I have to go now. I'll see you early tomorrow morning."

Richard called Amber downstairs; she had gone back upstairs to dig some more in the things of Richard's past. Then they left together on their majestic wilderness adventure. As they walked out the door, Richard handed Amber a pin-on bubble compass.

"If you ever get lost around here, travel in as straight a line as you can in a southern direction, and you should eventually come to the road in front of this place."

"How long would that take, Sir?"

"Depends on how lost you are and how far back you are. You might also have to cover some wet ground, swamps and such, if you keep on a perfect heading to the south."

"I won't get lost. Not today." As if there were plans in the working to get lost on some other day. Which there probably was, if Richard knew kids at all.

A slight wind had arisen, but in the protection of the deep forest it was not very noticeable. Except for the eerie noise that the wind made: a low moan which perfectly matched in wildness the darkness under the large pines. An old logging road, or maybe it was an old farm road, Richard wasn't sure, ran from the back of the front field deep into the forest. The path received more light and the walking was easy there.

A mile later brought the pair to a small field, smaller than the front field where his house was located. Five deer, startled by Amber's voice, ran past a large, grey, flat-topped boulder and into the swampy woods on the east side of the field.

"Did you see them?" asked Amber. "They kind of jumped as they ran, like their legs were springs."

"They run like that when they are not too scared. It is kind of a play escape, I think."

The path led past the field along a fence line on its western edge. The barbed wire of the fence had long ago rusted away, leaving tough sentinels of weathered posts to mark its fading existence. Walking out of the field and back into the woods, Richard and Amber came to an area of oak and cedar trees. Richard turned to the east onto a smaller trail, just a foot path, that soon became wet and spongy. The trees thinned here, and the grasses took over, lending the area a feeling of being a savanna. The walking was much harder here, so Richard stopped often, ostensibly to sight with his camera, but really to let Amber rest from the bumpy, soggy ground. She was not fooled.

"Thanks for the rests, Sir. I need them, walking over this stuff." The girl was eleven going on forty.

"There is a small creek up ahead. It is usually empty, except in the springtime like now, but there shouldn't be very much water."

"I'm ready again," announced Amber.

They continued, soon coming to Richard's prediction of a nearly empty creek—which was now rushing madly with water. Not quite a stream, but at least a foot of noisy water, and wider than Richard had ever remembered. So much for his knowledge of springtime runoff.

"We must have hit the water at its highest," said Richard. "Well, no sense in both of us getting wet feet. Flip your lucky quarter, Amber, and see who carries whom."

Amber looked at Richard with eyes like a teenager's after being asked if there will be boys at the party.

"OK, fine. I'll do the heavy lifting. I mean..."

"Stop talking... and let me get up on your back," ordered Amber. "I'll hold your camera."

"Yes, ma'am."

Amber, having been carried to the other side of the creek, slid off Richard's back and onto the ground. The trail continued deep into an Oz-like maze of moss-covered tamarack trees. It was the darkest in here, the ground damp and devoid of grass and even more spongy than the open swamp. The tamarack forest continued right up to the edge of this side of the lake, so when the trail finally opened, the lake was a sudden sight to the hikers.

"It's beautiful," said Amber. She still had the camera and wanted to take a picture of the "secret" lake. "Can you show me how to use this thing?"

"Let me fix the settings, then you can aim it yourself and take the picture." Richard started to show Amber some of the features of the camera, but without overdoing his instruction, he hoped. "Hold it real steady and push this button here."

The lake still had ice on its surface. Perhaps the last ice in the county. The lake's shallow waters froze down to the ground in winter, causing the ice to stay longer than in a deeper lake. There was a small island near the far shore. To the east was a steep hill, the only high land next to the lake, it seemed.

"Can we walk to the island?" asked Amber.

"Sure, I think so. Let me check the ice first. Not that the lake is deep, but I'd like to stay dry today." At least drier than his feet. "It's still solid, though a bit sloshy."

The effect of the wind was greater out on the open ice. Amber's light hair blew back as they neared the island. A crescent scar could be seen high on her right temple.

"What happened there?" asked Richard, touching the scar with his finger.

"My stepfather. It was the first time he had hit me like that. But I knew from watching him go at my mother that it would not be the last. I left the next day."

"I'm sorry."

Amber brushed her hair back down. "I'm not."

They explored the island together. It was covered in bent and twisted cedar trees, like those that might be found on the tops of high mountains, beaten and weathered by the sun, wind, and winter snows, but somehow surviving from generation to generation.

They found a fallen tree and sat and ate the cheese and crackers that Richard had brought. They shared the orange pop from Richard's water bottle. The lake was quiet out here. The island was a lonely place. Richard was glad to have the girl with him.

On the far northern shore a long line of whitetail deer came out of the swampy forest and walked along the edge of the lake, then quickly disappeared back into the bogs from which they had come.

"They remind me of films of the caribou I've seen on television," said Amber.

"That is just what I was thinking," agreed Richard. "The way the sun hit them made their coats look white like caribou, and they walked in a line like caribou, and there were so many."

"Like caribou," said Amber.

When the deer were gone, the lake seemed devoid of life again. Only the wind made itself known out here, speaking its language in the ancient cedars of the island. The two hikers sat and rested, enjoying the soothing sounds of the wind and trees.

"I have to tell you something, Amber."

"What's that?"

"A few days back I was out jogging in the national forest and I found a girl that had been murdered. I've been helping a state cop with the investigation since then."

"Is that why you found me?" asked Amber, making connections faster than a movie detective.

"Yes. The clues, different threads, led me to that apartment. I guess I was lucky." Lucky that he knew Tony de Medici.

"I was lucky, Sir." The girl took her quarter from her pocket and rubbed her thumb across the old man's face. Across the face of the old man on the quarter, not across the face of the old man sitting next to her on their tree. Amber started to cry. It was the first time Richard had seen her cry. Snot was running from her nose.

"What a mess, Amber. Here, let me clean your face." Richard wiped her nose with the sleeve of his shirt.

"Thank you, Sir," she said, as she put the old man back in her pocket, the old man of the quarter and the old man next to her.

They left the island after their lunch and walked back the way they had come from. It was already late afternoon and the air was beginning to cool. Richard had to repeat his carry across the swollen creek. At the small field where the deer had sprung away they walked over to the boulder and sat on top of its surface. The boulder was still warm from the heat of the daytime sun. A flock of Canada geese passed low over them, calling to each other as they flew.

Amber took a small paper bag from her pants pockets and spread on the rock a display of treasures she had found during their trip to the lake. Several leaves, a grey feather and a blue feather, two squashed bugs, half of a butterfly wing, a segment of petal from a white flower, a piece of cedar bark, and something so dead it was unrecognizable.

"I'll be ready for the microscope, Sir. I found some nice rocks, too." Amber emptied her other pockets of the various stones she had collected. Another hour and Richard would not have been able to carry the girl and her load across the creek.

"You have a good start to your rock collection," said Richard.

"See this greyish-white one here, Sir. This is a piece of chert, which is like flint, just not black."

Richard thought how he had become "Sir" not long after Amber had been at his home. It seemed formal, but he somehow knew that it was Amber's way of making a connection with him.

As twilight gave way to dark they left their boulder and walked back home along the grassy road. Richard was used to the dark, but it kind of creeped out Amber. Her terminology. As they walked, she asked about the girl and the investigation. Richard answered her questions, without getting too graphic. Still, a dead girl is a dead girl. Amber could and probably would fill in the missing parts. There was not much that Richard could do to protect her from the awful truth of what had happened.

Once back home, things lightened up. Amber stopped asking questions, at least about the investigation. Richard microwaved bowls of frozen vegetables and plates of frozen chicken for their supper.

The long day of fresh air and hiking had made Richard sleepy, so after the meal he laid down on the couch in the kitchen and was soon dozing off. In his semi-consciousness he could hear Amber moving about the house, sometimes coming into the kitchen and standing before the couch where he was resting. Then he passed into a deeper sleep.

Two hours passed and he awoke to a very quiet house. Amber had pulled a camp chair into the kitchen and was sitting in the dark at Josh's pre-conviction table, herself half asleep.

She awoke when Richard went to stretch his legs. "Are you rested now, Sir?"

"I feel much better, thank you."

Amber turned on the light and began to show him some of the things she had found while he had slept. A kid's fishing pole, a pair of wooden snowshoes, canoe paddles, a batteryless flashlight, Jeanette's old sleeping bag from when she was a child—when she was fourteen, the expensive hatchet that Richard thought had been lost while he was gone from his family, a rose-colored water bottle, old and worn fishing lures that must have been, thought Richard, from his own childhood and apparently carried about as he had moved from place to place. She had also discovered several torn, yellowed maps of the Boundary Waters Wilderness, marked with red dots and squiggly notes showing where the best fishing had been found.

"Can I have this stuff. It looks old, mostly, but I can fix everything like new."

"Sure, kid. These things belong to my family, so they are yours too." Richard and Amber were both surprised by what he had said. Maybe, felt Richard, he should not get too attached to the child. He tried to backtrack, "I mean, this is just old stuff anyway. I'm sure my children won't miss it any."

They spent the rest of the evening looking over the maps of the Boundary Waters, as Richard told stories of past excursions with his children canoeing into the wilderness up by Ely. Soon it was Amber's turn to fall asleep. Richard carried her upstairs to her bedroom and tucked her into her adopted sleeping bag.

"Sure, kid," whispered Richard.

CHAPTER 17

The soft murmur of voices, coming from downstairs in his kitchen, woke Richard. His muscles were more sore from yesterday's hike to the duck lake than if he had run miles. First he slowly moved his legs, to keep from cramping, then he stretched their muscles and those in his back. The older he got, the easier it became to acquire injuries for no apparent reason.

He could hear Amber talking to another, older, female voice. There were also deeper and darker Neanderthal-like utterances interspersed with the feminine conversation. Elsie had arrived as promised, early, and apparently with a male companion. Richard was compelled to leave his bed and greet his sunrise visitors. He put on his clothes from yesterday and climbed down his stairs.

"Elsie. You brought Thomas with you!?" said Richard.

"Eurr-ahh," said Big Thomas Thorson. "Her old truck, shifter problems."

"I had Thomas drive me over. He has grocery shopping and bills to do in Bemidji, so he can pick me up at the end of the day, unless you could drive me back to the farm later this evening."

"I can do that," said Richard as he watched Thorson push five of Richard's Amber-fried eggs, a Richard-hunted venison sausage, and two heavily buttered slices of Richard's breadmaker toast into his mouth, and wash it down with a mug of Richard's tea. The Irishman Thorson soaked up huge quantities of food, usually other people's, wherever he went.

"Ahh-err...right," said Thorson as he misted the air with tea and sprinkled with bread crumbs the pictures that Richard had taken at Rice Pond. Thorson continued to mist and sprinkle as he sifted through the photos, until he came to the tire tracks. "Uhh-err... pipe—for concrete—for conduit. Wires."

"The star-shaped cutouts are from pipe?" asked Richard. "Like at a construction site?"

"Yem. The pipe here must have been set facing up in the concrete, and then someone drove over its end, which would be just clearing the concrete. Result: star cuts on the tires," explained Thomas in a tone that suggested that every guy should know that. Then the big man rose, bade everyone farewell, and let himself out, trailing bread crumbs as he exited Richard's house.

Amber prepared another breakfast for herself, Richard, Elsie, and Elsie's four girls, as Richard explained the photos and the details of the case to Elsie. After wolfing down the morning's fare, Elsie's youngsters decided to explore outside, just like Amber had sought revelation the prior evening. Richard and Elsie talked about the sad discovery of Lennie Frontera in the cold waters of Rice Pond, and of the myriad developments that had unwound themselves since then.

"I spent a night camping alone at North Twin Lake, and then went running on the forest road the next morning. Near the end of the run I began to tire, so in order to rest and catch my breath I walked down to Rice Pond. That is where I found the girl."

"When you found her, could you tell if she had been assaulted?" asked Elsie.

"She had bruises on her neck, and scratches and cuts on one of her hands where she would have held on tightly to a rose. I found the flower in the water. A yellow rose."

"She must have been very determined, knowing that she would probably not live through the night," said Elsie.

"The girl, Miss Frontera, was wearing a pretty, blue gingham dress, a fact which has stuck in my mind for some unknown reason. She was pretty herself, with long beautiful black hair."

"Yes, she was," agreed Elsie, holding the photo of the Native girl resting on the clover of the trail into Rice Pond.

"She wore a delicate chain with a very old and worn cross. The cross was caught between two of her teeth, wedged in tight like a dead soldier's dog tag."

"What an awful waste," said Elsie softly, her voice a preternatural combination of sorrow and rage. A rouge of blood rose to the surface of Elsie's skin, up her neck and to her face, a red tide of anger which mimicked what Richard had heard in Elsie's voice from the previous night.

"I don't see why her attacker would do such a cruel thing," said Richard.

"It's the girl," said Elsie. "I believe that with the cuts from the rose and the cross bitten between her teeth, she is trying to tell the living something about her death."

Richard continued to tell his story to Elsie, about his giant black attacker: "Damn Jesus, Damn Jesus to hell," and the smelt-scaled fillet knife that Blister had dropped at the vehicle park above North Twin Lake.

And how Foster noticed the missing grapple hook, which led to Foster finding Chad Rochambeau's ID bracelet. Chad had been on Forest Road 2213, per his cow-licked white jeep, the day after Lenora's body had been carried from the frigid waters of Rice Pond. This led to learning that Chad and Lenora were lovers—had been, and also, conversely, that Chad and Blister had been enemies—still were.

There was the "lost" DNA evidence that should have identified Lennie's third attacker. The meaning of the lost evidence meant that someone in the sheriff's office or the district attorney's office wanted to protect at least one of Lenora's rapists. Since a Beltrami County protector of sex offenders must surely exist, then that person is how the black hulk knew where Richard's camp was located.

Antonio de Medici had found Euglena's hidden apartment turned prison, and helped to liberate its small captives: black Sassy and white Amber.

"Our Amber," said Elsie, glancing toward the little girl doing the morning dishes.

"Correct," agreed Richard.

"And later this afternoon we will ride over to the national forest and talk to another girl, the one that was attacked while jogging on the Paul Bunyan Trail near the state park," said Elsie.

Amber dropped the thick glass plate she was drying. It clattered off the sink and onto the floor, somehow not breaking. Amber looked like she might cry.

Richard took Amber by the hand and led her to a chair at the table. "You can tell us, Amber. What is it about the trail that frightens you?" Instinctively, Richard placed his hand on top of Amber's head, as he had with Lenora Frontera after he had laid her lifeless body on the grass of the old logging trail, as he had with his daughter Jeanette the day he recovered her from the predators' night.

Amber looked up with her dark green eyes and placed her trust with Richard, "Sir, two times Eugene took me to a shack, I think near that trail. A filthy place which they made me try to clean. It belonged to his partner, Odis Blister. Odis would brag that he lived on a trail that was used by girls for walking and jogging, and that he would stalk them from above. I heard him say that it was the Paul Bunyan Trail."

"Do you know how to get to the shack?"

"Not really. My wrists were taped to my ankles, like you found me in the closet, and I was thrown in the back of a cargo van, so I couldn't see much. I remember a driveway in big trees. There was a boulder at the entrance of the drive. I noticed it because it was pink granite with a large white band of quartz bisecting its center. An inclusion."

"I know what an inclusion is, my geologist girl. Well, now you are safe with us. You have friends."

Having spoken her fears, Amber seemed released from those fears. At least, that is how she seemed. She went outside to watch Elsie's girls play in the yard, as Richard and Elsie continued to discuss the events surrounding the case. Soon Amber led the four smaller girls to the front yard where a pile of clean straw was heaped, the remnants of last fall's archery target. The five girls were trying to dig a burrow into the main mass of the straw.

"My youngest there is Chloe." Elsie pointed to a tiny girl with short, white-blonde hair pulled to each side of her head and rubber-banded into floppy brushes. She was following a somewhat larger girl with sandy blonde hair. "The girl that Chloe is shadowing is her shipmate and protector, Rebecca. We call her Reb, as in Johnny Reb. Seems Reb's spirit is always in rebellion, hence her nickname."

Reb also had ponytails at the sides of her head, but unlike her little sister's, hers were long and braided.

"My two oldest are Catherine and Christine." Elsie pointed to a pair of slightly taller girls, one with bright, sunflower-yellow hair, and the other with darker, butternut-hued hair. "They are fifteen months apart, but because they are about the same size and both have yellow-blonde hair and look so much alike, they are often mistaken for twins. God knows they seem stuck to each other like twins." Catherine and Christine were about six inches taller than Rebecca, but just as slight of build and as graceful as the Reb.

When it came time for lunch, Elsie took a portion of what she had brought and carried it outside to a picnic table in back of the house. For a poor bachelor like Richard, Elsie's dinner was a veritable feast. She had made Spanish tacos from her own farm-raised beef. She must have heard Richard talk about how much he liked Mexican food. Richard wished that he could have a farm like Elsie's, or better yet, that he could have someone like Elsie. When everyone was filled, they carried the leftovers to Richard's fridge, and then were ready to drive to Teddy Zemm's home.

Elsie's four shades of blond girls rode on the rear bench seat of Richard's truck; Amber wanted the passenger window in front, the better to enjoy her newfound freedom. That left Elsie sitting next to Richard, which she seemed content with. Elsie placed her arm around him as they drove, her fine red hair brushing his face as she talked over the sound of the truck engine and the shush of air rushing past Amber's open window. Richard could not tell if Elsie's arm was in any way affectionate, or just an aid in conversation. Either way, he did not mind.

If Richard was to take Elsie and her flock back to Clearwater County tonight he would need more gas for the Chevy, so he stopped at Cindy Heath's store for a fill up. Miss Heath was in. She walked around the side of the truck as Richard was self-servicing his vehicle.

"Richard, I haven't heard from you for a bit. Anything new?"

Richard brought her up to date, ending with his plans to talk to Samantha's friend, Sally. Cindy wanted to go along. She still wanted to be a part of the solution, she said, for Lennie's sake. Cindy ran into the store, where Richard could see her say something to her boss and something else to her co-worker behind the cash register, and then she came out and yelled over to Richard that she would follow him in her own car.

Richard paid for the gas and for some chocolate—Heath bars, for himself and the girls, then found the manager he had talked to before, "Bob—Mr. Put-N-Go," and asked one other question of him, "What was Miss Frontera wearing the night she went missing from the store?"

Luckily, Bob's memory was much better than his crude efforts at covering his bald spot. "A heavy brown dress. Very long. I remember because it dragged on the floor and I asked her if that was practical for working in a convenience store, but she seemed to get around well enough."

"Thanks, that's all I wanted to know," said Richard as he veritably skipped back to his truck.

He could have driven directly from Tenstrike into the national forest and then south to Twin Lake and Teddy's home, but instead he took a circular route: first south on a crumbling section of the old Highway 71, toward tiny Pool Lake, then east past Turtle River Lake and Turtle River—where Richard knew an eagle had his or her aerie, and finally back north to Twin Lake and the Zemm home on Forest Road 2213. Final destination about a mile from Rice Pond.

By way of justifying his circular route, Richard explained that he wanted to try to get a picture of the eagle, which was partially true, but mainly he wanted some time to think about the blue gingham dress that Lennie had managed to get into prior to her death.

Toward the end of this broken section of old Highway 71, near Pool Lake, Amber yelled, "There! Over there! The inclusion." Her thin arm poked between the heads of Elsie and Richard, as Amber pointed to a large boulder next to a poorly maintained driveway.

It took a moment for Richard's mind to process what Amber meant by "inclusion," but his foot was already on the brake and he was turning into the driveway in question. One old man, a tough farm girl, and five children. And don't forget Cindy Heath—she had turned in after them. Not much of an army if the rapists were home.

A badly neglected shack, its one door slightly ajar, seemed to be deserted. Elsie stayed in the truck with the children, as Richard and Cindy checked the place. Richard took pictures of the outside of the shack, then crept inside, where he took a few more pictures.

The vile air in the shack stank of old urine and fear-induced sweat. A half-used roll of duct tape sat perched on the edge of a table left dirtied with moldy food. Tiny fish scales spotted the surface of a badly stained sink. A scarred football helmet hung on a peg set directly over a space heater, as if to dry the helmet of its perverted owner's sweat. The peg was driven into a heavy post at the back of the room.

Set against the front of the post was a vinyl chair with crooked metal legs; the chair faced the open door from across the space of the single room. Therefore, the chair was in front of the post, with the space heater and the peg with helmet on the side of the post. A folded cloth of blue cotton weave made an impromptu seat cushion for the chair. The cloth was the only color in the entire room.

"Let's go, Cindy, let's get out of here. We should never have stopped." Richard pushed Cindy, nearly frozen in place in disgust and shock, out of the filth of the shack.

Once outside in the light, Cindy finally spoke, "The shack is rape personified. I am so sorry."

"You are right." Richard figured she meant to say she was sad for her friend, but her sentiment came out sounding confusing. The filth of the cabin must have shaken her to her core.

CHAPTER 18

Amber looked back at the shack as Richard drove slowly, hearse-like, down the driveway, past the boulder with its quartz inclusion, and away. Richard thought that Amber's eyes held more sadness than fear. That would be good, or at least better. Fear could keep one from healing.

Elsie placed her hand on Richard's shoulder and pressed down hard, as if she needed to keep him from flying out of the truck. "It was rough in there, wasn't it."

"Yes. Cindy froze in place. I'm worried about her, Elsie. Have a talk with her when we get to Teddy's. Maybe you could..."

"I'll calm her," finished Elsie.

When the procession arrived at Teddy and Clara Zemm's home, Richard called the BCA office in Bemidji and left a message for Agent Kieran about the location of Blister's cabin. Then he made calls to his sons—Joshua and Foster, and to his friends—Chad Rochambeau and Tony, informing them of the discovery of the shack. He liked to keep his helpers informed, though in the case of Chad it was more in the line of letting an old friend know that something was being done to revenge his love's death.

With the news of finding the shack, Teddy Zemm lost his bad

temper and wanted to drive over and burn the place down. Clara held her husband's big hands until he was calm, or at least less agitated. Amber stuck to Richard's side until Samantha and Sally managed to pry her loose and drag her to their archery range to show her how to shoot Samantha's recurve bow. At first, Amber appeared awkward shooting the bow, but her arrows did find the target, if not the center of the bull's-eye. Soon she became smoother and more focused with her handling of the weapon. As pink-fletched silver arrows flew to their marks, things gradually returned to normal.

Joshua drove over with his dog, Barker, who promptly had a fit of barking at Richard's expense, as was usual. When things had become quiet again, Richard drove to the BCA office in Bemidji to drop off the probable cow-licked shirt that Richard had collected from Chad Rochambeau's jeep. Josh rode along with him, leaving Barker to play with the kids.

Michael Kieran was still out. Richard left the slimy shirt with Agent Jeff Haltman, Michael's BCA helper. Agent Haltman assured Richard that this evidence would not go the way of the DNA samples.

On the return trip Joshua reviewed the case to make sure that he was up-to-date with all the facts. "First, let's list all the people in the case. Lenora—murdered. Cindy—Lenora's friend and past teammate. Chad—Lenora's lover. Odis Blister—first suspect. Eugene Euglena—second suspect. Unknown protected rapist—third suspect. Unknown rapist protector—cop or DA. Any more?"

"Sassy, Amber, and Sally," said Richard.

~

An hour later and back at the Zemm's, Richard found Elsie, and together they found Sally and took her outside where they could talk in privacy. Elsie asked most of the questions about the attack, while Richard tried to be as inconspicuous as possible. Sally was more open than Richard had expected as she directed her answers back to Elsie.

"I was running on the trail north of the park," began Sally. "The blacktop turns to gravel just past the north side of the park, then after a mile or so the gravel becomes sandier and it gets harder to run on. I had already run several miles, so I turned around."

"Shortly after, on my return run, as I was passing through a dark section where the trees come close to the trail, I was struck down from behind. It was like I was crushed into the gravel. The attacker, a large black man, was wearing a football helmet which partially shaded his face, but I think I would recognize him if I saw him again." Sally had become restless and seemed anxious the more she talked of her ordeal.

"Do you want to sit down, Honey?" asked Elsie.

"No, I'm all right. I've covered… I started...so I need to finish."

"Then continue, Honey," said Elsie.

"I called Mr. Bede because I knew that his daughter had once been attacked. He defended her. I just wanted someone on my side, that's all. Someone to hear me."

"Of course," said Elsie as she touched Sally's thin arm.

"The man tore at my shorts. He tore them off me. My running shorts were actually ripped when I tried to put them on afterwards. Anyway, the wind had been knocked out of me and I was having a hard time getting my breath back and he was so heavy on my chest. I was a virgin and he raped me there on the trail and it hurt like hell. The gravel tore at my back and my rear, but I was just trying to breathe again. It went on and on forever."

A tear fell from each of Sally's eyes.

"He finished and got up," said Sally. "I thought he was done. But he dragged me off the trail and into the woods. He had tape there, where he tied my hands together behind my back, and he taped one of my feet to a small tree… a sapling. He wanted to tape my other foot, but there was nothing close that he could use, so he got angry and slapped me and called me a bitch. Then he slapped me some more. His slaps made my head dizzy. I was afraid that if I passed out that I would die. He might get madder and kill me." Sally took a deep breath and slowly blew the air from her lungs, loud like a kid might blow out her birthday candles.

"I guess I was lucky because he started to rape me again. My hands were caught under the small of my back and he was so heavy, he was trying to put all of his weight on me. My back muscles started to cramp real bad and I thought that my hands would break as he rocked on me."

Two other lonely tears fell from the eyes of the dark-haired girl. "I'm sorry...that night, once back home, I prayed to God that some day I would get a chance to kill that bastard. I believe that God hates rapists."

Elsie agreed.

Sally continued. "He crushed my breasts in his hands. They were bruised for weeks. He pushed my head sideways into the ground. Then he finished again. He got up and kicked me in my side, once, then again, then a barrage of kicks. He called me a bitch over and over, sounding like one of those rappers on the radio. I could tell he was a racist 'cause he kept calling me a white bitch." Sally stopped talking, leaned over, cleared her throat, and spit a blood-tinted pink liquid from her mouth. In the stress of reliving her ordeal, the girl must have bitten her tongue or the inside of her cheek.

She straightened her back and for the first time looked directly into Richard's eyes.

"As I was passing out from his kicks, I could hear people bicycling on the trail. It sounded like a family. When I woke again, it was dark and he was gone. I knew that the bicycles had scared him away from the trail, because I was still alive. I tried to move, but I couldn't. I laid there for what seemed like forever, trying to move. My hands were still taped together behind my back and my foot was still attached to the sapling. I scrunched over to the sapling and turned in to it so I could cut the tape off my wrists. I used a sharp piece of gravel. It took forever. When my hands were free I pulled my head to my ankle and bit the tape away with my teeth."

Sally pushed her dark hair back from her forehead with both her hands, took a deep breath, closed and opened her wet eyes for several moments—like slow eye blinks, then continued. "It was black dark out, but I felt around on the ground and found my clothes. My shoes were still on my feet. I put my shirt back on, but I had to hold my shorts on as best as I could because they were ripped open. I walked out of the woods and onto the trail. I was going to walk home, but then I started to run. I felt like the darkness was hiding me, which was good. I still like darkness even now. How does that song go? 'Hello darkness, my old friend.' Anyway, my arms hurt too much to hold my shorts to my waist, so I wrapped the torn cloth around my waist and tied a knot to hold them up, and ran like that, half-naked. It hurt to run, but not really much more than it did to walk, and somehow I felt better when I ran, like it gave me some kind of power. I made it all the way back to my home, running."

"Where you told your mom, and then the hospital thing and the cops," said Elsie.

"Yes. A bad aftermath: with the police. But I'm glad that I told."

Richard had been made invisible during all but the end of the girl's story. Now, he put his hand on the top of Sally's head and told her that he would help if he could. His promise.

Elsie gave Sally a hug and said, "Don't worry, you are not alone. You have friends."

As Sally turned to leave, she could sense that Richard had something else that he wanted. "What is it?" she asked, as she took his arm in her small hand.

"Sally, you said that you were struck from behind. Is that exactly how it seemed to you? From behind?"

Sally thought for a moment, and then said, "I was struck from above, like a rabbit might be struck by a hawk."

"Like a baby fawn might be ambushed by a mountain lion," added Elsie.

CHAPTER 19

Sally's dismal story had been exhausting to Richard and had left Elsie both pensive and angered. She wanted to retreat to the relative calm of Richard's home.

"Look at Sally with the other girls; she appears to be so happy and secure," said Elsie. "She must be very resilient."

Richard knew from his experience with Jeanette that a girl or woman might look normal on the outside, she might not even act the way that others expect a rape victim should act, but deep inside she is suffering a storm of fears and emotions. Poor handling by the cops or the so-called sexual assault advocates, or even indifference from teachers or from friends, could do irreparable damage to her psyche.

"Flowers will grow back in a field after it has been burned, but don't believe that there are no ashes underneath," said Richard. "With God's help and friends, she will be all right," he added.

Richard made his rounds prior to departure. There were plans made with Joshua and Foster to call them later. Teddy Zemm said good-bye and offered his help again. Clara gave Richard two Mason jars of rhubarb preserves: the really sour kind that Richard loved so dearly. Samantha and Sally had drafted Cindy Heath into their games, which Cindy was evidently enjoying very much. Cindy said that the girls wanted her to stay for a while longer, and anyway Clara Zemm had decided that she should make supper for her trio of guests: Cindy, Samantha, and Sally.

Amber rounded up Elsie's four little charges and got them into Richard's truck and sat in back with them to help keep them still. As young children are wont to do, they had gotten worked up by their trip to the national forest lands and the newness of Richard's friends.

Though with the passenger window clear of Amber's presence, Elsie again sat in the center, next to Richard, and again placed her arm around him, this time closing her eyes and resting her head on his shoulder. Even the thick skull of Richard could tell that this meant something more than mere friendship. He was as ecstatic as he was surprised. He kissed the top of Elsie's head, breathing deeply the sweet feminine fragrance of her red hair. It had been a long time.

Then he remembered that he had an impressionable audience on the back bench. He looked in his rearview mirror; Elsie's girls were busy watching every new thing fly by their windows, but Amber was smiling back at him. Richard readjusted the mirror to the road just passed, shaking Amber's mischievous image from its reflection if not from his consciousness.

There was company waiting for them at his place. Sitting on the porch was Tony and two unfamiliar faces: a matching set of young Native girls, except that one had cropped hair like a 1920s flapper, while the other's flowed nearly to her waist. Tony gave Richard a hug, then Elsie one too as he was being introduced, and then shook the hands of all of Elsie's towheads, who said "hi" shyly and ran off.

Amber said hello, but not much more. Perhaps Tony reminded her too suddenly of her recent past in the closet.

Tony knew how to break the ice. "My little sister, the girl with the party dress, she asked about you when she found out I was driving up to visit you and Richard."

"Tell her that I'm much better," said Amber. "And I still hope to be able to go to the museum with her some day."

"I'll give you our number before I leave. You can give her a call sometime after you get better settled here."

Amber agreed to that plan, then went to watch Elsie's girls when Richard asked her. Though Amber had been through a lot, Richard figured she could use a respite from the troubles of adults.

"I have captured more fugitives from Euglena," said Tony as he gestured with his hands, as in a magic act, toward the pair of Native girls. "I went back to Eugene's place and found them there, having been recently delivered by a gang member from Cass Lake. He said the girls were lost runaways from a reservation on a big northern lake. I asked around and was told to bring them up to Bemidji."

"Did you take them from the gang guy?" asked Elsie.

"Negative, I paid for them, Cash-On-Delivery, so to speak. Four hundred dollars apiece, which I think was the final payment, or was another payment; I couldn't really tell and didn't want to ask. But it will be no financial loss to my own personal expenses because I'll get reimbursed from a group of Native elders that live somewhere up north here."

The two Native girls, silent and static so far, took notice of Tony's reference to the tribal elders and became more than mildly agitated.

"The girls are worried about the opinions and reactions of the elders," said Tony.

"Did you stop by to visit, then?" asked Richard.

"I would love to stay here for a while, but I can't. I have to get back to the Cities pronto, before my parole officer can discover that I am missing. The only reason I am here is to drop off my runaway charges. One of the tribe's men will pick them up in a bit; I presume that he is a Native guy, but I'm not really sure. Name of 'Thorson.' Scandinavian? First name 'Thomas,' I believe."

Elsie laughed. Richard explained about Thomas Thorson. The girls on the porch became even more alarmed as Richard painted a verbal picture of Thomas. At the conclusion of Richard's soliloquy, Tony wished his Native girls good luck with Thorson and got into his car.

Before Tony left, he had one more item of interest, "I saw Chad Rochambeau in town today—in your town. Very early this morning. I recognized him from his picture on the web site of the Minnesota Bureau of Prisons. But I didn't recognize the girl that was with him."

"Was the girl very tall and athletic looking?" asked Richard.

"That's her," replied Tony, who then proceeded to drive away through the minefield of tire-cut ruts and frost-heaved holes that was Richard's path to his house.

Elsie ushered the pair of lost waifs into the kitchen and fed them something from what she had brought from her farm. They were truly ravenous with hunger.

Thomas Thorson arrived just in time to help them finish their meal. He said nothing to the girls he was to collect, but to Elsie and Richard he said, with half-cut deviled eggs stuffed chipmunklike into his cheeks, "There are two new construction sites in Bemidji—one by Highways 2 and 71—nothing there; the other is north a bit on 71 by the chain saw place. Going to be a flower shop. That place has freshly poured concrete with heavy conduit placed in it. That is where the star cutouts came from."

Richard thanked him for the information, then before Thomas could do any more damage to Elsie's larder, he shepherded Thomas outside to his vehicle and bade him farewell. The two Native girls rose as if from their last supper, followed with bowed heads, and silently got into Thomas' truck. As the truck pulled away, the pair of girls turned in unison and looked out the rear window and sadly waved good-bye to Richard, Elsie, and Elsie's children, as if they were family that would never be seen again. Thomas had yet to say anything to them.

Elsie put out a second supper and called Amber and her own blond children into the house. Once again Richard was delighted with Elsie's cooking. I should find a good cook like Elsie, thought Richard. "But I'd have to run twice as many miles," he said, out loud by mistake. He could see from of the corner of his eye that Elsie was looking down and smiling—not at the funny arrangement of her potato salad, he figured.

When the meal was completed, Elsie washed dishes as Richard read one of Jeanette's childhood picture books to the children. Elsie joined Richard in a short while and listened to the butterfly-festooned story that Richard was reading. When the story was finished, Elsie's foursome ran outside to play in the yard again.

Elsie talked of the forestry work that should be starting again soon, and she talked of her struggles with her new life at her grand-parents' overcrowded farmhouse. Richard was good at listening. The newly freed Amber was upstairs trying on some of the clothes that Elsie had brought her. There seemed to be a lot, and Amber would come down often and model another ensemble. At one point Elsie said to Amber something relating to taking her new old clothes to

Richard's truck in preparation for him driving them back to the farm in Clearwater County.

"You don't want to stay with a boring old guy like me," added Richard.

Amber did not take the news very well. "I am not leaving! Not, not, not!" She ran up to "her" bedroom and slammed the door hard enough that Richard was worried about hinges. Amber's breaking of the sound barrier caused Elsie to jump a bit in her seat.

After a reasonable span of time had elapsed, Richard followed Amber upstairs and went to Amber's door. He could hear her crying. He did not enter, but instead came back down to where Elsie was still sitting. "I didn't think that she should stay with an ex-con like me. How would that work?"

"But she sure doesn't want to leave," said Elsie.

"Maybe not, but she needs a mother and a family."

"I'll stay. My grandfather can watch over my few cattle, and my grandmother already takes care of the chickens. All I will miss over there is my tractor."

"Are you sure?"

"Believe me, getting out of my grandparents tiny house will be like a vacation."

Richard went back to Amber's closed door and spoke through it, hoping he would be heard over her sobbing. Evidently, the prospect of leaving her new home with its new bedroom of her own was causing her more grief than when she had been beaten by her captors.

He told Amber that Elsie was staying the night and so therefore she, Amber, would also have to stay. "Elsie says that she needs a rest from her cramped place, anyway."

A cessation of sobbing was the only reply. Richard again went back downstairs to Elsie.

Presently, Amber came down, red-eyed, a new outfit to model, and a hug and a kiss for Elsie.

"Thank you, Elsie," said Amber. "I'm sure you will like it here."

Amber was already digging in her heels for a more permanent solution than a solitary night.

Elsie was more noncommittal. "We'll see," she said.

Everyone was satisfied.

As evening wore on to the twilight of early night, it came time for Amber and the other children to go to bed and get some sorely needed sleep. Richard found some blankets and several old and now zipperless sleeping bags for Elsie's girls. Elsie made them a slumber area in one of the bedrooms, tucked them in as they fell directly to sleep—exhausted as they were from a full day of play and new places, then rejoined Richard in the kitchen where he had settled himself, knees drawn up, on the northern end of his favorite couch. Elsie was happy to commandeer the southern end.

"I started on this case with Foster and Joshua," said Richard, "and then I turned to Agent Michael Kieran, then Cindy Heath—Lenora Frontera's girlfriend and workmate. Sprinkle in phone conversations with my daughter Jeanette, and the assistance of Antonio de Medici."

"A lot of good people," said Elsie.

"And now I have evolved to you."

"If you have evolved to me, are you now a better species than you were before?" asked Elsie.

"Yes. I believe so."

"That's good."

"It seems the case is slowly yet inexorably being unraveled," said Richard. "This ordeal should soon resolve itself and leave me in peace."

"Your friend Tony...he seems a bit strange, but in a good way. Wouldn't you agree?"

"Absolutely. He knows people and about things, and can find out about stuff that one would think near impossible to discover, and he does so with a speed and accuracy that is astounding. I don't even ask him anymore how he does it, but I think that his multitude of family and friends is his strongest investigative asset."

"Do you think the police will find Euglena and Blister before they do any more damage?" asked Elsie.

"I hope so. But don't forget the third rapist, the one that got a gift of ruined DNA evidence."

"And the giver of ruined DNA evidence is also the fink that told your attacker where you could be found," said Elsie.

"Somehow this case leads to our veiled suspect," asserted Richard. At that, he reviewed the clues again, for Elsie's enlightenment, as well as for his own mind to process and reexamine. "Miss Frontera must have been abducted from her store and taken to Rice Pond. She was raped on the way or somewhere by the pond, and then she was killed. Before she died, she somehow changed from a long brown dress into a blue gingham dress. She crushed a yellow rose into the palm of her hand, and bit her crucifix into her teeth."

"Maybe she did," theorized Elsie. "Maybe she bit down on the cross so her attackers could not take it."

"That seems Draconian," said Richard. "But maybe so. From the very beginning, Miss Frontera has unraveled the plans of this gang of rapists. Their attack did not go exactly as they had expected. Chad Rochambeau's ID bracelet was lost at the pond, where Blister failed to retrieve it. Blister and his gang also failed to cover their star-cut tire tracks, which have, via Thomas Thorson, led to the construction site of the new flower shop. Blister lost his fishy fillet knife and he failed to finish off his previous victim: Sally."

"Odis Blister is messing up," stated Elsie.

"Correct. But so is Euglena. Tony de Medici is siphoning off his new recruits—the young girls that had been intended for his pimp show."

"Which in turn allowed Amber to show us where Odis Blister's trailside cabin was located," said Elsie.

"If the police can't catch these creeps now, then they are totally worthless," added Richard.

"Richard, I am bothered by your barber from prison, this Chad Rochambeau. How is he connected? Why is he on the forest road by Rice Pond the day after his girl was killed? Why is he up here now, apparently with Cindy Heath—who didn't even mention to you that she had been with Chad earlier today? Also, isn't it odd that Chad had a conflict in prison with both Euglena and Blister? Did those rapists attack Lenora as a form of revenge?"

"Chad Rochambeau is, indeed, a wild card. We need to talk to him again, but not just yet; I don't want Cindy to learn that we know that her and her wished-for boyfriend are under suspicion."

"Sally said that she was attacked from above," observed Elsie. "Your attacker from North Twin Lake and Rice Pond is falling from trees again, like he did at Point Park in Duluth. Odis Blister."

"Right. I should drive over to the forest tomorrow and check out Rice Pond. Maybe there will be some indication of how and where Lenora was attacked."

"And the section of trail where Sally was assaulted," added Elsie.

Having exhausted the possibilities of the connections relating to Miss Frontera's death, their conversation drifted off to other, more benign subjects. Elsie talked about her old farm and her newer, more constricted place at her grandparents' home. She talked about her four young girls: Chloe, Reb, Catherine, and Christine, and how much she loved them, but what a challenge it was to raise them, even with the help of grandparents.

"I should bring my tractor over here if I'm going to spend much time at your home." Perhaps Amber's will to form a new family was already having an effect on Elsie.

"You won't plow up my field of wildflowers, will you, Elsie?" asked Richard, not sure if he should be concerned or not.

"Of course not. But a veggie garden would be nice." Elsie went on to describe how she would set out the garden and all the different kinds of vegetables she would grow.

Richard quietly listened, watching Elsie's dark red hair as it swung across her pretty face. He wondered what her age was—twenty-five, or thirty-five—it was impossible to tell. She had given birth to four children, so she couldn't be too young, figured Richard. She was just so nice to look at.

Elsie may have read his mind. She scooted over to Richard and sat beside him, the both of them fitted into the depths of the end of the old couch. She kissed Richard as she let her hair caress and tickle his face. Her hands were strong but not at all callused as one might expect from farm work and chain saws. Her body was both firm and soft. Richard loved her perfect femininity.

Elsie rose from the couch, took Richard's hand, and led him to his bedroom and his bed, where she laid him down and undressed him. The last item of clothing to be removed from his person was a pair of dark blue silk boxers with red Valentine hearts and silver Cupid's arrows. Richard's long standing in total bachelorhood had lulled him into thinking that he could dress however he wanted, whenever he wanted. Elsie tried to stifle her laugh, but failed with a smile.

"I'm sorry," she giggled, as she removed his boxers.

"I'll have you know they are very comfortable and very cool," he defended, while failing to keep from laughing himself.

"Yeah, real cool," said Elsie, as she placed her hand over her mouth to keep her mirth from waking the household, and fell into Richard's bed and onto Richard. They kissed each other, trying to be serious.

At length, she pushed away from Richard, got back up, and stood next to Richard's bed, where she took off her own jeans and blouse, and everything else, and let her clothes fall from her body. There was scant illumination except from the moonlight which washed in from the single window, but Richard could see Elsie well enough. She slipped in next to him again and held him and kissed him. Time passed. There was no hurry.

After she had delivered a multitude of kisses to Richard, Elsie lay on top of him, pressed her small firm breasts onto his chest, and let her legs fall to either side of his form, and there, with her beautiful soft red hair swaying across his face, its fragrance enfolding his being, she made love to him. Richard loved her for it.

Richard loved her.

CHAPTER 20

The moment Thor had gotten that first call from his sister, he knew that he could not wait for the second as she had asked, but had instead hastily put together his own plans to reunite himself with his lost sibling—the last of his family. As soon as he hung up the phone he began to organize for his trip. It was too late to leave this evening, but an early departure tomorrow would be just as well.

Thor had saved a small amount of money during the three weeks of Amber's disappearance. He had mowed the lawn of the old hippie guy down the road from his place. Old hippie had paid him in eggs and quarters, a dozen of each, which was really good. Thor had also mowed the grass of Lady Nelson. Her lawn was too long, as usual, and she only had a dull push mower, the manual kind that spun from the energy of its wheels whenever little boys managed to push it fast enough. Thor would get a running start with the mower and crash it into the next patch of grass, like a halfback crashing into the other team's defensive line, making four or five yards each effort. Not much, but enough to earn first downs and win the game. The game in this instance being three more dollars.

Now Thor checked his money and got his clothes ready. A warm jacket would be smart. It was nice yesterday, but spring mornings and evenings could be cold. He wished his tennis shoes were newer, but beggars couldn't be choosers.

The kitchen didn't have much food. The hot lunch that his school provided was often the only real food that Thor and Amber could get in a day. They would pack in as much as they could, and other kids would usually offer stuff that they didn't want. They were proof that a child could grow on just one meal a day.

But today Thor had hoped for more. A small box of raisins, some Cheerios, and four slices of bread if counting heels. Thor always liked the heels. He made two rich sandwiches with the bread and sorghum, and placed the sticky creations into a sandwich bag, then put all the provisions into a larger paper bag.

A small plastic juice bottle was already sitting in his bedroom. Thor had tied a length of baler twine around its neck, so the bottle could be fastened to his belt. He filled it with water from the kitchen tap. He crept out to his stepfather's truck and found the Minnesota road map that he knew was there, then retreated to his bedroom to figure his route.

His dead father had left him a small jackknife and a compass, the bubble kind that hunters pinned onto the front of their jackets. He pinned the compass onto his shirt, then put his jacket on over it. Thor did not want to be too conspicuous. He was set for the morning. Then he took all his clothes off and took a hot shower and put his clothes back on. He wanted to be clean and quiet the next morning. Then he went to bed, real early. Then he got up and walked down the road and across the field to the farmhouse of his closest friends. Closest to his own home, if also to his heart.

The farm house held three friends that were boys and two that were girlfriends, that is, girls that were friends, not girlfriends, though the girls might not have seen it that way. His friends were outside playing in their backyard. Thor told them of his plans.

"I'm heading up north to Canada tomorrow, to join the foreign legion. I'll lie about my age and get in and be a soldier," lied Thor. He was hoping that his story and its direction would throw off pursuers when and if his friends were coerced into divulging his secrets.

The boys were impressed. The girlfriends were not so happy. They cried awful and hugged their little boyfriend soon to be lost to the army, and generally carried on.

Thor was taken aback a bunch. "I can come visit when I get my leave," promised Thor.

The girls were a bit pacified.

Then one of the boys said that he had an uncle that went to war. "I don't think he ever came back, though," said the oldest boy.

None of the boys could remember the name of the war.

The girls resumed their hugs and crying and carrying on. Thor had been made a captive before his enlistment. He tried to break free, but it was no use. He had to talk to the boys that evening with his two female appendages attached to his torso. It was not as unpleasant to him as he acted.

When his friends' mom called them into their house for the night, the boys shook his hand, then pulled their sisters off Thor. The girls kissed him as they were being removed. One girl gave him a dollar and the other gave him the remainder of a bag of M&Ms.

Thor walked back across the now dark field, down the dusty road to his home, set his internal alarm to four in the morning, got a glass of water, and went to sleep.

The water-turned- pee woke him in the middle of the night. It was a quarter to four. Close enough. Thor quietly got out of bed, put on his tennis shoes and left by the back door. He walked around to the front, crossed his yard, and turned to look at his old home. He wished that he could say good-bye to his mother, but drugs had taken her soul years ago. The drug mother was a stranger.

One of Thor's schoolmates had told him that drugs had been invented by liberals back in the 1960s. Before then there were only regular mothers and fathers. Mostly. Thor bowed his head, as if in remembrance of his past good mother and better times.

"I hate the '60s," said Thor to the dust in the road, as fat tears fell like bombs, cratering holes into the dust.

The little boy straightened his back, turned, and took his first steps to freedom.

"I have a family," said a small voice in the dark.

More steps south down the road.

"I have a sister that is waiting for me."

Thor kept walking. It felt good to be moving. Somewhere up ahead was a new home. He hoped. He was excited to finally be on the way, and he was scared.

In less than two miles he came to a crossroad. Just a bit farther south would be a small town where he might be recognized. Thor turned west onto the new road and walked another quarter mile to where the road crossed over a railroad. There he slid and stumbled down a steep embankment to the rails and turned south again. It was still dark, but the railroad was not as hard to walk on as he imagined it would be.

Two more miles and the sun began to throw its muted light over the curvature of the earth. Small flocks of sandhill cranes flew from the nearby refuge to the farm fields to the west. Thor was impressed by their size and their songs as they flew low over his head.

When his father was alive, he used to take Thor to the refuge to watch the thousands of birds that lived there. Thor closed his eyes and remembered his dad's face. He was no longer scared.

Both of the sticky sandwiches and most of the Cheerios had been eaten already. Thor's breakfast. That left raisins, M&Ms, and seven whole dollars. And about 132 miles yet to walk.

Up ahead was a trestle that crossed over a small river. Thor had finished drinking most of his water when he had eaten his sorghum sandwiches, so he made his way to the river to replenish his supply, as well as to wash his sticky hands.

"I should have brought a bigger canteen," said Thor, as if his juice bottle was a canteen and he was a soldier on a forced march.

His shadow, which was long-shadowing him from the sun just breaking through the tree tops, must have been the other soldier.

"Watch out for the bullets," yelled Corporal, no, Sergeant Thor, as slate-grey juncos flew low overhead. The tiny birds zipped into nearby bushes.

"That was close."

The forced march continued to the south.

"The Confederacy will soon be under our guns, boys," said the boy. "Just another...let's see," said Sergeant Thor as he checked his map. "Just another 125 miles or so."

The Sergeant mixed the raisins with the M&Ms into a type of trail mix. Thor's army travelled on its stomach, and its stomach was fast consuming the remaining provisions. Even a Union army sergeant was smart enough to do the math.

"We need to scrounge the countryside for more grub, soldier."

"Yes, Sergeant," said the soldier shadow.

"Do you understand me?" barked the Sergeant.

"Yes, Sergeant!"

Thor kept his eyes open as he walked. Spring was fresh on the land, everything new light green, but not very nourishing. Fall was the time for berries. More miles went by. Thor's legs were strong up to mile six. After that things became ever more problematic. He stopped at a field to rest. A few soybeans were still sticking to their plants, lucky survivors from last autumn's harvest. During a hunting trip one year, in the early fall, his father had showed him how he could eat the still green soybeans. They tasted like roasted soybeans, remembered Thor, only not roasted.

"Let's try these," suggested Sergeant Thor.

The old beans did not taste like the soybeans that Thor had eaten on his dad's hunting trip. They tasted like BBs, only harder.

Thor took a short nap, then pushed on south, farther down the railroad. The track did not seem as smooth as when he had begun. Soon, up ahead, he spied a pile of yellow.

"Must be a stash of gunpowder," said Thor's imagination. But he knew it wasn't gunpowder, he admitted to himself. Even his strong imagination was getting tired.

The yellow was corn, apparently spilled from a railway car. Thor tried some. It was hard, but chewable. It was starchy, but edible.

"Manna from heaven," said Thor to his flagging troops.

His pockets and the paper bag full of corn, Thor resumed his hike.

"I pray that the Rebs are as tired as we are, or the battle will not be for us, I fear."

The railroad crossed a small blacktop road and many gravel paths to old farms. Since his first steps this morning, Thor had not seen a single person. Nobody. He felt all alone in the universe. Nothing but the wind, his shadow, and thousands of birds as they flew back and forth to the refuge. Now, up ahead, were some buildings. The first tiny village that he would have to pass through. A few houses, two bars, and a gas station with bait. At the gas station Thor bought another plastic bottle of juice and two big sticks of jerky. He would have a second canteen and some protein. Then he walked back to the tracks and sat at its right-of-way and had his feast. The salt on the jerky was great and the juice was sweet. Thor could not believe how hungry he had become during his long walk. He had covered one-tenth of the distance, eaten all of his food—the trail mix disappearing during the last two miles, and had spent one-third of his money. He had pockets of hard corn, memories of his father, and a desire to get to his sister.

The bank to the rails was steep here. Thor leaned back to rest his tired body. He needed a miracle or stronger legs. He decided to pray. He knew he was a Lutheran. His mother used to take him and his sister to church long ago, before she switched her faith to drugs, but Thor knew he was still a Lutheran. He had eaten enough hot dish to become a permanent member.

He couldn't remember any prayers, so he made one up.

"Dear God, please send me a horse. Soon. Amen and thank you."

His eyes closed and he napped again for a short while. When he awoke there was a train sitting in front of him. Not the horse that he had requested. Thor jumped to his feet. Big black cattle were being loaded into a box car toward the north end of the train. At the other end was the engine, pointing south.

"So much for prayers," said Thor to his soldier shadow, who was now standing at attention on the east side of Thor. "But with a bit of human ingenuity, we can make do."

It was a short train. An engine, a few cattle cars, some flatbed cars in the middle, and two empty freight cars with open sides.

"Which should we take, soldier?" asked Thor.

"Take one of the freight cars," answered the shadow.

Before Thor could question why shadow had answered him, the train jerked into motion, which in turn jerked Thor into motion. He grabbed his bag of corn and ran to the first freight car. It was moving very slowly, but with one hand busy with the bag of corn, Thor could not pull himself into the open door of the freight car. He held onto the edge of the opening, wondering if he should drop the corn. Just then a huge hand reached down and caught him by his wrist and pulled him through the air and into the freight car. The hand belonged to a large man with a white beard and long mustache.

Before Thor could cry, speak, or jump from the train, the man with the huge hands spoke.

"Howdy, pardner. My name's Earl." Earl walked back to his spot at the other side of the car, near to the other open door—the one facing the fields, and sat down.

"I like to watch things as they go by," said Earl.

"Me too...my name is Thor...I am going home."

"Where might that be?" asked the big man.

"Puposky, Minnesota." Thor remembered that Amber had first travelled to St. Paul, in the Twin Cities. "That is a suburb of St. Paul," added Thor.

"I know where Puposky is," said Earl. "Those suburbs are really getting far out in the country now."

"I suppose so," agreed Thor.

"By the way, I don't suppose you have some grub you can share?" asked Earl.

"Sure do. I have a whole bag of corn here."

Earl looked at the corn. "This is good stuff," said Earl. "See here, no blue stain or nothing. Nice and clean."

"I ate a bunch already," said Thor. "Go ahead and have what you want."

As Earl snacked on the corn, he took a chunk of cheese as big as a loaf of bread out of his own pack and broke off a pound or so for the boy.

"Swiss cheese from Monroe, Wisconsin. Best in the world it is. Baumgartners."

At first Thor believed that the old man had said "bum gardens," and almost laughed at the old guy, but then realized that Earl had said the name of some place. "Thank you," said Thor. He took a bite of the cheese. It was the best Swiss he had ever tasted.

The old man told stories of his travels around the country. Places he had seen and jobs he had worked at. Troubles he had gotten into and out of. Old girlfriends. Earl said he liked the country the best; he was getting too old and tired for the cities. They sat and ate their corn and cheese and watched the countryside go by as the steel of the train wheels clicked against the steel of the tracks.

At a pause in Earl's story, Thor told some about himself and his sister. He didn't get into too much detail, but who could Earl in his bum gardens tell anyway? The story about his sister leaving to find a new home, her long awaited call after more than three weeks, this journey to be reunited with his only surviving family member.

Earl got some dust in his eyes, which caused them to water.

"Your story brings back hard memories, son," said Earl.

Thor told about the memory of the face of his dead father. He told of his mother whose soul had died of drugs many years ago, the mother who was still up north a way.

"I wish that I could have said good-bye before she drifted away," said Thor.

Earl got some more dust in his eyes.

"I remember when drugs started," said Earl. "People argued that drugs were no worse than alcohol, as if more bad was no worse than some bad."

For an old man, Earl was pretty smart, thought Thor. The train wheels clicked on. Earl told more stories. The train slowed to go through a bigger town. The name of the town was marked on a sign set along the railroad.

"I wonder who would try to steal a river," joked Thor, "but at least the weight of the water must have made him fall."

Earl thought that was pretty good. The train wheels clicked on. After more miles of fields and woods and a few swamps, the train slowed again.

"Not to worry," said Earl. "The train is slowing to cross on over to the east track, which is good for you because that will put you a bit closer to your new home in Puposky."

Thor checked his map. Sure enough, a spur track went east of the main line.

"There are two more small towns up ahead, but you need to get off at the first one," said Earl.

"How come?"

"The train won't be going to the second town this early in the growing season. It will pick up more cattle, then turn around and go back."

The train wheels clicked on. Thor started to doze off. He could hear Earl tell him that he would wake him at the next stop. Then all there was left were the clicks of steel.

"Wake up, boy!" said Earl, not quite shouting, but louder than talking.

Thor jumped to his feet.

"The train has already turned and is about to take off," said Earl.

Thor went to the door and was about to jump.

"Here, don't forget your bag of corn," said Earl.

Thor took the bag of corn in his left hand, shook Earl's big hand with his right, told him thanks, and jumped just as the train jerked back into motion.

"See you again someday, Thor."

"Yeah, see you again, Earl."

The old man pointed to the east. "That way, boy. If you ever ride on my iron horse again, ask for me. I'll be around."

"Iron horse?" Thor remembered from school. "Yeah, trains used to be called iron horses." Thor wondered if God had answered...

Thor waved good-bye to the white beard as it waved back, then he turned and resumed his journey. His legs were strong again, from the Swiss cheese and the nap and the fact that his map said he had gone over half the distance. The sun was at his back, which put his troops in the lead, so Thor just followed his soldiers.

At first he thought he could make it to the next small town, but after a while he realized that would not be possible. Just as well, there were good places to hole up for the night along this lonely section. Even with his jacket, it was getting cold. Thor was worried about freezing as he slept in the night.

Up ahead was a narrow field that came down almost to the tracks. A large haystack sat near the bottom of the field. Only in books had Thor ever seen a real haystack. It was as if he had been transported back a hundred years. Maybe two hundred years. Thor cut through the woods to the field and its haystack. Where the field edge met the woods was a pile of rocks. Water sounds were coming from the rocks. An actual spring. Thor blessed his good luck as he filled his canteens. He climbed up the side of the haystack and made a home for himself on a flat spot. His troops had already abandoned him, complaining about the lack of sunlight.

Thor fell directly to sleep, as a puppy after a hard day of hunting. He dreamed of iron horses and wind in his hair, freedom and hope for a new home.

CHAPTER 21

Thor knew it was morning, though the sun had not yet arisen to burn away the dense fog that had rolled down the hill in the middle of the night. He did not want to leave his warm castle of straw, but he would have to if he was to get the early start that he had planned.

"Wake up, soldier. We need to break camp and get moving if we are to escape the enemy advances," said Sergeant Thor, as he sat up to scan the hazy fog for said enemy advances.

The soldiers of his camp grumbled their displeasure.

"Well, just a few more moments then," acquiesced Sergeant Thor as he fell back into the warmth of the straw.

The boy soldier drank the spring water from his canteen. It was still cool. He found his bag and reached inside for a handful of hardtack corn. It was gone, replaced by a nice chunk of Swiss cheese wrapped in waxed paper.

"Thanks, Earl."

As cheese breakfast was eaten, accompanied by the songs of birds hidden unseen in the cover of the fog, Thor reviewed his progress to date and planned his march for today. His sister had given him strict orders not to ride the train, talk to strangers, steal from anyone, or get into any vehicles of any kind.

"Two out of four ain't bad, men," said Thor. He figured he was halfway to hell already, and he still had near seventy miles yet. For the second time that morning he sat up.

"We really must be on our way," said Thor, more for his own self than to motivate his men.

Too late. The snaps and creaking of dried lumber and the soft thuds of large hooves were approaching the haystack. Someone was driving a horse-drawn wagon to his bivouac area. Thor rolled down the mountain of hay just as the wagon pulled up.

Thor's Civil War era imagination had turned reality. On the spring seat of the wagon was a lightly bearded man dressed in black pants, white shirt, and straw hat. Next to him was a young woman wearing a plain, light blue dress, and a gauze bonnet which covered most of her yellow hair. Both of them wore clunky black shoes.

"Good morning, young man," said the man.

"Good morning," said Thor.

"One of the children thought that they had seen a boy climb up the haystack last night and go to sleep there," said the young woman.

"Yes, ma'am," admitted Thor. "That was me."

The man smiled and the woman gave a little laugh.

"I'm not a ma'am," said the young woman. "My name is Sadie. This is my older brother, Moses."

Even their names were from the 1860s, reasoned Thor.

"My name is Thor, from up north."

Sadie and Moses both laughed this time. Of course Thor would have come from the lands to the north.

"Where might you be heading to?" asked Moses.

"I'm going home. Near Puposky."

The young woman said something to her brother, but Thor could not make out what she was saying because her speech sounded kind of foreign, like German maybe. These folks must be recent immigrants come to homestead the wilderness.

"We are not familiar with this Puposky," said Moses.

"It's just north of Bemidji," said Thor.

Brother and sister looked blankly at Thor, then the sister said that they knew where Bemidji was located. "Kind of far from here, is it not?" said Sadie.

"I can march most of seventy miles in a day," boasted Thor, not mentioning the iron horse part of his ability.

"We are going east too, though not so far, of course," said Moses. "Climb on and you can ride a few miles with us."

Sadie moved over to make a space between herself and Moses, as Thor grabbed up his cheese and pulled himself into the wagon seat. A civil war era wagon was not a vehicle, a fact which Amber would certainly have to concede. Besides, it was the 1860s. Amber must have only been referring to modern times when she set down her rules.

Moses snapped his reins, which set the pair of horses into motion. Horses? Thor wondered if God had answered...

The seat of the wagon put Thor higher than he would have thought. This was a great place to watch the scenery slowly go by. Thor looked back to make sure that his men were safely ensconced on the bed of the wagon.

"Thank you for the ride," said Thor. And to offer help of his own he provided his free advice. "You know what? If you had electricity, you could light up your place and work past sunset."

Sadie and Moses were smiling again. "If God wanted us to work later, he would have made the day longer," said Moses.

Thor remembered his long hike of yesterday, from before sunrise to after sundown. One long day of work was certainly enough.

"I agree," said Thor.

Moses drove the wagon up the narrow field and onto a dirt lane. Ash trees lined both sides of the roadway, their branches touching each other high above the trail, forming a green tunnel for the wagon. The sun was cutting away the last of the fog. Two deer stood not far from the edge of the road and watched the wagon as it passed close by. Apparently horses were not as scarey to wildlife as cars.

"I have some really good Swiss cheese from bum gardens. That is in Wisconsin."

Brother and sister smiled at each other again. Thor thought that Moses and Sadie were apparently very happy siblings. He smiled too.

"Do you want some?"

"That would be nice," said Sadie, as she took the cheese from his hands and cut it with a knife taken from a basket at her feet.

"This is really good," said Moses. "Just like the old country."

Thor told them about his long journey to reunite with his sister.

Who could they tell anyway? They were not even in the correct century. He left out most of the stuff about his old home. Thor figured these peaceful people would not be able to understand the legacy of the '60s. The 1960s, not the 1860s.

"You love your sister very well," said Sadie.

"Very well," agreed Thor. "I will protect her from now on, as soon as I get to our new home."

"Home is a gift of God," said Moses, not stated as a fact but like a compliment.

Thor nodded his head in agreement. These simple people were smarter than one might expect.

Sadie told about their home, and work, and life.

Thor asked Sadie, "Do you spend most of your time barefoot and in the kitchen?"

"Some. But I wear shoes. And at other times I work in the fields plowing behind the horses. A great deal of hard work and sweat, but I like the exercise. I help in the gardens. I raise bees in my hives. We all work together to collect and boil the maple syrup from our trees. The best taps are on the steep hillsides where only young people such as myself can easily walk. We raise trout in a spring-fed pool, too."

"I took some of your water from a spring I found in the woods, near the haystack that I slept on. Thank you for the water," said Thor.

"It is not our water," said Sadie. "You can thank Him," she said, as she poked a finger toward the Heavens.

The horses pulled onward for miles and miles. Flesh and blood horses were not as fast as iron horses, but this was still a great start to the second day of his march. Sadie and her brother Moses had a seemingly endless supply of stories for their young friend. The dirt path finally led to a gravel path. This new road looked more like an official county road. A Ford truck with rounded fenders, like from the war years of the forties, passed them going in the same east direction. This must be the transition area between the two centuries, figured Thor. Soon they came to a small town and a feed store.

"This is as far as we go," said Moses. "We thank thee for your good company."

"I thank thee for the ride," answered Thor. He half expected that the ride would be God's doing too, but neither Sadie nor Moses said anything more about the Heavens.

Sadie opened her basket and took out a sandwich as large as a saucer and as thick as a pie and put in into Thor's bag. The dark bread was obviously homemade and heavy.

"I made this with lettuce, honey, and slices of our trout. It will be satisfying. I promise."

Thor wanted to know if Sadie and Moses were Mennonite or Amish, or if they really were settlers.

"What kind of people are you?" he asked.

"Just children of God," said Sadie.

"Oh, of course. Well, good-bye, and thank you again." He waved to his friends as he resumed his journey.

His map had him cut south through the town, then east once more. There was traffic here, but not much. The smooth blacktop was easier to walk on than the railway. There were more fields along the road, and barns and cattle. His legs were sore from yesterday. Twelve miles would be farther today than yesterday. Thor refilled his canteens at a creek in a swampy area of a field and ate his trout sandwich as he walked. Before long he was hungry again.

"I figure sixty more miles, men," said Sergeant Thor. "Pick up the pace." Thor's legs were dragging along as fast as they could. A group of horses came to the fence of their pen and stared forlornly at the boy, jealous of the freedom of open spaces and motion. Six miles brought him to another small town.

"There are millions of small towns in Minnesota," said Thor to his men. They were following behind again. They marched through the town and back into the countryside. More fields, more cattle, a few more horses, more swamps and woods, more miles. He came to another, larger small town. There was a park here with a clean stream. He refilled his water again. Walking used a lot of water, and he didn't even have a radiator. In the middle of the town was a "sportsman's" cafe. He figured he must have been a sportsman before he had been a soldier. He went inside.

A black man with wide shoulders and a big belly was cleaning off a table. A tall Caucasian woman was cooking food. From their sweet talk, Thor could tell they were husband and wife. A little brown girl with beautiful black curly hair was taking a plate of food to one of the customers. He thought she was maybe five or six years old. Thor found a seat and table near the back of the cafe where he could keep an eye on everything: the black man, the little girl with the shiny hair, the woman cook, and the big window at the front, as well as the other customers.

The little girl came to take his order. She did not have a notebook to write down his order. Of course not, thought Thor, she is too young to be smart enough to write. He did not want to spend much more of the last of his money, so he just ordered a piece of pie and a glass of milk. The little girl listened to Thor, took an order at another table, then went into the kitchen to tell the cook. Thor could just make out what she was saying. "The boy wants a pie and milk, mama."

The little girl served the other people their food, then brought Thor his milk.

"I don't recognize you from school," said the girl.

"I'm from up north," said Thor. "I'm walking over to my new home where my sister is waiting." Thor had already blabbed to half of northern Minnesota, so talking to one small waitress wouldn't matter. "I have less than sixty miles left to go."

The little girl talked to him for a while. She seemed much smarter than her size. Then she left to get the pie. When she returned she had a small plate with the pie and a larger one with a hamburger, French fries, coleslaw, and scalloped potatoes.

The first thing Thor said was, "Fries and scalloped potatoes?" The second was, "I'm sorry, I only ordered pie."

"This always goes with the pie," said the girl. "No extra charge."

Thor and the girl talked as he ate. She got him another milk when his first ran low. "Free refills on milk, too," she said. Thor ate his pie. It was blueberry. He had not even asked for any specific kind. Just pie.

"Blueberry is my favorite," said Thor.

It took him a long time to eat all the food, but he knew that his body would need it all. He asked for his check when he was done, and the little girl told him, "Twenty-five cents."

"But I had milk, too," said Thor, thinking that twenty-five cents did not seem nearly enough for pie.

"Oh, that is right. That will be thirty-five cents."

Thor paid the full account and left. As he passed the big window in front he waved to his new friend.

She smiled and waved back, then whirled around as she ran back to her mom's kitchen, her curly hair bouncing as she ran.

"Pretty good grub, boys," said Sergeant Thor. "Now let's get out of this town while the sun is still shining. God only makes so much daylight, you know."

Again more miles, cows, trees, and stuff to see and find. Nature was all around. Thor's legs were soon tired again, but not a desperate tired. Now the kind of tired that he could walk a thousand miles through to get to his sister and the new home she had found for them.

He came to another small town, turned north a few hundred yards as his map instructed, then east onto another blacktop farm road. Three or four more miles brought him to a sharp turn in the road. He was moving north now. On his left was the sun. There was a tiny lake on his right, as well as his company of soldiers. Up ahead was a pink church. At least it looked to be pink.

"Maybe it was sunburned today," said Thor.

As he walked up to the church he could see that there were graves all around the building, as if this had been a battle site and the fallen soldiers had been buried where they had died. The church seemed to have been added later. Farther down the road, far past the church, and sitting separate from the others in an open field, were a pair of crosses with circles in them.

"Seems this place is abandoned," said Thor to his men to bolster their flagging courage. "We better check it out." The sun would set soon and it was already getting cold. There would be no haystacks tonight.

Thor found a basement window in back that was open and let himself down onto a counter. It was a Lutheran church, so it was all right for him to enter, because he was Lutheran. He explored the church. The lights did not seem to work, but he found a flashlight in one of the cupboards in the basement kitchen. He found lots and lots of reading material, but it was mostly religious stuff. He found some satiny gowns that might make good blankets.

In a wood rack Thor found a large glass bottle of pop. He had a hard time getting the cork out of the bottle, but he finally succeeded. It was grape pop. Thor liked orange and root beer better, but as before, beggars could not be choosers. He was very thirsty again, so he drank all of the pop. It was really good, though more bitter than grape pop should have been. Now Thor was really getting tired, so he took his gowns upstairs and made a bed on one of the pews.

The next he knew, weak sunlight of blue, green, rose, and violet was filtering through the windows of the church. Thor's head was a bit dizzy, but he felt good and strong and ready for a hike. Maybe he could make it home today?

Just then he thought he heard water running in the kitchen down in the basement. A burglar?

"Who would break into a church," whispered Thor angrily to his soldiers. "Let's get the bastards."

Thor's first step was a bit unsteady. Perhaps he had drunk too much grape pop last night. What? He wasn't even thinking steady. He supported himself with the oak back of the pew as his head cleared. Revived, he slowly crept downstairs to the basement. Someone was definitely in the kitchen. Thor could not guess what the person was doing, but from the continuous sound of a running faucet, he figured they were stealing a lot of water.

Thor stepped into the kitchen. His dizzy head had made him braver than he was. He spotted the thief. She was washing her hair in the sink. One weak light over the sink illuminated the scene. The thief had short, reddish-blonde hair, a long, plain brown skirt, ugly shoes, and a bare back.

"Don't turn around," commanded Thor.

The thief shrieked and turned around. She was very pretty. She had nice pointy breasts. Thor looked at her face, then her breasts, then her face again, and so on.

"I told you not to turn around," complained Thor, as if it was the young woman's fault that his eyes were glued to her breasts.

"Who are you?" asked the woman, as she found a hand towel with which to cover her chest.

Thor was a bit flustered, what with the image of the girl's breasts burned onto his retinas, but he could answer. "I'm, um...Smith, John Smith. I'm on my way home and I got tired and cold last night, so I stayed here. Upstairs."

"Why here?" The woman could see that this was just a boy.

"I'm Lutheran. You are too, I suppose."

"I was. Not anymore. Now I am a Catholic nun."

Thor had stared at the pointy breasts of a young nun. He would certainly go to hell now.

"I'm sorry," said Mr. John Smith Thor.

"Come on over here," commanded the pretty nun woman.

Thor was staring at her face now. He walked to the sink, where the girl turned him so she could better see his face, somehow holding the small towel over her chest as she did so. Thor kind of hoped for towel slippage. He was going to hell, anyway.

"You have pretty eyes," said the woman. "Nice green and flecks."

"Thank you."

"They look kind of familiar. Have I seen them before?"

"I don't think so. They've been with me the whole time." Damn, why did I say that? "I'm sorry, the pop has made me confused."

"So, you are the culprit who drank the bottle of wine."

"Wine? In a church?" Here comes hell again.

"Communion wine. It is all right, though, the wine was not yet blessed," said the woman to better chase away the awful look on the boy's face. "Now go over there and turn around while I get dressed."

On the next sight of the woman she was dressed with a white blouse, a jacket of sorts, and a nun hat, as well as her previous skirt.

"My name is Sister Catherine. I presume you are Thor."

John Smith had been busted, though for the life of him he could not figure out how. It was the wine or God, of that Thor was sure.

"You have your sister's eyes," said Catherine with a smile.

Forget wine and God.

Sister Catherine explained how she knew Amber. Thor explained about his journey to his new home with his sister over by Puposky.

"I came here this morning to open the church and air it out," said Catherine. "My sister is getting married this afternoon." Catherine looked at the silver watch on her wrist. "I have to go back home yet, but if we drive fast enough I think that I can get you as far as 89.

"Great," said Thor. If he could get a ride to Highway 89, he might be able to make it to his sister yet today.

Way back on the railway embankment, in despair and exhaustion, Thor had asked God for a horse. Instead he got a train, a wagon, and now a car. Thor and Catherine walked to the rear of the church, where an old car was parked.

"It is a '68 Mustang," said Catherine, as Thor got in. "Buckle up."

A mustang? Thor wondered if God had answered...

Catherine slowly drove away from the pink church, past the two crosses with their halos, toward the east and Amber.

"Those crosses look lonely out there," said Thor.

"A woman visits them often. Some people say her daughter and grandmother are buried there."

Sister Catherine followed the road around a sharp curve, past a tall hill covered in children who were sliding into a pond, then picked up speed until the telephone poles snipped by as fast as fence pickets. Thor leaned to the side a bit to check the speedometer. The Mustang was going a mark or two less than 115 miles per hour. Sister Catherine hit a sharp rise in the road and they were airborne for a while. Thor's stomach stayed in his chest for longer than that while. They were to 89 in less than an hour. Catherine crossed the highway and pulled over to let Thor out onto the continuation of Highway 32.

"Tell Amber that I came back into the bus station to find her and give her a ride to my church, but she had already gone. I hope she made it OK."

Amber had told her brother about the closet and the duct tape. "She made it OK," said Thor.

Catherine took a long, light chain from inside her blouse and put it around Thor's neck. "I want you to have this. It is a Celtic cross like the lonely crosses back at our church. It will bring you peace." Then she gave Thor a hug and kissed the boy's cheek.

"Thank you," said Thor.

"And Thor? Don't tell Amber about my breasts. All right?"

Thor promised not to tell about those things, and got out and waved good-bye as Catherine spun around in the road and flew back from whence she had come. Thor resumed his march. Several miles east on 32, then turn south on 15 for four miles, then Arctic Road.

"Come on, men," encouraged the Sergeant. "I will make it home today if we have to walk all night," said Sergeant Thor with a great determination. "Arctic Road is our destination."

Miles rolled by. There were more forests here than before. His legs were tired and sore, and he was hungry. He was used to missing breakfast, but he needed more food for this much exercise. So close, and yet so far away.

A pickup passed him going in the opposite direction. It was a Chevy with big tires. Thor had seen the faces of two kids in the truck, not much older than himself, it seemed. The truck turned around and came back, passed him, and pulled over. The two guys got out and walked to the back of the truck where they leaned against its tailgate. Thor readied himself for a fight. Bigtires, the driver of the truck, was tall and had dark hair trying to escape from the top of his shirt.

The other guy had a bad scar on the side of his forehead. He had straightened his back rather slowly when he had exited the truck, and walked like he had just been in a car crash.

"Do you need a ride," asked Bigtires.

"I can make it," said Thor.

"Want a beer or some chew," asked CarCrash.

"No thank you," said Thor.

Bigtires dug in a cooler set in the bed of his truck. "Oh, here, I have a bunch of pop left. Orange, root beer, or grape?"

"Not grape," said Thor, as Bigtires handed him an orange pop.

"Where you headed?" asked CarCrash.

"Over near Puposky," said Thor. "On Arctic Road."

"Then you'll need our ride for sure," said Bigtires. "Two mean old dogs live on Highway 15. They'll eat you if you try to pass."

"Jump in the back seat," said CarCrash as he added another snuff can to its brethren of empties in the bed of the truck.

The tires hummed down the blacktop as the two rednecks told their stories to the boy. Thor tried to tell about his journey, but it did not seem believable to Bigtires and CarCrash. Hell, it would not have been believable to Thor if he had not been there himself. The truck drove faster as the boys drank faster. Thor directed them to the gravel road that he needed to find.

"You can let me off here. I want to walk the rest of the way to my home." Thor got out and thanked the boys.

"You must live in the log home on the north side," said Bigtires.

"I guess so," answered Thor as he walked away.

"Well, take it easy," said Bigtires. "Good luck." And he left.

More woods and trees, and a small swamp, but less than a half mile to go, then a field of wildflowers. Thor could see a big log house on the far side of the field, set up against the forest. Thor turned onto the path that led to his new home.

A small girl flew out of the house and started to run down the bumpy path that cut through the middle of the field.

CHAPTER 22

His gentle dream was about waking in the morning with a woman in his arms. When Richard awoke, he was holding a beautiful, red-haired woman in his arms. What seemed like eons of crushing loneliness had left him in a single night, and had been replaced by…what? Love? Looking at her face, peaceful in her sleep, he realized he was lucky—he had fallen in love with her during their work together on the Clearwater River, but had somehow not realized that she had fallen in love too. Hell, he had not truly realized that he had succumbed.

Elsie opened her green eyes and looked at him. "Else," she said.

"What else?" he said, not so intelligently.

"You can call me 'Else' instead of 'Elsie.'"

"Because you love me?" he said with a mischievous smile.

"Because I have trusted you to love me," she answered.

"Oh," he said, a million miles closer to Else than he had been a moment before.

They got out of bed together, dressed, and went downstairs to where Amber and the children were sitting at the kitchen table, each child already positioned in their respective sites. Amber gave Else's children the cereal which they were clamoring for, as Else picked through yesterday's leftovers trying to find something much more substantial for the adults, eleven-year-old Amber apparently included in that group. Richard sat at the end of the kitchen table, gazing out the south window overlooking his field.

"The field is really greening up out there," said Richard. "The rain we got performed its miracle."

Else came over to see what Richard was looking at. What she saw was not corn, wheat, or pasture. "It just looks wild to me."

"That is correct," piped in Amber. "We like the wildflowers better than anything else."

Richard wondered to himself, did Amber just say: "anything else," or "anything, Else"? "That's right," said Richard, "we like the colors of the wildflowers better than anything else."

Richard surmised that the intense fire of this spring's burn had allowed the orange-tipped Indian paintbrush, his favorite flowers, to become prolific, but he was just guessing. There were also thistle and Canada goldenrod, but they would not flower until much later in the summer. Several types of butterflies liked the thistle—Richard couldn't quite remember which ones, and honey bees liked the heavy flower heads of the goldenrod—which Richard would be allergic to except that goldenrod was not an airborne pollen—if he left it alone, it left him alone.

Patches of small, white, daisylike flowers grouped themselves at random throughout the field, as did congregations of bright yellow puccoon—splattered like butter amidst the Indian paintbrush and the mysterious white flowers.

Wild strawberries would be hiding in the field also, tiny white flowers with fuzzy yellow centers, which would later produce tiny but intense berries. Richard had never before noticed the small wild strawberries until one day when Joshua and Foster, themselves then small and wild, had pointed them out to their dad.

"There are tiny wild strawberries out there which can be picked later this summer," said Richard to nobody in particular. "But you have to have a lot of time to collect very many because they are so small. I never used to have the patience."

Two bird feeders offered entertainment outside the front window of the kitchen. One was a cedar house with two sides of clear plastic so the level of seed could be easily monitored. The other was no more than the flat top of a tall section of cedar log, set upright about eight feet in front of the kitchen window. The cedar log still had its bark intact, which made it seem like the trunk of a cut-off tree.

Several male purple finches, looking as if they had been dipped in raspberry wine, were squabbling over the black sunflower seeds in the house feeder and on the platform of the cedar log. Two nuthatches, with snow white breasts, were scampering headfirst down the side of the log. One stopped to push a seed into a crevice in the rough bark, where it proceeded to hack it open. Among all this commotion a chickadee flew in, snapped up a single seed, and flew off to a high branch of a tree at the edge of the woods. From far across the field, an airborne flash caught Richards eye. Perhaps the underside of the marsh hawk that frequently hunts his field in the summer.

Richard picked up his binoculars, always ready on the table, and scanned the edge of the field. He knew that there were bunches of marsh marigold blooming in the saturated soil of the roadside ditch, but they were lying too low to be visible from the house. His mailbox shot into view in the glass of the binoculars, then just to the right of the mailbox—the entrance of the long path which dissected his field as it weaved its course to his home.

A tatterdemalion was walking toward the house. "It seems we have a lost waif approaching," said Richard, still holding the binoculars to his eyes as he followed the progress of the small child in the field. Amber ran to Richard's window, pushed her way in front of him, and shrieked, "He's here." Then she sprinted through the length of house, leaving the door open for the honey bees and hornets, and vaulted off the porch to run down the path toward the lost waif in question. The distant child, upon seeing Amber's fast approach, began his own run toward her. They met in the middle of the field of flowers, and fell, literally, into each other's arms.

Amber brought the child home. "This is Thor," she announced. "My little brother." Little Thor was two inches taller than his sister.

"Do you have any other siblings?" asked Richard, trying to hide the mild concern in his voice.

"No, Sir, he is all I have." A comment that might be truthful in more than one meaning.

This Norse god of thunder, thought Richard, was evidently in dire need of nourishment. Else must have been reading Richard's mind.

She sat Thor down and got him a plate of the "adult" food and a glass of milk. He ate like a stray dog. Yet though dressed in rags, Thor's eyes were the same bright green as his sister's, his light hair fell regally to near his shoulders, and, while obviously starved, he held himself, as his name implied, in a grand and noble manner. He thanked Else most graciously for the food.

"Sweet Amber, I am guessing that you will owe me for some long distance phone charges," stated Richard.

"Yes, Sir," agreed Amber. Then, "Else, can Thor have another glass of milk?"

Richard thought, "Else? How did Amber pick up on the change from Elsie to Else?" In the new public state of his home, Richard had not yet used that term of endearment. "So I did hear, 'anything, Else.' Is this a conspiracy? Women!" Aloud, he asked Thor, "Did you have a long walk to get here?"

"I figured 137 miles by the map," said the slight Thor. The look thrown at him from his older sister caused him to wince. At least Richard now knew that Amber's place of escape was 137 miles in some direction from his house.

Else cleaned and put away the kitchen, as Amber showed Thor around the big house, with "her" bedroom upstairs. Thor was regaled with fanciful stories of house-eating porcupines and house-whacking woodpeckers. Amber then took him outside to the yard surrounding the house and the forest surrounding the yard to show him how truly wild this place was. Afterwards, Else shepherded Thor to the shower and threw his clothes, ragged as they were, into the washing machine, and found him a few clean items that seemed masculine enough for a boy to wear, and, with Amber's flip-flops, made Thor presentable.

Clean and wet-headed, and dressed in something better than rags, Thor was looking nicer every moment. He found his sister and together they went outside again, to sit on the bench by the garden and talk with each other. Richard could see them from the west side window of the kitchen.

Amber was doing most of the talking, it seemed. Twice she wagged her finger at her brother as if to emphasize a point. Presently, Thor put his arms around his sister and gave her a hug. That seemed to shut her up. After a while Richard looked out the window again. Mighty Thor was evidently sleeping on the bench, while Amber entertained Else's children with what appeared to be a botany lesson in Richard's flower garden.

Richard said that he wanted to drive into town to talk again to Agent Kieran, to update Michael on the case, and vice-verse. He called Michael to make sure that he would be in town today. Michael said he would. He also informed Richard that his shirt-turned-towel, used to wipe Chad Rochambeau's jeep, did indeed contain evidence of cow slobber. In turn, Richard informed Michael about the construction site at the new flower shop and the star-cut conduits buried there in the new concrete. Michael said he would have them checked out. Richard agreed to meet with Michael at the BCA office after noon.

Joshua and his dog Barker stopped by. He needed to pick up his stereo and speakers for a party he was having this weekend. Barker played joyfully and quietly outside with the children, until Richard came out, then the dog went into another of her crazed barking fits. In retaliation, Richard chased Barker twice around the house. Retreating to the stillness and quiet of his home, Richard asked Else if she would like to go into town with him, but she had to decline.

"I'll call Mr. Thorson and have him drive me over to my farm," said Else. "My truck is ready, and I can get the rest of the children's clothes." She added that Clara Zemm had called and wanted to know if all the children could come to their place again to cheer up Sally; therefore could Richard please drop off their newly expanded brood of six on the way to Bemidji?

Even though it was quite a deviation from his route, Richard agreed.

Joshua finished loading the stereo equipment, then talked to his dad for a short while, asking about Else's move to his place and if it might be permanent. Richard was noncommittal in his speech, if not in his mind. Joshua left. Richard soon followed, his truck packed with its load of freshly cleaned children, including sleepy-eyed Thor. Else kissed Richard good-bye and hugged him as tight as she could, as if she would never see her man again.

The sky was sunny and windy, the kind of day that was either cool or warm, depending on whether one of the fleeting cumulus clouds was obscuring the sun. Richard drove first to the intrusive rock in front of Blister's filthy shack, but the driveway there had freshly dug star cuts in its dirt, so Richard passed it by, not wanting to destroy the marks or to meet with whomever had made them.

Samantha and Sally were happy to see Amber and her brother. Amber proudly introduced Thor to the others, telling them the story of how he hiked dozens of miles to reunite with his only sibling. Thor beamed in his sister's attention and admiration.

Else's small children found the kitchen of Clara Zemm and stuffed their cheeks with fresh oatmeal cookies and washed the goodies down with cold milk. Then, with their internal burners refuelled, flew back outside to the semi-wilderness of Clara's backyard and gardens.

Teddy Zemm was still angry about the attack on Sally and the death of Lenora Frontera. Richard assured him that the predators would soon be caught and peace restored, though Richard knew that peace would never fully return to Sally, and peace could never be brought to Lenora. Not on this earth.

When Richard left the Zemm home and got into his truck to leave, Sally ran over to say good-bye. "I wanted to get you alone so I could tell you thanks for listening to me the other day. It is a big weight off my shoulders knowing that you and Else care about...about things."

Richard didn't really have the faintest idea what to say. Without thinking, he tried, "You have friends that love you."

That worked. Sally's face brightened and she patted his arm and told him to be careful.

Richard remembered his daughter back when she was fourteen. A few individuals befriended her after she had been attacked, and later during her ordeal with the county legal institutions. At the time these people seemed so important to Jeanette. Later they would drift slowly away from her, leaving Jeanette again with her family as her support. But those people, at a critical time in his daughter's trials, those few new friends, were sorely needed by Jeanette.

"Could you come over to visit Else and I sometime? We would love to have you."

"Absolutely," said Sally a bit too loudly, freezing Else's four children in their tracks for just a moment. Then softer, "Yes," as she backed away from the truck to let Richard leave. "I will come over to your home soon. I promise."

Richard drove, alone, to where County Road 20 passes the edge of Lake Bemidji State Park, and then followed it east to its intersection with the Paul Bunyan Trail. Pulling his old truck just off the road, into a grassy area used by joggers as a parking spot, he walked north to where Sally had indicated she had been attacked.

The dark constriction of trees was easy to find. Richard searched the area, walking up and down that section of the trail and into the edge of woods that flanked the trail. The area appeared tranquil in the daylight, cool and shaded compared to the main trail. The kind of place where a bicyclist or jogger might stop to rest on a hot day. It belied the evil that had recently struck there. Then he saw the tree stand. It was obvious, once one knew where to look, hovering heavy over the trail.

Grey weathered boards were nailed as steps leading into a large basswood tree. The steps led to a wide stand made of two-by-six planks. Richard climbed the steps and stood on the platform. The large leaves of the overhanging branches hid him.

As he stood on the platform, a family passed by on their bicycles. A mother in the lead, a young daughter, a slightly older son, and the father—pulling one of those baby bicycle carriages. Richard could see two little bald heads in this one. "A good start for a family," thought Richard. The bicyclists had no idea he was above them.

From that perch it would have been easy for Blister to fall onto his prey and crush the wind out of Sally's small chest. It was a perfect place for the rapist to stalk the girls and young women that ran and walked and roller-bladed on its path. In disgust and sorrow, Richard descended the basswood and abandoned the site.

Michael Kieran was in his office, as he had said he would be. When Richard arrived at the BCA building in Bemidji, Richard told him about seeing fresh star-cut tracks at Blister's shack. Michael said that he would ask the sheriff's department to send someone out there to investigate. Maybe he would go out later himself and take some pictures of the marks. Michael added that the construction site of the new flower shop had pipe set in concrete that seemed to match the star cuts left at the trail into Rice Pond.

"If the marks at Blister's shack match those from Rice Pond, and they all match the pipe at the new flower shop, then we will have a three-way connection," said Michael.

"If you do go to Blister's shack yourself, pick up a blue gingham cloth that is there," said Richard. "It is being used as a cushion for a chair set at the rear of the shack. It seems to me that it might be the same pattern as the dress that Lenora was wearing when she was killed. Though I don't see how that could be," he added.

"I can do that," agreed Agent Kieran.

"After dropping the children off at Teddy Zemm's home this morning, I drove over by the state park and walked the section of trail north of there. There was a tree stand over the bicycle path where Sally had been assaulted. Blister must have used it as a perch from which to drop onto Sally's back."

"In Duluth, Blister sat in trees, so I imagine, with his increase in age, he must find a tree stand to be more comfortable," said Michael sarcastically.

"Did any of his previous victims have bruises on the side of their necks?" asked Richard, as Michael's BCA underling, Jeff Haltman, came into the office and joined them.

Agent Kieran introduced the Bemidji home office BCA agent to Richard, not knowing if they had ever met before, then answered Richard's question. "No marks like we found on Miss Frontera, but all of his victims had been knocked around."

"Euglena had a reputation for liking to slap around his females. He believes that helps to keep them in line," said Richard.

Agent Haltman added, "The autopsy indicated that the bruise was from pressure, like Blister was pushing Miss Frontera's neck away, or her head into the ground. The bruises on the edge of her lower lip were from a string-like item. Like a fine jewelry chain. So from that we can surmise that Blister was pushing Miss Frontera's head down or away as he tried to pull her chain and cross from her mouth."

"But Lenora had bitten down so hard the chain bruised her lip and its cross was wedged between two of her teeth," reasoned Richard.

"I don't think that helps us much. Why would a woman do that to herself?" said Agent Haltman.

"She wanted to keep the cross, even if it meant her life. Or she already knew that she would be killed and it did not matter what she had to do to keep the cross in her possession," said Richard.

Agent Jeff Haltman excused himself and went to his own office down the hall. The conversation was coming to an end and Richard had errands yet to do in town, but he had one last question for his friend Michael Kieran.

"Did your lab in the Cities ever determine how the DNA evidence from Lennie had become compromised?" asked Richard.

"They didn't find any chemicals, so it was either accidental—put in a hot car trunk for too long, for example, or it was heated for a short time in a microwave, long enough to destroy the DNA but not so long as to make it evident that it had been cooked."

"Would a cop know how to do that?" asked Richard.

If the question had bothered Agent Kieran, he certainly did not show it. "Probably," he answered.

Richard already knew in his heart what had happened, he just wanted to know whose side Agent Kieran was on. He was still on Lennie's side.

CHAPTER 23

It was already late afternoon and Richard had a few more chores to do in town. He bade farewell to the BCA agent, Michael Kieran, and left to complete his errands, picking up a repaired chain saw from the local fleet store, and buying four gallons of milk that he placed in a cooler set on the floor of the rear bench seat. The cooler was needed to keep the milk cold during the drive from town to home, but was also needed to keep the broken driver's seat from sliding back into the rear seat. Perhaps some day Richard would get that old seat fixed. Maybe. Probably not.

After groceries, Richard drove past the construction site of the new flower shop. "New Home of Magnum Flowers," the sign read. He pulled off onto the gravel edge of the side road he was on and watched the work that was ongoing at the new building. The shop was near completion. Already there were plants and vases of flowers in the shop's windows. Two delivery vans were waiting at a side door of the business. As Richard watched, a black-haired girl came out of the store and loaded a box of plants into the back of one of the vans. She was wearing a blue gingham dress.

Richard instantly said to himself, "There's Lenora. What is she doing here?" But, of course, Lenora's body was much too cold to be walking around in the world of the living and breathing. A crushing sadness flooded Richard's mind as he realized his wishful mistake. The gingham-dressed girl walked back into the flower shop, leaving him with images of a girl with long black raven hair floating in a pond.

Richard forced himself to shake the apparition of Lenora's ghost from his mind and to drive to the flower girl's van and wait for her to come out again. When she did, Richard walked over to her and asked if he could ask her a question. Richard did not yet know what to ask.

"Who are you?" she asked, seeing that Richard was a bit unsettled, though not knowing that it was her resemblance to Miss Frontera that was doing the unsettling.

Richard told her who he was, and about Lenora Frontera and his finding her dead at Rice Pond, and how much she looked like that girl, and could he just talk with her for a while.

"I am helping a state cop that is working on this case," he said, once again trying to bolster his status by using his connection with Michael Kieran.

She said that her name was Peggy Raphael.

She could have been the younger sister to Lenora Frontera, except that Miss Raphael's black hair was exceedingly fine and her skin just a half shade lighter.

The delivery girl was visibly shaken, but she controlled herself with an iron will that Richard could see was already taking control.

"I know who you are, but I cannot talk here," she whispered. "Leave now, before you are discovered. I'll call you later tonight." The flower girl closed the cargo gate on the van and walked back to the store. She turned at the door, "I promise," she said, and went inside.

Richard left as instructed and drove to the Zemm homestead and its surrounding national forest lands. The children were enjoying their stay with Teddy and Clara, playing and socializing with their new friends Sally and Samantha. Thor was helping Teddy spread leaves as compost between the rows of the vegetables. Amber rode out of the woods on Samantha's bicycle. The fair skin of her face was flushed from the heat, and small beads of sweat had formed on her forehead. Catching the sunlight, the scattered beads looked like a disarranged tiara. When she spotted Richard she rode over to him.

"I went down to the lake to see what it looked like," said Amber by way of an explanation, though Richard had not asked for any.

Amber slowed her bicycle—Samantha's bicycle, and stopped next to Richard. He wiped the sweaty crown from her forehead with the palm of his hand, then wiped the royal perspiration onto the front of his blue jeans, and finally kissed her now bourgeois, if somewhat drier forehead.

"You need to get into better shape, Miss Tour de France, if you get this exerted just riding down to the lake."

"Yes, Sir, but I rode very fast," she defended.

"I suppose you did, Amber. But the grade of the road is uphill from the lake, so if you learn to use the lighter gears you could make the job easier on yourself."

"But that would be no fun," stated Amber.

"No, I imagine not."

Else came out of the cottage and walked over to where Amber and Richard were standing. "I thought you had been dragged off by the wildlife," said Else to Amber's reddened face. "I was just about to round up the posse." Else stroked Amber's white-blond hair, pushing wild strands back away from the child's face as she did so.

"I'm sorry, Else."

"Nevermind. Now go inside and ask Clara for some lemonade. All the others have already had a glass."

Amber did as she was told.

Else turned to Richard and put her right arm around his waist as they walked toward the flowers in Clara's garden. Richard could get used to this kind of reception.

"What did you find in town?" asked Else as her arm pulled him toward where she wanted him to go, her thumb caught in the belt loop on the far side of his waist.

"Michael informed me that the cow slobber was cow slobber. Also that all the star cuts probably match Thomas Thorson's conduit at the new flower shop."

"Does that help us?"

"Actually, it does. I think. I went to the flower shop and sat in my truck watching the building. A Native girl came out, dressed in gingham just like Lenora." Richard did not mention that the gingham ghost looked like Lenora, though he was sure that Else could guess that was so. "I talked to her and told her who I was and that it was I who had found the missing convenience store girl. She will call later and then come over to our place to talk."

"I have a feeling she will know something," said Else.

"I'm sure the gingham is the exact same pattern and color as the dress that Lenora was wearing." That Lenora finished her life in.

"The gingham dress and the conduit give us a positive, if as yet unexplained connection to Lenora and Rice Pond," said Else.

"Right."

"Anything else from your agent friend?"

"I asked Michael about the DNA evidence. He knows that it was tampered with. Which is good. Not the tampering, the knowing and acknowledging."

Else stopped in front of a bed of moss roses, their small flowers stained various colors of pastels. "They are lovely, aren't they? I like the yellow ones the best."

Else's thumb still caught in his belt loop, Richard turned into her and looked into her eyes. "I like the green ones the best." He kissed her mouth, then licked his lips. "Chocolate...chocolate fudge. You and Clara made fudge, didn't you," he accused. "Wait, let me kiss you again."

Else tried to push him away, grimacing in a fake expression of disgust, but her thumb kept them stuck together like one squirmy creature. "You just want another taste of fudge," giggled Else. "I can tell...well, you will just have to wait and have some with the kids."

Richard persisted in his efforts to obtain kisses and fudge. Else persisted in squiggling away. They fell, crumpled onto the grass, tied together at the belt loop. Else ended up on top, trying vainly to do a push-up off Richard's chest, but was pulled down in a bear hug.

"No kisses for you, guy. Absolutely forbidden."

"Just one more," said Richard. "For old times sake."

"You mean for old-timer's sake, don't you?" said Else.

Richard kamikazied in for a quick kiss, but Else turned her face at the last moment, leaving Richard with ear and soft red hair on his lips. He continued his efforts at getting that second kiss, until Amber rode by on Samantha's bike, then he had to abandon his efforts. Still stuck on his girl per her thumb, he awkwardly helped her to her feet to show her how gentlemanly he had now become. Else was still wary.

Thor came out of the Zemm cottage, looking rested for a change. Else said that he had taken another nap soon after Richard had left for the trail and town.

Richard called him over. "You look much better now that you have gotten some sleep under your belt. How do you feel?"

"Pretty good. But I'm still hungry. I should have taken more food with me when I left for your place."

"Did you walk the whole distance?" asked Else.

"I didn't want to take any rides from strangers." Apparently, most every man and woman in Minnesota is kin to Thor. "If my bike had not been broken I could have taken that. I'll miss my bike."

"That's all right, my sweet little triathlon man, we can get you a new one in town," promised Else.

Thor had a look on his face like he didn't know if he should really believe her or not. Soon, the scale must have tilted slightly to trust, as a small smile formed where disbelief had previously held sway.

Richard decided to visit Rice Pond again. The sight of the flower delivery girl had shaken him, and he needed to go where he could think. He extricated Else's thumb and told her where he was going and that he would be back soon. As Else told him to hurry back to her, he caught her by surprise and kissed her again and got his second taste of fudge.

CHAPTER 24

The trail to the pond had gotten much greener the last few days. Richard drove past the trail and parked in an old logging cut on the far side of the Forest Service road, then walked back across the road to the beginning of the path to Rice Pond. He did not want his old truck to be visible from the road or left at the trail to Rice Pond. It was unlikely that the killers of Lenora would be bold enough to come back again to the pond, but not impossibly unlikely.

The leaves of the trees had grown larger and were doing a better job of shading the path. Spring was coming on fast. This made the trail more enclosed than before, but in a cool and comforting way. Wild irises—northern blue flag—were growing in great numbers in the wet soil along the edges of the trail, some standing in water, their swordlike leaves seeming to protect the stems that held their showy flowers. In places where the trail climbed above the dampness of the surrounding woods, wild roses displayed their pale pink flowers. In late summer and early autumn, the hips that would grow from the flowers would be ready to be picked for the vitamin C that they held in their small red fruits.

Rice Pond was still mostly grey and brown, but green from the shore seemed to be edging its way into the water. The color shift was only an illusion, of course. It was the temperature of the soil and of the water that was determining where, when, and how fast the plants would grow.

Lenora's memory was present at the pond. Richard stopped for a short while to pay his respects. He would always regret that he could not have been here a few hours before he found the girl. Maybe he could have saved her. Then he would have been tried, sentenced, and sent back to prison, but she would be alive.

"No good deed goes unpunished," said Richard to the reeds where he had found the rose and the girl.

Richard continued his hike. Half a mile or so around the south side of the pond the trail widened into a small glade, which might have once, a long time ago, been a loading area for logging machines, but which now only grew flowers and grasses. From the entrance into the glade Richard studied the opening in the trees, the sunlight as it shifted over the grass, and the taller plants as they waved in the breezes that fell into the clearing. On the other side of the meadow was a shaded path indicating the continuation of the trail. Richard walked into the center of the clearing, stood in the bright light that washed the glade, and felt the warmth of the sun on his face. It was a beautiful place, a place where a romantic could take his girl for a secluded picnic.

Richard turned and looked back to where he had just come from. A tree stand was just barely visible from this direction. Something white was lying below the stand. Richard walked back and picked it up. A white blouse, long sleeved, with frilly cuffs and collar. Blood, too fresh to be Lennie's, but too old to be since Richard started his hike, covered most of its front.

Days earlier, under this very tree, Lenora must have fought her attackers and had managed to keep the evidence that was working to damn the damned. Somehow Richard felt this, knew this to be true. Now another girl had been attacked here too, and very recently, as proven by the fresh red blood on the torn blouse.

Startled by the sound of men approaching, Richard dropped the blood-stained blouse back onto the forest floor. Though it had been years since he had heard the voice of his hated roommate Eugene Euglena, he instantly recognized his evil noise as it seeped through the trees of the forest. Richard turned and ran away from the clamor, slowing only when the harsh sounds lessened.

A faint path led into the woods, recently walked and just barely visible in places, but generally cutting back north toward Rice Pond. Richard's trailing skills would never be as good as those of his son Joshua—with Joshua's sharp eyesight and vigilant patience. But they were adequate, practiced from last autumn's bow hunting season where he had followed wounded deer to where they had bedded down to recover or die.

A crushed patch of grass, or a broken flower, or a snapped twig showed where the owner of the blouse had walked. Whoever it was, they had been too tired or too injured to keep their passing a secret. Every thirty yards or so there would be a drop of blood on the path or a smear of blood on a sapling. Most of the traces of blood were low, left on the brown leaf litter of last fall or on the new green grass, but some of the blood was higher. The fleeing subject must be injured around their shoulders or head.

If there was not a hunter in Euglena's gang, Richard doubted that they would be able to follow this trail very well. It was marked well enough by blood and broken plants, but the sign was too spread out for a nonhunter to be able to track easily. More probable that Euglena was searching blind, sweeping widely through the forest tangle as if on a giant Easter egg hunt.

It dawned on Richard that there were no scuff marks in the old leaves, or sharp dents left from a boot heel or shoe. He guessed that the person walking somewhere up ahead of him was barefoot as well as shirtless.

He also guessed that the person he was tracking was a female. The torn, white blouse and the bloody handprints were girl-sized, as were the naked footprints. But if the fleeing prey was a girl, she was a girl who could keep on a fairly straight track. The path of escape led generally to the north, but also seemed to weave from time to time as if its maker was trying to find a place to hide.

Richard came to a dense tangle of broken trees where the girl must have rested for a while, perhaps thinking that this would be a good place to hide. A patch of blood showed where she had laid in the leaf litter of the forest floor. Richard wondered how much blood she had lost. Animals could sometimes lose a great percentage of their blood and still keep moving, but humans were more susceptible to shock from lack of blood and the attendant loss of heat.

The girl had evidently crawled away from her abandoned hiding place, ruffling a trail under the worst of the fallen trees. Then she had pulled herself up, leaving blood on a higher branch, and had started to walk again.

Richard continued to track. The girl's trail began to wander. She may have gotten tired, or shock from lack of blood was setting in, or she might even be suffering from exposure without her shirt and shoes. "No shirt—no shoes—no service," thought Richard. Though the blood and Euglena's presence suggested service of a kind that no sane person would ever want.

Most of the girl's blood was bright red, but some was pink, like a deer might leave if wounded in the chest. Traces of the pink blood had been left higher than the bright red blood. A few small branches and leaves had been painted with smears of the pink stain. Richard doubted that the girl could have gone so far with an injury to her lungs. The pink blood remained a mystery.

There was a spray of blood against a short bushy birch sapling, a spray like a chest wound. That would agree with the pink fluid, but no human could be wounded in the lungs and keep going like this. Richard studied the ground in front of the birch bush. The girl's feet had scuffed the leaves here, and there was blood on the ground too. She had fallen, probably against the bush, then onto the ground.

Richard felt sorry for the quarry, but also admiration. She was tough, whoever she was.

Richard prayed that the girl's trail would soon lead to her hiding place, or at least to where she may have collapsed from exhaustion or lack of blood. He needed to find her before Euglena could become an issue.

The trail continued toward the pond, then veered to the east, then at one point almost curved into a circle. If the girl was smart, she would try to find a place to rest. Euglena would not be able to find her stationary any better than if she was moving around.

The blood sign became more sparse. She must be coming to the end of her energy and was slowing, which ironically was leaving much less evidence of her passage.

An aspen sapling, its smooth bark as white as parchment, must have been pushed aside or used to steady the fleeing girl. A bloody hand print had been left on it at about waist height.

Richard could easily discern the blood-stained swirls of the girl's fingerprints. As he knelt down to look closer, a grouse thundered from the forest floor, causing Richard's heart to thunder in return. Someone ran off through the trees, breaking branches as they fled from the commotion. The someone was only a yearling doe.

Richard continued to follow the blood-blazed trail deeper into the forest. Soon he was following the trail only by the leaves the girl had turned with her bare feet as she had walked through the woods. A tough trail to follow. Richard was worried that he might lose her track.

The path came to another of the small clearings cut for the benefit of wildlife and hunters. Huge, round bales of straw dotted the field. New hay was growing tall around the forgotten mounds of straw. The small, secluded field was idyllic—serene and peaceful.

A bloodied girl, dressed only in a skirt and a black bra, was in the small meadow. She had seen him and was now trying to run away. Definitely not a doe this time. Richard followed in pursuit. She fell and before she could get back up, Richard caught her by her hair.

CHAPTER 25

The bloody white blouse belonged to a French-American girl, Suzanne Johanna de Lafayette. Another "de," but no relation to our Italian-American "de Antonio." By the time she was seventeen, Suzanne had already completed most of the courses offered at the community college in Grand Rapids, courses taken while she was still in high school. Every year the good schools around Grand Rapids turned out several outstanding young men and women, but Suzanne de Lafayette was head and shoulders above the best. No contest.

There was another side to Suzanne, however, that many people had come to discover and love over the years. Suzanne's mom worked for a nursing home in the area. When Suzanne was young she would sometimes come to the nursing home and wait for her mom to get off work. One day, when she was seven years old, she brought in a book that she was reading. "Hatchet." She decided to get some of the residents together in a corner of the television room and read a couple chapters to her audience. They loved it. From then on she would bring in books to read to them.

After a time, there came to be more people coming to listen to her read than there were watching television. So besides her young friends, Suzanne came to have many older friends, too. At any one time, she might tell the residents of the rest home that she would have to skip an evening to be with her young friends, but at other times she might tell her schoolmates that she could not do something because she had plans with her older friends. That was Suzanne. The older men and women loved to listen to Suzanne read her books to them, but what they loved the most was to have someone young come to visit them. The book was just an excuse to be together.

This first summer away from home she was staying at a dorm at Bemidji State and taking her first classes after an early graduation from her high school. Suzanne's parents, Thomas and Martha, were rich in pride for their only daughter, but poor in finances. They had helped as much as they could, but Suzanne had to provide for most of her college expenses. She had taken a job at a local Bemidji tavern, north on old 71.

Suzanne wanted to major in history. She was skilled in most every subject, but history was her true love, that is, besides her boyfriend, John Bridger. She had met him one evening at a promotional meeting for new members at the Grand Rapids biathlon club. They were both still in high school, and John remembered her from one of his classes. She said that she knew how to ski, but had never fired a gun before.

John Bridger, acting the big man as teenage guys are wont to do, told her that he could teach her how to shoot and convinced her to join the club. She did.

She was a good student and, to his great dismay, she could soon ski better than him and shoot better than him. A fact that she would gladly demonstrate every time they went out together on the snowy trails north of Grand Rapids. John was two years older than she was, but due to Suzanne's brains and work ethic, only one year ahead in class. In her sophomore cum junior year in high school he went off to college at Bemidji State. Suzanne finished her high school courses a year later and then pursued him to BSU. Now he was her fiancé.

Suzanne de Lafayette was a small girl. Wiry, with long smooth muscles. Dark walnut hair fell several inches past her shoulders. Dark olive skin. She was sometimes mistaken for a Native girl until she looked at you. Dark blue eyes, the blue like one of the deep Minnesota lakes on the Iron Range. As far as she could tell from her efforts at genealogy, she was all French. She was also all American.

Suzanne had first made love to her boyfriend John Bridger when she was fourteen, a fact and an age that she herself finds ridiculous, but with no regrets—especially since she was raped just a year later. Two drunken predators had abducted her from the streets of Grand Rapids after she had gotten off her part-time job. They had taken her out into the forests and had repeatedly raped her. Then they had tied her to a tree and played a game to see who could extinguish the most cigarettes on her naked body. When they went back to their vehicle to get more beer and cigarettes, Suzanne bit through the twine that held her to the tree and fled into the forest.

A search party had found her two days later—bug-bitten, cold, hungry, and dehydrated, but alive. She had stayed with the living by covering herself with an insulating blanket of dead leaves and by concentrating on warm dreams of John Bridger. Simply put, she had willed herself to stay alive.

The predators that had attacked her were caught and tried and sent to prison. Some in the state media wrote sympathy pieces for the rapists—how sorry the citizens of Minnesota should be because the poor boys' lives were now wrecked. After her ordeal, Suzanne had noticed that the media in Minnesota always did sympathy pieces for rapists. And also that special interest groups came out of the woodwork like rats, complaining about the awfulness of death penalties for predators, stating that it was the predators' parents, environment, or their schools that were the real cause of the violence, while yet others insinuated that the victims must have been at least partially at fault. The media jackals, as she and Gov. Jesse called them, made her sick.

Suzanne had also noticed that only a rape victim's death was ever adequate enough to bring out "true" compassion from television and newspapers. The media did not care about the girls and young women that were raped and left alive. Those were the imperfect victims, as were the females that did not make a really good story, like young girls not over the age of eighteen, prostitutes, lower class working girls, women with children, minorities, gang-rapes, white girls raped by minorities, girls that had been drugged or had been gotten drunk, runaways, whatever stories that could not be worked well. Politically incorrect victims. Imperfect victims.

From then on, Suzanne's aim during the biathlon became ever sharper. Her muscles during the skiing became ever stronger. She had vowed to herself that she would never again be a victim. At least not without putting up a struggle.

One might wonder how a girl could be brutalized twice in as many years, but in our culture with so many females being attacked, it is inevitable that some will be attacked on more than one occasion. The same night that Else had made love to Richard, Suzanne had once again been forced to fight for her survival.

~

Early last evening, Suzanne had driven north on 71 to the tavern where she worked. She had locked the door of her Malibu and was walking through the dusty parking lot. Suzanne was only seventeen, but she had lied about her age to get the job. She needed the money, and though the place was sleazy and the owner was always hitting on the waitresses, it paid better than most of the businesses in the area and she needed the money for books and tuition.

Ahead of her Suzanne saw the two black men, one a giant, the other thin and greasy. But she did not see in time the white boy that was coming up behind her. He grabbed her and put his hand over her mouth. She bit it and he let out a high-pitched yelp. Suzanne turned to run, but the white boy held her long enough for the two blacks to come up and grab her. She kicked at the men and screamed for help.

If any males in Beltrami County had heard her, they had minded their own business and had driven away from the trouble. Suzanne fought as violently as she could. Twice she almost broke free.

The three men forced her into a dirty white van and the white boy drove away, with the two blacks in back to guard her. The black giant was so strong that Suzanne gave up any hope of escape while imprisoned in the van. They soon came to a neglected cabin near the national forest. Suzanne was new to the Bemidji area, but she had a general idea of about where she had been taken.

The greasy black attacker dragged her from the van and to the cabin that Suzanne could now see was just a broken-down shack. She kicked up with both of her legs at the door, a foot on each side of the entrance, and tried to push herself free of her captors. The giant yelled to his greasy comrade not to let her go, and then the smaller black spun her around and hit her in the face with his fist. Suzanne could feel her nose break and its blood soak the front of her blouse. The men did not try to hide their identities. The greasy Euglena, the giant Odis Blister, and the white boy, who was not really white but was maybe Mexican and perhaps part oriental with some white mixed in—was alternately called Alberto, Rodriguez, or Junior.

Suzanne figured that they would kill her when they were finished with her. Their willingness to use violence did not bode well for her survival if she did not fight. She would have to escape. But how?

Once in the shack they forced her onto the floor, as Euglena and Junior argued over who would be first. Junior said that he should be because the girl was an Indian and he liked to knock around Indian girls. Euglena dismissed his reasoning and raped her first, tearing the buttons from the front of Suzanne's blouse as he pulled it off her, and scraping her breasts as he pulled her bra from her chest. Odis sat on a wooden chair at the back of the cabin, leaned against a support beam, and watched. He had put on a football helmet.

Junior raped her next. Before he was finished he pulled out and rolled her over and sodomized her. Suzanne could feel blood on her rear. When Junior saw the blood he exclaimed with glee that he had gotten a virgin. He pushed her head into the floor as he continued to rape Suzanne. The man called Alberto Rodriguez Junior had a strong desire to hurt her. Euglena said something about damaged goods not being worth as much and that Junior should take it easy on the bitch. Suzanne wondered if the greasy black had plans for her that were worse than death. Could she be broken to a predator's will? She doubted it.

Sometime during the rapes and the sodomy, her skirt and shoes had been removed. Now, like our Amber in Euglena's closet, she was completely naked. They made her stay that way as Odis Blister fried eggs on a dirt-encrusted stove. Alberto Rodriguez Junior put her on his lap as he ate, raping and sodomizing her as he filled his face with eggs, calling her his whore. Blister got mad at something that Suzanne could not discern and threw the last of his eggs on her, getting her hair sticky from the yolks. At that, Junior turned angry and started to slap Suzanne until she felt like she would pass out, then he picked her up and threw her face down on the table and forced her into oral sex. She resisted again, but Alberto would choke her until she passed out and then choke her again when she came to.

She must not have regained consciousness at one point, because when she did come to, Junior was pushing on her chest in a clumsy effort at resuscitation. She felt one of her ribs break and she cried out. She had to survive. She relented. The smell and taste of the sodomy gagged her. Euglena and Blister were laughing at Junior's antics and Suzanne's pain. With a growing desire for revenge, Suzanne willed herself to survive so she could someday kill these bastards.

She prayed, "Dear Baby Jesus, let me live so I can exterminate this vermin."

Junior noticed the old cigarette scars from the old rape. He lit himself a cigarette and smoked it down as he continued to rape her, and then he crushed the stub into the tender skin between Suzanne's armpit and breast. Four more cigarettes were extinguished that way, Suzanne screaming in agony each time.

Junior noticed second the gold string earrings that Suzanne had pierced through her ears. He took them in his hands and pulled them off, their metal wires cutting through Suzanne's earlobes as they were ripped away.

The senselessness of the ripped earlobes angered Suzanne, not that being raped, beaten, and sodomized made sense either. But the ruined earlobes triggered a rage in Suzanne. She slapped Junior across the face with her right hand, then again with her left.

That was all the violence she would get to give. Euglena hit her in the back with his fists until she fell to the ground. The pain from her broken rib sent her mind reeling. Junior stepped on the first hand that had slapped him and rocked on its knuckles. Suzanne would not even be allowed the privilege to fight this vermin one-on-one.

Odis Blister had yet to rape her, or to do anything but beat her and mess her with eggs, and to wear his stupid football helmet. There seemed to be other plans for his needs.

The men told her to get dressed, which she did as best as she could. Blister had thrown her shoes to burn in the cabin's wood stove, where they gave off a burnt rubber smell. Good to cover the smell of these bastards, thought Suzanne. Suzanne had to hold the front of her blouse closed because its buttons had been torn loose. The men were still laughing and joking and did not notice that Suzanne had swept a thin-bladed fillet knife from the table and had tucked it into the folds of the front of her blouse, where she held it as she held the front of her torn blouse closed.

The men took flashlights from the center of the egg-spattered table, loaded her into the white van, and drove to someplace in the forest, to a wide trail in the woods. Suzanne thought the trail might be for snowmobiles, or left from an old logging operation. She was not sure where she was at.

Odis walked off first, the feeble light from his flashlight bouncing into the darkness. Then sometime later the other two rapists escorted her down the trail toward where Odis had gone. A few minutes later they began to slap the back of her head and kick her legs while they ordered her to run down the trail. Suzanne did not ask why. She took off running.

A hundred yards or so she realized that Blister must be waiting up ahead. That was his perversion, she figured, to wait in ambush. She slowed to a fast walk and tried to scan the trail. There was an opening ahead where the path got wider. Night was coming on too quickly and she could not see very well in the woods, but it was lighter where the path opened up. Still, she did not see Blister. Her sixth sense told her that he must be there, but her other senses could not locate him.

Then she heard a tiny noise—a scrape; it had come from a high tree overhanging the trail. She could see a large form—like a great bear in the tree. She knew that she could not go back because the other two were behind her, so she pretended that she had not seen the ambush and kept walking straight ahead, her head pointed down to the ground but her eyes looking up at the waiting beast.

Blister, head helmeted for action, fell from the tree as Suzanne passed underneath. Suzanne jumped forward, not backwards as her would-be rapist might expect, and as she did so she spun around and swung the fillet knife overhead in a long arc into the center of the giant's back. He screamed like the stuck pig that he was. Suzanne whirled around and ran like a deer. Blister had just enough adrenaline left to grab the edge of the fabric of her bloodied and buttonless shirt, but Suzanne pulled free and slipped out of her blouse and made her escape.

After she had put a distance between herself and her attackers, she left the trail and hid in the undergrowth. She could hear Euglena and Junior running after her. They had apparently not spent any time in being concerned about their fellow bleeding rapist with the knife in his back. Like tiny searchlights, the beams of their flashlights swept past her, scanning into the trees of the forest. Suzanne was hiding much closer to the trail than the men expected, so they overlooked her as she lay frozen at their feet.

The tough, hollow stems of horsetail scraped against her injured skin, but its touch was as a soft caress compared to what violence would happen to her if she was caught. A musky pollen itched her nose and tried to make her sneeze. Though her nose was broken, she pinched her nostrils closed with her fingers until the urge to sneeze came under her control.

She could hear them talk. They were very angry. Junior left for a while to extract Suzanne's knife from Blister and to take the bleeding pig back to the shack. When he returned Suzanne was still pinned to her hiding place, unable to move because of the close proximity of Euglena.

Suzanne decided she would have to hold tight like a baby fawn, running only if about to be stepped on. Twice the men came so close she thought she could smell their filth. The beams of their lights swept high above her recumbent form, sweeping the branches of the forest as if they were searching for a perched owl or a treed raccoon, instead of a half-naked, injured girl. After a long while, an eternity to the frightened fawn of a girl, they moved back down the trail, closer to where their van was parked. Evidently they would block her path of escape as they continued to search for her.

Suzanne vowed to herself that she would survive to kill the men that did this to her. They had no right to steal her freedom and her dignity. Her body was her right. These three would not live fat and pampered in the state's prison like her other attackers were doing. They would pay if she could help it. They would damn well pay.

Quietly she rose from her hiding place in the primordial horsetail plants and slid deeper into the forest. Somehow the ankle of her left foot had been badly sprained and now it was swelling and causing her trouble. If she had to run again, she would be in great trouble. As if she was not already in great trouble.

Her nose, pushed slightly to the right when broken by Euglena, throbbed with pain and caused her eyes to water. She was bleeding from innumerable small cuts on her chest and arms, cuts which she must have gotten during her dash into the forest. She was concerned about how much damage the rape and sodomy may have done to her young body. The fresh burns on the sides of her breasts were tender and painful, enough so, she knew, that shock would be a possibility.

Thankfully, the cold of the night kept the insects away. The little crawly ones, not those with their flashlights. But half-naked, clothed only in skirt, panties, and bra, she might die of exposure. She did not want to curve back to the trail and maybe run into the rapists, but she did not know if she was walking in a straight line either. She walked for a long time.

The walking kept her warm, but she knew that it would also drain her energy. She would not be able to walk indefinitely. Drops of blood marked her slow passage, and at times she had to steady herself by grasping saplings, all of which she knew was leaving a trail. She didn't think the vermin trying to find her could follow a trail with much skill, otherwise they would have already found her. But she worried about the marks of blood she was leaving on the baby trees and the drops of blood that were falling onto the leaves of the forest floor.

Suzanne hid in a tangle of blowdowns for a while, but she realized it was not enough of a hiding place, so after a long time she crawled from under the brush and branches. She was getting tired. She was in pain. She was intensely thirsty. As she slowed her pace, she could sense that the drops of blood were fewer and farther apart. Either her wounds were clotting, or she was running out of blood. The thought that she might be running out of blood struck her as funny.

Suzanne whispered to herself and the wind, "When I get a chance to kill the vermin after me, that will be more funny that losing all my blood." The wind whistled in agreement.

Even in the dim darkness she could see well enough to notice a shiny smear on the ground. She bent down and ran her finger through her own old blood. She had circled back on her trail.

Suzanne decided that she needed to rest. She searched for a home to hide in as she walked along. It was almost too dark to see, but that was to her benefit—the better to stay invisible from the ugly pair of remaining pursuers.

The forest opened into a small field, maybe just one or two acres. An odd place and an odd size for a field. Maybe a clearing made for grouse or deer? Several round bales of straw, like sleeping elephants, dotted the field. One of the bales sat next to a slight depression in the ground. With a great effort, Suzanne rolled the round bale onto the depression. She tunnelled under the straw until she reached the edge of the makeshift cave, then lay down on her naked stomach and backed in under the bale. She fit, with elbow room to spare. In a few minutes she was warm. As she fell asleep, she hoped that she would not snore like her boyfriend John Bridger always kidded her she did. She didn't think she did, but she wasn't really sure.

Pleasant thoughts of John Bridger and six hundred pounds of clean straw kept her warm throughout the night. She needed to rest, but her sleep was fitful at first. She awoke at every sound, it seemed. But finally she did sleep, succumbing totally, the warm straw and total exhaustion doing their jobs.

In the morning she awoke to clear skies and sun. Thank God it had not rained, the depression under the straw would have become a cold bathtub. She peered out from under the straw, viewing the field from the same vantage point as the field mouse that was sitting a few inches in front of her face, rudely staring at her with its dark, beady eyes. "Get out of my way little mouse," she whispered. "I have to pee really badly." The mouse ran off. Suzanne moved, everything hurt, she rested, she moved again. The process repeated itself until she was free to pee.

The bright sun reflected off a nearby lake, sending signals of blue patches to Suzanne. She was so thirsty, from long hours without any liquid and loss of blood, but drinking untreated water was not safe. She hiked the short distance to the sparkling reflections, to a small, weedy bay connected to a small lake or pond. With parched throat she peered longingly into its shallow depths. For many minutes she stood at the edge, pondering the chances of getting sick if she would take a drink, then at length gave in to her intense thirst and rationalizations of clean springtime water. Satisfied after filling her stomach with the cool water, she retreated to her burrow. She repeated the process four more times during the day.

Suzanne was afraid to leave the safety of her secluded hideaway for an extended period of time, besides, she did not know exactly where she was or in what direction she needed to travel. She prayed that college kids and cops might be looking for her body at this very moment. But most of all she did not want to run into the rapists again. She spent the day in her straw home, hoping that no wolves would come and blow her house away.

Toward early evening, resigning herself to another night under the straw, she decided to drink one more time from the lake. She thought that she must have had gallons of water by now, but she was still intensely thirty. She must have lost a great deal of blood during her escape into the darkness.

As Suzanne returned from the lake and walked into the field, it was already getting cold. She was almost looking forward to her straw home, her bed with the mouse. She did not notice the man that was fast approaching until he was at the edge of the field. She began to run, but fell, her ankle giving way as she tried to sprint toward the trees. The man ran after her and caught her by her hair.

CHAPTER 26

Slowly, "I—am—your—friend," said the man that had caught her in the secluded meadow.

She looked closely at his face; he let go of her hair. He took her again, this time by her arm, and helped her to her feet. He was an older man—not much hair and what little there was—was grey. Blue eyes that she read as either gentle or a killer's, or both.

"The rapists are on the main trail, so we need to get away from here," said the man.

"No," she answered. "I have a place where we can hide. We will be safe there." She led him to her straw burrow and showed him how it was situated.

The man glanced at her breasts, pushed up as they were by a black, too tight bra, then at her broken nose, and said, "Sorry, I haven't seen a strange, half-naked girl with a broken nose in a long time now, so I don't know exactly how to act." At that, the man smiled at her.

His smile both irritated her and calmed her fears. Whatever her reservations had been before, the girl felt compelled to trust in the old man. If she was wrong, she perversely figured, she would certainly only die. They got under the straw together. Two bodies made for even more warmth, though it was very crowded and they had to lay pressed tight to each other. The mouse would have to find another place to hide tonight.

"My name is Richard Bede."

"Mine is Suzanne. Suzanne de Lafayette, from Grand Rapids." She started to cry softly. She didn't know why...yes she did, she now had someone to share this ordeal with.

Richard acted as if he did not notice Suzanne crying, saying only, with yet another warm and irritating smile, "You really stink, girl."

As pissed as she was at the old man's clumsy efforts to cheer her, Suzanne had difficulty keeping from laughing, she certainly must have stunk to high heaven. At least she could share her misery with another human. That alone might bring a smile to her dirt-smeared face.

Richard explained about finding her bloodied white blouse and about recognizing, from his prison days, Euglena's voice when the do-ragged child molester/rapist/pimp had approached along the trail. Suzanne was not so sure she had made the correct decision getting under the straw with an actual convict, but what the hell.

Suzanne noticed Richard noticing the fresh cigarette burns on the side of her breast. The small round wounds were slowly leaking a pink-tinged watery fluid. The mystery of the pink blood was solved.

"Junior saw my old scars and decided new ones would be fun," said Suzanne as she showed the old man some of her old scars. "If I can help it, Junior will not get to spend his days in the comforts of a nice safe prison—like my first attackers—protected and pampered by the State of Minnesota. This bastard will pay," she spat.

Suzanne went on to explain about the previous attack on her, the media concern with the "poor boys" that had raped and scarred her, and the privileged treatment in prison that her abductors had been given by the state due to their status as sex offenders.

"At least the people of Grand Rapids were on my side, otherwise I would have been alone, or at least alone with my parents and my boyfriend."

Richard told her about the attack on his own daughter, Jeanette; how it was similar to Suzanne's earlier ordeal, but also how he thought it was different: how many people in the Bemidji area sided with the rapists, how the rapists were "punished" with just two weeks of sexual assault classes, how he was convicted for saving his daughter's life.

"Do not be too quick to defend yourself in this community," said Richard.

Then he told of how it was he came to be in this part of the forest, lying under a huge bale of straw with a shoeless, half-naked, cigarette-branded college girl. About the beautiful Native girl that he had found lifeless at the shore of Rice Pond.

"My family moved to Minnesota from central Wisconsin," said Richard. "We were drawn by the beautiful wildness of your north country. But we never imagined that we would have to contend with crime and violence."

"Welcome to the land of political correctness," said Suzanne.

"And endless sympathy for rapists. This has cost my family a great deal. And just when I thought I was free, I cross paths again with yet more scum."

Suzanne realized she was much the same as the old man. "I know just how you feel," she said.

Richard looked again at her ill-clothed top and the burns on the girl's breasts. "You better take my shirt. It is warm and I have a T-shirt underneath which will be good enough for me." Richard wiggled out of his long-sleeved shirt and gave it to Suzanne.

"Thank you very much, Sir," she said, graciously accepting the shirt which might be too warm under a quarter ton of straw and which would most likely stick to the pink fluid leaking from her burns. But at least she would be presentable. "Thank you."

The "Sir" made Richard lonely for his new guests back at his log home in the field near Puposky. He missed Amber and Thor.

Richard needed to change the tone of the conversation. "Tell me the good things," he said.

The abrupt change angered her. "Well, let's see, recently I've been abducted, raped, branded and tortured, beaten and broken, and now I am being hunted by perverted killers, it seems."

The old man did not react, which Suzanne thought was good.

"I'm sorry, you mean the good things from my previous life. Well, I have a man in my life that I love very much, parents living back in Grand Rapids that I love very much, and a multitude of friends that I love very much. I guess I really am lucky. If I can survive tonight and get out of this forest alive, then I will be really, truly lucky."

"You are, really lucky about your love, that is, and you will be truly lucky also, when you get out of this predicament in one piece, if somewhat broken of course."

Suzanne took over from there, telling the old man about her mom and dad, her boyfriend, her other friends, her exploits in high school. She talked about her new school at Bemidji State University and what a great opportunity it would be. It was good to be able to talk about her past life and her future plans.

Later into the evening the conversation trailed off, replaced by a deep quiet; Richard, lying next to Suzanne, was soon asleep, much to the girl's astonishment. As time passed and the sun shifted lower in the sky, Suzanne left her straw hideaway to drink from the lake. Once returned to her...their hiding place, she debated whether she should wake Richard so she could have someone to talk to again. She decided to close her eyes for just a few minutes before she woke him. Soon she was asleep herself.

When she awoke, it was light again, though the morning sun was still below the tops of the trees. Wet dew hung on the grass in front of their burrow. The scent of the straw, with the cool dampness of the new day, was stronger now and itched her broken nose—which she could not even scratch.

Suzanne was thirsty again. She crawled from under the warm straw, and as she did so, crouched half out of her lair, heard Euglena's ugly voice yelling for Junior. The greasy rapist had seemingly appeared from nowhere and had spotted her motions.

Suzanne was momentarily frozen in place. Richard changed that. He scrambled from beneath the bale of straw, taking Suzanne by the wrist and pulling her with him, away from Euglena's voice. Suzanne was stumbling from the strain on her injured foot and could not keep pace. Richard put her arm over his shoulder to take some of Suzanne's weight off her sprained ankle. Like a painful sack race, Suzanne ran and hobbled and jumped away with the old convict.

Junior's voice could be heard in the distance. There was a single shot and the whine of a bullet as it flew high over the heads of the old man and the girl. Suzanne directed Richard to the small bay of the lake she had found and out onto a short peninsula of land.

Richard realized that they would be trapped unless they acted quickly. "Can you swim?" he asked.

"Not very well. Besides, we would be sitting ducks out there on the water," said Suzanne.

"Then we have to work back up this peninsula and sneak around the lake. I recognize this as the south side of Rice Pond, so if we follow the shore west from here it will lead us to the forest road," reasoned Richard as he turned to run back from where they had just come. But Euglena appeared in front of them, running after them and running out of breath. He was armed with a dirty fillet knife like the one Suzanne had shoved into Blister's back, like the one that Blister had earlier used in his attack on Richard at North Twin. Richard took Suzanne by the wrist again, spun toward the lake, and ran to its edge. They were trapped. And if Junior could home in on Euglena's yelling, then the old man and girl would have to contend with Junior's gun as well as Euglena's knife.

Richard looked again to the lake. A beavers' den had been built by a colony of the furry rodents, just off the tip of the land. The water was shallow and clear both near the shore and for some distance into the pond. Richard saw a green stake and its green metal tag—which he knew was the marker for a beaver trap. Not man deadly, but strong steel. Richard knew that the beaver trap would be chained to the stake, hidden in the muck and debris of the bottom of the pond. Grabbing one of last year's cattails as a pathetic weapon, he led Suzanne into the shallow water and around the stake with its green tag, placing them behind the trap and facing the shoreline.

Suzanne did not see the rusty iron as it hid arachnidlike at the edge of the pond. "What the hell are we doing? You can't do anything with a cattail, for God's sake."

Euglena did not see the trap either. He splashed headlong into the water after his quarry, amazed when Richard threatened him with the soft cattail, and laughed the same mean laugh he had the night before when Junior had crushed his tobacco firebrands into the sides of Suzanne's breasts. Then he stepped into the steel jaws of the trap.

The jaws snapped and Euglena screamed. Though not a huge trap, like those for bears or coyotes, the ragged steel bands of the trap bit hard into Euglena's shin. He fell face first into the pond. Suzanne brushed past Richard's shoulder and stepped on the back of Euglena's neck, holding him under the water with the weight of her burnt and violated body. Euglena struggled to escape, his hands and forearms sinking into the soft goo of the pond as he tried to push up from the bottom, while his leg was held tight by the trap as he tried to swim. Richard watched, unable to force himself to save the life of such an insect as Euglena.

Only the untimely arrival of the other predator, Alberto Junior, kept Suzanne from drowning the trapped rapist. Junior, barely visible between the tall pines and still far up the peninsula, fired two shots from a revolver, their bullets falling impotently farther out into the pond.

"We have to go, Suzanne." For a third time, Richard took her by her wrist and led her from danger. With the heel of her uninjured foot she kicked at Euglena as she was pulled away, snapping his head sideways like on an overcooked turkey neck.

"We will have to work up the peninsula until we are near Junior," said Richard. "Stay behind the larger trees and stay about twenty yards from me. He can't aim at both of us at once. When we are close, distract him, and I'll try to charge." Richard separated from Suzanne. "Just don't get killed," he added.

It took timing to work together without getting shot. Luckily, the killer rapist was still out of range; his bullets travelled the distance to them, but they lacked any accuracy. The gap was rapidly closing. Richard was amused to see that he was still armed with his cattail.

Junior had gotten into range at the same instant that Richard and Suzanne had worked their way to a small treeless space—a pretty glen at any other day—a death trap today. This was not good. They would have to rely on Junior coming to them, on Junior splitting the distance between them. But he was not doing that. He had slowed to a walk and was now approaching the white pine that Suzanne was hiding behind.

"We need to retreat," called Richard. But Suzanne was unable to move without giving Junior a clear shot at her.

Junior stopped and took careful aim at the part of Suzanne's face that was peering out from the side of the tree. Junior shot, taking bark from the tree where a moment before Suzanne had been watching the rapist approach for the kill.

As if in echo, there were two other shots. Richard turned toward the firing and looked into the dark forest from where Junior had just come. In his mind's eye he thought he saw a grey ghostly figure, a Southern civil war soldier, camouflaged by the soft, dappled sunlight filtered through the canopy of forest. Many of Richard's ancestors had fought for the Union, but a few died for the Lost Cause. Perhaps a ghost from the Rebel side of his family's history had come to give him assistance in this latest battle. The soldier would kneel and fire a shot, then stand and run through the wilderness, and again kneel and fire and run again toward the battle to repeat the action. Richard was reminded of stories of the ferocity of the fighting of the Battle of the Wilderness. Closer the soldier came. The reinforcements were...Else.

It was Else. Dark blue denim jeans. Grey, long-sleeved flannel shirt, black logging boots, grey cap with a faded red bill. Her wavy red hair pulled tight behind her head in a Civil War pony tail. Else looked the part of a Confederate foot soldier as she charged the enemy. While she ran, Else was working the bolt on an old, long-barrelled .22 rifle, firing intermittent shots at Rodriguez.

Junior retreated under Else's fire.

Else made it to the pines where Richard and Suzanne were taking cover.

One quick introduction, "This is Else, Suzanne," said Richard as he took the rifle, only to have it taken from him by Suzanne.

"Hi," said Else.

"The girlfriend I told you about," said Richard.

"Hi," said Suzanne.

Junior, courage restored, was returning, firing madly toward the trio. He had run about forty yards away, and had yet to reclaim much of that distance.

"I don't think the sights are set correctly," said Else.

Suzanne aimed at some imperceptible mark fifty or so yards away on a sun-bleached stump, fired, worked the bolt to bring another shell into the chamber, adjusted the windage and elevation of the rear peep sight, and repeated the process two more times in succession until Richard could see the small blemish that Suzanne was aiming at as she put the last shot into its center. The cold and snowy training of the biathlon was clearly imprinted onto Suzanne's nerves.

Again working the bolt, Suzanne swung the old varmint rifle in an arc toward Rodriguez, making a slight scraping noise as the brass cartridge was shoved into the steel barrel. The sound could be heard clearly in the panicked silence of the forest.

Rodriguez had come slightly closer to them as Suzanne had made her corrections on the sights of the rifle. He had fired and reloaded and fired again. Richard pulled Else to the ground to get under the bullets that now sounded like angry bees. Suzanne calmly stood her ground, jerking back just once, slightly, at the sound of one of Junior's shots. Bright red blood seeped from a fresh gash cut into the skin on the edge of her left shoulder.

Suzanne's chest rose with a breath and she froze; she could feel a trickle of the clear pink fluid run down from the side of her breast into the black fabric of her bra; Suzanne's only movement was a slow, imperceptible squeezing of her index finger on the trigger.

The shot was not as loud as Richard had expected, the sound of the small explosion being pushed out and away with the flying bullet, toward the rapist.

As on a Hindu woman at a holy festival, a red spot appeared high between Alberto's eyes. He fell slowly to his knees and sank back as if he was stretching his quadriceps before a foot race. The small bullet had entered his forehead and had bounced around the inside of his skull, tearing deadly paths through his pornographic mind until he was dead. Suzanne had already chambered another shell.

Euglena had been sneaking up behind them during the deadly dual. Now close, he made a charge at the old man and the two girls. Suzanne saw the movement and swung the rifle toward the rapist and fired. But Richard had also seen Euglena, and Suzanne's swing of her rifle, and had pushed the barrel up and to the side, sending the shot harmlessly into the sky. "Don't shoot another rapist," he ordered. "The jury."

Intent on Richard's back, Euglena did not notice Else as she stood and shifted her weight from rear foot to fore. The heavy-booted farm girl kicked the rapist's balls into the crack of his ass. Euglena, hands over his ears as if his head and not his crotch was injured, dropped his fillet knife and limped off into the trees toward the forest road and his dirty van.

"I'm sorry, Suzanne, but if our district attorney decides to try you for defending us, you will not want two dead rapists to explain to a jury, especially since one was not armed with a gun," stated Richard, illuminating the reason he had deflected the shot.

Then, to Else he said, "Remind me not to ever cheat on you, girl."

Else hugged her guy and smiled as Suzanne laughed. "I've been looking for you for hours," said Else as she hit him for the second time this week with her little hammer of a fist. Then she hugged him again, with equal parts relief and affection.

"I love you too," said Richard.

They walked out of the forest together, leaving Alberto Rodriguez Junior to rot in the woods. Euglena had made his escape in his van and was nowhere to be seen. Free of unnatural predators, the forest seemed beautiful and serene once again.

Richard drove Suzanne, with Else following in her own old truck, to Teddy Zemm's place, where Else had left the children and where Richard could use a phone.

Richard had a feeling that things weren't over with his former roommate, the presently balls-busted Euglena.

CHAPTER 27

Richard called Agent Kieran and told him who he had found in the woods—Suzanne de Lafayette, and what had happened to her. "They put fresh burns on her body, and I think on her mind too. She really wanted to kill each and every rapist, which may be a good thing. Extermination just might be in order."

"The Star Tribune out of Minneapolis and the newspaper from Grand Rapids have already picked up on your missing college girl," said Michael. "They have been using a high school photo that is really striking; the girl must be really pretty."

"I'm sure she is, sans a broken nose," said Richard.

Michael ignored the remark and continued to explain about the situation. "The story broke faster than usual because some guy had seen the abduction and had called a reporter he knew from the Star Tribune, and that kicked things off." Michael did not have to add that the clever Bemidji-area man did not try to stop the abduction. "Then from the newspaper reporters the story moved on to television, even before the first printing was off the press."

Michael also did not mention that the Bemidji paper did not have anything as yet about Suzanne, though Richard could guess as much from the exclusion. The district attorney probably did not have time to write the story for them.

"I have to get Suzanne to the hospital for attention to her injuries and for the sexual assault kit," said Richard. "I know a doctor there that I can trust to get the collecting done right. Dr. Luther. But first let's meet at Blister's shack, to look it over before the local cops step on everything."

Richard told Michael to meet him at the large boulder in front of Blister's driveway. Then Richard made a call to Joshua, connecting through to Joshua's cell phone. He was in the woods with his brother Foster, down by the mergansers' camp on North Twin, searching for signs of their missing father.

"I found a girl that had been abducted from a local tavern parking lot," said Richard, as if finding dead and injured girls was as common as finding pennies in the dirt.

Joshua scolded his dad for getting more deeply involved in the mystery, though he knew it was not his dad's fault who crossed his path; but Joshua was relieved that this time one of the good guys was not killed. Just broken and mutilated.

"You were worried that another woman would be attacked before the cops did their job and found the perverts," complained Joshua.

"And they're not caught yet. Though one is dead and another might be dying, for all we know," added Richard. And on their way to hell, for all we know. God would sort them out.

"They are not caught yet," continued Joshua's complaining, "though they had already been caught years ago and let out of prison by the system."

"Forget the system. All we need is self-defense."

"Like this Suzanne girl," finished Joshua.

Chad Rochambeau was called next, to let him know that one of Lenora's killers had been killed. Richard figured that Chad was using a cell phone, but he couldn't tell if that phone was in the Twin Cities area or if it was again near the herd of cow-slobber cows in Beltrami County. Next Richard called Cindy Heath to say the same, guessing that she was most likely standing next to Chad as she spoke. That would make sense because they had both loved Lenora.

Tony de Medici was contacted at his mother's house. A little girl answered the phone "hi," who passed the phone off to a slightly older girl "hello," who gave it to Maria de Evangilista, who said she loved him like one of her own sons and missed him and ordered him back home—to her home, "I have so many kisses for you," and who then reluctantly gave the phone to Tony.

Richard told the story over again to Tony, about the abducted girl with the precise aim.

Tony told Richard that word on the street was that certain elders of the Native community were hunting Euglena for stealing young Native girls and selling them into prostitution. "The Cities will be a mucho dangerous place for your greaseball for a very long time into the future," said Tony.

Lastly, Richard called and briefed his oldest son Terrie, who had the only real money in the family. "Keep in touch with Joshua and Foster," requested Richard, "and hunt up a good lawyer for Suzanne, just in case."

Terrie was upset that his dad had gotten more deeply involved in "his mess," as he called it, meaning his dad's mess. "If you were still on probation you would already be history. You need to get a greater distance from your mess. Lie low for a while."

Richard remembered the prophecy of Cassandra.

Else made a short call to Thomas Thorson. Amber, wordless, held back from the rest, appearing even paler than her usual translucent self, holding onto Thor Tollefson as if her brother might get lost in the confusion. Else's four little blond girls continued to play in the yard, oblivious to the adults, the impending danger, and any possibility of evil in the world.

Richard took the phone back when Else was finished, calling the Bemidji hospital and finding the thin-shouldered nurse that he knew worked there. "Have our doctor, Luther, get a sexual assault kit and be ready to take samples as soon as I bring in this girl that I have. Her name is Suzanne de Lafayette. She looks like one of our Native girls, but is French-American," added Richard.

Clara Zemm was trying to calm her husband, who was angry at the news of another woman being attacked, though Teddy Zemm was somewhat mollified that one of the rapists had been killed. "Serves the bastard right!" said the pair—Clara and Teddy—in that unison gained from a long life lived together.

Else gathered Amber, Thor, and her own four girls, and loaded them all into her pickup to take to Richard's house.

"While I was searching, the kids spent yesterday afternoon and last night here with Samantha and Sally, so I'm sure they are totally exhausted by now," said Else. "They will need a nap."

The kids looked refreshed. Richard suspected that it was Else that needed the nap. "I think you are right about the nap," said Richard as he kissed Else good-bye. He added, "I don't want Suzanne to be in trouble, but I'm glad that you did not shoot Junior. A poor farm girl from another county would be an easy target for our legal system here, especially since you had not been bodily injured yourself."

"I would be labeled a 'jack pine savage,' wouldn't I," suggested Else with a smile.

"You are a savage," said Richard, again kissing Else. He guessed that Else had read the "jack pine savage" term in one of the old news articles about Richard and his defense of his daughter, Jeanette.

"By the way, you should know that I called the police yesterday evening when you did not return," said Else. "I drove to the entrance of the trail to Rice Pond, where I saw more of those star-cut truck tracks pressed into the mud."

"But you did not see my truck, of course."

"It was so close...damn."

"Well, it ended all right." Except for the riddled brain of one of the rapists.

"The cops drove to the trail and I think down to the pond, but they said that nobody was there, so they left."

"The rapist gang may have parked across the road or even next to my truck," said Richard. "And I'm sure that at some point they must have taken their stabbed comrade away from the area."

"After the cops left, I had your boys come over and we phoned everyone we knew and searched every place that we could think of. All night. I'm so sorry I didn't find you sooner." Else did look upset and worried, perhaps feeling that for a second time she was unable to protect someone she loved.

As Else took his face in her hands and softly kissed him, Richard answered, "You and your little rifle did just fine."

Suzanne and Richard drove to the rock at Blister's shack. The drive was made in silence except when Suzanne told Richard that she would have to wait in the truck. She looked more tired than she had been under the straw. The stress of the past hours, the present drive to the shack with its nightmare memories, and the future with the police—all these things were straining her young nerves.

Agent Kieran was already there, leaning against the boulder with the quartz inclusion. "I have something to show you," he said, and led Richard down the drive and to the shack. The door was more open than shut, creaking arthritic as it swung lightly in the slight breeze. Inside, Richard could see Odis Blister slumped back against the beam at the rear of the shack. A silver arrow with bright pink feathers was sticking out the front of Blister's chest. From the depth of the impact, Richard guessed that the arrow had Blister stuck to the beam.

"He is deader than dead," said Kieran.

Walking inside, Richard picked up the gingham-patterned seat cushion. The blue cloth had fallen onto the dirt of the shack's floor. As he had believed, it was a torn dress that had been used as a cover for Blister's chair.

"Lenora put on a dress like this one, before or just after she was raped," said Richard. "Either her attackers had her clothe herself in gingham for their own perverted reasons, or Lenora was trying to tell us something."

"We will probably never know," said Agent Kieran.

As Richard left the shack he stopped before the crusty stove at the front of the single room and picked up a small coin that had fallen onto the floor.

"A hard way to get wealthy," said Michael.

"Harder than you know," returned Richard.

Suzanne was still sitting in Richard's truck. Her head was resting on the top edge of the back of the seat, wedged between the seat and the passenger door. Her eyes were closed. Her right fist was entangled in her hair, pulling on it ever so slightly, as if she needed to feel herself to know that she was still a living entity on earth.

"I have to get her to the hospital," said Richard, as he opened his creaky door, the noise of which momentarily opened Suzanne's eyes. "The county deputies can find us there if they need any information that you can't tell them."

At that, Richard drove away with his injured girl, but not without first stopping at the edge of the forest near where the muddy path leading to North Twin Lake passes close to the Zemm home. There, Richard walked through the woods to the rear of Teddy's garden and found the target that Samantha and Sally had used for their archery practice. He collected all of the pink-fletched silver arrows that were sticking out of the target and carried them back to his truck, putting them behind the rear bench seat, sticking them into the cross ribbing that held on the seat cover. Mission completed, Richard at last drove his battered and bruised Suzanne to the hospital in Bemidji.

The thin-shouldered nurse had done as she had been instructed. She had found Richard's Doctor Luther and she had gotten a sexual assault kit ready. With the nurse's help, Doctor Luther took samples from various places in and on Suzanne's body and from her clothes, and placed the various samples into the vials of the sexual assault kit. Richard told the nurse to hold the samples and to give them to BCA Agent Michael Kieran, only to Agent Michael Kieran, and to nobody but Michael Kieran.

Suzanne's boyfriend, John Bridger, had arrived after the samples for the kit had been taken. He had earlier arranged for the hospital to call him if his girl had showed up at the emergency room. John was a stark counterpoint to the dark French girl. His hair was sandy blond, his skin light—with freckles on his nose, his build strong—with wide shoulders and long legs. John raced to embrace his girl when he saw her.

"Suzanne, where have you been? What happened to you?" he said through a not-so-manly wash of tears.

Suzanne held her arms out to stop him. "No, not yet John. One of my ribs is broken."

Doctor Luther checked her chest as well as the rest of her. Suzanne would have to be wrapped in bandages for her ribs. One of Junior's bullets had grazed her right shoulder, leaving an angry furrow that looked much worse than it was.

"But other than my ribs and the ugly bullet scar and the broken nose and the fresh burns and the awful night of being attacked, the doctor says I am not seriously injured," complained Suzanne, quite justifiably.

"I'd like to get my hands on those bastards," threatened John. "I'd kill them."

"No you won't," said Richard. "Your job is to be here, free, for your girl. Can you do that?"

Apparently John Bridger was smarter than he was angry. After a bit he agreed to the logic. "I can do that."

"Thank you, John," said Suzanne. "I love you too."

Doctor Luther gave Suzanne a salve for her burns, antibiotic shots for the rape, and an anti-pregnancy medicine. Then he took Suzanne's nose between the palms of his hands and put it back to the center of her face. The sound of cartilage against bone was clearly audible. It would heal, but there would always be a bump on the bridge of her nose where it had been cracked. Suzanne did not flinch, cry out, or even complain as the doctor shifted bone over cartilage. Either she was as tough as Richard thought, or she was hurting too much to feel such a minor pain.

A small army of deputies arrived shortly afterward, with their own sexual assault advocate in tow—a twenty-something female. Richard had advised Suzanne to make one short statement to the local police, explaining in general what had happened, but to then ask for a lawyer when the heavy questions started to come.

Suzanne agreed to do so, not asking why, not having the energy to ask why. Initial statements were given by Suzanne and Richard, mostly by Suzanne, and then Suzanne was taken into another exam room where a second sexual assault kit was used to take a second set of samples, this time for the local authorities.

After the second exam and second set of samples, Suzanne was led into a small waiting room. It smelled of stale cigarette smoke and bad coffee. The smells upset her stomach, but she was too tired to complain. Officer G. Mandible and two other deputies were waiting for her.

Officer Mandible started. "We understand that you work at the tavern up on 71, correct?"

"Yes. I need money for college."

"You are only 17, correct?"

"I need money for college."

"Just answer our questions. No expanding on your own. It will go quicker that way." As he spoke, Officer Mandible tapped the clicker of his ballpoint pen on the glass top of the coffee table that sat between himself and Suzanne, as if to emphasize his words in little metallic ticking sounds.

"Yes," said Suzanne.

"Now, juveniles going into bars is a serious offense in this county, as I'm sure you may know. I'm not sure if the district attorney will charge you for that or not. We will have to see...um...on how well you cooperate and such. Correct?"

"Yes, I guess so." Suzanne really needed to rest. She could feel the big cop-heads pressing in on her.

"You shot Mr. Alberto Rodriguez. Is that correct?" The other two officers nodded in agreement.

"Yes. I did."

"That was Rodriguez Junior. Correct?"

"Yes. I believe so. When I was being raped last night I heard the other two call him Rodriguez and Alberto and Junior. So he was a junior, I suppose."

"We will get to the alleged rape later," barked G. Mandible.

Suzanne's frayed nerves caused her to jump visibly in her seat.

"For now just stick to the facts," ordered G. Mandible.

"It is a fact I was raped. Do you want to see what a cigarette does to a woman's breasts?" asked Suzanne, her anger using up a little more of the little bit of energy that she had left.

If the cops were moved by her outburst, they did not show it. The radio of one of the silent officers crackled. The officer answered it and then stepped out into the hallway for his conversation. Suzanne felt the officer wanted privacy from her ears. G. Mandible waited.

Presently, the officer came back in and spoke to Officer Mandible. "The district attorney wants to know where the rifle came from. He said he needs that information for his case."

G. Mandible turned to Suzanne and asked her about the rifle. "It is important that we find out about the rifle, for your sake. Do you understand? OK? Where exactly did you get the rifle from?"

"Did we finish talking about the rape?" asked Suzanne, equal parts exhausted and pissed off.

Officer Mandible explained about the rape. He seemed to know a great deal about such things. "Here is what the deal is. OK. You are underage, a minor. You work in a tavern. That is wrong, but maybe if you cooperate we can forget about that. Anyway, you are around alcohol and presumably drink some. I don't know. But it makes sense. A lot of juveniles do that kind of thing. So anyway you drink some, then somehow you connect up with someone, with Junior. You go to his place. There is some stuff going on. Alcohol. I don't know, I'm just saying. You are tired. It is late for a juvenile girl such as yourself. It is late for someone such as yourself and you must be tired. It makes sense. Maybe you do something you regret, then you panic and start making some false accusations. You want to blame the guy. Your sex was an indiscretion. It is dark out and there is alcohol. You spend time at the tavern where there is alcohol. That's not right, but maybe we can go easy on you there if you tell us the truth. You already lied to get into the tavern. So we know you lied. Anyway, it is dark out and maybe some sex takes place and you later panic and want to blame someone. So you maybe are confused by the alcohol. I don't know. I wasn't there. But it makes sense. There is the lateness of the night and the alcohol and the darkness. You can't see too good. The alcohol maybe affects your vision. It is really dark out and you have sex with someone. Maybe consensual. Maybe it is someone else, but you think it is some other guy like Mr. Rodriguez. But you are not sure. You can't be sure. But you panic and accuse people, maybe innocent people who later get hurt by your indiscretion."

The other two officers nod their heads in unilateral agreement with G. Mandible. Suzanne does not nod—she does not agree and cannot be coerced into agreeing. There is no bilateral agreement.

"So, you are a juvenile, maybe not used to alcohol, it is really dark outside, you can't see who you are having consensual sex with, then you panic and blame someone else. An innocent person. Then you lose yourself in the forest and when your friend comes to find you, you shoot him. But we can maybe forget about the alcohol if you can just cooperate. OK. Where did you get the rifle?"

Suzanne's eyes were open, but they had lost focus. The monologue and the big cop-heads were weighing in on her. Somewhere deep in her mind she heard Richard's last message.

"I want a lawyer," she said.

"You are not arrested," said G. Mandible. "Let's just talk some more. OK? Did Richard Bede give you the rifle? He is a convict, which you may not have known, but we can forget about your being with a known convict and maybe forget about the alcohol, if Richard Bede gave you the rifle. OK?"

"I want a lawyer."

"You are not arrested yet. We can't tell if we want to arrest you if we don't know what happened, so you must cooperate. That is why we need to know about the rifle. OK?"

Suzanne's eyes closed, her head fell back against the cushioned seat she was sitting on, and she became as silent as the mouse of her first night under the straw.

G. Mandible, with his nodding heads as witnesses, intensified his interrogation of Suzanne.

Suzanne's silence.

"Where did you get the rifle?"

Suzanne's silence.

"Where did you get the alcohol?"

Suzanne's silence.

"Where did you get the bullets?"

Suzanne's silence.

"Where did you have consensual sex?"

Suzanne's silence.

"We know you lied...cooperate."

Suzanne's silence.

"Alcohol...maybe forget...where did you get the rifle?"

Suzanne's silence.

"Consensual...rifle...some sex...rifle sex...dark night...outside sex consensuals...maybe...where...alcohol...sex...maybe sex."

Suzanne's eyes felt good to remain closed. She remembered when she was a very little girl and a very mean dog had bitten her on the calf and had held on and torn her flesh. The dog bite had hurt her. But she survived.

The cop noises sounded like they were a long way off.

"Rifle?"

Suzanne's silence.

"Alcohol...maybe not trouble...forget about..."

Suzanne imagined that she could hear the heads of the other two officers nodding in agreement.

"Bede rifle."

Suzanne's silence.

"Richard Bede...and rifle."

She remembered now as she sat hurting, flashes of red and green light behind her closed eyes, the mean dog and the pain it had caused her as its teeth had torn at her calf.

"Rifle? Richard Bede? Rifle? Richard Bede? Rifle?"

Her ass hurt, and her breasts hurt from where she had been burned in the shack, the pink fluid was leaking from her body and sticking to Richard's shirt, and her vagina was sore, and her head hurt from the big cop-heads pressing in on her, and her nose hurt, and her broken rib was still broken, and her ankle hurt where it had sprained, and her feet hurt from running barefoot through the forest, and her legs hurt from the cuts made by branches as she had escaped into the darkness of the forest. But she survived.

Richard had been arrested for the murder of Odis Elvie Blister, presumably for having stuck an arrow into Duluth's missing pervert. John Bridger, having stated that he was Suzanne's boyfriend, and also two years older that his girl, had been arrested for statutory rape.

Suzanne had been escorted, partly led and partly dragged, by the two nodding deputies to the back seat of their police car. Somewhere between consciousness and unconsciousness, Suzanne de Lafayette had been arrested for the murder of Alberto Rodriguez Junior.

CHAPTER 28

The district attorney made a preemptive strike in the local paper, The Bemidji News, saying, "I don't think there is any doubt about it, he (Alberto Rodriguez Junior) was not in any way involved in an attack on the alleged female victim."

The newspaper went on to explain that the female in question, an underage college girl who had lied in order to work in a tavern, had apparently had consensual sex with an individual, possibly after she had drunk alcohol at the tavern where she worked, then had panicked at the possibility that her boyfriend might find out and had shot an innocent boy, the son of a prominent local businessman.

Thanks to the generous assistance of the district attorney and the local newspaper, many people in the community were able to make up their mind as to Suzanne's guilt, without the need to hear her side of the story. Others were not so sure. And yet others, those who had previous personal experience with the local legal system, or who knew friends or relations that had contact with the county law, believed just the opposite.

As further proof of the boy's innocence, the district attorney was quoted, "The family of the murdered juvenile has been in the Bemidji area for many years."

An unknown officer had told the reporter that the female arrested for the murder of the juvenile boy had a night of fun sex. "That was all it was, just a night of fun sex; then the girl panicked and killed an innocent boy to try to cover her indiscretions."

It was also revealed that the female suspect had been having an ongoing sexual affair with an older male, one John Bridger, who was foreign to the Bemidji area. John Bridger, the paper said, had been arrested for statutory rape when he had revealed that he had prior sex with the arrested murder suspect/alleged rape victim—a juvenile female college student—just seventeen years old .

According to the cop talking to the reporter, John was obviously guilty. "The male suspect is a college student originally from Grand Rapids."

As for Richard Bede, the Bemidji News stated that he was arrested for the death of a minority person—Odis Elvie Blister from Duluth. The motive given was that Mr. Bede had previously been convicted of an earlier vigilante action.

There was apparently no need for the local news to talk to the three suspects, since, as usual, the authorities were omnipotent in their knowledge of what had happened.

All three crime suspects: the juvenile murder suspect (Suzanne de Lafayette), John Bridger (the statutory rapist), and Richard Bede (vigilante killer of level three sex offenders), would be arraigned later that afternoon.

Richard had been kept in an isolation cell throughout the night. No water, no light, no window to anywhere, no toilet. Just cement floor with a drain, and a cement bed poured six inches higher than the cold floor. Richard knew that Suzanne would have been kept in a similar cell. He also knew that the dark isolation cells were very disorienting, and he hoped that Suzanne, already injured, raped, and tortured, would not suffer too much.

Two days after finding Suzanne hiding in the forest near Rice Pond, Richard was led into the courtroom in handcuffs and leg irons. John Bridger was already in the courtroom, trussed up in the same way as Richard. Suzanne, though a juvenile, was brought into the same courtroom in the same manner. Perhaps the judge was in a hurry to get to the country club, therefore the adults and the female juvenile would have to be processed together.

246

Pain flooded over John's face when he saw his girl chained nearly immobile, wrists and feet bound with steel links. For herself, Suzanne seemed quite calm, though her face was even more pale than Richard had remembered, perhaps still bloodless from her injuries.

John was the first to be called.

"Statutory rape of a minor. How do you plead?" asked the judge.

"But Suzanne is my wife," said John in amazement.

Suzanne stood as well as she could, chained as she was like the ghost of Christmas past, and spoke to the judge. "John and I were married just this spring, near Fort Campbell, Kentucky. John's older brother is stationed in the army there, so in the pretext of visiting him, we were able to go to a state where we could be legally married. We haven't told our families yet because we wanted a formal wedding after we both graduate from college, and also, I needed to be able to stay in the dorms because that is all I can afford."

"Last night the cops told me that they were arresting me for rape, but they never explained about it being my wife. I did not understand what was happening," added John.

"Silence!" shouted the judge at the defendant, as His Honor banged his little wooden hammer.

At that point, Richard's oldest and richest, Terrie Bede, entered the courtroom with a tall, well-dressed gentleman. The man's black hair was combed straight back from his wide forehead. His glossy black briefcase matched his dark hair and the lustrous sheen of his black suit. Richard's oldest son had hired a very good lawyer.

The lawyer introduced himself to the court, "Your Honor, if I may. I am Attorney James Carpenter, from Minneapolis. I have recently been retained to represent all three of the defendants present today in your courtroom." Then the lawyer produced a certified copy of the marriage certificate proving that John and Suzanne were husband and wife.

The judge was disturbed with the interference, but the case against John clearly had to be dropped.

"I should charge you for contempt for causing all this confusion, young man," complained the judge.

John kept his mouth shut, as his instincts and intelligence told him he should, but he really was guilty of contempt.

Richard was arraigned next.

"How do you plead?" ordered the judge. "Are you guilty of the willful murder of Mr. Odis Blister?"

"No! I am, your judgeship," came a small voice from the rear of the courtroom.

It was Thor. He was standing in front of Else, who was trying rather unsuccessfully to hold him in place. "I shot an arrow into him because I was afraid he might come after my sister and take her back to his closet."

Before anyone could ask about sisters and closets, there erupted another admission.

"No, the boy is lying," boomed a deep voice from the other side of the courtroom. The World War II veteran Teddy Zemm was shaking his fist in the air as he spoke, face red as blood.

"I killed that pervert for what he had done to all those girls."

Big Thomas Thorson stood next, "Argh, uerr... I think the tribes may have killed Blister for helping Euglena sell our Native girls to pimps. But you will never find out who from the res," he added.

The judge banged his hammer, like a child trying to force a square peg into a round hole. "Silence in my court!" he screamed.

Terrie's attorney calmly broke into the commotion, "Your Honor, I request that the Court allow BCA Agent Kieran to present some evidence that he has on this matter. If I may, Your Honor."

The judge was placated and grateful to have an officer of the court, Attorney Carpenter, show the proper respect to the court and to guide the proceedings away from the spectacle of multiple confessions. "You may," said the judge.

At that, Attorney Carpenter waved Agent Kieran forward and whispered something to him, then allowed Michael to speak for himself.

"My name is Agent Michael Kieran. I work for the Minnesota State Bureau of Criminal Apprehension, and am presently assigned to investigate the white slavery ring headed by Eugene Euglena and assisted by Odis Blister and, we believe, the recently deceased Alberto Rodriguez Junior. Euglena and Blister are level three sex offenders, while Rodriguez had a juvenile conviction for forcible rape."

Agent Kieran produced three manila files from a battered state briefcase and placed them on the defense table.

The district attorney interrupted Michael's dissertation of the facts. "Objection, Your Honor. Mr. Rodriguez is, was, a juvenile, and as such deserves the protection of this court."

Attorney Carpenter countered, "Mr. Rodriguez is deceased, and therefore no longer has that protection. Besides, it is Mr. Bede that is being charged here."

"Continue, Agent Kieran," said the judge. "But I order you to leave out any references to Mr. Rodriguez." The court did not ask to see the manila files, the connections they may reveal apparently not germane to this case.

Michael continued, "The initial investigation of your own county coroner was unable to determine if the knife wound to Blister's back was the killing agent, or if it was the arrow. However, your coroner did determine that Blister was killed between noon and 4 p.m. of the day in question."

Michael looked at his watch as if the time on its scratched face would confirm what he was saying.

The BCA agent continued. "I can testify that Richard was with me at my office during that time frame. We were going over the details of the murder of Miss Lenora Frontera. I should add that Mr. Bede has been helping me in some small ways with that case." At that, Michael signalled the end of his testimony with an intense silence.

An established time of death and the alibi of a state agent made for an insurmountable obstacle to conviction. The district attorney did not want a check in his loss column.

"I, the State, withdraws its case against Mr. Bede."

The case against Richard was dropped. Suzanne de Lafayette was arraigned last.

"How do you plead, young lady?" asked the judge, clearly peeved that two criminals had escaped the justice of his court.

During the first two aborted arraignments, during the multiple confessions of Thor, Teddy, and Thomas, and during the recital of information from Agent Kieran, more and more citizens had been pushing their way into the courtroom. Now the seats were filled and people were standing in the aisles.

Unknown to the district attorney, a reporter for the paper in Grand Rapids had caught wind of the rape of one of their hometown girls, and of the charges that were being brought against her, and had already printed in the Grand Rapids' paper a long article this very morning, the same morning as the district attorney's statements in the Bemidji News.

Suzanne was a champion biathlon skier, a cheerleader, and the best scholar that Grand Rapids had to offer, in short, a darling of the community. And a past victim of sadistic rapists. The city of Grand Rapids was in an uproar. For the second time in a dozen years the district attorney had failed to do his homework and had misjudged his ability to control the information to the press. He had wanted to protect the reputation of a local businessman, but Junior's too close involvement with level three sex offenders had made that task nearly impossible.

A heavyset woman let her opinion be heard, "Let Suzanne go. She only defended herself."

Then louder, from a weathered old farmer with brown arms, a red neck, and a glaring white forehead, "What is wrong with this city?!!"

A small woman with piercing black eyes and matching black bible, leading a tight group of fellow church ladies, ranted to the Heavens above, "God shall smite the devil."

The church ladies, "Amen," sung as pretty as Richard remembered the Supremes.

Several college students, mostly young women, grumbled their complaints to nobody in particular, looking in all directions, their sentiments a curious mixture of sympathy and politics.

At that point, various and sundry citizens of Grand Rapids began interjecting their own feelings into the mix of college noise until the courtroom had been thrown into a cacophonous din.

Attorney Carpenter stood on the seat of his chair and faced the crowd with arms up and palms facing the angry audience. "Calm down. Calm down, please!" The people quieted. Then, still high on his chair, he turned and faced the judge.

"Because of the negative comments made in the local paper by the district attorney, I have filed a motion with the State of Minnesota to change the venue of the trial for my client, Suzanne de Lafayette, i.e. Suzanne Bridger, to the city of Grand Rapids."

"Objection, Your Honor. I can't win there," wailed Foat the Goat, i.e. the district attorney.

The judge did not know what to do. The district attorney would lose if the case was moved, but de Lafayette's attorney would most likely be able to force a change of venue through the state appeals court. The judge did not want the district attorney to have to lose a case. Bad precedent.

The district attorney was thinking the same thing. "The State will withdraw its case against Miss Suzanne de Lafayette… I mean, against Mrs. Suzanne Bridger, until further investigations can be completed."

Two large deputies took Suzanne out of the courtroom and back to her jail cell.

CHAPTER 29

The case against Suzanne had been dropped. At least for now. It took two more hours for the jail personnel to process the three ex-defendants and to release them. Suzanne was the last to clear. When she walked out onto the lawn next to the old section of the courthouse, John was at last able take her in his arms and hug her, which she dearly loved though the pain to her ribs was clearly hard for her to bear.

Attorney Carpenter had some odd news for the newly reunited couple. "You were both suspended from school when the charges were first announced in the paper. I can get you reinstated for this autumn, but summer classes will be out of the question. That also means that your room at the dorms, young lady, is no longer yours."

"You will stay at our home," said Else.

"Now it was 'our' home," thought Richard. Just two weeks ago Richard had a huge, empty house all to his private self.

"I will accept on one condition," said Suzanne. "I claim the first shower when we get to your place." Suzanne was still in the smelly clothes of the rape, unshowered yet from her ordeal.

"I second that condition," said Richard, holding his nose as he smiled at Suzanne, who, at that particular point in time did not want to be smiled at by anyone—not even her former comrade under straw.

Back at home a succession of showers were taken: Suzanne, John, Richard, then the children who had to wash Zemm garden dirt from their every pore, and finally Else, who had spent the last two days either hunting for or worrying about her man. Good providence that Richard had replaced his old water heater with a huge electric model that could pump out hot water for as long as there was coal in North Dakota.

John and Suzanne took the last spare bedroom. Though the sky was still daylight, they turned in after supper because Suzanne was hurting from her cracked rib.

Attorney Carpenter called to inform Richard that he believed that the district attorney would reinstate the charges against Suzanne after things had quieted down. "Since Junior was armed and firing at the time he was killed, it is unlikely that a jury would find Suzanne guilty of murder, but they might default to a lesser charge such as assault."

"That would still ruin her young life, besides being grossly unfair," said Richard.

"It would be good if a stronger connection between Junior and the other two rapists could be established."

"The sheriff's office should be able to find a connection easy enough...but of course the district attorney won't let that happen," said Richard, stating the obvious as it occurred to him.

"They will also try to make it seem like Suzanne had sneaked back to Blister's shack and had finished him off with the arrow. Even if they can't prove that, raising the issue as a possibility, however implausible, would make a conviction for killing Junior much more likely."

"When two murders are submitted to a jury, they feel obligated to choose one of them," surmised Richard.

"That is correct," said the attorney.

After the conversation with Attorney Carpenter, Richard reviewed in his own mind the events of the past two days. Just two days ago he and Michael had felt that the case was almost concluded. Now a new girl, Suzanne, was stuck in a mire of murder charges for defending herself from the worst kind of predator. Tired of thinking, Richard cleared his mind and calmed his spirit.

After the children had been put into their sleeping bags and the house was quiet, Richard lay on the couch in the kitchen to watch one of his favorite shows: about a girl who gets weekly instructions from God who comes to her in varying personas. Else joined him on the couch, which was slanted toward the front from old age and too much duty as a bed. She had to hold tight to Richard if she was to stay in place. Richard loved the fragrance of her red hair—his favorite sensual indulgence, and the cool softness of her skin as he kissed her lightly on her face and neck.

They held each other to the end of the show, and then Else turned off the television and the lights. Else whispered that it would be safe down here since any intruders would have to turn the lights on in the stairway before coming downstairs, giving ample warning. The kitchen was shaded softly by muted starlight entering the curtainless windows of the kitchen. For a time they lay together and watched as hundreds of fireflies pulsed in the field before the house. Richard unbuttoned Else's blouse and kissed the bare savannah between her breasts. The fragrance of her skin was warmer than the fragrance of her hair, and he breathed her deep into his lungs.

Else rolled Richard onto his back and sat on his waist and finished undressing herself as best she could from her perch. Her naked body, a gift of God as nature itself, was beautiful to watch as she moved in the starlight. Then she undressed Richard, kissing his shoulders, chest, arms, hands, and belly as she took off his shirt and the rest of his clothes. Else regained her seat on Richard's waist, her legs holding his hips in a tight grip. Leaning over, she pinned his shoulders and arms, then swooped in to kiss him quickly on his mouth.

She continued her game, more play than love making, sometimes kissing Richard and sometimes missing, when her hair would sweep against his face or tickle his eyes so he would have to close them from her form. At times, Else would lean down and brush her hair against Richard's face in quick, light, sweeping motions, back and forth and back and forth again. Richard wondered how it was she did not get whiplash.

At times Else would come to a sudden stop and she would peek from between the hair framing her face and peck him with another of her kisses, or sometimes kissing him longer before pulling away. Richard kind of enjoyed being teased, especially when Else's kisses were part of the bargain.

Else lay flat on Richard, length of body against length of body, her hands curved under Richard's shoulders as she was propped up on her elbows, her hair now forming a tent over Richard's face as she kissed him on his lips, or his eyes, or his forehead and cheeks… as she pleased. Else's feet bumped ceaselessly against Richard's because she was rocking them back and forth, ankles against ankles and insteps against insteps. Else had yet to "make love" to Richard, but she had created love for him to enjoy.

Else wiggled higher up along Richard's body until the center of her chest was even with his face. Then she gently pushed his face to the side and laid her chest over his ear, holding her weight lightly over him. Richard did not understand this at first, but then he could hear the beat of her heart. Alive. Strong. Perhaps full of love for him.

Drifting off together into a satisfied ecstasy, Richard and Else were returned to common life when there was a knock on the east entrance door. The two lovers quickly dressed, kicking their underwear under the couch and checking their buttons and zippers. Richard went to see who had come to visit so late. It was the delivery girl from the new flower shop. Again, with the same blue gingham dress and the black hair, she reminded Richard of Miss Frontera.

"I heard about your troubles," she said. "When you were released I decided to drive over after work and talk to you in person. As I may have told you before, my name is Peggy Raphael."

Richard led the delivery girl into the kitchen and introduced her to Else, who was busy trying to smooth her fiery hair with her hands. Richard told Miss Raphael about the recent events at Rice Pond and about the district attorney trying to charge everyone in an effort to protect the reputation of Alberto Rodriguez—Junior and Senior.

"That is why I never came forward after Rodriguez tried to rape me," concurred Miss Raphael. "The assault happened at the downtown store. I was working late one night, preparing roses for Valentine's Day, when Rodriguez Junior came into the cutting room. I heard a noise at the last second, which was Rodriguez sneaking up behind me, and so I picked up the large cutting shears—the kind that can trim the bottom off an entire bouquet."

"I think that I can tell where this story is going," said Else.

"But there is a twist," continued Miss Raphael. "Alberto grabbed me from behind and put his hand over my mouth. I was wearing one of those gingham dresses, which are a kind of uniform for the female workers at all of the Rodriguez flower shops. I held the shears at my side, hid in the pleats of my dress so Alberto could not see them. When he forced me onto the prep table and lifted my dress up, I stuck the shears into him. They struck him between his shoulder and chest, plunging in all the way to the finger holds. There was a torrent of blood."

It appeared that Miss Raphael was becoming tense just telling the story. Else got her a cold glass of milk and half a Hershey bar that one of the children had left in the freezer. "But you did not go to the police?" asked Else, more to help Peggy continue her story than to discover the obvious.

"No… I remembered how the police and the paper had treated Mr. Bede's daughter, and I was just a Native girl, while Junior's father was rich. But it was not that simple. After I had stabbed Alberto with the shears, he backed off, crying and screaming that I had attacked him." Peggy Raphael took another drink of the cold milk to calm her nerves, and then continued, "Now, for the twist: Junior's father, Alberto Rodriguez Senior, appeared from behind the window that separates the prep room from the sales floor. It is a kind of one-way window, where customers can watch their flowers being made up, but we can't see into the sales area. Obviously, Senior had been behind that window so he could watch his son rape me. Anyway, Rodriguez Senior threatened that he would have the police arrest me for assault and attempted murder of his son if I went to the authorities. I was so upset… I couldn't think straight… and who knows? I just left and drove to the reservation."

"But you still work at the flower shop?" asked Else.

"I told my old Auntie, who I live with, and she talked to some of the elders in the tribe. A really big man, a lighter-skinned Native, came to our house the next day and talked to me. He said rumor was that Rodriguez Senior was bankrolling a scheme to sell rural girls to pimps in the Cities. Rodriguez Junior had found this Euglena guy, who was the connection. I don't know where Blister came from, but it seems that he is the loose cannon who killed Miss Frontera and has caused the Rodriguez's business plan to go awry."

"Do you remember the big man's name?" asked Richard.

"Thomas. That is all he called himself, I believe. He has kept in touch with me since then, but he never uses his last name. After a while I figured that he wanted some anonymity."

"Well, let me ask you this: did Thomas eat anything while he was at your place?"

Peggy held both her hands before her face and laughed. "My old Auntie brought out a plate of cookies and fry bread, and a cereal bowl of hamburger fixings for the fry bread, and three sodas for us. This Thomas ate it all, even drank the three sodas, and then asked us for coffee. When Auntie brought out a cup and a pot of coffee, he drank the whole thing. Auntie and I still laugh about that sometimes."

"Thomas Thorson," said Else, smiling.

Miss Raphael finished her story, "Thomas asked me to go back to the store and keep my eyes open for things... for information about Senior's white slavery business, which is a poor term because many of his victims are Native. Anyway, that is what I have been doing since then. I went back to work the next day after talking to Thomas, just two days after Alberto's attempted rape of me, and acted like nothing had ever happened."

"Have you found out anything?" asked Else.

"Some, I think. But not much. I discovered that Junior had a strong fixation on those gingham dresses. The flower girls would find sticky stuff on them some mornings when the shops opened. He also had a thing for dark-haired girls. Junior and Euglena use the company vans to transport their captives; I have figured out that much. The night that Miss Frontera was killed... Alberto had taken one of the vans."

"Can I see that van? Do you know which one Junior drove that night?" asked Richard.

"I do, and you can. I have a key for the store. And in the store are keys for the vans. Come around tomorrow evening after closing time and we can look at the one that was used that night."

Miss Peggy Raphael continued to talk to Richard and Else. She had a lot to talk about even though she did not. Else and Richard let her converse late into the evening. It was midnight before Peggy tired. She asked if she could just stay the night on the couch. Else said that would be acceptable and got her some blankets. Then Peggy called her Auntie, spoke briefly over the phone, and, while Richard and Else were still talking in the kitchen, curled up and fell asleep in released exhaustion. Else cut off the light and led Richard, now also exhausted, up to their bed to make tired, if not leisurely love, Else stating most mischievously, though perhaps truthfully, that she had to make hay while the moon was shining and her man was still free.

Else had her lover lay on their bed and close his eyes and rest, as she undressed him, undressed herself again, and sat upright on his hips, her legs straddling him as she slowly rocked, like a mother might rock a cradle, late into the night.

Richard rested his hands on top of Else's thighs, feeling their soft and gentle motions as she made love to him. He thought he fell asleep like that, or half asleep, his dream a reality, or his new love a dream.

CHAPTER 30

Before Richard had arisen the next morning, Else had gotten up and had fixed their flower shop girl, Miss Peggy Raphael, a light breakfast of granola and half a grapefruit smothered in sugar. Peggy had also awoken early because today she had to work from noon till closing, and she wanted to talk to Else before leaving for the flower shop.

Miss Raphael had grave misgivings concerning Rodriguez Senior's future treatment of her now that another female would-be victim had killed his son. Rodriguez Senior would undoubtedly hate Suzanne for defending herself from one of Senior's gang of predators, especially when that gang member had been Senior's own perverted son.

"Would that hatred transfer from Suzanne to me?" worried Miss Raphael.

Else thought that she was being paranoid—justifiably paranoid. "You will have to be more careful than ever. I think you should maybe consider quitting, or at least contact Thomas and see what he says."

"It was already weird enough working there after I had stabbed Rodriguez Junior with the shears."

"I believe it is time for you to retire from the flower business. For your own safety." Else unconsciously punctuated her remarks by sticking her knife into the grapefruit she was halving.

The household's half-dozen children ran pell mell into the kitchen, captured Peggy, and took her outside to play catch. Thor had found an old scuffed football from former times hidden in the closet of Foster's bedroom. The team walked around the field in front, using Richard's mowed track as their nature trail, throwing and kicking the football as they went.

Richard was the next to descend. He peered out the front kitchen window to check on his bird feeders and saw Miss Raphael playing football with the opposing team.

"Peggy and the children, with their football, remind me of when my four were younger and every day we would walk around the glacial mound in the middle of Roche-a-Cree State Park, back in Wisconsin. We called it 'our mountain' because it was steep like a mountaintop."

"I bet you guys even had a football," said Else.

"Exactly. That is what jogged my memory. That is the exact same football that we would throw to each other as we circumnavigated our mountain. Spring, summer, fall, and winter. We got so good in the elements that we could catch in driving sleet or sub-zero cold."

"Like the Green Bay Packers," said Else, mischievously smiling in mock derision.

"I think that Peggy just got tackled by our team," said Richard, as he stood watching out the kitchen window. Peggy was half sitting and half lying at the far edge of the field, facing the house, as if she were trying to crawl back home. With six children on the opposing team, maybe she was.

John and Suzanne Bridger were the last to arrive in the kitchen, interrupting Richard's vigil over Peggy and her rivals. Richard still thought of Suzanne as "de Lafayette," of the family of straw-concealed "de Lafayettes."

Because of her broken nose, her eyes had blackened like soot; she looked liked the raccoons that would sometimes raid the sweet corn in Teddy Zemm's garden. Her ribs hurt so much that she could not breathe well, so she lay flat on the kitchen's couch and let her husband feed her. He would have to bathe her and dress her too.

Though Suzanne was in pain from her broken nose and cracked rib, and recovering from the insult of the rape and the county district attorney's treatment, Richard had to press forward and talk about a plan of defense for Suzanne.

"I've been cleared from all unpleasant legalities, per BCA Agent Kieran's alibi, and John is free thanks to his marriage to his lovely bride here," said Richard, as he waved a dramatic hand in front of Suzanne's nasty-colored face.

"Thanks," said Suzanne, graciously accepting Richard's theatrics at her expense. She was in greater pain but better spirits than she had been yesterday on the courthouse green.

"But our legal savior, Attorney Carpenter, has warned me that the district attorney is posturing in such a way as to be able to again charge Suzanne with Junior's murder. And he may also charge her for the premeditated murder of Odis Blister, claiming that Suzanne had somehow trailed Blister back to his shack and had finished him off."

Richard's words took away Suzanne's smile. Now her face was ashen under black and blue.

"Why would he do that?" worried John.

"To win a case against an outsider," said Else. Suzanne, from Grand Rapids, Minnesota, being the outsider.

"Also to protect the reputation of the Rodriguez business," said Richard. "If Suzanne is painted as the culprit, then the rapist status of Junior can be replaced with that of an 'innocent boy.' Historical revisionism. The forensics—the DNA—will be on our side. But the district attorney will have a courtroom strategy to get around their uncooperative forensics," added Richard.

"Will the DNA tests be unusable, like parts of the testing were for Miss Frontera?" wondered Else. "They would not dare again, would they?"

"They might and they would. But Doctor Luther took our own set of samples and gave them to Michael. That is our insurance for the forensics," said Richard. "Our main concern, however, is Blister."

"Why would Blister's death be more of a concern than Junior's?" asked John. "Suzanne killed Junior, not Blister."

"But it is also a fact that Suzanne put a knife into Blister's back," explained Richard. "If the district attorney can suggest that she might have followed him to his shack and finished him off there, then the jury will have two murders to choose from: Blister's as well as Junior's. It will be their duty to determine which one Suzanne is guilty of."

"That does not make any sense," said John, caressing his wife's forehead more to erase his own worries than to sooth his wife.

"No, it does not, but that will not make any difference," said Else. "Richard was convicted for saving his daughter's life. Her life had been threatened by a gang of rapists, but the district attorney portrayed the predators as a bunch of innocent toddlers. You are not in Kansas anymore, John." Else went on to explain what had happened to Richard after his daughter had been raped. "If the district attorney tells a lie often enough, it will become the truth. At least in this town."

"We will have to show that Suzanne could not have walked all the way to Blister's shack, and then we have to find who it was that killed Odis Blister," said Richard. "Of course, we may or may not want our mystery archer to go to prison, depending on who he or she is, so that will very likely create another problem," said Richard.

"I feel doomed," moaned the discolored Suzanne from her supine position on the couch.

"You have friends," said Richard. "They will keep you safe."

Bad news taken, John guided his wife outside so Suzanne could lie on the bench next to Richard's flower garden. Richard had not had time to plant vegetables, but had strewn flower seeds about in the hope that they would take care of themselves. Most had. Now it was a perfect place for Suzanne and John to calm their fears and to be with each other. Perhaps the springtime sun would warm Suzanne's spirits while it warmed her body.

As John led his battered wife outside, Amber and Thor came back inside, to the kitchen where Else and Richard were still sitting. Amber fixed herself and Thor more bowls of cereal which they proceeded to eat in unchildlike silence.

Else found a notebook and turned to a blank page. "Let's list the possible suspects, who could have killed Blister, and why."

Richard started, "There is Chad Rochambeau—Miss Frontera's lover; Chad was present in the Chippewa Forest the day after Lenora was murdered. If his jeep had not been so cow-licked, we never would have known he was there that day."

"Don't forget Cindy Heath. She also loved Lenora."

"We can blame Eugene Euglena or Alberto Rodriguez Junior," conspired Richard. "They must have wanted to get rid of their loose cannon."

"And why didn't they take Blister directly to the Bemidji hospital after Suzanne had put that fillet knife into his back? In a court of law their lack of action would make them look guilty."

"That is a good point," said Richard. "Remind me to mention that to our lawyer, Jim Carpenter."

Else and Richard continued to formulate their list of suspects. Who else would want Odis Blister dead? Who would not? There were all his former victims: known and unknown, and the people who loved those victims. The list included most of the citizens of Duluth because of his victims there and because of the damning publicity after his Park Point attacks.

The Natives had to be suspected, including Big Thomas Thorson. Perhaps his Irish temper got the best of him for once. And the as yet unpublicized fighter of crime, flower delivery girl Miss Peggy Raphael with the rapierlike shears. She may have gone to the shack to pay back Junior for trying to rape her, and ended up killing Blister instead.

"The silver arrow," said Else.

Richard thought about that for a moment. "The silver arrow. Yes, that is the key: the silver arrow with the pink feathers."

"Who could have gotten the arrow and also wanted the predator dead?" asked Else.

"Teddy Zemm hated the bastard for what he did to his niece's friend Sally. Or what about Sally herself? Or Samantha? Those girls obviously had access to the silver arrows, and either one could have ridden Samantha's bike over to the shack. Samantha is a deadly shot with her little bow. But how would they know where the shack was located?"

At Richard's last comment, Thor jumped up, spilling the last of his cereal and milk, and angrily reentered his plea of guilty. "I shot the arrow into him! I did. Why won't you believe me? I did it all by myse…"

Thor's second effort at confession was cut short by his sister, as Amber literally dragged her brother outside by the scruff of his neck. "Don't you ever…ever…ever…," said the Viking's sister. "Do you hear me?" The east door slammed shut and Else and Richard were left in stunned silence.

"Well, where were we?" said Else, smiling at Amber's handling of her brother.

"That leaves dear Antonio de Medici, a known vigilante," said

Richard. "He seems to have no fear of rapists and is always messing with their business. But how would he have gotten the arrow?"

"Well, how does Tony find out about or do any of the things he does? He just does."

Richard had long ago stopped asking how, so Tony was definitely a suspect. But Tony would have to be an informal suspect, so to speak; his convict status would make him too easy of a target for the local authorities. "Consider Tony, but do not mention his name."

"We have a dozen or so good suspects, with a few thousand extra possibilities," stated Else.

"These should be enough to work with," said Richard. "Our guilty culprit is most likely hiding somewhere on your list."

"You have forgotten another main player... Michael Kieran, your BCA Agent," offered Else.

Richard stood blank faced as he considered the possibility, then, "Michael does seem to go after the predators with unusual zeal. Most cops are more careful of their careers not to step on so many toes. But not Michael. He has fought the system long and hard to protect our Minnesota girls." Richard recounted the many times that Michael had gone against local powers to defend the defenseless.

Richard decided that he should check on his computer to see if there was anything there that might be enlightening relative to Agent Kieran, but his poor Internet skills brought no luck, so he called his daughter Jeanette, a far better computer detective than he, and asked her to try to find something...anything. While he waited for Jeanette to get back to him, he used his own computer to run down Else's list of the most probable suspects. Not much to add.

Jeanette called back after a few minutes. "Hello, Dad. It's me again. I found something that will be of interest to you."

"Shoot."

"Michael Kieran has four children from his first, only, and current marriage. They are all doing very well except one: a daughter who is presently living in a mental health institute just south of Minneapolis. It was hard to find out why she is there because she was a juvenile, sixteen years old, when she entered. But I was able to cross check an item that was referenced to her commitment—a felon who was ordered by the courts, as part of the terms of his conviction, to stay away from her. So I ran that individual and found that he had been convicted of raping and torturing a sixteen-year-old Caucasian girl. The young Caucasian girl must have been Michael Kieran's daughter," concluded Jeanette.

"How many years ago was the girl attacked?" asked Richard.

"Twelve, so she would be 28 now."

Twelve years ago would put it near to when Richard's daughter had been attacked. "Michael's daughter must have been profoundly affected to yet require institutionalization after all these years," stated Richard.

"A man cannot imagine what it is like to be raped. It seems to go on and on forever," said Jeanette. Jeanette had said exactly, word-for-word exactly, that same thing a dozen years ago to her father during the first call from jail that her dad was allowed to make to his family. Today, Richard wondered if Jeanette realized that she had repeated, verbatim, what she had said back then.

Jeanette finished, "That is all I could find. The prison sentence of the rapist would have expired last year, while Kieran's daughter is still in the prison made in her mind by that rapist. I am guessing that because of his daughter's ruined life, your BCA friend has grown to hate all predators."

As if on an unseen signal, father and daughter abruptly stopped discussing the case, substituting instead talk of Jeanette's two children and her experience working on the suburban police force near Green Bay. At the end, Richard thanked her for her help and told her that he loved her and missed her.

After his talk with Jeanette, Richard worked the screen of his computer while the new information about Agent Kieran sank in. Michael would indeed be another suspect for Richard's inquisition. As he thought of how the case, two days ago nearly concluded, had now become a maze, Richard entered Else's name and crossed it with Clearwater County. He wanted to see how large her old farm had been before she had lost it during her divorce. Instead, a story about a murdered girl came on the screen. Else had an older daughter. An older daughter that had been "lost" by Else's ex-husband in a late night poker game. The story said that the next morning Else had found her firstborn girl—raped, beaten, and lifeless—in the woods behind their home.

Before he could be arrested, the man that had won Else's daughter was found floating in a remote section of the Clearwater River with a string of small holes in his skull and large chunks of meat missing from his decaying body. The locals presumed that the holes appeared to be from a hay pitchfork, while the missing meat resulted from the efforts of the resident snapping turtles. Else's husband had run off, last seen in southern California. Else had petitioned the court for a divorce, without the missing husband, and had gone on with her life as best as she could.

Richard turned off his computer and went back to the kitchen. "How old was she?"

Else let the plate she was drying slip back into the wash water. She stood directly in front of Richard, close enough that he could discern the separate specks of green that haloed the deeper green irises of her eyes. "God gave Elizabeth to me; I loved her on earth for thirteen years. Then the evil of men took her from me."

The intensity of Else's love and hatred startled Richard. He tried not to let it show. Instead, he took Else in his arms and held her.

She said, "I started to love you when the men on your crew first told me how you went to prison for saving your daughter's life. Now you are mine forever."

Else did not discuss further her oldest daughter or the evil that had happened to her or about the rapist with the line of pitchfork perforations in his skull. That all could come later. Instead Else talked about the plans she had for herself and for Richard, and about his new additions to his family. Richard held her the entire time she talked. In the end, Else returned to the present case, "Other than my past, what did you find on the computer about possible suspects—real or imagined?"

"I was having trouble with my own computer snooping, so I called Jeanette. She discovered in short order that Michael Kieran has a daughter that ended up in a mental institution as a result of a sexual assault." Richard told the rest of the story, as well as he knew. Else seemed too saddened for anger.

"If this was a fictional story, it would seem way too improbable," said Else. "The extent of the damage that these insects cause is beyond the comprehension of most people."

"I agree, Else. Minnesota has 10,000 lakes, and, it seems, 10,000 predators doing their damage to our children."

Else was anger personified, and getting angrier. "Each and every pornographer should be hung for what they have started."

John Bridger interrupted the thoughts of Else and Richard by walking into the kitchen. He wanted to get a bottle of ice water for himself and a pillow for his young wife. "Suzanne is sleeping outside; she is really tired from her injuries."

The moment broken, which may have been just as well, Richard finally let go of Else.

"I have to go into town to talk to Michael," said Richard. And then direct to Else, "I'll call you later. I love you, Else."

Richard called Agent Kieran and arranged to meet with him at the small park downtown by the waterfront. For what Richard had to ask, the open spaces of a public park would be more private.

Before Richard could leave, Amber found him and pulled him into the relative privacy of the living room. "Sir, will Else's daughters be my sisters? I am just asking because I never had a sister before."

"God! Women!" is all that Richard could say as he kissed the top of Amber's head.

CHAPTER 31

The first of the Canada geese had arrived at the small park downtown on the south shore of Lake Bemidji. Soon there would be dozens of pairs of the large, bold birds. Richard wondered about the enduring fidelity of goose and gander; they stayed with each other for life, finding a replacement only if one of the pair should die. If only most human couples would be as true to each other, human goslings would be the better protected for it.

Agent Kieran arrived tired and worn looking. He had been busy with the forensics of the case, working late into the night.

"There is one set of fingerprints on the arrow that killed, or helped to kill, Odis Blister, and they are not Suzanne's, so that is a plus for us," said Michael.

"Do you know who they belong to?" Richard tried not to show his concern, but he is not a good actor.

"No. But they are very small, a woman or a tiny man."

"The bruise on the side of Blister's neck? What about that?" asked Richard.

"I wondered about that, too. So I had one of my agents up here, Jeff, do a somewhat informal autopsy, with the help of your doctor Luther, and they determined that someone either had held Blister's neck in a powerful grip, tight enough to crush the artery that goes to the brain, or had somehow crushed the artery with a garrote of some kind."

"A strong cord would certainly be needed if a smaller person was to generate enough force," said Richard.

"But the garrote theory doesn't seem to fit because there is not a complete encircling scar on Blister's neck. Most of the circumference of the cord seems to be missing. Either way, the crushed artery seems to be the actual cause of death."

"Which explains why the local coroner could not determine which puncture wound had caused death," said Richard. "Neither had."

"That is correct."

"So a man with half a very powerful grip had crushed the life out of Blister," said Richard.

"Add the fingerprints to the equation, and the evidence seems to point to a woman with small but immensely powerful hands," said Michael.

"Maybe a farm gir…," Richard did not finish.

Michael either did not hear Richard or did not dare acknowledge the half-uttered conclusion.

"I had also sent a blood sample to the BCA lab down in the Twin Cities," said Michael. "It seems that Blister's system was loaded with digitalis—enough to stop his evil black heart. The digitalis may have contributed to Blister's death, since Blister was bleeding from both his front and his back at the same time the digitalis was coursing through his system."

"And then someone closed the artery to his brain," completed Richard.

"Exactly."

The list of suspects had not gotten shorter—the list of causes of death had gotten longer. Enlarge the maze. Richard summarized and theorized, "Level three sex offender Odis Blister was killed by a fillet knife wound to his back—per Suzanne de Lafayette—who is really Mrs. John Bridger, then Blister is also killed by an arrow shot into his chest—pinning him to the beam in the shack, then Blister dies of digitalis poisoning, and finally, Blister's death is assisted by a lack of blood to his brain caused by a crushed artery in his neck."

"Precisely," agreed Agent Kieran, though the term "precisely" hardly applied in this instance.

"So now, who is our prime suspect?" asked Richard, to Michael and of himself.

"You started the list with Suzanne; why don't you continue and see where that goes," said Michael.

"Let's see, Teddy Zemm has a powerful grip that can crush a man's neck. I also suspect that he may have a heart condition, which could explain the digitalis."

"Did Mr. Zemm know where Blister's shack was located?" asked Michael.

"He had never been there, but he must have gotten a general idea of where it is located from listening to the others talk."

"Possibly Mr. Zemm, then."

"Cindy Heath could have shot Blister with the arrow, but where would she get the digitalis, unless she 'borrowed' the medicine from Teddy Zemm's cabin."

"Could Cindy have crushed Blister's artery?"

"Not likely," reasoned Richard.

"Probably not Miss Heath, unless she found a way to kill that we are not yet aware of."

"Thomas Thorson is strong enough to crush a pervert's neck, or head or chest or legs for that matter, he really is that strong," said Richard.

"From what you have said before, it seems to me that Mr. Thorson is an information gatherer, not a main player...but I could be wrong."

"Chad Rochambeau fights for keeps," continued Richard, further enlarging his list of murder suspect friends. A fact that was not lost on his mind or his heart. "Neither Euglena nor Blister would be safe around that young boxer."

"Once again, did Chad know where Blister's shack was located?"

"He may have found it during his search for Lenora. Maybe his search-mate, Cindy Heath, led him to the shack."

"Then Mr. Rochambeau is on the list, perhaps in conjunction with this Miss Heath," said Michael.

"Neither will be on the list, not officially. Just the list in our minds," asserted Richard.

"Let me guess: Mr. Rochambeau is a convict. Is that the reason for your need for exclusion?"

"Correct. One mention of the word 'convict' and the local cops will trot off with their blinders in place."

"Anyone else?"

"Euglena or Junior or both together could have decided to silence their loose canon," said Richard. "The district attorney won't include Junior as a suspect, and Euglena has yet to be caught for his parole violations from the Cities."

"Mr. Euglena and Mr. Rodriguez will be on the top of my official list. Hell, they'll be the only ones on my list." Michael laughed at his private joke.

Richard nodded his head in relieved agreement.

Michael continued, "The DA might not want Euglena charged and kept in Beltrami County because of what Eugene might say about Junior's involvement in their white slavery ring. He needs to silence Euglena's voice in order to protect the Rodriguez business."

There was a break in the conversation as Richard watched a pair of lovesick Canada geese waddle past. Then he told Michael, rather humorously, "Our little Thor has already confessed to the murder, so let's not forget him." Richard had omitted Tony de Medici, Samantha's friend Sally, the flower delivery girl—Peggy Raphael, and Else.

"What about yourself, Richard?" asked Michael.

"Yes, I could be a suspect, I suppose. But I have a much better suspect."

"And who would that be?" asked Michael.

Richard answered the question with a question, "How much do you love your daughter, Agent Michael?"

Michael did not answer. He directed his gaze out onto the lake. He pitched pebbles into the edge of the water, he hummed softly at the geese, he studied black-edged cumulus clouds as they floated by. It was as if the conversation about the case had not been taking place. Enough time to run a mile ticked by.

Finally, Michael looked at his one and only convict friend. "Yes, I suppose so. But I didn't. Though I can't guarantee that I never would have."

"What is her name?" asked Richard. "Your daughter."

"Elizabeth... and I loved her so... I still love her. For me and my wife, she was perfect."

Richard wondered about there being two lost Elizabeths, Else's

Elizabeth buried in the ground of Clearwater County, and Michael's Elizabeth buried in the childless halls of a mental institution in central Minnesota. "I guess we can be suspects, Michael, but we better not tell the district attorney. He would reincarnate the Spanish Inquisition to get his two vigilantes."

"That he would," agreed Michael.

The list of suspects was forgotten. Richard listened as Michael spent the next hour talking of his daughter Elizabeth, a family history from birth to her status as a beautiful young lady. Childhood injuries and illnesses, accomplishments and victories. But not much past the day her young life was frozen in time. Still, Michael's eyes were bright and he was so proud of his girl, as he talked and told the stories of her growing-up.

Michael had a wallet of badly creased photos, a little blond girl on a small bicycle—Michael holding the handlebars to steady her, a small, pinafore-dressed girl hopping off a yellow school bus—metal lunch box in hand, a very pretty but not yet fully developed young lady standing next to a shy boy—her first real date, a somewhat more mature teen beauty dressed in an expensive chiffon dress—when she was someone's bridesmaid. Michael's wallet held more memories than money.

"Elizabeth crashed her bike soon after this photo was taken, but she got right back on and rode away. By late afternoon my girl was covered in bruises, but she could ride that bike."

"I know about stubborn kids," said Richard.

"The school bus was during her first-grade year. Elizabeth almost had to be held back because she missed so much school for asthma and such, but we homeschooled her, which helped."

"I homeschooled my two youngest for a long time. Now I wish it had been longer."

"The shy boy is a doctor now. Something to do with pediatrics and bones."

Richard had nothing to add. Evil destroys the future of good and innocent people.

Michael put his memories away and closed his wallet, if not his heart. "The lives of all the predators in Minnesota are not worth one hour of one life of a single one of our young girls," said Michael.

"I agree."

"There are other memories, too," said Michael, as he placed his hands on his knees like an old man about to tell a story about the good old days.

"The first time it happened was when I remembered helping my girl with her Spanish classes from the community college. I really loved assisting her with her new language."

Richard wasn't sure he understood what Michael was trying to tell him, so he kept his mouth shut and his heart open.

"At first I didn't think much about it. Then a few weeks after the Spanish lessons, I bought a small Honda motorcycle for Elizabeth and taught her how to ride it."

One of the last new pleasures of old men is to teach their sons and daughters how to drive.

"After the motorcycle, the memories came faster and faster. My daughter went on to the University, she had loves found and lost, she met a perfect guy and married, had two healthy babies, got a great job in Minneapolis. Her and her husband built a beautiful house in the country."

Richard was beginning to understand what Michael was sharing with him.

"You still travel to the canoe country every year?" asked Michael.

"Every year, thought it is getting harder and harder to get any of the kids to go along. They have their own busy lives now."

"Well, when Elizabeth's son and daughter got older we started a family tradition of canoeing together each summer in your beloved Boundary Waters. Two adults and one child in each canoe."

As if in agreement with his trips to the wilderness, a family in a sailboat blew past the shore.

"I remember it all: everything that my Elizabeth missed out on because..."

"My life froze the day I went to prison," said Richard. "I thought that when I came back home that it would start up again, but it didn't. I will forever be lost in the past, trying every day to begin from the day I was taken from my family."

"Yes, I understand," said Michael.

"But yours is a thousand times worse," said Richard. "Your mind has created memories of everything that should have been your daughter's life."

Patting Michael's shoulder and saying good-bye to the old cop, Richard left Michael at the edge of Lake Bemidji.

Before today, he had believed that he truly hated the predators. Now Richard realized how he himself, a dumpy old dad that long ago had been caught in a bad situation where he was forced to save his daughter's life, and had been torn from his family and sent to prison for doing so, was just a weak ember compared to Michael's firestorm of hate.

Michael would hunt predators till the day he died, then continue to hate them from Heaven or hell.

CHAPTER 32

Lake Bemidji State Park, on the northern side of the lake, would allow Richard a chance to recover from the intensity of Michael's memories. Richard drove there and used one of the wooden stalls to dress into his running clothes. He would try to cover a middle distance today, about five miles, long enough to relax but not so far as to become exhausted. He ran out of the camping area, onto the tree-lined trails, then up onto the raised, old railroad right-of-way of the Paul Bunyan Trail. From there he ran north to where two lakes constricted the trail into a high, narrow ridge. He would not go as far as the ambush site of Sally's attack.

Two and a half miles out, the same back, Richard finished his run along the north shore of Lake Bemidji. Far across the lake were the city, the college, and the small park with the geese where he imagined Michael might still be—lost in the twin memories of his daughter's past life and her missing life.

The one shower on the beach, supplied directly by a ground well, made Richard clean and cold. He then drove back to where he had started, to Bemidji, to meet with Peggy Raphael at the flower shop. Peggy was waiting at the now closed store, sitting on the hood of a blue sports car which matched, however accidentally, the uniform of the blue gingham dress she was wearing. Dark hair and brown skin, she again reminded Richard of Lenora. The feeling was eerie and gave Richard a tragic sense of loss for the girl he never knew.

Peggy led the way to a white van coated with dried mud and dust. "This is the one that Rodriguez used the night Miss Frontera went missing," she said. "It hasn't been washed or emptied since then."

Moving slowly and deliberately, like a ghostly double of Lenora, Peggy unlocked the cargo door on the side and slid it back along its track.

Inside was a box of wilted yellow roses. Two crumpled gingham dresses were stuffed under the passenger seat. Blue. Richard went back to his truck to get his camera, then took several pictures before climbing into the cargo area. Part of the end of Lenora's life had been spent in this van. Richard could almost feel her presence.

Lenora Frontera had left messages at the pond: the yellow flower, her cross—crushed into the space between two of her teeth, her lover's bracelet. Perhaps the blue gingham dress had been a message too.

In the van, Richard found what he believed were other messages, certainly left there by the doomed girl. Scratched into the flat metal of the support post next to the cargo door was a drawing of a cross. On the front of the cross was hung a primitive Jesus—his holy head circumscribed with a Celtic halo. Down lower, jammed into a space where the post was welded onto the sheet metal, were four Heath bars, each badly broken and each with a short section of rose stem inserted into their wrappings.

"Another pair of messages," concluded Richard.

He took several pictures of Jesus dying on the cross and photos of the chocolate. He took the roses with him, the broken chocolate, and the two dresses. Nothing else seemed evident to him, though he was not an expert in forensics, so something unnoticed might yet be hidden there.

Peggy had been shuffling through the contents of the front of the van as Richard had checked the back. "I found this knife," she said. "Do you want it?" Peggy held out a dirty fillet knife.

"Yes, I'll take it to my contact at the BCA office. Agent Michael Kieran. He has been collecting all of the physical evidence for his lab down in the Twin Cities."

"Do you want me to clean the fish scales off it?"

"Leave them on. They are probably the same scales that were on a knife that Blister had tried to use earlier." Richard did not add that the intended use in question was attempting to stick the knife into Richard's body at the camp at North Twin.

"Did you ever see anyone with Junior during any of the times he came to this shop?" asked Richard.

"He was usually by himself, but twice he had a skinny black guy with him. I remember that the guy acted like he was God's gift to women. And also, the black guy had something, like a woman's black stocking, tied over the top of his head."

"Euglena."

"That's it. Oh, yes, then another day, there was a girl with Junior. Very tall. She seemed way too classy for him; that is what I remember thinking."

"Did you hear her name?"

"No, I don't think so. You have to remember that I was trying to be as unobtrusive as possible in my spying."

"You did well," said Richard.

"We should leave now," said Miss Raphael. "Though it is secluded back here, I don't want to take a chance that someone will see us going through this van together."

Richard told Peggy to be extra careful the next few days. Taking the rose-stemmed Heath bars with him, the two blue dresses, the knife with its fish scales, the box of wilted yellow roses, and the pictures in his camera, he drove north up Highway 71 to Bob-The-Manager's gas and convenience station.

Cindy was in. She came out to Richard's truck when she saw him park, and climbed into the cab. Apparently she no longer cared if the manager saw her leave her post.

"Come to bring me news, I hope," she said. Cindy looked tired, with eyes that were darker than Richard had remembered. The strain must be wearing on everyone by now, so why should Cindy be any different?

"I just finished inspecting the van where Lennie spent part of her last night on earth," said Richard.

A sad "Oh" was all Cindy could say.

"Lennie had scratched a picture of a cross, one with a Jesus hung from it. Do you still have Lennie's cross and chain?"

RICHARD LORY

If Cindy was surprised that Richard knew she had her dead friend's cross, she did not show it. She pulled Lenora's cross from deep inside the neck of her dress and unhooked its tiny latch and handed it to Richard.

"Does your store carry tins of shoe polish?" requested Richard. "Dark...black or burgundy."

Cindy left and returned in a moment, handing a polish tin of dark burgundy to Richard. He opened it and spread a miniscule amount on the back of the cross. Another, older cross appeared, also hung with the body of our Christ, a Celtic halo framing Jesus' tired head, exactly as Lennie had scratched on the post of the van.

"This is the cross that Lennie had drawn on the inside of the van. She is going to her death, and she takes the time to draw this Celtic Christ," said Richard.

He held up the polish-stained image for Cindy to see. He then continued, "Under the scratched drawing of Jesus and his cross were four candy bars...Heath. Lenora had broken them to bits while they were yet in their wrappers, then had taken sections of rose stems and had set a single broken stem into each candy bar wrapper, thereby, I believe, connecting the roses of the flower shop with the Heaths. Lenora then placed the rose-stemmed wrappers under the scratched drawing of her Personal Savior."

Cindy's eyes had fixed on her knees. She held her hands together in her lap. Her lips moved, but she did not speak.

Richard continued, "You said before that the bastards who killed your friend would someday have to pay."

Miss Heath looked up and across the highway, to the darkness of the trees where the Chippewa Forest began.

"Not a singular bastard."

Cindy did not take her eyes off the forest.

Richard continued, "According to the time sheets that your boss showed to me, you were supposed to work to the end of closing the same night that Lennie went missing. But instead you checked out an hour early." Richard took the chocolate-as-message from his pocket and set them on her lap and closed her fingers around the broken bars. "Heath is you."

Cindy started to cry softly as she wistfully studied the dark forest. She did not look at the old man sitting next to her.

282

Richard continued, "A convict friend of mine saw you and Chad together, a fact that by itself means very little, but with the rose and the cross and the broken bars… you could not have Lennie's love, so you turned to Chad. You fell in love with him, but he still loved Lennie. So somehow you found Junior, or Euglena, and arranged for them to take your problem away. Which they did. They took away Lennie."

"I didn't mean for her to die. I thought…"

"I also know that Chad was near the attack site the exact day after Lenora was murdered," said Richard.

"I was with Chad that day, showing him where to drive. He was so worried. He had heard about Lennie being missing, and had driven up from St. Paul to try to find her. I told him that Cindy might have been taken by some creeps that live near the forest, and that I knew about where their cabin was. Of course, this was all before I heard she had been murdered."

"What were you going to do if you found your perverts?" asked Richard.

"I didn't want Chad to get in trouble with the law again. So…"

"So you had a pistol, young lady. Your .32 is registered with the state. You were going to kill your own hired men before Chad had a chance to beat them to death," said Richard.

"Yes. I carry my gun sometimes late at night at the store. But I… we…did not find the men who had killed my friend. Otherwise…"

"You wanted to kill the rapists in order to save Chad's life, even if it meant that you would lose your freedom and your last chance at love. You would lose Chad in order to save him."

"Yes, that is what I intended," said Cindy as her eyes moved from the forest to the old man sitting next to her.

"You have to break it off with Chad," said Richard. "If he ever found out… he might try to revenge Lennie's death on you, and then his life would certainly be ruined forever."

"Yes, I will…I…I will."

"Also, if by chance Suzanne Bridger is charged again, you will have to tell what you know."

Cindy dropped her gaze to her lap again. She smoothed her dress with her hands. More tears than Richard thought humanly possible were streaming down her face, but she did not make a sound.

Finally, "Yes, I will tell if I am needed." Richard handed the old cross back to her. She refused to take it, "You can have it, Richard. I don't deserve it anymore." She stepped from the truck and stood rigid in front of the store, love lost from her life. She was a poor reflection in Richard's rearview mirror.

When Richard pulled his truck into the Zemm's drive, Teddy was tending his wife's flowers in the back garden. He was glad that his young friend had stopped by on such a nice evening. The old veteran shook the hand of the younger veteran. Teddy's handshake was strong as an anvil, though his face seemed to have eroded into yet deeper creases. Richard talked for a while about the fishing luck that his sons had not been having lately, and about the various projects that needed to be done in and around his log house. Teddy again showed off the flowers that his wife had gathered and planted over the years.

Richard stopped to admire a bed of tall flowers. Interestingly, he had not seen such a collection of the pinkish-purple flowers since he had been incarcerated at the state prison at Moose Lake. A convicted murderer there had told him that the flowers were highly poisonous. Apparently and luckily, none of the other convicts knew about the flowers' characteristics as a murder weapon. Just like the plants at Moose Lake Prison, these plants of Clara's stood tall in deadly spikes of thimblelike flowers.

"Do you know the name of these flowers?" asked Richard.

"Those are foxglove, the source of digitalis. We maybe should not have them growing here, what with the children and all, since the leaves are poisonous, but we figured that Samantha was too old to be doing something as foolish as eating flowering plants. And the violet flowers, as you can see, are such a nice addition to the garden."

"They are very striking," agreed Richard.

Teddy Zemm added, "But now that you have Else's little ones, I think that I will put a woven wire fence around them, just to be safe."

The two men moved on, from Clara's flower garden to Teddy's larger garden of vegetables.

"Did I see you coming from the hospital the other day, Teddy?"

"You probably did. I have been making regular trips to the clinic for treatments for cancer. But it seems to be under control now. I was lucky—the medicine worked. I am tired now, as you can see, but the doctor says that I will be feeling better soon."

Seemingly changing the subject, Richard said, "I have to find out who killed Blister, just in case the district attorney tries to recharge Suzanne for murder."

"Yes, I suppose so."

"I can tell you that Blister was killed by knife, by a silver arrow with pink fletching, by a crushed artery in his neck, and also by an overdose of digitalis."

Teddy laughed long and hard. "I'm sorry, Richard, but someone really wanted that bastard dead." Then, "I almost wish I was dying from cancer still, I would take the blame and spare your Suzanne the scrutiny. I will yet if you want me to."

"I don't think that will be needed. But thanks."

Teddy's garden was off to a good start. Loving care and strong hands had done their miracle. Clara joined them and asked if Richard could stay for supper. Else probably had food ready back home, but Richard said that he would like to stay and share a meal with them; it is always good to spend some time with the greatest generation.

CHAPTER 33

The night was late by the time Richard returned from the homestead of Teddy and Clara. Everyone was already asleep, Suzanne—convalescing from her injuries, the sextette of children—worn out from a day of hard play, and Else—lying naked in the center of Richard's bed. Richard undressed to his boxers, climbed in next to Else, kissed the top of her head, and then, as is his usual male custom, turned away from her to find his own sleep space.

Else, though evidently in a deep sleep, drew close to Richard and put her arm around him and threw her leg over his hips. She nestled her face into the nape of his neck. The next morning Else was still holding onto her man.

Else took a shower with Richard, a quite pleasant if somewhat embarrassing endeavour considering the resident witnesses present in his home. Perhaps, Richard reasoned, the shared shower had been intended to put Suzanne at ease since the extent of her injuries would necessitate that she be washed and dressed by her husband.

"Could you please wash my back, Madam?" requested Richard.

Else complied. For all he knew, it may have been years since the exact center of his back had received any attention. His arms weren't so flexible like when he was young.

Then it was Else's turn to be cleaned. Richard scrubbed her back, then moved to her shoulders, then her legs and calves. He lifted each leg back like a farrier shoeing a horse and washed between Else's toes. She was very ticklish on her feet and could hardly stand upright as she giggled like a schoolgirl. Then Richard reached around from behind and started to wash Else's front. That ended his kind administrations.

"Oh, no. I can get that stuff," protested Else.

After the shower, they got dressed in the clothes that they had the foresight to bring with them. Richard tried to help Else again, but his efforts were no more appreciated than his washing of frontal body parts.

"I can put my own clothes on, thank you," laughed Else. "I've been doing so since I was little." Richard wasn't so convinced.

Since the only shower was downstairs, there was no way not to get caught as they left. As one might expect, all the children were sitting at the kitchen table, staring at the bathroom door just down the hall. Apparently, man-with-woman baths were a curious phenomenon.

Thor wondered at the arrangement, "I don't remember my mom ever taking a bath with a man."

Else teased, "You mean that she was always dirty?"

Thor thought about that, and then at length, "Well, yes, I guess she was." Thereby ending Else's attempt at levity.

John and Suzanne were next at the shower, as all of the children resumed their vigilance of the front of the bath door.

Else's youngest, Chloe, had an inspiration as she flopped her side ponytail brushes back and forth, "They are saving water."

Reb liked her sister's reasoning, but the older children were still skeptical. There had to be more to this than mere conservation.

Leaving the pack of children in the kitchen, Else went upstairs to get her socks and shoes, while Richard settled himself before the phone in the living room.

The impending situation concerning Suzanne's legal status had to be clarified. Richard called his son Terrie in the Cities and asked him if Attorney Carpenter had any new news about the case.

"Jim says that Suzanne must go to court in Bemidji tomorrow," said Terrie. "The district attorney may charge her for the murder of Odis Blister. Or maybe not. It all depends on whether the deputies up there can find and capture Euglena."

"Why does charging Suzanne with the murder of Blister depend on capturing Euglena?" asked Richard.

"The district attorney needs Euglena to testify against Suzanne, though that seems totally illogical to me because Euglena is a known convicted predator."

"He needs Euglena in custody so he can arrange a statement from Euglena that does not suggest another killer of Odis," said Richard. "Otherwise, the district attorney's proceedings against Suzanne could be interrupted with Euglena being caught during the trial and him fingering another suspect."

"That would humiliate the district attorney because it would show that he had charged and tried an obviously innocent person, your Suzanne."

"Of course we already know that Suzanne could not have killed Odis," stated Richard.

"Yes, that is a reality. But as you know, the district attorney will form another reality in the controlled environment of his courtroom," said Terrie.

"So Euglena must be under the DA's control before there can be a trial," concluded Richard.

"Absolutely."

"What about Junior?" asked Richard.

"Suzanne will definitely not be charged with killing Junior."

"Because Junior had a gun?" asked and stated Richard.

"That, and because the DA wants the Rodriguez name to fade from the public's memory as quickly as possible."

"Of course," said Richard, newly enlightened. "No need to stir up bad publicity if you will probably just lose anyway."

Richard told his urban-loving son Terrie to stay in close touch with Attorney Carpenter in order to monitor the progress, or lack thereof, the legal situation; especially in regard to the machinations of the district attorney. Then Richard made two more calls, first to Chad, then to Anthony de Medici.

Chad was glad to hear from Richard, at least until Richard told him that Cindy Heath was ending her newly formed relationship with him. Still, he took it better than Richard had expected. Maybe Chad loved Cindy only because she was a connection to Miss Frontera. Lennie was still his true love.

"Did you find anything more about who had abducted Lenora?" asked Chad.

"You must have heard by now that two of the rapists have been killed," stated Richard.

"That still leaves one."

"I know that you and Cindy were hunting for Lenora the day after she went missing."

"We just wanted to find her, that's all."

"Cindy would have killed those responsible. That was her plan."

Several moments of phone silence, louder than any words might have been. Then, "I didn't know that."

"I believe you," said Richard. "Just keep Cindy away from our last remaining perverted survivor."

"I will."

"And, Chad..."

"Yes."

"I know how much you loved Lenora. But you need to stay free for your mom. That means no trouble. Understand? No trouble."

Chad did not ask why Cindy was ending things with him; and before he could inquire about the reason for her actions, Richard told him not to bother trying to find out. Chad dropped the entire issue. Convicts, more than others, know when to retreat into themselves.

The de Medici son was next. Tony had discovered some further information concerning Euglena and the status of his future. "Do you remember Sassy, the small black girl that was in Euglena's apartment with Amber?"

"Of course."

"Well, she has four brothers—all in the military: two marines, one quartermaster in the army, and a nasty-assed army ranger. Sassy's mom pressed the story from Sassy and passed it along to her family military. All four soldiers came back home on leave and are waiting for Euglena to come back to the Cities. They'll make him ugly when he does."

"Do you think that Euglena knows about this?"

"Most likely. So he is trapped up north," said Tony. "Per Sassy's military and the Natives and the State cops."

"Where he will lay low and wait out the storm," figured Richard.

"But Euglena can't afford to do that," said Tony. "He has other problems he needs to attend to, namely, he had already sold Amber for an extremely high price, so he must produce the body—'habeas corpus'—so to speak, or his own corpus will be finished."

"He would certainly not try to recapture Amber, would he?" asked Richard.

"He would. He might. He very likely will. To be forewarned is to be forearmed. So take care," said Tony.

Else had to be informed about the impending danger caused by Euglena's debts of flesh. Richard left the living room and its resident phone, and went into the kitchen where he found Else and Suzanne spying on a band of rose-breasted grosbeaks feeding on the cut-off section of cedar tree trunk. Richard sat across the table from the pair and waited for them to turn to him. Then he gave them the bad news about Euglena's possible impending invasion of their castle.

"The home will have to be defended," said Richard, "but no guns, no firearms can be allowed in this place, per my ex-con status."

"I've been planning to go back to my grandparents' farm to get the last of my things. So my sweet love here," said Else as she pointed an accusing finger at Richard, "could drive me and the kids over to the farm today. That would give us time to figure out what to do."

That still left the question of what to do with Suzanne.

Else added, "Meanwhile, John can take Suzanne back home to her parents in Grand Rapids."

Richard dropped the other bomb. "The lawyer says that Suzanne must be in court tomorrow."

"That is all right," said Suzanne. "I need to stay here for at least another day, anyway, because I'm hurting too much to go back home to Grand Rapids just yet."

Else had the solution. "I will call Thomas Thorson to come over with his rifle and post guard in front of the property while Richard and myself are gone."

Richard knew that his house would have to be emptied before nightfall. John would have to take his covert bride away to safety. Else would have to take her brood back to her grandparents' crowded farm. Amber and Thor would have to go with her or be taken over to Clara and Teddy's cabin in the forest. Richard would then be left alone to prepare for his next visitor. But for now Richard would say nothing. One more set of daylight hours could be enjoyed in peace.

Else put the day's activities in motion. She had Richard hook up his trailer so she could bring her tractor back to his land. Then she packed a cooler with picnic food, and organized the children. Her tractor was sitting on her grandparents' farm northeast a few miles from the rural town of Clearbrook, not far from where Richard's crew had been cutting downed and drowned trees from the Clearwater River.

Since Richard had never been to Else's farm, she directed him, taking the northern road to her grandparents' place.

North on Irvine Avenue three miles to the tiny hamlet of Nebish, where the village's most prominent feature was a large, beautiful, white wooden Catholic church standing guard on the curvy road, then west on Highway 32 past a string of lakes: Island, Balm, and Clearwater. Richard stopped at a dam on the north side of Clearwater Lake. A river by the same name, their work-site Clearwater, spilled through a concrete tunnel there, rushing under the highway with the force of a giant's fire hydrant. Local boys would sometimes swing on a rope into the water on the lake side, take one last breath of air before their fated self-immersion, and then allow themselves to be shot through the tunnel and downstream into the river.

Richard stopped at the lake and let the children fish at the river's edge below the dam. He always kept two fishing poles in his truck for just such "emergencies." He would have to remember to pack more poles in the future. Else's four girls were elated when Amber caught a pumpkinseed bluegill on a rubbery grub-tail. Thor rigged the other pole with the same arrangement and helped Else's children take turns catching their own brightly colored sunfish—a dozen of which were soon swimming in a large yellow plastic fish bucket. The children continued to fish until the bucket could not hardly hold any more, then they hunted pearly clamshells along the river's banks.

From Clearwater Lake it was only a short distance to Else's farm. County 11—the ridge-running blacktop where Richard had jogged just days before—turn off 32, then four miles more. The farm was both bucolic and run down, as is common with so many of the old northern farms. Else's tractor was parked next to a faded red barn that seemed to be wider than it was long, having had lean-to's added to its sides decades after the original structure had been built.

Else hugged her grandmother, her grandfather, and her tractor, with seemingly equal affection.

"Farmers and their tractors!" said Richard.

The cooler of food was unloaded and the children were ushered into the farmhouse to clean themselves for lunch. The grandmother told Else that a "legal" man had called for her and that she should call him back right away, which she did. After the phone conversation, Else came back into the dining room where Else's grandparents and Richard were getting to know each other. Else announced that she had decided that she wanted to take Richard on a private picnic.

Just the two of them.

CHAPTER 34

Else prepared and packed a small dinner for herself and Richard from the contents of the large cooler. Then she had him drive a few miles to where a green cemetery had been carefully mowed out of a hayfield. A tall pink church was located south of the cemetery, about a hundred yards away, as if the living believers did not want to be too close to the ghosts of their deceased brethren.

The cross at Elizabeth's grave was also Celtic, like that of Lenora's. "My grandmother, my father's mother, had given Elizabeth a ruby ring and a silver chain hung with a Celtic cross," said Else. "That was just prior to their deaths. One too old to live and the other too young to die."

"I'm sorry, Else." Richard took her hand in his.

"Elizabeth's great-grandmother is right behind us."

Richard turned slightly and looked to his left. Another Celtic cross faced the cross of the grave of Else's oldest daughter.

"I'm not sure in what century the necklace had been crafted, but family legend has it that the cross had been handed down for some several generations." Else set fresh flowers against the grey stone of Elizabeth's Celtic creation. "I had a local stonecutter make a cross just like the one that she had worn."

"Lenora's cross was Celtic too," said Richard. "It is almost as if there is some meaning in that coincidence."

Else spread a blanket next to her daughter's grave and set out the picnic she had prepared. "I try to spend time here when I can. My memories seem to be both softer and clearer here." Else ran her hand over the grass on her oldest daughter's grave. "This ground is where my Elizabeth is resting."

Else talked about the case and Suzanne's troubles if Euglena should fall into the district attorney's hands. She talked of the land and her farming. She looked close into Richard's eyes and said that she loved him. This last sentiment seemed to have come from out of nowhere.

Else lay next to Richard and presently she fell into a quiet sleep. Richard lay next to her and brushed the dark red tresses away from her too-canted ears and watched her as she slept. When she awoke, she led Richard deeper into the hayfield, trampled out a small hiding place in the tall grasses, set down the blanket, and told him that they would have to make love.

Richard agreed. And knew something was wrong.

Else removed the cut-offs and blouse she was wearing, then her faded blue tennis shoes and white socks. She pulled Richard forcefully on top of her and wrapped her legs around Richard's waist and held him with an intensity that bordered on violent. She tried to kill him with the passion of her kisses. She cried as she made love. She even licked the sweat-salt from his chest so, she said, she could remember the taste of her man. Richard could only ride out the storm. When Else was exhausted she again went into a gentle sleep, her beautiful naked body next to Richard. He held her and caressed her and wished that time would come to a stop and remain forever frozen.

After a long while, Else opened her tear-reddened green eyes and spoke, "The phone call I returned was Carpenter, Terrie's attorney. My ex found out that I was moving in with you and he is trying to get custody of the girls on the grounds that you are a convict and we are not married. I will have to remain here at my grandparents' farm when you leave for home."

An old heart can break too.

"Will you ever return?" asked Richard.

"I wish I could say. I would never leave you for any other reason. But my four girls?"

"I guess that I am down to Amber and Thor," said Richard, sadly accepting his fate.

"No, Richard. I'm sorry. Terrie's attorney also informed me that the district attorney is planning on causing you trouble over those runaways. Amber and Thor will have to live with Teddy and Clara Zemm if they are to be kept from their drunken mother and their cruel new father."

"Of course." Richard would have to be resigned to loneliness once again.

Else reached behind her neck and undid the light chain. "This is the cross that was Elizabeth's. I want you to wear it for me as a sign of our love, so we will always be connected in this sign." She placed the silver chain around Richard's neck and fastened the clasp. Now he had two crosses, Celtic twins, Else's Elizabeth's, and Miss Lenora Frontera's. Two dead girls.

Richard remembered that his own daughter had been wearing two crosses the night she had been attacked. A female Satanist had torn those crosses from Jeanette's neck to keep as souvenirs of Jeanette's defilement. The local authorities never charged that female rapist with her crime: setting up Jeanette to be raped. They had not even made that female rapist return the crosses to Jeanette. Richard would never forget or forgive. Though the Satanist might be too stupid to realize the danger she was in, her life would be on a precarious edge until Richard got his daughter's crosses back in his hands.

Else stood up and stretched, her arms reaching for the sky as the muscles in her legs tightened, forcing fresh red blood to the rest of her body. Tiny jewels of sweat glistened like clear sand quartz on her chest and shoulders. Sunlight, catching her lap from hipbone to hipbone as she twisted her body, revealed that she was a true redhead. Richard was amazed that a woman could be so unself-conscious.

Else put on her socks and tennis shoes and walked into the field. At least her feet were covered, though nothing else was. The hay was mostly timothy, with some clover. The grass was a few inches higher than her rather knobby knees. She had to hide when a car came down the road in front of the cemetery. She fell to the ground and lay flat on her stomach until the danger had passed. Richard sat and watched her as she explored the area around the blanket. After a while, another vehicle came down the road, a stake-bed farm truck, and Else crawled on hands and knees back to the blanket and Richard.

Richard had fallen in love with Else. Very much in love. He would have liked to be able to tell her so in some poetic and memorable way. What he said was, "This is going to be really hard on my sex life." He then imagined that Else would say how much she also loved him and wanted to stay with him forever and live happily ever after... and so on, and so on.

Instead, she agreed, "I know it will."

Else and Richard dressed and left the field, first stopping to say good-bye to Elizabeth. Else rearranged the flowers on her fallen daughter's grave, ruffled as they had become by the afternoon's wind. Else's love of her daughter was both beautiful and sad.

Else put her arm gently around Richard's neck and with both her hands turned his face toward the pink church. Else had already called it the pink church, but she asked, "What color is that church?"

"Pink," said Richard.

"The church is white," she said "Some people even see it as white. The church is painted with white paint. Every year. White barn paint, my love, to be exact."

"I don't get what you are saying," said Richard.

"Others in the congregation, in my church there, they see it as pink. Always. Morning, evening, middle of the day. Put a light on it at night and they see it as pink." Else, still holding Richard's face, kissed him lightly, gently, lovingly on his cheek. "Superstition says that any man or woman who has lost a loved one to some evil will always see the church pink. War, crime, accidents. Senseless losses, I guess."

Richard turned toward Else, against the force of her hands, looked into his girl's beautiful green eyes, put his arms around her and held her to him for a very long time. "Why for us, Else, does your church have to be pink?"

"I don't know, my love."

~

Once back at the farm, Else found Amber and Thor and told them of the developments, that Else and her children could not go home with Richard, and that they, Amber and Thor, would have to live with the Zemms for a while at least. Thor was visibly shaken at the loss of his mother-in-training, Else. Tears collected in the corners of his eyes, but he steeled himself and stood straight and tall as befitting a Viking.

Amber stated calmly that she did not care. What she meant was that neither Heaven nor hell would keep her from her new father for long, so she wouldn't sweat the details.

When time came for Richard to leave, he did not know what to say. He held Else for a moment, kissed her face and ears, tousled her hair with both his hands. Then he let go, abruptly, and left with Thor and Amber. Just left. What could he do?

Richard drove home on the same high route that Else had earlier directed him when she had led the way to her Clearwater County farm. Else's grandfather had cleaned the sunfish that the children had caught and had wrapped them in newspapers and ice. Richard could cook them for a last meal with his newly acquired and soon to be lost son and daughter.

Suzanne had decided that she wanted John to drive her back to her parents' home in Grand Rapids, despite the ache to her ribs. She wanted to visit with her family and her many friends in the event that tomorrow's court date should not go well for her. Suzanne's decision sparred Richard the need to expel his new boarders.

Since Suzanne and John had to drive east toward Grand Rapids, she and John would deliver the newly reunited brother and sister to the forest home of Teddy and Clara. As he had been just a few days earlier, Richard would once again be free to rattle around in the great loneliness of his large home.

John Bridger, seeing the mist of pain on Richard's face, took over the duties of frying the sunfish and sent the old man outside to relax in his garden. Richard walked his yard and inspected the many types of wildflowers that grew along the edge of his field.

Tiring from the long day and the abrupt loss of so much family, he sat on the bench near his flower garden. There he silently prayed to Jesus and His Father that Suzanne would be spared any further harm from rapists and lawyers.

CHAPTER 35

Toward evening the whine and venom of mosquitoes chased Richard from his garden and into his home. Remarkably, there were pumpkinseed bluegills left from the supper that John had prepared. Richard ate some of the crunchy fish as John and Suzanne loaded their car. Suzanne looked more tired and battered than she had two days ago. Richard suspected that the worry of tomorrow's court date was weighing on her.

Suzanne came into the kitchen and lowered herself onto the couch, letting her husband finish the packing that he had wanted to do by himself in the first place. "My ambition is greater than my strength."

"It will take time. Just give yourself some time."

"I suppose so. But I think that half of my trouble stems from knowing that the system is against me. I don't understand why that should be."

"Remember, Suzanne, you have friends who love you."

"That I do. I have John, and my parents, and lots of friends."

"And look at all those citizens that came to the court for you."

"Yes, that was great," agreed Suzanne. "But I have another person to be thankful for, too."

"And who is that?"

"I am thankful for you."

"And I am glad that I could offer my assistance. But remember that there are many good people that are trying to end this thing."

"That is true," agreed Suzanne, as her husband came to collect his bride for their journey back home to Grand Rapids.

John shook Richard's hand and thanked him for helping his young wife. Suzanne hugged Richard till her ribs began to hurt, then took his right hand in both of hers and squeezed it tight. "We will have to meet under a bale of straw again someday," she said, fighting a losing battle to hold back the tears.

"That we will," said Richard. "And Suzanne, after the court date tomorrow, check with the college about your classes. I think you can be reinstated for your summer classes yet. You and John can stay here if you would like."

The mention of returning immediately to BSU and the offer of a place to stay put the light back in Suzanne's eyes.

Amber had already said good-bye in the garden, but she had to say good-bye again in the kitchen. "I am not going to lose another parent, so don't get too comfortable living by yourself."

Suzanne laughed in approval and support of the little girl's intense determination.

Thor said that he would follow his sister wherever she went, so Richard knew that he would be seeing the boy again someday. They left Richard on the porch of his empty house, watching the car as it disappeared down the field road.

Tony had not been heard from for some time, so Richard decided to call his walking-mural friend.

Antonio had an update on his prior warning, "Euglena only has until tomorrow night to put meat on the table. Otherwise, his flesh creditors will consider him late for a bad debt."

"So he will have to kidnap Amber tonight or tomorrow?" asked Richard.

"Tonight," asserted Tony. "Euglena will figure that Amber will be in court tomorrow, where he can't touch her. You will have to be ready tonight for his possible, or probable, arrival."

Richard informed Tony about the departure of Amber and Thor and the others. "The house feels like an old leaf basket with a single acorn rolling around in it."

"Are you saying that you are a nut?" asked Tony, voices of children echoing in the background of Maria's home.

Richard was jealous of the de Medici home, of the sounds of friends and family. "Going from an empty house, to a completely packed house, to empty again in just a few days would make anyone a bit crazy. I miss them already."

"At least no one else will be in danger when Euglena shows up to collect his runaway slave."

That left Richard with one minor concern—per his own persona. "Antonio, I am really tired. At the least I need a nap."

"Euglena won't strike until after darkness, when he thinks that everyone is asleep. Rats don't skitter in the daylight."

"So I can take a nap now?"

"You can rest until sunset, Richard. Then be ready." Tony had to go for some fresh mysterious reason, leaving Richard with a horrible phone noise in his ear.

Richard brought down his bow from his bedroom upstairs. The Hoyt, a compound bow bought from his son Joshua, maxed out at a weak 44 pounds. Nevertheless, Richard had taken several deer with the weapon. Next, he picked four of his newest and straightest arrows and twisted thin-bodied razorheads into the threaded holes in the end of each arrow. Then he set a chair in the hallway in the center of the house, facing toward the east entrance door.

Euglena, if he came tonight, would have to walk through that opening. Richard unlocked the door, opened it wide, went back to sit on the chair, and practiced drawing the bow a few times.

Usually, Richard never pulled the string with just his fingers, but instead always used a bow release—the triggerlike grip that attached to the string of the bow. The release made it easier to hold against the weight of the string as it was pulled back. But the release was still missing from the time he had shown Amber how to shoot the bow. He would have to rely on his bare hands tonight, something he had not done for several years, maybe not for several decades for all he could remember. But since he would have to aim down the arrow because the weak moonlight would not allow the use of sights, then perhaps the mechanical release would have been a hindrance anyway.

The doorway framed a rectangle of illumination in the wall. An intruder would silhouette himself in the opening. In an hour a near full moon would add its colorless light to the effort. Richard shut and locked the door, then laid on his second favorite couch, the newer one in the living room, and slept.

The sound of a motor and squeaking car springs woke Richard. A sedan was bouncing down the path in Richard's field, its headlights off, but moving too fast for the ruts and holes that plagued his drive. Friends, family, and UPS men had long ago learned not to drive so fast on his path.

Richard unlocked the front door, yet left it closed, and then sat on the chair that he had pre-positioned in the hallway. He nocked a sharp arrow in the bow. He could hear that the car had stopped a short distance from the house and its engine had been turned off. There was a long silence. Autumns spent bow hunting for deer had taught Richard about patience. Still, Suzanne's life might depend on the outcome of tonight's events.

While Richard had slept, the moon had arisen in the southern sky. Now its light, reflected thousands of miles, was streaming through the windows. Richard knew that the doorway would be lit if and when the driver of the car should gather enough courage to enter his home.

Silence—long and deadly. A wait of a few minutes seemed like an eternity. At length, Richard could hear a faint scuff of shoe against wood as someone walked onto the porch, and a louder clunk when that person's foot struck the loose plank that covered a hole in the floor of the porch. Another interminably long silence passed.

The door pushed open a tiny crack. Richard wondered why his intruder would not think it suspicious that this door was not locked. Why do rats walk into traps? They just do.

Richard slowly pulled his bow back and aimed for the side of the entranceway. If by some chance it was a friend, he did not want to let an arrow fly to an innocent target. Richard knew that he could not hold the bow steady for more than one minute. One, three, five, seven seconds passed. Ten. Fifteen seconds. Soon Richard's arm would tire and his accuracy would be affected.

The intruder pushed the door open the rest of the way. Richard could see the moonlight reflected from the rag that Euglena always wore on his head. Euglena's right arm was cocked at the elbow, as it would be if he were holding a pistol.

There were no threats from Richard. No clever sayings. No fair warnings as in the movies. Richard relaxed his fingers and the bow's string slipped its bondage, catapulting the arrow toward the intruder. The arrow struck the rapist with a loud slap. Euglena was rocked back by the force of the arrow. His pistol clattered onto the porch with an unmistakable, heavy metallic sound.

The dying rapist of little girls stumbled down the stairs and fell onto the patch of lawn before the porch. The moonlight illuminated the scene outside quite well.

Richard was surprised that the arrow had not gone entirely through Euglena. It had instead stopped just out the back of the rapist, leaving the arrow—with its now bloody razor—protruding about four inches past. Bone, perhaps the rapist's sternum, must have slowed the arrow. Euglena was struggling to get to his feet, but had only been able to rise onto his knees.

At that very moment, with an arrowed rapist about to die on the grass, another set of headlights turned onto Richard's trail and came toward his house. "Damn," said Richard. There was no time to move Euglena or clean the blood that he must be losing. "I really did not want to go back to prison," said Richard, again aloud and to nobody, unless perhaps to Eugene. "Not over another dead rapist."

Richard evaluated his situation as the vehicle came closer. Would his actions qualify as self-defense? Euglena had been armed with that pistol. But Euglena did not get a chance to shoot, and the arrow had hit him while he was still on the threshold of the doorway.

"Is a threshold considered in your home or outside of your home?" wondered Richard.

The vehicle in question turned out to be a truck with a badly cracked windshield. With great relief, Richard recognized the pattern in its glass—a spiderweb belonging to Thomas Thorson. Fortunately, Thomas was alone. The big man pulled up and got out of his truck, leaving his engine running and the headlights bright shining onto the macabre scene in front of Richard's porch.

"Er-ahhh," said Thomas. "I saw the car pull into your drive and decided to come investigate." Thorson walked around to the front of Euglena, grasped the arrow just above the fletching, and pulled it out of the rapist in one swift and tremendous jerk. Eugene fell over dead.

"Christ, Thorson, you should have warned me you were going to do that," complained Richard.

"This rat will start to stink soon," answered Thomas as he picked up Euglena's carcass, with no more effort or concern than if it had been a bag of trash, and threw it into the back of his truck. "I have a hole it can go into."

"What about Euglena's car?"

"Ahh-er," answered Thorson. "Go to bed, Richard. The car will be gone before you awaken."

"Just like that? Go to bed?"

"Yum...errr...by the way, nice shot."

Thomas left.

Standing on his porch, bathed in the cold, illuminating light of the moon, Richard wondered at the events of the last few days. Three dead rapists. Stabbed, poisoned, arrowed to a post, and garroted; shot in their pornographic mind with a small rifle bullet; trapped by steel jaws, drowned near to death by a barefoot and breast-burnt college girl, crotch-kicked by the ghost of a Confederate soldier, and run through by a razor-tipped arrow of the soldier ghost's lover.

One dead female citizen. Several other girls and women injured by the evil. One young lady, Cindy Heath, had ruined her own life by her foolish contact and conniving with the predators. Lives trashed, ended, and ruined. Suzanne and Sally might recover, or, like Richard's and Michael's daughters, they might not ever be quite the same.

Jeanette had never fully recovered from the effects of the rape on her young body and mind, the handling of the police, the bad press, and the lies of the district attorney. Michael's Elizabeth must have fared even worse. Richard prayed that life would be better for these latest casualties. It had been like... no, it was—a war of attrition. Sassy, Sally, Amber, Cindy, Suzanne, Peggy Raphael the flower girl, two Elizabeths. And Lenora lost forever.

Richard spent the next hour hosing down his porch. He was not as tired as he might expect—the fact that Euglena was off the Earth, probably under the earth by now, meant that Suzanne's future could not be ruined by the county attorney, and that fact alone had buoyed his spirits. A strong, fresh wind was blowing from the south, bringing with it a promise of a warm day tomorrow. Several deer entered the field at the far edge. They nibbled on the new grass and played in the wind that kept the insects away.

After Richard had washed away most of Euglena's tainted blood, he sat on his kitchen's couch and stared out the window and watched as the deer came to taste the salt lick in his front yard. A great horned owl landed in the ancient birch near the east side of his home and hooted messages into the night. A nervous crow answered, perhaps giving away his position to the enemy. Fireflies winked their sexual messages to each other in the warm air above Richard's field. Summer was fast on its way.

Later, he left the animals to play in the silver wash of moonlight, while he lay himself to rest and slept peacefully through the night.

CHAPTER 36

The next day was sunny but cool, more like autumn than spring. As Richard had slept, the south wind had given way to a light northern breeze, breaking last evening's promise of a warm day. High pressure had moved in to trip up the onrush of summer. Richard would have loved this morning's weather if he had not been so apprehensive about this afternoon's court date for Suzanne.

Clad only in cotton boxers, a sweatshirt, and a well-broken-in pair of loafers, Richard walked out onto his porch and into the bright fresh air of the morning. Euglena's car was gone. Every drop of his spilled bad blood had disappeared. The arrow, no longer straight per its deadly impact with Euglena's chest, was stuck in a Christmas wreath nailed to the log wall. Other than the slightly bent arrow, no trace of Euglena's sudden demise existed.

Thanks to Thorson, the carcass of Euglena was gone, stuffed down a deep hole somewhere in a swamp, or farmer's field, or hidden in the deep forest of the vast expanse of northern Minnesota.

A dark brown woodchuck dashed from the pasture of Richard's backyard to the safety of a pile of aspen firewood. Mr. Woodchuck had been spared the talons of the resident owl because this particular woodchuck exposed himself only during the light of the day, when the owl was sleeping.

After a shower and a breakfast of Else's leftovers, Richard was ready for the morning. He drove over to Teddy's place first. Clara and Teddy were inside having their morning coffee and going over the seed catalogs that each spring seemed to decorate every table and flat surface in their home. Amber and Thor were still sleeping, holed up in a back bedroom of the Zemms' small house. Teddy had started a small fire in the wood stove to cut the chill.

Richard talked to Clara for a time, about his suspended situation with Else: losing Else to her ex's threats. The ex with the poor morality as well as poor poker-playing talents.

"Amber and Thor will have to stay with you and Teddy for a while longer, if that would be all right. I can help you out with the extra expenses, and there are a lot more clothes for them at my house. Else saw to that."

"Don't you nevermind," said Clara. "It is a joy to have them around. For one thing, it seems that they are more help than they are a hindrance. And Teddy's spirits are on the rise, I believe at least in part because of the children."

"Their previous home life must have been a challenge, but they seem well adjusted. Amber has a strong personality that kept them going in hard times. I'm glad they are not getting in your way."

"Thor likes to help my Teddy with the garden work. The boy is getting stronger by the hour, I swear."

Clara went on to voice her concerns relative to the county district attorney finding Euglena and using him against Suzanne. Without his going into details, Richard assured her that Suzanne's situation would resolve itself. When finished, he asked Teddy to go outside with him to the garden.

"Your tomatoes are off to a fast start, considering that we have not had any really hot weather yet," observed Richard.

"I keep them covered with floating row covers."

"Is that the material that lets rain and sun to the plants, but keeps the bugs out?" asked Richard.

"Yes. Works real well. And not too expensive."

"Must save on the bug spray," theorized Richard.

"They are uncovered at present only because I was cutting back their leaves and suckers earlier this morning."

At the end of the row of tomatoes was Clara's batch of foxglove. They were fenced round with heavy chicken wire, just as Teddy said he would do. Richard stopped there as if to admire the violet-speckled flowers. "Something has been nibbling on these plants," said Richard. "Um, yes… rabbits."

"Seems odd that rabbits would have stripped handfulls of leaves without leaving one single bite mark," said Richard as he moved away from the foxglove flowers, stopping next before Samantha's target of straw. "All of Samantha's arrows are gone."

"I think maybe Clara picked them up and put them somewhere. Probably did not want them to get wet," asserted Teddy.

"But she forgot the bow," said Richard as he leaned down and picked up Samantha's recurve and pulled the string back. "This thing has good poundage for a kid's bow."

Teddy did not answer.

Richard gently returned the string of the little bow to its normal resting state, absorbing its kinetic energy into his arms. He knew that a bow should never be released without an arrow nocked to absorb the force. Twice more he pulled the string back, held aim at the target on the center of the bale of straw, and then slowly returned the string to straight.

"Dammit, Richard, do you know or don't you?" asked Teddy of his friend.

"Yes, I know. Do you?"

"It was Sally or Samantha, I'm sure of that, but I can't figure which one," said Teddy. "Then again, I don't think I want to know which one." Teddy had become agitated, nervously wringing his big hands.

"I can't say too much about who Blister's killer might be, but you have to consider that your list of suspects is probably way too short."

"Sally would have the hate, I'm sure," said Teddy, as if he had not been listening to Richard. "But Samantha has the strength and the accuracy."

"It is unlikely that Sally or Samantha were involved in any way."

Teddy rubbed his huge hands together in continued agitation. "But you said that you knew who killed that rapist?" asked Teddy.

"Yes. And you don't need to know. Better that way."

"Oh, of course," said Teddy, not looking satisfied with Richard's answer.

"You can stop trying to solve the mystery. You will never get it unravelled anyway."

"But what about Suzanne? We can't allow her to be blamed for a killing that she didn't commit."

"She will be free if the county deputies can't determine the hole where Euglena is hiding. No rigged testimony—no trial."

"So?" wondered Teddy. "The cops are bound to sooner or later find this Euglena pervert."

"Euglena is gone and will not be found," said Richard, stated as done fact.

Teddy was confused, then perplexed, then bewildered, and then finally, his eyes shining like last year's Christmas lights that were still decorating the front of his cottage, enlightened. "You glorious, God-loving bastard! The county district lawyer will never find his rapist friend because he ain't to be found! But are you sure?"

There was no better answer to Teddy's last question than there was to his first. Richard just walked on, followed by Teddy smiling like a fat raccoon in his sweet corn patch.

The children had finally dragged themselves out of bed. Amber ran to throw her arms around Richard. Thor followed—as expected, and also threw his arms around Richard—as not expected. It was a good reunion.

"Sir, I'll be home soon, after the system forgets about me again," said Amber.

"Just don't get this old convict in trouble with the law," requested Richard.

"I won't, Sir," said Amber.

The little blond girl was wise beyond her years. Richard was glad that these two orphans had adopted him.

"Samantha lets me ride her 12 speed," said Thor as he ran off to get the bike. "Wait here and I'll show you how good I've gotten."

"My brother is having a lot of fun over here, and I think that he has a crush on Sally."

"Really?"

"You should see his face when she comes over," giggled Amber.

Richard could just imagine. Thor and Sally were of different ages, Sally maybe four years older, guessed Richard, but Thor was actually the taller of the two.

"I'd like to see that," said Richard.

"They are so cute together. Sally is three years older than my brother, but Thor is already bigger than she is. As a couple, they are a good match."

"I'm glad that things are working out over here," said Richard.

"But Thor would really rather be living at your place. He might not say it or show it, except for the hug you got which really surprised me. He misses you."

"Maybe we can be a family again someday. The district attorney will forget about you two as soon as you are no longer of any use to him." The use being to harass Richard as much as possible.

"Someday better be near," asserted Amber.

Thor rode up on Samantha's bicycle and had Amber sit on the seat while he gave her a ride around the garden. "I've been practicing peddling double like this to make my legs stronger," yelled Thor with more breath than one would think possible.

"I am very much impressed," said Richard, which he was. Thor seemed to be going from little boy to young man, the transition phase being skipped.

Richard drove to town after his visit with Teddy. He parked in the lot that used to belong to the old Food-for-Less grocery, bought two tacos from a shop near there, and ate in peace in his truck so he could think of what to say to Suzanne's lawyer later this afternoon.

After lunch, Richard headed to a sports store where he purchased several lures that were on sale, future presents for Joshua and Foster. As was his usual habit, he checked the backpacks and sleeping bags.

Back at his truck, he inspected the lures he had just purchased, waiting for the time to come before he would make his way to the courthouse. He listened to a garden show on the radio as he waited. When the gardening advice ended, he drove downtown to the old county building.

Suzanne and John were already there, waiting in the lower hall of the courthouse, not far from the huge oak doors of the main court-room. Suzanne was frantic with worry. The last time she had been here she had been arrested and thrown in a dark jail cell as a reward for having survived the gang rape of her young body. Suzanne gave Richard a quick and nervous hug, and then stammered out several nearly unintelligible questions.

"Whoa, slow down, Suzanne," said Richard. "No need to panic."

Jim Carpenter, the attorney that Terrie had hired for Richard's group, came to join them. He had one large black briefcase and no assistants.

"I think the district attorney will charge Suzanne, even without Euglena in custody, figuring that his deputies will find the rapist soon," said Attorney Carpenter.

Suzanne was visibly shaken by the lawyer's words. Holding tightly onto her young husband's arm with both of her hands, she spoke, "We can't... John. We can't..."

"You will not have to," said Richard, answering Suzanne's broken statement. "I have information that indicates that Euglena will not be available to give any choreographed testimony for the county district attorney. Not today. Not tomorrow. Not ever."

"What does that mean?" asked Attorney Carpenter.

"It means he is dead," said Richard abruptly, ending any clever plans he may have had to impart that information in a more subtle manner.

Suzanne was rocked back on her heels. Attorney Carpenter had a puzzled look on his face. John was busy keeping his wife standing on her feet.

"Are you sure?" asked Suzanne.

"At this point, my dear Suzanne, I must limit any further inquiry," informed Richard, sounding kind of lawyerlike himself, he thought, perhaps to match the surrounding courtrooms.

The lawyer had finally comprehended the situation and as such had refrained from asking any further questions. He did, however, make one statement—one legal statement: "As of one hour ago you, Richard, have been another of my clients."

"Why?" asked Suzanne.

"Attorney-client privilege," said Richard.

Attorney Carpenter gently ushered Suzanne into the courtroom and led her to a desk in front.

John and Richard were left standing in the hallway. "Are you sure that Euglena will not be found?" asked John. "Is he really dead?"

"I believe my information to be quite accurate," assured Richard, still stuck in his lawyer's impersonation.

Else soon joined them. She was wearing a dark green dress that perfectly matched her dark green eyes.

"My other green-eyed monster," said Richard.

"What?" asked Else, her frayed nerves causing her to bark her short question more than ask it softly as would have been her usual manner.

"Oh, nothing, Honey. Just a wild thought," said Richard.

The court was convening. Richard, John, and Else went in and sat on one of the benches near the front of the courtroom. Though not as crowded as before, there were again many concerned citizens from Grand Rapids. Suzanne had friends.

The judge asked the district attorney if he was prepared to bring a case against Suzanne. The district attorney said he was. Then, as a formality, the judge asked if the attorney for the defense had anything to add.

Attorney Carpenter said that he did. Several items, in fact.

"I have a young lady here who is from the business that is owned by Alberto Rodriguez Senior," said Attorney Carpenter. "She has valid testimony relating to a white slavery ring that Senior and Junior were assisting. She will demonstrate a connection between the Rodriguez business, Eugene Euglena, and Odis Blister."

As Attorney Carpenter had been talking, Miss Peggy Raphael had risen from her seat at one of the back benches and had walked to the desk of Attorney Carpenter.

"Your Honor, I saw Blister and Euglena meeting with Rodriguez Junior and Rodriguez Senior," said Miss Peggy Raphael. "On several occasions. I can also tell you that Junior tried raping me once, while his pervert dad was looking on, but I stopped the sexual assault by stabbing the junior Rodriguez in the chest with a scissors. You can check his autopsy if you don't believe me."

The district attorney did not like the prospect of having a Native girl, an alleged rape victim at that, testifying against his case. But he really wanted another conviction for his wall. No self-defense or any other type of vigilantism would go unpunished in his county. "I must object, Your Honor," he said.

"I have another witness, Your Honor," said Attorney Carpenter. "Miss Cindy Heath."

Cindy stood and came forward to take Miss Raphael's place next to Attorney Carpenter.

"I am ashamed to say that I had arranged for Euglena, Blister, and Rodriguez to kidnap a friend of mine, a rival for a man I loved, and take her away forever. I am so sorry. Because of me, they killed my best friend." Cindy collapsed to the floor. Barely audible from the crumpled mass of humanity, "Put me in prison forever, Your Honor, I don't deserve to live."

Chad Rochambeau, having arrived late at the court, had been standing at the rear of the room as Cindy was confessing. His mean, tough brother, Trent Rochambeau, was with him. Chad walked to the front where Cindy was laying, picked Cindy up in his strong arms, and carried her out. The bailiffs parted as Trent Rochambeau led the way out of the courtroom.

The district attorney turned to one of his assistants and whispered, "This confession would hurt my case. Still, she would be a suspected felon, at best. Even with her confession in my way I could win this thing." And out loud, "I object, Your Honor. Hearsay," said the district attorney.

"I would like to call next, Your Honor, Minnesota State BCA Agent Michael Kieran," said Attorney Carpenter.

Michael Kieran came forward and spoke, "I have evidence that one of the vans used in the Rodriguez business had also been used to transport Miss Lenora Frontera to her death, Your Honor. Miss Lenora Frontera, just prior to her death, had scratched a drawing of a Celtic cross on the inside of the van. This is the same cross that Miss Frontera had bitten into her teeth the night that she was raped and murdered. Miss Frontera had also taken and held a yellow rose, same as the yellow roses that were in the van in question."

The BCA agent paused for a time to let the judge assimilate what had so far been relayed, then he continued. "Miss Frontera had also, probably after she had been raped, clothed herself in a dress from the van, a gingham-style dress that is used by the Rodriguez business as a type of uniform for their female employees."

The district attorney hated facts. But he likely could still force a conviction in this county if he brought in enough uniforms to back his case. "Circumstantial evidence, Your Honor. I object. Besides, Your Honor, we are only interested in Odis Blister, aren't we?"

"I agree, Your Honor," interrupted Attorney Carpenter. "Odis Blister is our only interest. Therefore, my next and final witness has testimony that would attest to Odis Blister's character, or lack thereof. I will just call her Sally, since she is a juvenile and as such may need the protection of the court."

Sally came forward, walked to the front of Attorney Carpenter's desk, and turned to face the citizens assembled in the courtroom. The young girl was wearing an elegant and extremely expensive looking blue satin dress. Hollywood ladies would have paled in comparison.

"The man that was killed in his shack—he is the one that had raped me and tried to beat me to death. I lived only because I was able to escape and hide in the cover of darkness." As the small girl spoke, a shock wave pulsed through the people assembled in the courtroom.

The district attorney was visibly annoyed. "I must object, Your Honor. A juvenile? She is much too young to be credible."

At Attorney Carpenter's prearranged hand signal, Sally spoke again, "My father owns one of the auto dealerships in town. One of my uncles owns the trailer sales west of town. Another uncle owns the welding shop up the highway a little way. He employs over two dozen men. Then I have a rich aunt in banking. Shall I discuss my mother's side? Did I mention how many generations my family has been in this area? Should I continue, Your Honor?"

"The State withdraws its case!" squeaked the district attorney.

The judge dismissed the case against Suzanne, with prejudice, which in this instance was a very good thing because it meant that Suzanne could never ever again be charged for the rapist's death. She was forever free. At least from the district attorney if not from the lingering effects of the assault on her by the dead rapists.

Everyone gathered on the lawn on the west side of the court-house, seemingly under the protection of "Justice"—the oversized bronze statue of a well-bosomed, strongly muscled lady—armed with her terrible swift sword held high above her metal head.

The elegant blue satin Sally found Richard in the crowd and gave him his fourth hug of the day. "I have to go now. My mom is taking me over to Samantha's home, but I wanted to thank you again for your listening to me and my story. And thank you for the other girls, too." At that, Sally walked away to a blue Mercedes that matched her dress, turned to wave good-bye, and, with a bright smile on her impish face, yelled, "If you ever need help or money, come let me know."

Suzanne was emotionally exhausted but happy. John had to all but hold her up to keep her from collapsing. Else spoke to Richard, telling him that the river work would not start for another nine days at the least; she had been checking the level of the water.

Richard hoped that Else's desire to get back to work was less a concern to make money than it was to be with him again every day. Chad Rochambeau spoke briefly with Richard, and then he and his brother left with a shattered Cindy Heath in tow. Agent Kieran was nowhere to be seen. Richard figured that this victory was for Michael just one more ending of another battle of the ongoing war that he would forever wage against the predators of the world. Michael would for a time retreat to his old memories.

Attorney Carpenter was gloating over the way he had handled the case: a kick to the balls of the district attorney.

Richard walked to his truck to leave. Else caught up with him. As if by magic, her four little ones were now with her. "I will miss you, Richard. Please do not forget me." She kissed him, splashing his face with salty tears, and then turned and ran away, her young ones having to run hard to keep up with her.

Else's last good-bye and sentiments did not sound very promising to Richard. He would have wished for more hope.

~

The field in front of his home was filled with the bright colors of flowers. A solitary marsh hawk glided low over the ground as it hunted for unwary mice. If Richard must be alone, he decided, then he would be truly alone. He would take down his green-painted canoe from the beams in his living room and make a trip into the wilderness up near Ely. He packed his gear in the truck and tied his canoe into the truck's bed. A perpetually readied cardboard box of camp food was thrown onto the back seat.

Tomorrow he would drive to the Cities to visit his son, Terrie, and stay a night with Antonio and his kind and loving mother, Maria Evangilista de Medici. He would drink a glass of her forbidden wine, eat her tomato-packed spaghetti, and kiss her face until she cried for mercy. He would be with a family again for a single night, and then, refreshed, he would leave to be alone in the northern wilderness. He was looking forward to both.

Late that night his daughter called just to have someone to talk with. She often did that when she was worried about something or had a problem to work out. Usually, Richard was unable to figure out what Jeanette's worry or problem was, but his listening always seemed to help. Richard listened. It was good to hear Jeanette's voice again. When his daughter had talked herself out, they said good-bye in their usual way, "I love you." "I love you, too." "Good night." "Good night."

"And, Jeanette…"

"Yes, Dad."

"God bless."

CHAPTER 37

The last thing Richard remembered from the previous night was the talk with his daughter. He must have been exhausted from the events of the past days and the relief and release he felt when Suzanne was given the papers making her a free woman. He awoke on the kitchen's couch dressed in boxers and T-shirt, so he had gotten that far anyway. Cereal in cold milk for breakfast, a hot shower, and bright sunlight had brought him back to the living.

Richard walked out onto his porch and observed the field in front of his house. After having so many people living at his home recently, the emptiness was nearly overwhelming. Maybe, thought Richard, one of his sons would call just to talk. That would be good.

Through the birch trees that lined the county road at the front of his land, Richard caught glimpses of bright reflections off a vehicle. It was not throwing much dust, as a car or truck would have done, nor was it traveling very fast. A bicycle. There were two children on the bicycle, a young boy standing on the pedals, with another child sitting behind him on the seat. The pair turned onto Richard's rutted path.

It was at least twenty miles from Clara and Teddy's home in the Chippewa Forest. The children must have left before sunrise.

As the pair approached the house, Thor was the first to speak.

"I rode most of the way here, but Amber thinks she is faster, so she wanted to do some of the biking, too."

"Hello, my runaway Hansel and Gretel."

Thor and passenger Amber looked at Richard with matching blank expressions. Apparently the fairy tale had not been read to them in their previous childhood. Richard made a mental note to get the book from the library.

"Teddy and Clara must be frightened to death about your missing status. We need to call them right away," said Richard.

Amber already had that issue arranged and taken care of. "They were still sleeping when we left, but we wrote several messages back at their house. Each message is in plain sight where they can't miss it. They will know where we are as soon as they awaken."

"That's good," said Richard, a little bit relieved. "Clara should be calling soon."

As the bicycle rolled to a stop, Amber slid off the seat and walked stiff-legged over to Richard.

"Sir, I will always come back." It was not a promise. Amber had stated a fact.

"I know you will." Richard took her again by the hair of the back of her head, as he had done the first day they had met, and pulled her close to his tired eyes and looked into the fresh clear green eyes of the girl, and lightly kissed the top of her forehead. "But you're still in trouble."

The phone rang. "That must be Clara," said Richard. "You two busy yourself with something while I try to get you a reprieve for your escape."

After calming the jangled nerves of Clara, Richard went outside to watch the children. They had found his compound bow and several arrows. Thor was trying to pull back the string, but he did not have quite enough energy left after the bicycle marathon to make it to full draw. This bow was several pounds heavier in draw than Samantha's bow.

Thor's sister added her strength to his and together they pulled the string past its let-off point. Amber stepped away. Thor, aiming carefully at the center bull's-eye, let the string slip from his fingers. The arrow rocketed just over the top of the bale of straw and into the woods behind.

Both children quickly looked toward the house, but not before Richard had stepped back behind its corner. Believing they had not been seen, they ran into the woods to find their errant arrow. Soon Thor was waving the arrow over his head as if he had found gold. Lucky that the arrow had not ricocheted off a tree or they would be looking until Christmas.

The children spotted Richard as they walked out of the woods. Apparently, with incriminating evidence safely in hand, they felt no need for confessions. To be children and not to be caught red-handed is to be innocent.

Thor gave his found prize to his sister and ran over to Richard. "Want to play some catch?" more told than asked Thor. "I have your football from the other day."

"Sure," said Richard. It was nice to have the feel of a football again, throwing it back and forth to an eager child. But soon Thor tired; his majority percentage of the work of the bicycle ride had caught up to him. The grid-iron teammates sat on the garden bench in the shade near the back wall of the house.

"I can see that you need a nap. The ride must have been rough on you."

"Not as bad as I would have thought. The hike from my old home must have made my legs stronger, and also, my sister took over for me whenever I got too tired. That helped."

Richard turned on the bench to face the young Viking head on. "Thor, I need to ask you for a favor."

The little boy thought for a while. Thor always seemed to think before speaking, maybe the result of being ejected from the house by Amber when he let on about the distance. He said that a favor would be all right with him. "Sure. What do you need?"

"Thor, do not confess again to the killing of Blister. OK?"

"But I really did shoot him…because…to protect my sister. You see?"

"I know you mean well, but your confessions only bring attention to the real killer. Do you understand?"

Thor sat in silence. Richard imagined that if Thor was a cartoon character, the side of the boy's head would fade open and reveal sets of wooden cogs gearing past each other. Then finally, "I won't try to confess again. I promise."

No more was said on the subject. Thor laid himself down on the open end of the bench and was soon deep in the good sleep that comes from physical exhaustion and the sudden release from fears. Richard watched Amber as she continued to practice with the arrows. At Teddy's home she could not pull back the string on Samantha's bow. Now, just a few days later, she was able to use Richard's bow. She had surpassed her brother in that aspect. There must have been a lot of work and practice involved in her recent and rapid improvement.

The poundage of the draw of Richard's bow was very light, but even that light weight would be great for most eleven-year-old girls with slight builds. Amber did not seem to struggle unduly. As she pulled the string back, the muscles of her back and shoulders rippled like the waves of a small pond. She was using his wood and metal string release, apparently newly found. The release gave her fingers a much greater combined strength. Richard had wondered where his lost release had gone to. Now he knew. The arrows flew one by one toward the red bull's-eye of the target. One of the arrows ticked the nock end of another one which was already stuck in the red center.

"Don't shoot so many at a time," suggested Richard. "Four will be plenty. You are too accurate for more, or you'll be splitting all my arrows."

"Yes Sir," said Amber, looking back toward Richard, a warm smile on her innocent face.

She rested the bow against the tomato cage and walked over to the bench and sat next to its old occupant. She patted her brother's leg, then pushed his feet a bit away from her to give herself more room. Thor was oblivious to the world, and would be so for some time.

"I am getting a little bit better. But I need a lot of practice."

"I am very impressed both by your increased accuracy and your improved strength," said Richard.

The man and girl sat together and listened to the small noises of the garden. Spring bees were already buzzing in the fresh clover of the lawn. Tree frogs were piping to each other in the woods beyond the yard. A pair of chickadees flitted by and landed on one of the arrows sticking from the bale of straw. Richard said that the black caps of the little birds reminded him of the slicked-back black hair of the lawyer that had defended Suzanne.

The bright smile faded from Amber's young face. "Sir, Suzanne cannot be charged again. Am I right?"

"You are correct."

"Good," said Amber, as a slighter version of her previous smile reappeared.

"I also told your brother not to confess again. It is not good for others to hear what he was saying."

"Yes, Sir. It does sound awful."

"Thor agreed not to confess again when I explained to him that his words might bring unwanted attention to the identity of Blister's real killer."

Amber's slighter-version smile disappeared, replaced by the look of serious thought. "Sir…"

"Yes."

"I did kill Blister."

"Yes, I know."

"And I'm not sorry for doing so."

"I know, my little protagonist."

A confused look crossed Amber's face. "I'm not an agonist, Sir, I believe in God. But I'm not sorry for Blister."

"Agnostic, my dear Amber. You are not an agnostic," corrected Richard.

"What?" screeched Amber, her small nerves stretched a bit too tight.

Thor stirred slightly on his bed side of the bench, but there was no chance that he would awaken.

Richard tried to clear the semantic confusion. "An agnostic is someone who believes that the existence of God cannot be proven. An agonist, which is correctly related to the word protagonist, is someone who is torn apart by inner conflict."

"I'm not torn apart, Sir. Not inner or outer."

"No, I suppose you're not," said Richard.

"I got rid of Blister. I'm telling the truth. When the other kids were playing, after you left for the forest, I took Samantha's bow and one of the arrows and rode Samantha's bike to the shack. I had also picked pocketfuls of leaves from Clara's foxglove flowers."

"Yes, Amber, I figured that." Richard smiled at his little charge, a perhaps inappropriate smile considering the severity of the scope of her confessions.

"Sir, this is the whole truth. You see, I knew that the leaves were very poisonous because I heard Mr. Zemm talking about them when Else brought her little ones over to his place."

"Yes."

"I was going to pretend that I had come back to Blister's shack out of fear, then I would make Euglena, Blister, and Rodriguez a pot of black tea. They had always made me make them coffee before. So I would make tea instead and then I would throw in the poison leaves. When I got there I found Odis sitting by himself against the beam at the back of the cabin. So I cooked him a big pot of tea and poisoned him."

"Yes, Amber, I believe you."

"I really did that, Sir; I'm telling you nothing but the truth. Odis was hurting so bad that he did not think about how I had arrived out of nowhere. He was always stupid, anyway. Odis was very thirsty from the blood he had lost, so when I fixed the tea, he drank the whole pot. After that, his heart began to hurt and he realized that I had done something to him, so he cursed me and tried to go after me. I took the bow, but I was shaking so bad that the arrow fell, so I pulled the string back and let it strike against his throat."

"That injured the artery in his neck," concluded Richard, being enlightened as to how Blister's artery had been crushed.

"I picked up the arrow and went to leave, but at the door I turned. Blister was still alive. I wanted them, him, to never be able to come after you again. So I tried once more to string the arrow, which I did, and I… um…the arrow stuck him to the beam, I believe," said Amber in her little girl's killer voice.

"Yes, of course."

"Sir … you do believe me? Don't you?" asked Amber, her voice barely audible now.

"What have I been saying, Amber? Yes, Amber, I believe you. I believe you. I believe you."

"I really did it, Sir."

Richard reached into his pocket and took out a worn quarter. One of those state quarters. New Hampshire. Live Free or Die.

"I found this at Blister's shack. You must have dropped it there when you pulled the foxglove flowers from your pocket." Richard gave Amber back her quarter. "I'll trade your lucky quarter for my string release. Is that a fair enough deal?"

Amber finally believed she was believed.

Richard hugged the little girl. He then held her at arms length and gazed into those green eyes again, "I knew these things before you told me, Amber, but please, never tell anyone else. Promise me."

"I promise, Sir. And Sir… what will God think when I die and go to Heaven?"

Richard laughed. "God will think that little girls have a right to protect themselves from feral animals. Now take off and leave an old man alone."

Amber jerked to turn and fly away, then she stopped abruptly and jerked back to Richard to hug his neck and kiss his cheek.

"I love you, Dad." And off she ran.

Freshly adopted Richard wondered at his little green-eyed girl monster. Her plight reminded him of his own situation with his "first" daughter. Amber was too little to be a politically correct suspect. The authorities would never ever consider her for any involvement in Blister's death.

Amber shot an arrow, which shattered the nock of the previous arrow.

"Amber, just shoot one at a time…or better yet, spraypaint little dots as targets on the straw." Richard would have to make a note to buy more arrows at the fleet store.

It seemed enigmatic to Richard that he had shot an arrow into Amber's abductor because he was afraid for the Viking girl if that predator was left alive. Likewise, his Amber did not shoot her silver, pink-fletched arrow out of revenge, or even out of hate, but because of fear. Fear that her new, adopted father would be attacked again and killed, leaving her and her brother alone once more.

Between hate and fear—fear was the more dangerous killer.

A few more arrows flew to the target on the bale of straw, then Amber set the bow back into the tomato cage and walked back to the garden bench and sat again between her sleeping brother and the old man. She took a deep breath, then blew the air out of her lungs like a whale coming to surface.

"I'll have time to practice later," she said.

"Yes, I suppose so."

"Did I ever tell you how smart I am?"

"No, but I figured as such."

"I plan to go to college someday. Probably Bemidji State, then a masters degree from Duluth or the University down in the Cities."

"Those are good plans," agreed Richard.

"I've been teaching myself how to use your microscope. And I've started another rock collection. I even found a chuck of bituminous."

Richard had to think about that for a while. "Oh, yes, Foster had a cast-iron forge when he was younger. Made those curved pulls that you see on our doors. Anyway, that is why we had some coal. I think that the forge is still in the basement. You can use it if you would like. Outside, of course."

"I would, thank you. I'll have Thor help me carry it up when and if he ever wakes." Amber rubbed the top of her legs with both her hands, then released another breath of whale exhalations. "Sir, I am sorry about your friend."

"And who would that be," asked Richard.

"Lenora," said Amber.

"Of course. The friend I never knew."

"You got to know her. She could have been your daughter."

"Like you?"

"Sir, I am your daughter." Amber slapped his arm as if to remind him to not make that mistake again. "Are you listening to me?"

Richard turned to cough to cover his smile and to extinguish the laugh that was trying to escape. Once again safely under control, he turned his face back to Amber's.

"Sir, I'd like you to know that you helped Sally a great deal. We thank you for that."

"I only listened to her story, that's all," wondered Richard.

"Yes, Sir. You and Else listened to her and cared."

"Oh."

"Now you must talk to Cindy Heath. She is a victim too, though partly a victim of herself. Her pain is a sign that there is still a good person inside of her."

"OK, I can do that, I suppose."

"And we must call Sassy, too. She could not help me when I was in the closet, because she could not help herself. I need to tell her that I am all right now."

"OK, we can do that."

"Also, your Else still loves you. She will come back."

"I wish I knew that for certain."

"Are you listening to me?"

"I'm listening...I...just."

"We can have Else and her four girls come over and go with us to the Lutheran church in Puposky. I found out where it is from the church lady down the road from here."

"The church lady? Oh, yeah, you're right."

"Or we could drive over to Else's farm and go with her to her pink church," said Amber.

"Don't you mean Else's white church? The one by the hayfield and the cemetery with the two Celtic crosses."

Amber looked at him like she was wondering how older people ever made it from day to day.

"You are, again, correct," said Richard. "I remember her church as being pink too."

Richard wondered about a world in which eleven-year-old girls had to see white churches pink.

Richard changed the subject. "You said that Thor was three years younger than Sally. I also know that Sally is three years older than you. Can you do the math?"

"Yes," said Amber. "Fourteen minus three equals twins."

"That is what I thought," said Richard.

Amber explained, "When our real father died, Thor could not cope well. I had to take care of him. People noticed, so I started to say that he was my younger brother. But now that he has a new father, he can grow into a man. He is already trying to take care of me, instead of the other way around."

"I see."

"Every boy needs a father," said Amber. "Dads are like fertilizer."

"I'll take that as a compliment, I think."

It was Amber's turn to change the subject.

"Then there is the flower girl, Miss Peggy Raphael. She is a fighter, not a victim. That is good."

"That is good," agreed Richard. "She knows how to use her mind, as well as her shears."

Amber rolled her eyes at his smart-assed remark, but she clearly concurred with his sentiments. "Peggy is not a victim."

"That is good," again said Richard. "By the way, I was planning a canoe trip to the Boundary Waters. Would you and your brother like to go along with me? But first I was going to the Cities for a day or two and visit my son there and stay with Tony and his mother at their home."

"Thor and I would like both trips. We accept." Amber thought for another moment, then, "Can we visit Michael's Elizabeth when we are down to the Cities? Maybe...I don't know, but..."

"That should be all right. It couldn't hurt, I suppose."

"Good. We will visit Tony and your son, then Elizabeth, then go on our canoe trip," planned Amber. "I've never been in any canoe before."

Their conversation left one person unaccounted for. "But what about Suzanne?" asked Richard. "She was really hurt during her forced ordeal. Will she ever be the same, you think?"

"Suzanne is more of a fighter than any of us. The more she is beat on, the tougher she becomes. And she has family and friends and a whole community that loves her. She is definitely not a victim."

Yes, Suzanne would be safe, but Richard needed to know about Amber. He ruffled her white-blond hair as a prelude to his serious question. "And what are you going to be, Amber?"

Amber immediately knew the answer to his question. "Sir, I am going to be a geologist."